Acclaim for

# FERRARELLA

"Marie Ferrarella is a charming storyteller
who will steal your heart away."
—*Romantic Times*

"A pure delight…"
—*Rendezvous*

🐦 🐦 🐦

Praise for

# SCHULZE

"Ms. Schulze smoothly develops
a warm and wonderful love story."
—*Romantic Times*

Dallas Schulze is an author with "talent and flair."
—*Affaire de Coeur*

## MARIE FERRARELLA

began writing when she was eleven. She began selling many years after that. Along the way, she acquired a master's in Shakespearean comedy, a husband and two kids (in that order)—the dog came later. She sold her first romance in November of 1981. The road from here to there has had 155 more sales to it, with 144 being to Harlequin. She has received several RITA® Award nominations over the years with one win for *Father Goose* (in the Traditional Category). Marie figures she will be found one day—many, many years from now, slumped over her computer, writing to the last moment—with a smile on her face.

## DALLAS SCHULZE

spent her childhood debating the relative merits of being a Playboy bunny or a nuclear physicist. When she realized that the former would require her to spend her life in high heels and the later would call for more than rudimentary math skills, she looked around for an alternative career choice and found it in her love of reading.

She sold her first book when she was twenty-four and hasn't looked back since.

She currently lives in California with her husband and one very large, very spoiled cat named Chloe. When she's not writing, she can be found waging a halfhearted war with the weeds in her garden or making quilts.

Dallas loves to hear from readers. You can reach her at her Web site www.dallasschulze.com or contact her at dallas@dallasschulze.com.

# Marie FERRARELLA
# Dallas SCHULZE

## California Christmas

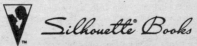 Silhouette Books

Published by Silhouette Books
**America's Publisher of Contemporary Romance**

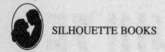 SILHOUETTE BOOKS

ISBN 0-373-23028-1

by Request

CALIFORNIA CHRISTMAS

Copyright © 2004 by Harlequin Books S.A.

The publisher acknowledges the copyright holders of the individual works as follows:

CHRISTMAS EVERY DAY
Copyright © 1993 by Marie Rydzynski-Ferrarella

A VERY CONVENIENT MARRIAGE
Copyright © 1994 by Dallas Schulze

**Printed in U.S.A.**

# CONTENTS

Dear Reader,

Do you remember that very special feeling you'd get Christmas morning just before you walked into the room where the tree was? How you were full of hope and anticipation? Do you recall that rush that went through you as you came into the room, hoping that the one thing you wanted most in the world would be under the tree, waiting for you, hidden just beneath a thin wrapping of paper?

That special feeling was what Sara was looking for in a relationship. But it's not realistic to hope each day is like Christmas. For one thing, if it were, it would lose its specialness. For another, every single day of the calender year can be special in its own unique way when you find someone to love who loves you back. This was what Sara came to learn when she met and allowed herself to fall in love with Nik Sinclair. All the Sinclairs have always been near and dear to my heart. I hope, after reading this installment of their story, they will be to yours, as well.

Wishing you love,

*Marie Ferrarella*

# CHRISTMAS EVERY DAY

## Marie Ferrarella

To Mary Ann Johnston,
a one of a kind lady

# Chapter 1

What Sara Santangelo liked about life was that if you looked hard enough, there were usually choices. She had one now as she deplaned at John Wayne Airport. She could either drive up to Eagle Rock, a development within Newport Beach, and see her father, or she could go to meet the man who was going to be her employer during her temporary stay in Southern California. It never even occurred to Sara that the man might not give her the position. To her it was a foregone conclusion.

As was her choice. She'd face her father later.

Depositing her suitcases in the car she had just rented, Sara decided to drive to Sinclair's, the restaurant co-owned by her new cousin-in-law, Julia.

By nature Sara was not a coward. But it was just that, almost fifteen years after her parents' breakup, there was still too much emotional baggage for her to unpack. This close to seeing her father for the first time in over a decade, and suddenly the tips of her fingers felt icy and the pit of her stomach had contracted into a tight, angry knot.

Perhaps after she managed to get things in gear at Sinclair's, Sara reasoned, she'd feel more like facing the man who had broken her heart and walked away from her and her mother when they had needed him most.

After all this time, it still hurt.

Raymond Santangelo hadn't just divorced his wife, he had divorced his daughter, as well. There had been a handful of visits in the first year and perhaps a dozen cards and notes. And then nothing. A stark, empty nothing.

It was hard for Sara to feel charitable toward him after that.

With the address memorized, Sara easily found her way to Sinclair's. Pacific Coast Highway's serpentine route hadn't changed all that much in the past fourteen years, and she was blessed with a photographic memory that absorbed everything around her, cataloging it all away for future use.

It was a nice-looking restaurant, Sara decided as she pulled up in the parking lot. She would have expected nothing less from something that Brom was involved with. Her cousin had begun by wanting to remodel the restaurant at his Tahoe casino and had wound up remodeling his life by marrying Julia Sinclair, the woman who had taken on the task of bringing a touch of class to a heretofore drab restaurant.

Sara had been duly impressed with both Casino Camelot and Sinclair's/Tahoe when Brom and Julia had shown her around yesterday afternoon. Impulsively stopping at Brom's house en route to staying with her father, she had left as emotionally fortified as she could for the long-delayed meeting ahead.

Her father had called a week ago, having tracked her down through relatives who kept tabs on the nomadic life she led. Sara spent six months in one place, a year with another firm, nine months with a third. She left when things threatened to turn stale. Or serious. She always stayed clear of anything serious. It was a war wound, left over from her parents' divorce. That was the way she had thought of her parents' divorce. As a war.

The conversation between them on the telephone had been painfully awkward. Raymond Santangelo had been diagnosed as having a clogged left artery. He faced the possibility of intensive heart surgery. And he was facing it alone. He'd asked that Sara come to stay with him until he recuperated. She had wanted to say no, but the word that had come out of her mouth had been yes.

So here she was, dealing with ghosts after all these years.

Sara sat for a moment in the rented tan Mazda, thinking. Beyond the building the ocean peacefully communed with the shore less than a half mile away. She could see Catalina in the distance, its form distinct against the horizon like that of a proud whale sunning itself beneath the golden rays. It was one of those perfect days that Californians liked to brag about.

But Sara wasn't really thinking about Californians or the weather. She was thinking about her life. And her cousin's.

Brom had it all. A tiny spark of envy flickered within her soul before it went out again. A home, a family and a lucrative business. Sara laughed softly to herself as she thought of it. She'd never have guessed that he would turn out this way. Out of the assorted collection of cousins who huddled beneath the giant family umbrella, Brom had always been thought of as the black sheep. But his roots went deep.

Why shouldn't they? A touch of uncharacteristic bitterness framed the question in her mind. His parents had never divorced. He had been one of the lucky ones. His world hadn't dissolved right before his eyes.

Sara took a deep, cleansing breath, then consciously shrugged off her mood as if it was a physical thing, like a heavy sweater being shed as the day warmed. There was no reason to feel this way. She liked her life. She had toured the country in the past six years.

Hell, she'd toured the world and enjoyed it all to the hilt. She spoke two foreign languages and could order dinner in three more. For some people, roots were good. For others, herself included, they just tended to tangle things up. She liked living out of a suitcase. That way, nothing owned her and she was free to come and go whenever she pleased.

Freedom meant a lot. Freedom to do. Freedom not to be hurt.

She tried not to think about what had brought her to Southern California in the first place.

Time to meet the man who was going to be her boss for as long as she let him. Sara got out of the car and absorbed her idyllic surroundings for a long moment. Composed, she crossed the parking lot and pulled open the heavy oak door that led into Sinclair's.

There seemed to be almost a hush as the door drifted back into its frame. Sara felt as if she had entered a church.

No, a dwelling out of the pages of time was more like it, she decided, looking around. Crossing the threshold of Sinclair's/Tahoe had instantly catapulted her into Arthurian England. This restaurant didn't go back quite that far.

The journey stopped at the brink of Queen Victoria's time. The ambience was pleasantly old-fashioned, but not stiflingly so.

"How many in your party?" the woman at the reception podium asked.

Sara turned, startled. For a moment she had been so lost in her reverie, she hadn't noticed that there was someone else here. She felt no embarrassment at having been caught daydreaming.

"Just one," she said with a smile.

*And it's been that way for a long, long time.*

She had no idea why that made her feel momentarily sad. She decided that her father's call had set everything temporarily on its ear. It was going to take some effort on her part to get everything back on line again.

But she had done it before, she thought cryptically. No reason to suppose she couldn't do it again. Practice made perfect.

Jennifer Sinclair Madigan picked up a tall, dark green menu. For a change there were no catering arrangements to see to. Which was fortunate, because Ginger had called in sick this morning, leaving the hostess podium unattended. Once this had been Julia's position, until her sister married Brom and moved away. Now Jennifer manned it when she wasn't busy trying to juggle several other responsibilities, as well.

She glanced down at her small waist. There was no sign yet. But with the new baby coming, Nik was definitely going to have to hire someone to help out around here.

Jennifer offered the dark-haired woman a genial smile and turned. "This way, please."

Sara laid her hand on Jennifer's arm before she could go any farther. "Oh, I'm not here to eat."

Jennifer looked at the attractive woman quizzically. "Excuse me?"

Sara scanned the dim room as her eyes acclimated. She could discern more details now, and tried to decide which restaurant she liked better, the one in Tahoe or this one. It was a hard choice.

"I'm here to work," she replied, preoccupied. "Maybe." She tossed in the qualifying word as an afterthought. Better not to sound too confident. Employers hated an overconfident employee. She didn't mind playing a part in the beginning.

Jennifer studied the petite woman more closely. She had short black hair and animated dark eyes. She looked like a cross between a dark-haired Tinker Bell and a gypsy.

The description immediately struck a chord. Those had been Julia's exact words on the telephone yesterday when she was describing Brom's cousin. Which had been just after Nik had accidentally destroyed the accounting disc and it had flat-lined on them. A single, eerie white line lying horizontally across a blue field had announced the death of five months' worth of accounting information. In desperation, Jennifer had called Julia to ask if the accounting firm they used had a branch office in California. Brom had promptly volunteered Sara.

Jennifer felt like embracing the woman. "You're Sara."

A mouth that was wider than her delicate oval face

dictated split into an even wider grin. Somehow it looked appealing, Jennifer thought.

"How did you know?" Sara asked, surprised.

Jennifer shifted the menu to her other hand and took the smaller woman's hand in hers. "I'm Jennifer," she said warmly. "Julia's sister. Brom's sister-in-law," she added for good measure.

This was the surrogate mother, Sara thought with a touch of wonder. Brom and Julia had been quick to set Sara straight about the baby when she had commented on how much the little girl looked like a combination of Julia and Brom.

"And A.J.'s—"

"Aunt." Jennifer finished the sentence tactfully, but firmly.

She had carried Aurora Jennifer under her heart for nine months, had given her sister the supreme gift of a tiny life as only one woman could do for another. But now the ties had to be put in their proper place. The baby had Brom's blood running through her veins. Brom's blood and Julia's love. It had begun that way. There was no need to alter anything else with biological details just because Julia was unable to conceive. A.J. was their daughter, not hers.

Sara looked at Jennifer for a long moment through eyes that were filled with genuine amazement. She couldn't quite comprehend that sort of a sacrifice, that degree of selflessness which the situation required. She had never known anyone capable of that before. It took her breath away.

"They told me all about it. Julia and Brom," she added quickly. "The baby's beautiful."

"This way." Jennifer gestured for Sara to follow her through the dining room into the kitchen. She stopped one of the waitresses at the threshold between the two rooms and asked the young woman to take over the desk for a few moments.

That done, Jennifer allowed herself a moment to bask in Sara's compliment. "The Sinclairs make beautiful girl children. Boy children, however," she said as they entered the kitchen, "tend to turn out just a little surly around the edges."

The kitchen, as always, was a beehive of activity. A rather warm beehive, since the air conditioning was being temperamental again and the repairman was over an hour late.

Nik looked up just as Jennifer concluded her pronouncement. He allotted one curious glance in Sara's direction, decided she was some new friend of his sister's and continued with his work without missing a beat. The knife flew over the carrot on the chopping block. Tiny pieces emerged, popping out like a well-rehearsed marine drill team.

"Jennifer, I'm busy."

He was going to have that chiseled into his tombstone—and soon—if he didn't start slacking off. Jennifer shook her head. "So what else is new?"

He spared one dark look in Jennifer's direction. He didn't have time for intrusions, or to act polite. Maybe he'd even forgotten how. But they were shorthanded today and he had a party of thirty coming in at noon above and beyond the usual large crowd of diners that the restaurant enjoyed. Polite would only get trampled to death in the rush.

Jennifer nudged Sara forward. Sara's eyes were glued to the flying knife as it reduced a stalk of celery into confetti before her eyes. "This is the lady who might change some of that for you."

Nik had no idea what Jennifer was talking about. His mind was on half a dozen different pots and ovens at once. Blotting the sweat from his forehead with the back of his wrist, he looked at Sara. He didn't remember calling the temporary agency. Had Jennifer?

"Do you cook?" he asked Sara as he moved to one of the myriad of pots on the seven stoves in the kitchen.

As a rule, Sara frequented take-out places, not supermarkets. "No, but I burn pretty well." Intrigued, drawn by the aroma, Sara peered into the huge pot that Nik was attending. The aroma was almost seductive. Her salivary glands stood at attention. "I don't know tomato paste from poster paste."

Nik replaced the lid on the pot firmly and looked at Sara as if she had just declared a preference for drinking furniture polish over aged wine. "Then why—?"

Jennifer was quick to jump in. Nik became more irritable when things became obscure. "She's here about our accounting mess. You remember, Nik. This is Brom's cousin, Sara."

No, he didn't remember. Not really. Life was becoming more muddled for him than mulligan stew. He remembered a disc dying and Jennifer saying something about calling Brom for a recommendation. Then he vaguely remembered Jennifer talking to him while he had been supervising the pastry chef's newest creation. But as to the exact words, they eluded him. He wondered if he had agreed to something he was going to regret.

His sister and Sara remained standing there, waiting for him to make some sort of acknowledgment. Nik sighed. He didn't have time to leave the kitchen, but he couldn't just hire the woman on the spot, either, even if Brom *had* vouched for her.

He waved toward the door. "Yes, I remember," he lied. "I'm a little busy right now." Now *there* was an understatement, he thought. Nik looked over toward where the new apprentice chef, Chris, was slowly filleting a tray of halibut. "Why don't you have something to eat in the dining room and I'll come out when I can?"

Sara knew when she was being dismissed. Turning, she glanced toward Jennifer as they walked out through the white swinging doors.

"Is he always that friendly?" She'd met corporate heads filing chapter eleven papers at court who were more cheerful than the broad-shouldered man in the apron.

Jennifer led Sara over to a cozy booth close enough to the kitchen for Nik to easily find Sara. "He used to be a lot more easygoing," Jennifer confided. "But after Julia got married and moved away, things went from bad to worse."

Sara looked around the dining room. It was deceptively arranged so that even when it was filled to capacity, it didn't appear crowded.

"Doesn't look all that bad to me," Sara assessed. In her estimation it looked about as busy as its sister restaurant in Tahoe.

Jennifer was tempted to sit and talk for a few minutes, but there just wasn't any time. If she had any to spare, she had to pop into the back office to see how Katie was doing. There was always someone on break, minding her daughter when Jennifer was busy, but nothing took the place of looking in for herself.

"No, the business end is fine," Jennifer agreed. "But

Nik's swamped and he's trying to do everything himself." She smiled fondly as she looked over her shoulder toward the double doors that led to the kitchen. "He has trouble delegating." That had been true of him since childhood. Everyone always relied on Nik to get things done. It had only intensified after their parents' death, when Nik had taken over being father, mother and sole provider for them.

Sara had gotten a good sample of the man's disposition in the kitchen. The man had been chopping, directing and mixing all at the same time. She supposed she could relate to not wanting anyone else's finger in the pie to mess things up. She felt the same way about some things herself. "So I gathered."

Jennifer resisted saying anything further. If she pleaded Nik's case too much, Sara might be put off. Or Nik might become offended if he found out. "Well, I have to be getting back to the front desk." Jennifer began to back away reluctantly.

Sara wondered if Jennifer felt obligated to entertain her for some reason. She waved the other girl's words away. "Oh, please, don't stay on my account. I don't need anyone to hold my hand while I wait for your brother." She looked around again. She was going to like working here. It had a nice feel to it. She set great store by her initial reactions. "I like my own company."

Jennifer studied Sara for a moment longer. *Yes, I think you do.* She placed the menu she was still holding on the table before Sara. "Order anything you like. It's on the house. Lisa'll be here in a few minutes to take your order."

"What was that terrific thing Nik was making?" Sara

asked suddenly as Jennifer turned away. "That big pot he didn't want me looking into?"

Jennifer stopped, smiling. "Nik gets possessive about his work. That was beef Stroganoff." One of the specialties of the house.

"Beef Stroganoff," Sara repeated, as if memorizing the words as she attached them to an image.

After Jennifer left, Sara perused the long, slender menu. It was an impressive selection, she thought, with an equally impressive price range. She scanned the large dining room. Something, apparently, to appeal to everyone. She closed the menu, her order already decided upon. She'd have the Stroganoff.

Sara had finished her meal, consumed three glasses of mineral water and had found several different ways to fold her napkin before Nik finally emerged out of the kitchen, worn around the edges, with a streak of flour on his cheek.

Without any empty chatter to pave the way, Nik sank into the booth next to Sara as if he was collapsing beside an old friend who didn't require any niceties. He sighed and stretched his feet out before him. The last time he'd sat down, he mused, was the day before Halloween. Nineteen ninety. Or, at least, it felt that way.

He closed his eyes for a moment, absorbing the sensation of not being on his feet and moving. When he opened them again Sara was looking at him quizzically.

"Sorry," he muttered, straightening. With very little encouragement he could probably fall asleep right there, sitting up.

Sara held her glass between her hands, rotating it slowly on the table. She had all but given up on him. "I should hope so."

Her reply had him narrowing his eyes. "What?"

Maybe the pending trip to her father's had her unduly antsy and short-tempered. Whatever the reason, she didn't feel very forgiving at the moment.

"I don't like to be kept waiting more than an entire season. When I first sat down, this was a tall candle." She pointed to the stubby yellow waxed candle flickering in the bowl in the center of the table.

Glancing at his watch had become second nature to him, as involuntary and unconscious as breathing. As he did so now, he realized that Sara had been sitting here over an hour. He'd still be in the kitchen, working, if Jennifer hadn't come in and all but pushed him out.

Nik dragged a hand through his light brown hair. He really didn't have the time to conduct an interview. The irony of it struck him. It was like being given a time-saving device and not having the time to read the manual in order to make the device work.

"Listen," he began, "today's rather hectic—"

Sara leaned closer and looked at him knowingly. "Do you really think tomorrow will be any better?"

"No." He didn't even have to think about it. It had been like this for the past six months. And while he blessed his patron saints for watching out for his business, this pace was going to burn him out soon. "I don't."

She rested her case. "I didn't think so. Jennifer told me how well business was going," she added when he raised a brow. She laced her hands together, her eyes on his face. It was a nice face, she thought, strong and broad and sincere. "I'll make it easy for you. Tell me the salary you're thinking of, point me toward the work and I'll give you my answer." She smiled. "That shouldn't take us too long."

Rather than be pleased at her solution, Nik held it suspect. He was always suspicious of things that were too easy. "Are you always this slipshod?"

Her eyes held his for a long, pregnant moment. Hers were the color of hot chocolate on a cold, toe-freezing winter's morning. Or maybe caramel, warm, melting caramel, sliding slowly downward along a mountain of ice cream.

Nik roused himself. He had definitely been slaving over a hot stove too long.

Sara's smile tightened just a smidgen around the edges. "Never. The word, Mr. Sinclair, is fast. I have always been fast." At times she resented having to defend that gift. "Fast does not mean sloppy, or careless, it just means being blessed with quick reflexes and a quick mind."

And obviously, Nik thought, a large ego. There was no room in his operation for something like that. It was just asking for trouble. His doubts multiplied.

"You seem to think a lot of yourself, Ms.—?" He didn't even know her last name, he realized.

"Santangelo," she supplied.

She moved her napkin aside, deciding to dig in and take this man down a little. She didn't know why she felt challenged, but she did.

"A positive image always helps," she told him. "If I don't think well of myself, why should you?"

Nik supposed it made sense in a simple sort of way. He rose and gestured toward the back. "You have a point, I guess." He began to lead the way to the back office, then stopped abruptly. Maybe Brom hadn't filled her in completely. "Listen, this isn't going to be a permanent position."

Nothing ever was, which was just the way she liked

it. Sara shrugged carelessly in response. "Good. I'm not looking for anything permanent."

Anticipating an argument, Nik continued quickly, walking her through the kitchen. Force of habit had him scanning the area to ascertain if everything was proceeding as usual.

"This is just until I get everything back on the disc that was blown up and in general get things under control again." Her words replayed themselves in his mind. "Why aren't you looking for anything permanent?" Nik held the back door open for her.

Sara stepped out into the narrow corridor, brushing against him as she passed. She felt a shimmer of something warm and pleasurable ripple through her. She looked up in surprise and saw by his expression that he had experienced the same unsettling reaction. Just random chemistry, she told herself. Her eyes held his. Or maybe not so random. She wasn't altogether certain she wanted to find out.

After a beat she realized she hadn't answered his question. "I'm here on family business. When that business ends, so will my time here."

That was an odd way to put it, he thought. He was already aware that he wasn't dealing with an average woman, no matter how vague his memory of the gender—outside of his sisters—was as a whole. "You make it sound like you're serving a jail sentence."

The knot in her stomach twisted a little tighter as she thought of what lay ahead of her this afternoon. She wasn't very good at confrontations.

"Close, but not quite." It was bad enough she had to go through it; she didn't want to talk about it, as well. She changed the subject. "So what is it that you

want me to work on? Your books, or your program, or
what?''

''I think it's in the realm of 'or what,''' Nik answered
in a moment of weakness as he opened the office door.

Candy, a college freshman who worked at Sinclair's
part-time, was on the floor, playing with Katie. She
looked up, startled and then pleased. She got up slowly,
like smoke rising in the air, her eyes on Nik. Candy ran
a hand over her picture-perfect hair, gave Nik a sensuous look that drifted right over his head and smiled.
The invitation was so blatant it would have knocked
over a more receptive man. Nik appeared completely
oblivious to it.

''I guess I'd better be getting back to work,'' she said
in the best imitation of Marilyn Monroe that Sara had
heard in a long time. ''My break's over.''

Sara was tickled that Nik was apparently unaware of
the come-on. She decided right then and there that she
was going to like working for him.

''You run a nursery on the side?'' She nodded toward
Katie.

The little girl was clutching a fat crayon and seriously
decorating a huge sheet of paper in front of her. With
a sigh befitting an artist, she lay the crayon down and
appeared to survey her work.

Sara had been an only child, but there had always
been cousins galore of every size and shape while she
was growing up. Instinct took over. She crossed to the
little girl and picked her up. She smelled of apple juice
and baby shampoo.

Katie's cornflower blue eyes opened wide as she
studied Sara's face. A smile broke through as she obviously decided that Sara was to be trusted.

The little girl was going to break a lot of hearts when

she got older, Sara thought. She turned toward Nik, who was watching her quietly. She couldn't tell if he approved or disapproved of her holding the child. "Everywhere I turn, there seem to be babies associated with you people."

"That's because we're so family oriented," Jennifer told Sara as she looked in the doorway. She had seen Candy leaving and had come to check on her little girl. Jennifer looked from Nik to Sara. "Everything okay here?"

Sara jiggled Katie on her hip and the little girl laughed. "Couldn't be better," Sara answered.

Nik, Jennifer could see by the expression on his face, wasn't completely sure about that yet. She wondered if his disquietude had to do with Sara's qualifications, or just surrendering a piece of the control in general.

With the front desk at a lull, Jennifer took the opportunity to steal a few minutes with her daughter. She crossed to Sara. "I see you've met Katie."

Katie stretched her arms out to her mother. "Yours?" Sara asked as she handed the child over. Jennifer nodded, brushing her cheek against the tinier one. Sara turned toward Nik. "Where are yours?"

Right now the only way he could have children, he thought, was to send away for them through a mail-order house.

"I don't have any." He nodded toward his sister. "Raising Jennifer and Julia was enough for me, thanks."

Which wasn't completely accurate. Lately, seeing Julia with her family and Jennifer with hers, a longing had risen within him, a longing in the form of a faint voice that echoed, *Where are mine?*

But it was usually blotted out by the sound of pots

and pans. When it wasn't, he tried not to pay attention to it. Someday he would do something about it, but not now. He was far too busy.

Raising them? Sara looked at Nik dubiously. "You don't look old enough."

"He wasn't," Jennifer confirmed.

She set her squirming daughter back amid her colorful chaos. Nik had had the room transformed into a giant play area for his niece. He had left only a few bare essentials to identify the fact that this was also an office where all the business transactions were conducted.

"But he managed, anyway," she added fondly. She looked at Sara. "So, are you taking the job?"

Nik noticed with annoyance that Jennifer had completely bypassed his input in this scenario.

Sara always went with instincts. Instinct told her to take the job. Prudence told her to go more slowly than she was normally accustomed to. Nik didn't look as if he was up to her normal pace.

"I don't really know what it is yet." Blocks crashed in an orchestrated avalanche as Katie clapped her hands together. "Is she going to be my junior helper?"

Jennifer laughed as she got down on her knees to clear away the debris. "Not if you're lucky. You're going to have enough trouble as it is."

Sara wasn't quite certain whether or not Jennifer was joking. "Trouble?"

Jennifer nodded toward her brother. "Because of Nik."

*Now* she thought of. bringing him into it. To be insulted. "It's not my fault," he protested darkly. "It was the damn computer."

Sara moved toward the desk that was pushed against

one wall to maximize space for Katie. She looked at the dormant computer. "Uh-huh, famous last words."

Jennifer joined her. She switched on the computer and it hummed to life. Within a few moments the single, lonely white line appeared. It lay rigidly stretched out across the screen. Jennifer pointed toward it. "He did that yesterday."

"Any backup discs?" Sara had a feeling she already knew the answer to that.

Nik hated admitting that he had made a mistake. He wasn't used to making them. Despite all the responsibilities that were laid across his shoulders he had always made the right choices, done the right thing. In short, he had always handled everything well. The fact that they now needed an outsider to handle something he considered to be a key part of the restaurant really grated on him.

He scowled at the machine. "No."

"I see." A challenge. Sara nodded thoughtfully. Because Jennifer was more receptive, Sara turned to her with the next question. "Any paper files?"

Jennifer nodded at the towering file cabinet. "Lots. In there. We keep the drawers locked so that Katie isn't tempted to create her own version of a ticker-tape parade in here."

"Very wise. Also a tremendous relief." Sara circled the file cabinet like a magician contemplating the best method of making a tiger appear before an audience in place of a lady. This was the kind of thing best tackled early in the morning, when she was fresh. Right now there was something weighing too heavily on her mind for her to concentrate. "I can start tomorrow morning at about nine or so."

Just like that? Was she desperate, or careless? Nik

couldn't make up his mind. "I haven't quoted you a salary," Nik reminded Sara. The woman was going faster than Julia ever had. His head began to hurt again.

Sara looked at him, surprised that he would think of that as a deterrent. "I'm Brom's cousin. I don't figure you'll insult him or me by paying me minimum wage. Besides—" she shrugged her shoulders in a gesture that was beginning to make Nik feel oddly itchy "—I'm not taking it because I need to make a living at this moment." She had more than enough saved to see her through this episode, had never needed much to begin with.

"Oh?" Nik asked skeptically.

"No." Her wide mouth turned up in a broad smile. "I'm doing it as a favor."

Nik crossed his arms in front of his chest and pinned her with a look. He'd be damned if he was going to be pitied. "For whom?"

"Brom," she answered easily. "And Julia. She said that you were desperate."

Julia always exaggerated even the simplest of things. "I'm never desperate," Nik informed Sara before she began laboring under the wrong impression.

Jennifer weighed the matter quickly and thought that this was a safe time to override Nik. Sara was going to find out, anyway. She nudged him out of the way and moved closer to the other woman. "We're desperate."

Nik knew when he was outnumbered. What did it matter? It was only temporary. They were both in agreement on that part.

Sara began to carefully pick her way through the scattered blocks. "Fine. I'll be here tomorrow, then." She stopped at the threshold. "Oh, one more thing. I need the day after tomorrow off."

Nik stared at her. She was nervy, he'd give her that. "Already?"

"Already," she answered cheerfully. "Those are my terms." She waited to see if he'd turn them down. If he did, he was a fool.

"We'll take them," Jennifer answered for both of them, afraid to let Nik say anything.

But it wasn't good enough. Sara looked at Nik. "Okay with you?"

As much as Nik hated to admit it, he really had no other choice. Sinclair's couldn't go on indefinitely without some sort of up-to-date accounting system. With business being what it was, he had no time to feed the damned information into the miserable computer again, and neither did Jennifer.

That left him with only one viable alternative.

He sighed, Lee surrendering his sword to Grant at Appomattox with whispers of "The South shall rise again," echoing in the background.

"Okay by me." The words sounded as if they were being forcibly dragged out of his mouth.

Sara laughed as she exited. "It's going to be great working for one of the less popular seven dwarfs," she mused aloud, closing the door behind her.

Nik scowled at the door. He gave the arrangement one week, tops.

## Chapter 2

The smile on Sara's lips slowly faded as she slid behind the wheel of her car. There were no other stops she needed to make. It was time to see her father.

A hollow feeling seeped through her like seawater into the hull of a ship that wasn't quite airtight.

"No more excuses, Saratoga, you're a big girl now. You can do this."

Sara jabbed her key into the ignition and turned it. Anger and anxiety faced off within her like pro tennis players at a Wimbledon play-off. Gripping the wheel, she gunned the engine and peeled out of the parking lot, hugging the road as if the car was part of it.

Nik winced when he heard the noise, certain that it was Sara driving away. Just what he needed, an Indianapolis 500 trainee.

He eyed Jennifer as she prepared to leave for a consultation with a catering client. "Brom say what Sara does in her spare time? Stunt driving for movies?"

Jennifer slipped her purse strap onto her arm. Affectionately she patted her brother's cheek. Her fingers touched a tiny bit of stubble Nik had missed shaving this morning.

And that wasn't all he was missing lately, she thought. Life was whizzing by him. "She's probably just in a hurry to see her father. You grumble too much, Nik. You're getting too stodgy and cranky in your old age."

Old age. The phrase rankled him a little more than it should have, perhaps because he felt it was merited. He resisted it all the more for that. Nik gave Jennifer a black look. He was only thirty-five. Why did it feel as if he had already lived an entire lifetime?

And why, at the same time, did it feel, with all this responsibility he had to shoulder, with all the work he had to do, with all the family around him, as if life was mysteriously passing him by?

"Watch it, Jenny, I'm only five years older than you. If I'm old, what does that make you?"

"Still young and happy." Her expression softened slightly as concern edged its way in. She wanted him to have the same things she did. If anyone deserved happiness, he did. "Maybe you should take the time to enjoy life before it's too late."

Nik frowned. Not that again. He wasn't in the mood to listen to another verse of "Poor Overworked Nik" being sung in the key of Jennifer. He knew all the words by heart. "I'll see if I can schedule it in by the end of the month," he quipped, turning away.

Maybe Jennifer was right, he mused reluctantly as he opened the door to the kitchen. Maybe he *was* working too hard. The problem was, he didn't know how else to approach life anymore except at full throttle. The little engine that could—did. And would undoubtedly continue to do so until it blew itself up.

Now there was a heartening prospect.

Nik sighed. Now his sisters had him doing it, making him feel that he was overdoing everything. He didn't feel overworked. Not *exactly.* Just a little harried, as if he was missing something by being here all the time. But for more than the past decade, in order to first make a living for them and then keep the restaurant going according to his high standards, this was all he had had time *to* do. Hard work had begat success, which begat more hard work. It was like being on a merry-go-round that had lost its Stop button.

He wondered if a vacation was the answer.

A noise in the kitchen caught his attention and thoughts of vacations dissolved like greasy dishwater before an emulsifier.

Nik strode into the large room and crossed directly to the new apprentice chef. He eyed the portion of halibut beneath Chris's knife critically. The fish looked as if it had been tortured to death.

"Unless you're trying to get a confession out of that halibut, you're going about filleting all wrong. Watch."

With a shake of his head Nik took hold of the long knife and went to work on the next piece of fish.

It had been almost fourteen years since she'd ridden down this path. Fourteen years bracketed by painful, lonely memories. Yet she remembered the way as if the route was forever painted onto the pages of her mind. The car moved as if it was on automatic pilot. There was no hesitation at corners, no fumbling with written directions, indecisions on whether to turn left or right. Sara never forgot anything.

She set her mouth hard. No, she never forgot anything. Not the good times, or the bad.

She was almost there already, she realized. The trip from Sinclair's to her father's house had gone by much too fast to suit her. She had secretly hoped for a blowout or a traffic snarl to delay her, to give her just a little more stalling time.

"Coward," she muttered under her breath. "What are you afraid of?" Her voice rose over the sound of the music on the radio. "He can't hurt you anymore." She was clutching the steering wheel so hard that her knuckles were literally turning white. She eased her hold, though the tension refused to go. "You're past that, remember? He has his life and you have yours. You're just doing a good deed because you happen to be kinder than he ever was."

If that's all there was, why was her throat constricting like wet leather left out in the sun as she approached her father's development, for God's sake?

Annoyance bubbled within her like unattended boiling water on the stove, threatening to overflow. She needed to be strong, to be self-confident now of all times, not suddenly fighting with shadows from her past.

Needing to distract herself, she started flipping to different radio stations, searching for heavy metal music that would fill the car and take up the space in her brain. Sara desperately wanted to be anesthetized by the time she reached her father's door.

She wasn't.

Sara parked across the street from the familiar address and shut off the engine. Instead of opening the car door and getting out, she remained where she was, waiting for the feeling to return to her suddenly numb legs. She sat for a long while, just staring at the tidy-looking house. Her father lived in a single-story stucco house. The walls were dove gray, with white paint accenting the wood trim. It appeared to be freshly painted.

It was just the same as when she'd seen it last. Fourteen years and he hadn't changed the color scheme, she thought. At least her father was steadfast about some things.

Bitterness rose in her throat, bringing with it a sickly taste. Sara forced it down. No recriminations, she had promised herself before boarding the plane. Recriminations would only serve to rip open tender skin that covered wounds that had never properly healed. She didn't want to hear his excuses, because they weren't any good.

There *were* no acceptable excuses as far as she was concerned, no reason in the world for a man to turn his back on the daughter who worshiped him.

Sara closed her eyes and searched for inner strength. She'd come this far; she couldn't fall apart now. "C'mon, Sara, remember Drama One. You can carry this off. At least your conscience will always be clear."

She knew that if she'd turned a deaf ear to her father's plea, justified or not, she would carry the burden of that guilt with her no matter what the outcome of the operation. It wasn't in Sara to walk away from a plea for help no matter how much she might want to.

Woodenly Sara emerged from the car and slammed the door behind her. The three suitcases she always traveled with were butted up against each other in the trunk, but for the time being she left them there. It was almost as if, subconsciously, she was denying the fact that she had agreed to stay with her father for the duration of his surgery and recovery period. If her suitcases remained in her car she might still feel as if she was just passing through. She wanted to hang on to that feeling a little while longer. It might make the first few hours here that much easier to handle.

She glanced around for traffic on the street and then crossed to number five Avalone.

That was all she was doing, Sara assured herself. Just passing through, the way she had through all those dozens of other places that had floated by in the past six years.

"Just another adventure, Saratoga. No more, no less." She pressed the doorbell.

As she stood there, waiting for a response, it was as if there were two completely different projectors in her mind, vying for the same screening space. One reel was filled with scenes from her childhood, happy scenes with her parents, with her father, taking trips, going on family outings together. All her happy memories.

The other held only a single vivid scene. It was the moment her father had, for the last time, walked out of the house he and her mother had once shared. He had promised Sara that he'd return the following weekend. He hadn't. Week after week she had waited, hoping, praying. But he had never come.

She felt the ache inside her chest building again. Damn it, she wasn't that young girl anymore. *She wasn't.* Sara blinked back the tears that had begun to coat her lashes. She had grown light-years away from the girl who'd cried, who had felt so abandoned.

The door opened.

Sara sucked in her breath as the tall man in the doorway moved forward. The eyes were the same. A soft brown. But where they had once resembled those of a small boy, twinkling with secrets and mischief, her father's eyes now belonged to a man who had been beaten down by something or someone. Apart from his eyes it was difficult for Sara to recognize Raymond Santangelo. He was thinner now and years older. The years were all there, etched on his face in lines of sorrow. His once-thick brown hair had thinned and his hairline was receding. Though physically tall, he somehow seemed smaller to her than he had fourteen years ago.

This was her father?

Sara wanted to deny it and run, to hold on to her last memories and close the door firmly behind her.

She remained where she was.

"Saratoga?" He whispered her name in hopeful disbelief the way a prisoner did upon receiving a long-awaited parole from the review board. Nervously he moved to take her hand, then stopped, running bony fingers through his gray-flecked brown hair.

Because her father was nervous, Sara found the resolve to be strong. "Hello, Dad." She forced a distant smile she didn't feel to her lips. "Funny running into you like this."

Raymond Santangelo was a policeman with eighteen years of service behind him. In his time he had faced down more than one criminal. And in all that time his hands had never felt this clammy. He brushed them against the back of his jeans and then found the courage to clasp his daughter's hand in his.

"Saratoga, you're beautiful."

She frowned. She referred to herself by that name at times, but no one else did any more. Most people didn't even know it was her legal name. "I'd rather you didn't call me that. It's Sara now."

She had suffered years of teasing because of that name. She had endured it without complaint because her father had named her after the town he had met her mother in. Sara had once thought it was the height of romance. After he left there hadn't seemed to be much point in Sara being reminded of it.

"Saratoga sounds too much like the racetrack."

Raymond nodded, uncomfortable at the reminder. Did she know, after all? Or just suspect? He'd tried so hard to hide it from her.

"Sure. Sara." His head bobbed again. "Sounds fine. Fine." Feeling awkward, needing somewhere else to direct his gaze, Raymond looked down at the doorstep. "Where's your luggage?"

"In the car." She nodded over her shoulder. The idea of going to a hotel was beginning to appeal to her. "I thought that I'd—"

But Raymond was already striding past his daughter, intent on reaching the car before Sara. At least he could carry her bags for her.

"I'll get them." He walked with a sense of determination as he crossed the street. "And you can park the car in my garage." He gestured behind him without looking. He was all right as long as he didn't see the accusing hurt in her eyes. Raymond spoke quickly. "It'll be a tight fit, but it's supposed to be a two-car garage and—" He reached the car and suddenly swung around, carried away by the emotions swelling within him. He'd missed her so much. "God, Saratoga—Sara, I'm glad you're here. I know this wasn't easy for you."

Sara reached the other side of the car and opened the trunk. "Easiest thing in the world." She purposely kept her voice as distant as the physical space she maintained between them. She saw her father raise his brow. "I buy airplane tickets all the time. This gives me an excuse to see Southern California again. It's been fourteen years.''

She wasn't unaware of the wince her words evoked from her father.

*Guilty? Good, you should be.* But the thought brought her no satisfaction.

"Yes, it has been a long time...." His voice trailed off with nowhere to go.

As her father reached into the trunk for the first suitcase Sara quickly stopped him like a no-nonsense nurse walking in on a patient about to light up a forbidden cigarette.

"I'll get them." She ignored the frustrated look on her father's face. "I'm not the one having heart surgery," she reminded him crisply. "You are. You're not supposed to be carrying anything heavy."

"Sure. Anything you say."

Sara didn't bother to comment. She took out the first suitcase and then the second. The third was a small case with a shoulder strap. Slipping it over her shoulder, she managed to pick up all three bags.

Raymond watched her helplessly. He licked his lips, wanting desperately to find the right words to break down the barriers that had grown between them. He knew that he deserved every bitter nuance that she tossed his way, but for far different reasons than she was aware of. He ached for the love he had been forced to turn away from so many years ago.

Sara walked back to the house. Raymond hurried so that he could hold open the door for her.

"You'll be staying in your old room." He pushed the door back and the doorknob bumped against the wall with a thud.

Sara crossed the threshold, valiantly shutting herself off from a fresh onslaught of memories. The familiarity clawed at her and she knew she shouldn't have come. But she was here and had to work with that.

"I don't remember staying in it often enough for it to be thought of as my room." She set down one suitcase to get a better grip on the handle.

"Are you sure I can't help…?"

She wanted to throw her arms around him, to cry, to beat her fist against him and demand to know why he hadn't said those words years ago, when he *could* have helped.

Her grip tightened on the suitcase handle as she straightened. "I can manage. I've been doing it for a long time."

Raymond faltered slightly before turning and leading the way toward the rear of the house. "I'm sure you have."

Sara looked around as she followed him. There was hardly any furniture in the living room and the dining room was completely empty. The faded wall outlined bright rectangles of color where once paintings and framed photographs had hung.

Raymond turned to see the surprised look on her face. "It looks pretty Spartan," she commented.

Her father nodded. His second divorce had been bitter and painful. "Joyce decided to take more than her share." He shrugged helplessly. "I thought she'd earned it."

*And what about us, Dad, Mom and me? Didn't we deserve more than we got?*

Sara moved around her father as she entered the small bedroom, careful not to allow the slightest physical contact between them. "Very sporting of you."

Raymond heard the hurt in her voice, the brittleness, and wished he had the words with which he could cut down the brambles that had grown between them. Now more than ever he regretted what had happened.

But he was an optimist at heart. Even in the face of darkness he always believed that there would be light. Maybe soon.

Sara tried not to look around as she placed the suitcases down next to the bed. Memories ricocheted from the walls despite her efforts, threatening a fresh assault. She had known this was going to be hard, possibly the most difficult thing she'd ever done. But she hadn't fully realized that it was going to rip through her this badly.

She'd never forgive herself if she cried in front of him. She braced her shoulders as she turned to face him. Searching for something to say, she wrinkled her nose. "It's dusty."

Raymond leapt on the neutral topic like a starving dog onto a bone. He ran his hand along the footboard and wiggled his fingers at the layer of dust that coated them.

"I never was much on cleaning." Self consciously he wiped his hand on his jeans and then shoved both hands into his back pockets. "I kept meaning to get a woman to come in to clean after Joyce left, but you know how it is." He shrugged as if to punctuate his statement.

Sara picked up a suitcase, placed it on the light blue bedspread and snapped open the locks. "No." Her voice was low. "I don't know how it is. And I probably never will." She shook out a sweater and crossed to the narrow closet. It was empty inside.

"I'll get you some hangers," Raymond volunteered quickly, anxious to avoid any emotional confrontation.

Sara laid the sweater over the back of the chair that was next to the white, lacquered desk. The furniture was intended for a young girl. A young girl, she thought, who had barely gotten to use it.

Raymond stopped in the doorway. His voice grew even more uncertain. "How's your mother?"

Sara tried to hold on to her anger. Her father had put her up in the same room she had occupied as a child and now he was asking about her mother. Didn't he realize how difficult he was making this for her? It was all she could do not to give in to the need to hurl accusations at him. If this was going to work she needed to keep everything, all her emotions, under wraps. Maybe he was doing this intentionally. Maybe he needed forgiveness, but she couldn't find it in her heart to give it to him.

"Fine." The word shot out as if it was a bullet. "She and Larry moved to Arizona three years ago."

Or maybe it was four. Sara had lost track after her mother had distanced herself from her daughter. It arose from the fact that each time she looked into Sara's face, her mother saw traces of her failed dreams there.

"He raises cattle. She frequents the artsy-crafty places. It works out." Sara felt as if she was reciting a human interest story about two people who were strangers to her.

Selectively, Raymond remembered soft laughter and better times. "I'm glad she's finally happy."

A blouse held tightly in her hands, Sara raised her eyes to her father's face, but said nothing.

The silence vibrated like an oppressive dirge within the room. Raymond wished he was on a stakeout, or somewhere where he had a clue as to what he was doing, what was expected of him. He had no clues here. He had no idea what to do or what to say next. The road between then and now was littered with so many mistakes he was at a loss as to how to begin to clear a path to his daughter.

Frustrated, helpless, angry, he gestured toward the kitchen. "Have you eaten? I could whip up a macaroni and cheese casserole. Remember how you—"

She didn't want to remember. Anything. "Yes, as a matter of fact, I have eaten. I had lunch at a place called Sinclair's on Coast Highway. Know it?" Raymond shook his head. His experience ran to fast-food places. Both his line of work and his finances dictated it.

Sara continued removing things from her suitcase. She hardly knew what she was handling. She just knew she had to keep her hands busy. She had a feeling that when she finished she'd have no idea where anything was.

She placed her nightgown in the bottom drawer of the bureau. "I'll be working there."

"Working?" Raymond's face brightened. It was as if the sun had come out after forty days of rain. "Then you're going to—"

"Stay?" She second-guessed him.

The word turned as if it were a knife in his gut. Raymond could tell by the way she said the word that she wasn't.

"No." She slammed the bottom drawer with finality. "But I don't like vegetating, either." Returning to the bed, she realized that there wasn't anything left inside the suitcase to remove. She closed it and lifted the second one onto the bed. "I looked in on Brom before flying down here. He's married again."

She wondered if her father even knew that Brom had been married before. Or that his first wife had died suddenly. Probably not. He was too busy with his own life to know. Or care.

On automatic pilot, she began to unpack the second case. "And his new wife's part owner of Sinclair's." She lined up a few tubes of makeup on top of the bureau. "Seems they need a temporary accountant. And that's me."

Her eyes met her father's in the mirror above the bureau. "Temporary." Her tongue wrapped around the word carefully, as if it was jagged. Her father looked away. "Just passing through. I don't like to stay anywhere for very long." A briskness underscored her manner as she emptied the rest of the suitcase on top of the bed. "There are too many places to see and too many things to do in life to let myself stagnate in one place too long."

It was his fault. All his fault. He'd known it for years. But for reasons other than she thought. Raymond reached out to touch her arm.

"Sara, I—"

Sara's head jerked up and she pinned him with a look that had her father dropping his hand impotently to his side. "Yes?"

Raymond Santangelo backed down from the slight, dark-haired woman the way he never would from a confrontation with any hood on the streets.

He shook his head. "Nothing. I'll leave you to your unpacking." He hesitated as his tongue nervously outlined the border of his dry mouth. "Maybe later you'd like to just sit and talk?"

Sara's immediate reaction was to refuse, to say no, they couldn't sit and talk now. Talking was something they should have done years ago when it still could have done some good. But she let her temper cool, and nodded.

"Sure. You can fill me in on your doctors' names and the rest of the details about your tests and diagnosis." It was the accountant in her speaking. She knew she was on safe ground if she just stuck to cut-and-dried details. Things she could maintain at an antiseptic distance.

Sara already had her back to him. She tried to sort out the clothes on the bed that were swimming before her as her eyes grew moist. Pressing her lips together, she curled her fingers into her palms, digging in with her nails. The moisture abated.

"Sara?"

Under control, she still refused to turn toward him. "Yes?"

He stood, looking at her back, remembering. And was grateful. "It's nice to have you here, even under these conditions."

Without realizing it he ran his hand over his chest. The small, nagging pain was with him almost constantly now. An irritant to a vital, active man who had once thought himself on the edge of immortality.

She turned and caught the unconscious movement. She refused to let it penetrate her wall. "These were the only conditions under which you could have me here," she answered quietly, her voice a single, steely note. Turning her back on him again, she returned to her sorting. "I'm a Culhane. And Culhanes don't ignore their responsibilities."

Raymond opened his mouth to say something, then shut it again. There was no point in it right now. "I'll see you after you've settled in."

* * *

Sara knew she would have slept better if she had slept on a bed of nails. Spending the night in her father's house had her tossing and turning for endless hours, haunted by thoughts, by memories. And by guilt. Guilt she felt she didn't deserve. But it gnawed at her anyway, like a hungry mouse at a huge ring of cheese.

She rose at first light, more dead than alive. Forcing herself to move quickly, she showered and dressed, hoping to leave the house before her father was up.

She succeeded.

Maybe it was the coward's way out, she thought as she made her way down to Coast Highway. But she just couldn't bring herself to sit across from her father over breakfast. Dinner had been hard enough with the ghost of years past sitting right there between them. She was good at small talk when the need arose, but last night she had had to dig deep to keep the stillness at bay.

The stillness and the hurt.

After a sleepless night she was in no mood to wage another war. Especially not when she had a full day of work before her.

Her stomach grumbled a protest. Sara was used to eating first thing in the morning. The beauty of working at a restaurant, she told herself, was that she could get her breakfast there.

Provided Mr. Personality didn't have some rule against employees eating on the premises. She thought of Nik, and her mood shifted from tension to amusement. He reminded her of the type who was accustomed to exercising complete control over things. She could relate to that. And enjoy sparring with him.

Anything to get her mind off the house on Avalone Drive.

When she pulled in to the gray, graveled parking lot,

there was only one other car there. It was a battered old car, vintage unknown. Its color depended on the side she was standing on. It had a red hood and beige right side and rear. The left side was black. The rickety car was a composite of accidents.

She wondered if it was Nik's. It was rather early to be here, but Nik struck her as the type to open up the place on his own. If it was his car, the man was definitely eccentric.

Her stomach grumbled again as she got out of her car. She rubbed it, as if that would stave off the pangs that were growing.

Sara knocked twice on the back door. There was no answer. With a sigh she knocked once more. Nothing. Time to find a fast-food take-out place, she decided.

She had crossed to her car and was just taking out her key when the back door of the restaurant opened.

A snowy head peered out. The man squinted at her from behind his glasses. "We're closed," the man announced, his spidery fingers splayed on the door.

Sara was back before him in a minimum of steps. "Yes, I know. But Mr. Sinclair wanted me to get an early start on the accounts." Before the man could say a word in protest, Sara had slipped her hand into his and was shaking it heartily. "I'm Sara Santangelo. I'll be working here for the next few weeks."

The old man blinked as he pushed his wire-rimmed glasses up his short, wide nose. His expression was still rather doubtful. "Mr. Sinclair didn't tell me nothing about anyone coming in here before him."

Easing her way in, Sara nodded as if this was to be expected. "He must have forgotten, Mr.—" She looked at the maintenance man. "I'm sorry, I missed catching your name."

He ran a coarse thumb beneath the suspender of his bibbed overall. "I didn't throw it." He paused, eyeing her. Sara outwaited him. "Sam," he mumbled. "My name's Sam."

"Sam," she repeated, her generous mouth spreading into a wide smile.

A beat later Sam closed the door behind them and followed her into the restaurant.

# Chapter 3

The two aspirin he had taken just before leaving his house definitely weren't doing the trick, Nik thought, disgruntled. More than that, they were making things worse. Instead of taking the edge off the pain that was pulsating in his neck like the rhythm section of a rock band, they were slowly, methodically, burning their way through his esophagus, creating a hole in his stomach.

At least, it felt that way.

The pain didn't put Nik in the best of moods as he pulled his '78 Mustang into the parking lot in front of Sinclair's. His disposition would have been judged surly in comparison to a wounded bear's.

Served him right for trying to stay up while his whole body begged him to go to bed. He'd fallen asleep in his recliner again last night, poring over his notes for the new recipe he was working on. A meal had to be choreographed just so, both for taste and appearance. Nik spent hours choosing and discarding different arrangements, searching for the perfect marriage of ingredients with the right visual complement of main course with side dishes.

There was a time he'd stayed up all hours trying to trim pennies from budgets that were already cleaved to the bone, in order to keep the restaurant running a little longer, until it turned a profit. Now budget worries were essentially a thing of the past, yet there always seemed to be something that kept him up at night.

Both Jennifer and Julia had been pleading with him to stop doing the actual cooking and just concern himself with the creative end of running the restaurant, but it was hard for him to let go. Hard to let go of any of it. He knew he had a very real need to feel in control of it all. It was difficult to break old patterns, even in the face of prosperity.

Nik shut off the engine. Massaging the back of his neck, he rotated it slowly, desperately attempting to alleviate the stiffness. It clung like a suction cup to a smooth glass surface.

He sighed, getting out of the car. Eventually the pain would taper off. What he needed right now, he decided as he walked toward the restaurant, was something in his stomach to coat it. The aspirin felt as if they were well on their way to burning a hole straight down to his toes.

It was tantamount to the old, closing-of-the-barn-door-after-the-horse-had-run-off theory, he thought sarcastically. But eating something certainly couldn't hurt any more right now than this miserable burning sensation going through him, and maybe it would help.

Slipping his key into the lock, Nik opened the large oak front door. Once inside he closed the door softly behind him. He felt the peace embrace him immediately.

The dim lighting cast shadows all around him, reinforcing the hushed silence. He could hear himself breathe here. Even the hum of the refrigerator wasn't audible. It was almost like a cathedral, he mused. In a way, maybe it was, to him. He'd done a lot of praying here, a lot of invoking of heavenly intervention to keep the bill collectors at bay and to spread the word through satisfied restaurant critics.

His prayers had worked.

Time to get the cathedral up and running, Nik thought, pocketing his key.

He didn't bother turning on any more lights. He could easily maneuver his way around in the dark. Every inch of Sinclair's was familiar to him. With long, sure strides he made his way to the kitchen. If he didn't eat something soon to quell this fiery stomach he didn't know if he could concentrate on his work.

It was dim in the kitchen, as well.

Nik stopped when he heard a noise coming from the walk-in refrigerator. Frowning, he flipped on the switch. There wasn't supposed to be anyone here except Sam. It wasn't like the maintenance man to just help himself to anything. It wasn't that Nik minded if the man fixed a meal when he came in early. It was just that he knew that Sam was a stickler about not taking what wasn't his. That meant that someone else was in the kitchen.

The door to the walk-in hung open like the mouth of a steely cave. From his vantage point, the first thing Nik saw as he approached was a very well-rounded, jean-clad posterior. The owner of said anatomy was bending over, examining the contents of one of the large metal pots that were kept stored there.

Nik glanced at his watch. It was too early for her to be here. He winced as the movement sent another arrow of pain shooting through his shoulder blades. "Change your schedule, Harri?"

Sara dropped the huge flat lid onto the pot and swung around. She'd been so engrossed in her explorations that she hadn't heard Nik approaching. Quick to recover, she gave Nik an intrigued smile.

"Harry? I look like Harry to you?" She glanced around at her posterior. "I must need more exercise than I thought."

It was her. The accountant. Sara. Nik was reminded of the pain in his stomach and neck simultaneously.

"From this angle you look just like Harri." He saw the dubious look rise in Sara's eyes as she followed him out of the refrigerator. "Harriet Sugarman," he clarified. "The woman who comes here to collect the restaurant's leftovers every morning."

Stopping at the pantry, he bent and opened the lower drawer. He dragged out an unopened two-foot-long loaf of white bread, laid it on the counter and expertly cracked it in half as if it was a mere egg. The white wrapper on both sides tore easily. Nik extracted two slices from the middle, then moved the loaf aside.

Sara stared, fascinated by the size of the loaf. She nodded toward the refrigerator. By her own cursory inventory, she had seen that there were a great many leftovers stored there. "Isn't that an awful lot of food for just one woman?"

Nik took a bite out of the bread before answering, feeling as if he was making an offering before a fire god. He managed a smile, thinking of Harriet and the work she did.

"Harriet has a large family." That was the way she

regarded anyone in need, as her brother or sister, Nik thought. There was a lot to be said for that sort of generosity. He did his own small part by throwing open his kitchen to her. He hated seeing food wasted.

Sara opened her mouth, but Nik wasn't in the mood to answer more questions. ''Actually, she collects food from local restaurants and supermarkets to take up to the homeless mission in Orange. She's usually here at nine.'' He took another bite of the bread for good measure and debated making a sandwich. ''I should have realized you weren't her.''

For one thing, from that angle Harriet didn't look nearly as firm as Sara appeared to be, but he decided against making the comparison out loud.

Nik glanced at his watch. It was only a few minutes past eight. ''What are you doing here so early, anyway? You don't have to be here before ten.''

He sounded as if he was annoyed with her, she thought. He was acting like someone who'd caught a poacher on his land. She wondered if he actually regarded this as his little kingdom.

Nik had surprised her before she'd had a chance to fix anything. Now Sara helped herself to a slice of bread, then proceeded to tear little holes out of the middle as she ate.

''I thought I'd get an early start. Okay with you?'' She raised large brown eyes to his face, waiting.

He shrugged. ''Fine with me.'' Nik watched as Sara wadded up the small pieces and popped them into her mouth. It was almost sacrilegious. He resisted the temptation to take the bread out of her hand. ''Who taught you how to eat? A sparrow?''

She popped another piece into her mouth before answering, then raised her chin, as if daring him to take a swipe. Her eyes laughed at his seriousness. "Big Bird, why?"

He moved the loaf back onto the butcher-block top. It hit the row of toasters, rattling them. "You can't savor it if you eat like that."

Sara stared at the slice in her hand. By now it was only a crusty frame surrounding a white-rimmed hole. "This is white bread, not escargot." As if to reinforce her point she held the bread up, dangling it before him.

This time Nik *did* take it from her, and then tossed the crust into the garbage. "Doesn't matter. All food should be enjoyed, or what's the point?"

Her slender shoulders rose and then fell in a careless shrug. She wondered if Brom had neglected to tell her that his brother-in-law was some sort of a fanatic.

"I don't know." She'd never been much for frequenting fancy restaurants and stuffing herself on rich, overpriced food. Sandwiches and Twinkies were fine with her, washed down with soda pop. "Fuel? Survival?"

Nik didn't care for either of the two choices she offered. The sigh he emitted hissed through his teeth as his hand clamped down on her wrist when she reached for another slice of bread. Their eyes held for a minute, hers defiant and amused as she waited.

"Have you had breakfast yet?"

"No, that's what I thought I was doing now." Her eyes indicated the imprisoned hand. When he followed her gaze, she wiggled the slice of bread she was still holding. "You can take it out of my pay."

Nik released her wrist. It was going to be a challenge working with this woman and not wrapping his hands around her long, slender neck. He looked at it now, letting the image play across his mind.

"Sit down." Nik motioned toward one of the stools that were tucked under a long counter on the side of the room. When work was hectic, some of the employees took their meals here. "I'll cook it for you."

Before Sara could say anything, Nik walked into the refrigerator. A moment later he emerged with a large bowl filled to the brim with eggs. He placed it near the closest stove.

Sara remained standing where she was. She didn't much care for being motioned off anywhere like a lowly servant. "Don't bother." Sara reached around Nik's side toward the pile of eggs in the bowl. "I can—"

For the second time in five minutes Nik caught her wrist. This time his grasp was firmer. He felt her pulse jump under his thumb. It made him wonder why. Maybe she was girding up for a battle. "You told me yesterday that you don't cook."

It figured he'd remember that. Sara shrugged, annoyed. She could certainly manage beating up two eggs, for heaven's sake. "I don't, but—"

Nik caught up the last word. "*But* I'd rather not see this kitchen in a mess before I even start."

Amusement was the best way to handle this bear, she decided. As if in surrender, she raised her hands in the air, away from any utensils or ingredients. "Wanna make your own mess, huh?"

He didn't particularly like being laughed at, not when he felt as if his neck was going to snap off and his stomach was the scene of an intense inferno. "Santangelo, go chew on an abacus until I'm finished."

Exasperated, he banged down the metal pan that was shiny despite years of use and pulled open a drawer beneath the butcher-block table.

"Are you always this charming first thing in the

morning?'' Sara watched him almost snap off the top of the antacid bottle and shake out two tablets. They bounced from his hand and landed on the table.

He reached for the tablets. Sara beat him to it. He raised a warning brow. ''No, usually I'm worse. Just ask Jennifer.''

Smiling sweetly, Sara offered up the prize, pouring the two tablets from the palm of her hand into his. ''Don't tell me I'm giving you heartburn.''

''No.'' He threw the two tablets into his mouth and chewed with a vengeance, wishing they could act instantly. Or, at the very least, make *her* disappear. ''The two aspirin I took this morning beat you to that.'' *This time.*

''Aspirin? You have a fever?'' Sara placed her palm to his forehead.

Nik moved his head aside. He didn't quite like the fact that her hand felt soothing. The rest of her certainly wasn't.

''No, a pain in my neck.'' He saw the slight flash of annoyance in her eye. ''Literally.'' Without meaning to, he ran his hand along the back of his neck and winced slightly. ''All the aspirin did was give me a burning sensation in my stomach.'' He turned back to the pan. ''Now, if you're finished taking inventory—''

Sara had stopped listening. Instead, she circled behind him. Nik felt as if he was being stalked. Before he could ask her what she thought she was doing, Sara was standing on her toes, placing her long fingers on either side of his neck.

She probed, her fingers surprisingly sturdy. ''Here? Does it hurt here?''

He tried to move aside, but he couldn't. Sara was

holding him in place. "I'm paying you to be an accountant, not a masseuse."

The man was a mule. She took a deep breath and discovered that his cologne created a very pleasing sensation, conjuring up all sorts of warm, sensual images within her. Probably essence of paprika mixed with equal parts onion powder, she mused.

Her hands remained firmly in place despite his attempt to shrug her off. "You're not getting a masseuse. This is something I learned from a chiropractor in New York."

Nik opened his mouth to protest being a guinea pig for her experiments when suddenly there was a sickening, crunching noise. It came from his neck. "Oh, God."

Miraculously, his pain was gone.

Nik took a slow, tentative breath, as if to test whether his head was still connected to the rest of him or had fallen off somewhere. He turned to look at her, his expression incredulous.

"The pain's gone."

Sara tried not to appear too smug, but lost the fight. She slipped back onto the stool. "Yes, I know. Works every time. *Now* I feel like I've earned my breakfast."

He stood a moment, flexing his muscles uncertainly, as if he expected something to pop off. What, he wasn't sure. "You do this often?"

She shook her head. "Not that many people I know get pains in their neck."

He eyed her for a moment. "I find that hard to believe." He had a few more choice things to add, but he swallowed them. He was best at just cooking, and decided to concentrate on that exclusively for the time being.

Sara watched, fascinated despite herself, as Nik created an omelet for her. His fingers seemed to fly from dicing ingredients on the chopping block to the frying pan and back again. Bits of ham, green pepper and what appeared to be three kinds of cheese, not to mention things that flew out in an array of interesting colors from containers on the spice rack, all met and melded on the sizzling pan in an edible rainbow.

Sara crossed her arms in front of her. It was a little like watching an artist create a masterpiece. Or, more appropriately like a magician conjuring something out of nothing.

Holding a corner of the plate through a towel he had picked up, Nik placed the dish before her. "There. Breakfast." He took silverware from the same drawer where he kept his antacids. He handed the knife and fork to her.

The omelet was huge. There was no way she could ever manage to finish it on her own.

"Aren't you going to join me?" She cocked her head as she looked at him. "This is way too big for me."

Getting off the stool, she opened the drawer he had just shut and took out another set of utensils. She offered them up to Nik.

He regarded the knife and fork uncertainly. He had a dozen details to see to before the restaurant was open for business. Details he liked attending to himself. He didn't have time to share a meal with a woman he found as annoying as he found attractive.

"I, um…"

The utensils remained aloft. A smile curved her mouth. "Or did you manage to poison this somehow when I wasn't watching?"

He took the knife and fork from her and sat down,

even though he'd had no intentions of doing either. "Of course it isn't poisoned."

She smiled wider, wondering if he even knew that he was sitting down. "Then there's no reason not to join me, is there?" She bent closer, her body suddenly very much in his space. "Unless you don't like the company."

Hot chocolate. Her eyes definitely reminded him of hot chocolate. That hot chocolate had been his favorite drink as a child seemed oddly disconcerting to him right now. "I'm not sure exactly *how* I feel about the company."

The answer pleased her. "Good. I've never liked being thought of as predictable." She tossed her head. The large hoops at her ears swung back and forth. "It's far too stifling." She scanned the length of the spice rack. "Have any hot sauce handy?"

He did, but he wasn't about to let her commit the ultimate sin by splashing his creation with a fiery red wave. "My omelet doesn't need any hot sauce."

*No ego problem here.* Resigned, Sara took a bite. It was like a warm surprise on her tongue, tangy and flavorful and light. She looked at Nik and saw that he was watching her reaction. She decided to play it straight. "This is good."

He relaxed a little. No matter how long he went on cooking, Nik knew that people's opinions would always matter to him. And one unfavorable critique canceled out a dozen praises the way a single swipe of a hatchet could cut down a year's worth of growth for a sapling.

He cut himself a piece of the omelet. "Of course it is."

She grinned as Nik swallowed. "No one's ever going

to accuse you of allowing a rampant case of modesty to get in your way."

Nik was about to put her in her place when Sam looked in. The old man pursed his lips as he regarded the two of them at the counter. "I see you found her."

There would have been absolutely no way to have missed her, Nik thought. "Yes, I did."

Sam pulled on his chin. Day-old white bristles poked out all along the bottom half of his face, pointy and sharp like the spines of a bristled porcupine.

"It was okay, my letting her in, then?" Sam yanked a little more on his chin as he looked uncertainly at Nik from beneath shaggy brows.

Nik was suddenly reluctant to give his tacit approval. He didn't want Sara's early-morning appearance to become a habit. He had no intentions of sharing breakfast with her every day. This was the time of day when tranquillity was supposed to reign supreme and he was allowed to enjoy his domain in peace and quiet. Still, he didn't want to make Sam feel as if he'd done something wrong, either. Sam tended to be on the sensitive side.

"Frankly, Sam, I don't quite see how you could have stopped her."

Sam took that to be a yes. He nodded his head toward the rear of the building. "I just come to tell you that Ms. Harriet's here."

Nik placed his fork next to the plate and rose. "All right, tell her that I set the breads aside for her in the back office. Everything else is in the walk-in. I'll help her out to the van with it when she's ready."

Given the choice of the omelet or following Nik, Sara opted to satisfy her curiosity. She was off her stool and had caught up to Nik in a few quick strides.

"Do you do this every day?" He looked at her, confused. Was she talking about breakfast? "Give away food?" she clarified.

Nik opened the walk-in and left it that way. He moved to the rear and felt the temperature drop. "Yes."

Sara nodded her approval. "Good thinking. It's a hell of a write-off."

Was that what she thought? That he was doing it for tax reasons? Was she the type of person who only did something if it benefited her? Nik had never cared for self-serving people. And he definitely didn't care for being thought of in that light.

"I don't do this for a write-off."

The annoyance in his voice didn't stop her. Sara didn't know exactly why, but somehow she'd known he was going to say that. And she was glad he had. "Charitable impulses?"

He pulled out a large cardboard box filled with yesterday's pastries. Let them eat cake, he thought cryptically. But there were more substantial items to accompany the pastries, and everyone should be allowed to indulge a sweet tooth once in a while.

"I don't like anyone to go hungry, even if they can't leave a sizable tip at the end of the meal." He fairly growled out the words, not enjoying having his motives examined under a microscope. He gestured toward the counter. "Don't you have an omelet to finish?"

There was a distinct edge to his voice. Maybe she'd satisfy her curiosity about Harri and the mission food another day. Giving Nik a smart salute, she retreated. "Yes, I certainly do."

The pain in his neck was gone, Nik thought as he turned his back on Sara, but the one in another region of his body was obviously just beginning.

\* \* \*

"You look like you've been dumped right in the middle of a blizzard."

With a page in each hand, Sara looked up to see who was addressing her. There were columns and scribbled entries dancing in her head.

Jennifer was on the other side of the room with Katie. They looked as if they had been there for a while. Sara hadn't even heard them come in or walk by her.

She dropped the papers on the desk. "How long have you been here?"

Jennifer grinned as she finished fixing Katie's braid, which had come undone. "Oh, long enough to hear you mumbling to yourself about the messes some people got themselves into."

Sara flushed, wondering if Jennifer had taken offense. "That long, huh? I didn't mean that the way it sounded." She looked down at the multicolored folders spread out all over her desk. There were many more housed within the top two drawers of the file cabinet. "It's just that this has got to be the most creative accounting system I've ever seen outside of a courtroom."

Jennifer picked up a file. She knew exactly how Sara felt. "Most of this is Nik's own way of keeping track. Once a month Julia used to sit down and try to make heads or tails of his system. After she left, I got the wonderful task."

She flipped open the file and took a deep breath. It wasn't fair to have Sara tackling this all on her own right from the start. It would take hours to unscramble Nik's notations. "I could sit down and—"

Ginger popped her head into the office, glancing at Sara curiously. "Jennifer, Mrs. Lorenzo's on line one about tomorrow's dinner party." She grinned at Sara. "Hi, I'm Ginger. You're new."

"Yes, I know." Sara laughed.

Jennifer glanced toward the telephone. She couldn't wait until the Lorenzo catering job was behind her. Mrs. Lorenzo called on a daily basis to change her mind about every detail. "Sara's here to reconstruct everything on those discs Nik blew up."

Ginger looked at Sara sympathetically. "Lots of luck." Ginger pointed toward the telephone. "Line one," she reminded Jennifer, then ducked out again.

Katie reached for the telephone. Jennifer just managed to place her hand on the receiver first. Jennifer looked at Sara apologetically.

"That's all right," Sara assured her. She'd been at this for over three hours now and was actually making some headway. "I think I can probably work my way backward from some of the older files and data discs."

As Jennifer picked up the receiver, Sara dug in again.

Twenty minutes later Jennifer hung up. Before her was a rather extensive list of last-minute changes that Mrs. Lorenzo had requested for her fiftieth wedding anniversary party. Jennifer's ear felt flattened. Mrs. Lorenzo had changed her mind about the main course. Again. And there were more waitresses to recruit now. Mrs. Lorenzo had informed her that twenty more people were being invited. She had calls to make and people to see. Still, Jennifer felt guilty about leaving Sara to cope with this paper storm all on her own.

Torn, Jennifer glanced toward the doorway and saw Nik standing there with a tray. Silently Jennifer moved toward her daughter and watched the scene unfold.

It was obvious to Jennifer that Sara was oblivious to Nik's presence as she sat, making notes on a large yellow pad. The woman appeared to be valiantly attempting to arrange the different files into piles that could be cross-referenced between inventory and accounting.

And it was just as obvious that Nik felt awkward about what he was doing. He had a determined set to his jaw that made him look as if he was about to enter a boxing ring.

Nik slid the tray onto the desk, nudging aside several folders. One opened and fell to the floor, a flurry of papers hitting the beige carpet.

Sara looked up, surprised. "You trying to make this job impossible?" With a sigh she bent to pick up the papers.

Nik joined her on the floor. With a swipe of his hands he collected all the sheets in a single, jumbled mess. "Don't get smart. That was an accident." He deposited the papers on the desk. Sara debated throwing them into the trash, then calmed down.

"I just brought you something to eat," he muttered needlessly.

There was a salad, a cup of coffee and, as she lifted the lid on the center dish, a succulent offering of sliced lamb with baby carrots and baby peas. She replaced the lid. "What, no dessert?"

He lifted a brow. "Sugar tends to make you sluggish in the long run."

"Never happen," she assured him. She nodded at the tray, curious. "Isn't this service a little above and beyond the call of duty?"

He didn't want her making more out of it than it was. If he was being honest with himself he wasn't sure what had prompted him to throw together a tray for Sara when he'd realized that she hadn't come in for anything to eat. It certainly wasn't because she looked as if she needed someone to take care of her.

Nik was already edging his way out of the room. "Just eat. You haven't taken a break or eaten anything since you sat down here after breakfast."

Jennifer hurried after her brother, catching his arm just as he moved beyond the door. "And since when do you notice when someone takes a break, unless they happen to be standing right next to you? Or in one of your pots? You're oblivious to everything that isn't on a spice rack."

He shrugged off her hand. "I notice a lot more than you think."

Jennifer leaned against the wall as she crossed her arms in front of her. Well, well, well. Maybe she'd better call Julia and get a little more information about their new employee. It had been a long time since Nik had shown an interest in a woman.

"Apparently," she murmured.

Nik saw the look that rose in Jennifer's eyes. He didn't have to stay and take this. He turned and headed toward the kitchen. His soufflé was almost ready. "I've got work to do, Jennifer."

"It's about time, Nik," she called after him.

He heard the grin in her voice. Nik turned just as he reached the kitchen, his hand on the swinging door. He knew he was going to regret asking. "About time for what?"

Jennifer laughed as she relished the scene. She anticipated Kane's expression tonight when she told him that the immovable object was finally being moved.

"Now that part's up to you, brother, dear. Just remember—" she eyed the office door behind her "—don't drag your feet."

Nik scowled. "Try to do something nice for someone and it gets blown out of proportion."

"If you say so." Jennifer's expression told Nik that she wasn't buying his protest.

He waved at his younger sister, dismissing her. "Go to work, Jennifer."

Jennifer laughed as she turned to reenter the office. At the last moment she looked over her shoulder. "You, too, Nik. You, too."

She heard Nik muttering under his breath as he walked into the kitchen.

# Chapter 4

The noise level in the kitchen had decreased a while ago as activity wound down. Most of the staff had already gone home. Nik looked over toward the large clock that hung on the wall near the rear exit. Ten-thirty. He had put in a fourteen-and-a-half-hour day. He was bone tired. It was time to call it a night.

He looked around for Antonio. Nik saw the silver-gray mane bent forward as the older man sat on a stool, entertaining one of the waitresses with a story. He was like an old fox, Nik thought, amused, always eyeing the young chickens wistfully. Antonio had been with him at Sinclair's almost from the beginning and everyone knew he was harmless.

Nik crossed over to him as he untied his apron. "Want to lock up for me tonight?"

He dropped the apron into the side bin, where all the day's laundry was collected. The waitress flashed an inviting smile at Nik, then sensibly departed, leaving the two men to talk.

Antonio remained seated on his stool. He regarded his former protégé with keen interest. "Getting old, eh, Nikolas?"

Antonio laughed, his booming voice rattling around the kitchen. He leaned around Nik's body to get a better view of the departing waitress before the door swung shut on her. Then, looking up at Nik, he patted the stool next to him.

Antonio Rossi was well into his sixties. He had started out as a busboy in an exclusive hotel in Naples at the age of ten. There he had worked diligently under the tutelage of his maternal uncle. Eventually he was running the kitchen at the same hotel. At thirty, his talents took him to America. He was the best backup chef Nik could have wished for.

Nik glanced at the empty stool, then decided that if he sat down now, he'd never have the strength to get up again. "I'll never be as young as you, Tony."

Nik turned to leave, but Antonio held up one finger, stopping Nik as he dug into his back pocket with the other hand.

"Wait." Rising, he pulled out his wallet. The cracked brown leather case was thick with photographs. "Did I show you the new picture of my granddaughter?"

Nik laughed and shook his head. Antonio had five children and twice as many grandchildren. And everyone at Sinclair's knew them by sight, thanks to Antonio's ever-present wad of photographs.

"No," Nik answered. Antonio began riffling through his wallet. "Not in the last fifteen minutes."

The broad shoulders, which appeared far too wide for his frame, shrugged as Antonio stuffed the wallet back into the recesses of his pocket. "When are you going to get pictures of your own, eh?"

Nik ran his hand over the back of his neck. He felt the knots that had been building up all day. "I've got pictures."

"Nieces." Antonio waved a dismissive hand in the air like a chess player pushing the pieces off a board. "They do not count."

Nik shook his head, amused. "You'd better not let Jennifer or Julia hear you saying that."

Too short to reach Nik's shoulders, Antonio wrapped a surprisingly strong arm around Nik's back.

"No offense to your lovely sisters or your charming nieces, but there is nothing like bouncing your own baby on your knee, Nik." A wide grin split the tanned face, spreading the well-groomed silver mustache. Tiny fringes of hair hung over teeth that were whiter than new-fallen snow as Antonio winked slyly. "Unless, of course, it is bouncing a pretty lady on your knee instead."

Antonio had enough energy for both of them. "You're a dirty old man, Tony."

Antonio looked pleased by the assessment. "Yes." He nodded his head as he hit his chest with one powerful fist. "But that is how I stay young."

His expression grew serious as he regarded Nik. "You work too hard, my friend, and do not let me work as much as I should." Antonio pushed the younger man toward the outer door, which led into the hallway. "Go, I take care of the kitchen for the last hour. Get some rest."

Rest. It sounded almost seductively alluring at this point. Nik nodded. He remembered muttering good-night as he left.

As the kitchen door closed behind him Nik looked down the darkened hall. He was surprised to see a beam of light pooling on the floor. It was coming from the small office. Jennifer and Katie had long since left the restaurant. Kane had come by on his way home from the precinct to pick up his wife and daughter. As for Sara, as far as he knew she had left at six. Or so he surmised. That meant the office was empty.

Curious, Nik walked down the hall and looked in. Sara was sitting hunched over the desk. Her shoes had been kicked off to the side and her bare feet were curled up against one another like two woodland creatures huddling for warmth. She was moving the toe of one against the sole of the other as she concentrated on the screen. It constituted the only movement going on in the room. Sara had her head propped up on one fisted hand and she seemed totally engrossed in the spreadsheet she had typed in on the computer.

Nik knew he should just walk away. It was late and he was asking for trouble. But he leaned his shoulder against the doorjamb and just watched her for a moment, fascinated by what he saw. Only a single lamp illuminated the room. The beam gently played across her features, dusting them with shadows and lights, making them seem soft. Sara looked totally unanimated and utterly docile. And almost sweet. Nik felt something stir, something very basic and strong.

It took him completely unaware.

He straightened, squared his shoulders as if a battle cry had silently sounded, then walked into the room. "Don't you have a home to go to?"

Sara turned to look in Nik's direction. She seemed so unfazed by his entrance it was as if she had been expecting him all along.

She thought of the house on Avalone Drive. And of her father. "Not really."

Nik's brows drew together as he plucked a fragment of a conversation from his memory. Had he misheard? "I thought you said you were staying with your father."

Sara sat up in her chair. Lacing her fingers together over her head, she stretched, flexing her body like a graceful cat trying to warm herself on all sides by the fire. Nik tried not to notice that her breasts were straining invitingly against the thin fabric of her sweater. Maybe he wasn't as dead tired as he'd thought.

She let her hands drop bonelessly to the desk. "I am."

Had he lost the thread of the conversation somehow? Didn't that mean she had a home to go to? "Then...?" He let his voice trail off as he waited for her to explain.

A quirky smile lifted her lips. "Doesn't necessarily make it a home, does it?"

Nik detected the defensive note in her voice and saw a similar look in her eyes before her expression melded into an amused look.

"I could ask you the same question, you know. It's what?" She twisted her wrist to get a better look at her watch. "Ten-forty. You've been here a long time."

She probably enjoyed arguing more than she enjoyed breathing, he thought. Nik decided to oblige her. He rested a hip against the corner of her desk. "I own the place. What's your excuse?"

"I won't be here tomorrow, remember? I thought I'd do as much as I could. Besides—" She pushed away from the desk. Suddenly he seemed to be crowding into her space, and she needed air. "I found your creative bookkeeping utterly fascinating."

He crossed his arms in front of his chest and tried to

get at the gist of her meaning. "Creative bookkeeping is a term usually reserved for people serving five to seven in Folsom."

The sound of her laughter drifted to his ears like snowflakes from the sky. "I didn't mean to make it sound as if I suspected you of having two sets of books." She tapped the closest file. "One set like this would be hard enough to come up with."

She looked at the sea of folders on the floor that she'd already gone through. A myriad of others fanned out across the desk. More waited within the metal cabinet drawers. She repressed a shudder. "Does the word organization mean anything to you?"

Nik had never reacted well to criticism. Now was no exception. He lifted a brow. "The restaurant is organized. It's just the paperwork that isn't."

"Now there's an understatement." She sighed, stretching again. She *was* tired. Lifting her head, Sara saw the way his eyes were gliding over her, and felt a warm shiver weave through. She was flattered. And just the tiniest bit on guard. "You're watching me."

"Sorry." Caught, he made no effort to look away. "You're the only thing in the room that's moving."

She let out another sigh and leaned over the keyboard. Pressing a combination of keys, she stored the material she had spent hours inputting. When she returned, she was going to have to look into getting all this set up differently. What Nik had, working from the old disks that remained and an old copy of the software program, was far too cumbersome.

Hitting the last key with a flourish, she leaned back. "I guess I've slaved enough for one day." She switched off the machine, then looked up at Nik. "You've gotten your pound of flesh."

He didn't care for the insinuation. ''I didn't ask for a pound of flesh,'' he reminded her. ''I just asked for competence.''

Saying thank-you probably would have killed him, she thought. Sara shrugged nonchalantly. ''Consider it a bonus.''

He still had no idea why she had come in so early or why she had stayed so late. As he'd said, it wasn't her restaurant. And the pay was good, but she wasn't working to impress him so that he would give her a raise. They both knew this arrangement was temporary.

The woman was a complete enigma.

Sara had told him the truth, but only in part. She'd stayed longer because his way of keeping records had been unorthodox and haphazard at best and it was a challenge to get things organized. She enjoyed challenges. But that wasn't the only reason she'd stayed here hours longer than she should have. She wanted something to occupy her mind. Something to keep her busy and to keep all thoughts of her father and tomorrow at bay. She didn't want to think about tomorrow. Not tomorrow or all the yesterdays that had been missed. She really didn't want to think about her father at all.

She suddenly realized that he wasn't wearing his apron. ''You going home?'' He nodded. She moved aside several files on the floor and opened the bottom drawer, where she'd tossed in her purse. It was time for her to go, too. She couldn't very well sleep here. ''I guess I've made enough headway for one day.''

Nik crossed to the doorway. He was about to leave, but something was holding him back. He looked over his shoulder at her and heard himself saying something he'd no idea he was going to say until the words came out. "Buy you a cup of coffee?"

White teeth flashed in a grin that was just the slightest bit off center. "Seeing as how you own the restaurant, that's mighty big of you."

He wondered if there was someone special in her life and if there was, how the man put up with her. "Do you ever give it a rest?"

Sara grinned even more broadly in response. Maybe he was right. She was sparring just a wee bit too much, even for her.

She ran her fingers through her cropped hair and laughed. "Sometimes." She turned her face up to his, amusement highlighted there at his expense. "Yes, I'd love a cup of coffee." Her eyes fluttered shut for a second as she envisioned the hot liquid winding down her throat and the heat pouring through her veins. "Warm and creamy and rich."

She made drinking a cup of coffee sound erotic. For a second, just for a second, he was tempted to touch her face, to let his fingers slide down her cheek and vicariously share the experience with her.

Nik fell back on the only thing he knew well. "I thought you didn't care for food."

Sara opened her eyes. "Coffee's not food, it's a religion. I couldn't live without it." Grabbing the straps of her purse, she lifted it from the drawer and followed him out the door. "Got any cappuccino?"

Because it was late and she was new, he decided not to be insulted by the question. "Yes, we have cappuccino. Since you're such a coffee aficionado, I'll give you a choice. Sinclair's has ten different kinds of coffee to choose from."

Without thinking she linked her arm through his and

laughed, her hair brushing lightly against his chest. The skin underneath his shirt tingled. He thought maybe it was the fabric softener he'd used with the last wash. "Ten? I think I may be in love with you."

The word echoed and vibrated inside him, startling Nik into silence. He began to wonder who this woman was and what she really thought. He had a feeling that there were layers here that needed to be peeled back before he had his answer.

When Nik and Sara walked into the kitchen Antonio looked up, surprised. He set the large pot he was holding down on the table as his eyes narrowed. "I thought I told you to go home."

Nik nodded at Sara. He saw the way Antonio's eyes slid appreciatively up and down Sara's well-rounded, diminutive frame. Lucky thing Antonio was a family man, he thought.

"Our newest employee wants some coffee," Nik explained.

"Temporary employee," she interjected. Dropping her hand away from Nik, she moved toward Antonio. She shook his hand warmly, both her small hands covering his. "Hi, I'm Sara Santangelo."

Antonio's face lit up. He knew it. "Ah, Italian."

And so was he, she guessed, by the look of him. "Half," she corrected.

Antonio was unabashedly prejudiced. He kissed his fingers, then spread them wide, as if the kiss had suddenly taken wing and sprung up away from them. "Always the best half."

Nik turned to Sara just then and saw that her cheeks were flushed, not in embarrassment—he didn't think her capable of that—but in fleeting annoyance. Why? He found himself wanting to unravel the riddle that she was beginning to represent.

Rather than recite the different types of coffee he had available, Nik picked up a menu that was lying on the side. One of the waitresses had brought it in. There was a small rip on one of the pages, which meant it was to be discarded. Nik liked things to be as perfect as humanly possible.

He handed the menu to Sara and pointed to the last page. He heard her anticipatory sigh.

"Mocha mint with whipped cream sounds heavenly."

"Mocha mint it is." Nik turned to where the well-polished row of coffee machines stood in the rear of the room like a vanguard of gleaming knights. They could produce five hundred cups of coffee at will.

Antonio grabbed Nik's sleeve. "You go outside with the pretty lady. I fix the coffee. Go." He was all but shooing Nik out of the room the way a farmer's wife shooed away an aggressive chicken in the barnyard.

Nik could see exactly what was on Antonio's mind, but this was no time to get in a discussion over it. Instead, he took Sara's arm and urged her toward the inner door that led back into the dining room.

She looked at the old man as he began to prepare two cups. "Does he order you around like that often?"

Nik smiled. "When I first started out, Antonio was working for an exclusive restaurant in Beverly Hills. I was his apprentice chef. All thumbs and eager to learn, with two kid sisters to provide for."

Sara heard the affection in his voice and it warmed her without her realizing it.

"He showed me the ropes. Stayed after hours to teach me things you don't pick up in cookbooks. He didn't

have to do that. When I got Sinclair's going, I asked
him to come work for me.'' Nik's mouth curved fondly
as he looked over his shoulder at the other man's back.
''He still thinks of me as that kid he took under his
wing. No harm in that. The way I figure it, I owe him.''

Nik led Sara to a secluded booth in the main dining
room. There were only a handful of couples left, all
lingering over their desserts or after-dinner drinks,
moved by the company and the atmosphere.

It all seemed suddenly and uncomfortably intimate to
Sara. She wasn't used to feeling vulnerable anymore. It
was probably just because she was tired, she thought.
Just tired.

She slid into the booth and waited until Nik sat across
from her.

*Now what?* she wondered, nerves jumping through
her like beads of water on a hot skillet.

She looked toward the door that separated the dining
room from the kitchen, hoping that Antonio would
come out with the coffee soon. When she turned back
toward Nik she saw that he was studying her. The beads
of water jumped higher on the skillet. This wasn't a
good idea.

Sara started to rise. ''Maybe I should just—''

For the third time that day Nik caught her wrist in
his hand. It was getting to be a habit, he thought. And
not a totally unpleasant one as far as habits went. Her
skin was silky soft and her hand felt almost frail in his.
Deceptive packaging. He found himself wanting her to
stay, although God only knew why.

''What's your hurry?''

''Nothing.'' She pulled her hand away, not wanting
the contact because it was too easy to let it happen. ''It's
just that I—''

She thought of the house, of her father possibly waiting up for her. By some standards it was still early. She hoped he'd given up and gone to bed. She was less in the mood to talk tonight than she had been this morning.

Sara shrugged and forced herself to settle back in the booth. "No, no hurry at all." She saw the kitchen door open and almost sighed with relief. "Ah, Antonio. You're a lifesaver."

Nik had the feeling she was a lot more serious than her smile let on. What was she afraid of? He certainly had no designs on her and even if he had, what could he do in a public place?

The older man beamed as he set down the two cups of coffee and bowed with a flourish. He moved the small cup filled with pitch-black liquid in front of Nik and a masterpiece of froth and sculpted foam before Sara.

"Your mocha mint, *signorina*."

"Sara," she prompted with what Antonio thought was a beatific smile. "Thank you."

She took a sip and sighed. It *was* heavenly.

Antonio took his leave, looking well pleased with himself. He winked conspiratorially at Nik as he passed him. Nik pretended not to see.

Toying with his espresso, Nik watched Sara. She appeared enraptured by the drink. He enjoyed seeing someone savor something so much. He wondered if she took the same delight in a really good meal. And if she brought her gusto to bed with her, as well.

Sara raised her eyes to his. "You're watching me again, and I'm not moving this time."

Nik leaned back, his hands bracketing the small cup of espresso between them on the table. Who was she? "You always throw that term around so easily?"

He'd completely and effectively lost her. She cocked her head and stared at him. "What term?"

He was thinking back to her declaration when he told her of the number of coffees the restaurant habitually carried. "Love." He sat, waiting.

The word, when he said it, brought a small chill to her as it danced along her shoulder blades and down her spine. She shrugged, taking another slow, appreciative sip before answering. "Sure. It's the easiest word in the world to say."

Sara leaned over the table and looked up into Nik's eyes. In the dim light it was hard to discern the color. But not the power. She could feel his strength even now. Anticipation hummed through her like the plucked strings of a harp. She ignored it.

"I love you," she whispered. The words spilled out into the darkness like a velvety liqueur amorously coating the sides of a glass. And then she shrugged carelessly, settling back. "See? Easy. Nobody means it."

He'd felt something tighten within him like a wound-up coil when she'd looked into his eyes and whispered the phrase. He knew it was utterly ridiculous, but for the space of that one moment it was as if he was gazing into a crystal ball and looking into the future. He didn't believe in premonitions.

And yet—

Nik mentally shook himself free of the mood.

He didn't like the fact that she seemed to take such a dim view of love. He'd never really been in love himself. There'd never been time. But he had hopes that, someday, love would find him. Everyone needed love.

"What makes you so sure?"

She was letting the atmosphere get to her, she

thought. She was feeling oddly unarmed right about now.

"What? That no one means it?" She thought of her parents, of what her mother had told her. *Don't trust anyone, Sara. Men lie just to get their way.* "Maybe they do, when they say it, for about three and a half seconds. After that—" Sara snapped her fingers "—it's gone, and with it, any obligations that might have been created by that declaration of love." *Like a father abandoning a child.*

It was too harsh a philosophy for someone as young as she was. "How old are you, Sara?"

Why was he playing twenty questions at this hour? "It's on that employee form you had me fill out." She paused. She could see he was waiting for her to answer.

Maybe he hadn't looked at the form. "Twenty-eight."

At twenty-eight he had buried two parents and had the world on his shoulders. Even so, he had never felt this cynical. "That seems awfully young to take such a dark view of life."

She didn't like being analyzed. Sara raised her head defensively. "You'd be surprised." She looked down into her cup. It was almost empty. "Besides, I don't take a dark view of life. I just see it as it is. That's why I try to enjoy myself when I can." She tilted the cup and watched the few remaining drops coat the bottom. Her mouth curved in a half smile. "This is a cup of coffee, not a dry martini, Sinclair. Why are you playing bartender and looking for confessions?"

"I wasn't aware that I was." He moved back slightly, giving her room. "I thought I was making conversation."

Who had hurt her? he wondered. Had there been

some man in her life who had made her so cynical? Had someone walked out on her? Or worse, stayed long enough to trample all her dreams?

The quirky smile was back. "You were asking questions. That's usually called prying."

The more she resisted, the more he felt he wanted to know. That in itself was unusual. Nik always gave people more than their share of space. "Only if you don't want to answer them."

Their eyes met and held. Sara knew that she didn't want him inside of her head. She gestured airily. "I rest my case."

At this point, he thought of just calling it a night. The conversation definitely wasn't going well. Yet, tired as he was, he was reluctant to relinquish her company. There was something about her that made him feel she needed someone to talk to, and he was the likeliest candidate around.

Nik decided a change in topic was in order. He stretched his legs out in front of him, still studying her. "So, you're going to be out tomorrow."

"Yes," she said slowly, wondering where this new line was going to lead.

"It's pretty unusual taking the second day at a job off." He watched the way the yellow flame from the candle on the table seemed to make love to her skin. The faint ache within him grew. Maybe he shouldn't have had the espresso after all. "What's so special about tomorrow?"

"Nothing. You're being a bartender again," she admonished, but this time she was smiling. Sara wished the topic didn't bother her so much. "My father's going in for surgery. He needs me to take him in, that's all."

Nik wasn't fooled by the indifferent tone of her voice.

She was hiding emotions behind it. The tension was there in her shoulders. "Serious?"

Her father had told her what the doctor had said. That there was always the possibility of a heart attack while on the operating table. She distanced herself from the feelings that were pounding on the closed door of her heart with both fists. She didn't need this.

"Maybe. It's an angioplasty. He has a blocked artery." She looked away as her voice drifted off.

She was trying to appear nonchalant, but she wouldn't have dropped everything and flown here if she didn't think it was serious. Nik's heart went out to her. He remembered what it was like, walking down those long hospital corridors not once but twice, having to deal with the fact that one of his parents was slipping away from him. He remembered the impotent frustration raging within him because there was nothing he could do.

He stifled the urge to take her hand in his. "What time is the surgery?"

She shrugged, as if the detail was too inconsequential for her to remember clearly. Nik waited. "Ten," she mumbled, looking away.

At ten o'clock her father would be stripped of all defenses, facing a surgeon's scalpel. What if—

No, she didn't care. She didn't. What happened in his life was his business, not hers. He'd forfeited her caring about him when he walked out on her.

Nik watched in fascination as emotions played over her face like neon lights going off and on along a marquee. "Want some company while you're waiting?"

His question took her by surprise, cracking the tight shell of her thoughts. She swallowed. The last thing in the world she wanted was someone there with her, offering her pity.

She took a deep, fortifying breath. "Are you planning on burning down the restaurant tomorrow?"

Talk about something coming from left field. Nik looked at Sara as if she'd just lost her mind. "No."

"Then you'll be busy, won't you?" she pointed out briskly. "But thanks for the offer." Fidgeting inwardly, she began folding her napkin into fours. "I won't be hanging around the hospital, either, actually. I'm just going to drop him off and then go shopping or something."

Sara sounded as if she was talking about boarding a dog at a kennel, Nik thought. For a moment he was annoyed at her flippant attitude. But then he realized that it was all only a facade. She was having a great deal of trouble dealing with this. He could see it in her eyes.

Sara looked down and saw that she was wadding the napkin into a ball. Carefully she laid it on the table and smoothed it out with the palm of her hand.

"California has some of the best malls in the country." If her tone was stretched any further to sound cheerful, it was going to crack right down the middle. Her eyes shifted to his, daring him to take exception. "Maybe I'll even drop by here later and work on the mess you left."

Before he could say anything, Sara rose abruptly. "Thanks for the coffee, boss. I'll see you the day after tomorrow."

And with that she quickly walked away from the table and toward the front door.

Nik sat, silently watching her as she left. Was she as brash as she let on? He shook his head. He knew the answer to that before the question had even posed itself to him. Nik knew hurt when he saw it. He'd lived through it more than once himself. Sometimes building up walls around yourself was the only way to deal with it.

But walls, he knew, kept you in as well as kept everything else out. He didn't think she was the type who wanted to remain in prison indefinitely.

## Chapter 5

The second night was even worse than the first had been. Sara woke up every half hour as if there was some sort of inner alarm clock ticking off the minutes within her. Each time her eyes opened, thoughts of the pending surgery would explode on her brain, haunting her. She tried to ignore it, reminding herself that she didn't care about her father anymore. He was just another human being on this planet. It didn't help.

At five she gave up all attempts at getting any additional restful sleep. Her father had to be at the hospital in less than two hours, so she might as well get up.

More dead than alive, Sara dragged herself to the bathroom, hoping that a shower might help restore some of her depleted energy. The blast of cold water that came out of the shower head when she turned the faucet toward *H* gave her an instant headache. It reinforced the tension that was throbbing in her temples like a bugle corps practicing for a recital.

The edginess within her was building. Sara tried to busy herself with the mechanics of getting ready, struggling to hold a tight rein on her thoughts. As she hurried, she found that she seemed to be all thumbs this morning. Sara shook her head disparagingly. It figured.

She was desperate for a cup of coffee and wanted to get into the kitchen to make one before her father was up. The doctor had forbidden him to have any food or liquids after midnight. Though she couldn't make herself forgive her father, it would be cruel to sit there drinking coffee in front of him when he had to abstain.

The hair dryer she was wielding with the kind of grace that a magician employed with his wand began to emit a tiny wisp of smoke. She saw it trail into the air as she glanced in the mirror. At the same time, an acrid smell assaulted her nostrils. The motor was burning out.

Muttering, Sara shut it off. She ran her fingers through her hair. It was still damp in places, but it would have to do. She sincerely doubted that her father owned a hair dryer.

She grabbed her purse from where she had hung it on the bedroom doorknob and, carrying her shoes in one hand, made her way into the kitchen, confident that she had time enough to make the coffee.

She was wrong.

Raymond Santangelo was in the kitchen, his back to the doorway. It brought back memories from Sara's childhood, when she would tiptoe downstairs early on a Saturday morning to find her father in the kitchen making breakfast for all of them. Her mother always liked to sleep in on the weekends.

Sara hesitated, fighting against giving in to the sentiments the memory created. She debated going back to her room. Her father turned around before she could make up her mind.

His wan face brightened immeasurably when he saw her. "You're up. Good morning, Sara."

He sounded so chipper, she thought, anyone would have thought that he was on his way to a picnic instead of a hospital operating room. Sara crossed stiffly over the threshold and walked into the kitchen. The room was too small and crammed to accommodate more than two people adequately. Sara felt almost claustrophobic being here with her father.

She nodded in response to his greeting. "Morning."

There was still a hundred miles between them, Raymond thought sadly, though his expression never hinted at the sorrow he felt. He gestured toward the coffee-maker. It was making spasmodic sounds as it used the last of the water to produce coffee. The pot was only one-quarter full. Just enough for one.

"I made you some coffee."

She remembered how much he always loved drinking coffee in the morning. It was he who had introduced her to her first cup during one of those early Saturday mornings they'd shared, sneaking it to her behind her mother's back. She'd been eight at the time.

Sara eyed the glass pot suspiciously. "You didn't have any—?"

He second-guessed her question. "Myself? No, some rules I can follow." He maintained a smile, though the edges appeared strained to her. "I'll just sit here and smell yours if you don't mind."

Raymond poured a mug full for her and placed it on the small kitchen table. Pulling out one of the two chairs, he sat down and waited for Sara to take the other seat.

Feeling awkward again, Sara lowered herself onto the chair slowly, as if she was trying to find the best way to sit on a keg of dynamite.

Raymond pushed the matching sugar bowl and creamer toward her on the table. Sara shook her head as she moved the mug closer.

It wasn't getting any easier facing him, she thought. She cupped her hands around the mug as if she was attempting to anchor herself to something real. If anything, it was getting harder each time she was alone with him. Her nerves were becoming more frayed.

In actuality, they were never really alone. There were always ghosts in the room with them. Ghosts and a myriad of jumbled emotions swirling within her, trying to storm through.

Her fingers tightened around the mug. There was anger—no, more than that. It was rage fibrillating through her, rage at having all her old feelings awakened. Time had numbed her a little. The years had worn away all the sharp edges. Seeing him, being here like this, honed those edges to razor-sharp points all over again. And they were pricking her.

If she'd realized it was going to be this bad, she wouldn't have come. Maybe she should leave now. Sara thought of the job she'd just undertaken. Unlike her father, she never left anything undone. She prided herself on always finishing what she started. She couldn't leave.

And what about Nik?

The unexpected question exploded within her brain, startling her. Where had that come from? Slightly unnerved, she pushed his image from her mind. Nik had no place in any of this, other than the fact that he owned the restaurant where she worked. It was just being here with her father that had thrown her so off balance, making her mind wander.

She looked down into the mug and watched the light from the fluorescent fixture overhead shimmer along the black liquid. There were so many things to say and no way to say them. So she sipped her coffee instead, and said nothing.

The liquid seeped through her and she pretended that it was helping to fortify her.

Raymond watched her expression, his own almost sadly hopeful. "Good?"

She set the mug down, but didn't release it. "Good."

He nodded toward the creamer and sugar bowl she had ignored. When he'd made that first cup of coffee for her all those years ago, it had been three quarters milk. "You take it black now."

She ran a fingertip over the mug's handle and realized that it had been glued together. There was a tiny crack where it had broken. Some things, even when fixed, were never like new again. "I don't like having my caffeine diluted."

She took another long sip and felt his eyes on her. It was as if he was trying to absorb her, as if by doing so, he could somehow make up for all those years he had let slip by.

*Too late. You can't do that, Dad,* she thought.

"I like mine the texture of motor oil in the morning."

His laugh bore only a faint resemblance to the loud, booming sound she recalled, the sound that used to make her feel so warm and secure.

"Then you're not disappointed." He didn't wait for her to say anything, as if afraid that if she did, it would negate the tenuous strands he was trying to work with, the ones he was desperately attempting to weave into a bridge that would span the chasm between them. "I always made the coffee at the precinct when I got in. Santangelo's sludge they called it." He smiled, remembering. "Among other things. But the pot was always empty by the time we went out on patrol."

He'd been a police officer when they lived in Tahoe. She remembered the time he had taken her for a ride in a squad car. She'd been so proud of him, so proud to be his daughter. Being a policeman was all he had ever known. Was he still a policeman? She realized that she didn't know. There was a whole segment of his life that was missing, that she had no idea about.

She looked at him through the warm mist hovering over her mug. "Are you retired now?"

"No." He leaned forward, eager to be engaged in any sort of a conversation with his daughter. "I'm on disability. But they're going to put me behind a desk when I finally get back."

He frowned. Behind a desk. It meant he was growing old, and he hated that. Part of his life had finally fallen into place, even after his second divorce, and then this had happened. He had tried to shrug off the weakness, the strange, nondescript numbness in his left shoulder. But he had made the mistake of mentioning it to one of the detectives. The next day he'd been forced to take a physical. The blockage in his left artery had been discovered then.

A desk job. Sara nodded, remembering how much her mother used to worry about her father returning home safely, even though Tahoe was a relatively peaceful place. "It's safer that way."

Sara saw something flicker in her father's eyes. An impotent anger. Passion filled his voice. Sara set down her mug and listened, compassion nudging at her though she tried to deny it.

"I didn't become a policeman to be safe, Sara, or to sit home and collect a pension after twenty years. I did it to make a difference. Punching keys isn't going to make a difference."

Instincts had her attempting to soothe him before she could stop herself. "Lots of ways to fight crime, Dad. Not everyone is Clint Eastwood." She realized what she was doing and emotionally backed away. "Even Eastwood's slowed down some."

The stillness returned and discomfort stirred again, like flies buzzing over fruit on a sticky July night. She searched for something more to say. "What precinct are you with?"

"Newport Beach."

His answer struck a chord. Jennifer had mentioned something about her husband being assigned to the Newport Beach precinct when she'd introduced him yesterday. "Do you know Detective Kane Madigan?"

Raymond looked at her in surprise. Madigan had been the detective who had recommended that he go in for his physical. But there was no reason to bring that up, especially if he was a friend of Sara's.

He looked longingly at the coffeepot, then forced himself to look away. Coffee wasn't what he needed now. A little luck was in order. Or maybe a lot of it.

"Yeah, I know him. Sharp guy." Raymond thought back to his impression of Kane when the detective first transferred to the precinct. "He was a real loner until about a couple of years ago."

Sara moved forward in her chair, interested. "What happened?"

"He got married." There was a framed photograph

of the man's wife and daughter sitting on his desk these days. Madigan, who had never shown any emotions before. It had stirred a lot of comments. "I guess marriage changes some people."

Sara remembered what her mother had told her about her marriage. How life had gone from happiness to sorrow. Sara's eyes met her father's. "Yes, it does."

The mood was back, closing the temporary opening between them as if it hadn't, for a glimmer of a moment, been there at all.

Sara took a breath, then set aside her mug. It was empty. She pushed herself away from the table. She wanted to get this over with. More than that, she wanted to be somewhere else, away from here.

"Well, if you're ready, maybe we'd better get going." She started to rise, but something in her father's eyes stopped her. A wariness she wasn't prepared for. Whatever else her father had become, he had always been an unshakable rock. The man before her was far too mortal for her liking. "What?"

A strange, nervous smile played across his thin lips. He shrugged without being conscious of doing so.

"I don't know. Maybe I'm scared." He raised his eyes to hers. "Kind of funny, huh? I've been in some pretty hairy situations, been assigned to some precincts where every minute on patrol could have been my last and I never really turned a hair. I loved it." His tongue caressed the very words as he thought of his professional life, of living on the edge where he had to depend on his own instincts to help him survive. "The excitement, the uncertainty. The thrill of beating the odds and making it through another day. I loved it all."

On the streets he felt as if his fate was in his own hands. Now it was in the hands of some strange surgeon he'd met twice. He looked down at his hands, not really seeing them.

"And now I'm scared." He whispered the words.

For a fleeting moment the urge to comfort him was almost overwhelming. Sara wanted to put her arms around him and say it was going to be all right.

But she couldn't.

It was as if she was paralyzed, as if her emotions were immobilizing her, turning her to stone as surely as if hot lead had been poured all over her.

"Think of it as another challenge." Her voice sounded so brittle it made her cringe inside. And yet she couldn't help herself. "From what you've told me, the odds are in your favor this time. You'll make it through this, too."

It was the best she could do, but she couldn't shake the guilt, even though she told herself he didn't deserve more.

Raymond rose and nodded as he smiled at her. He hadn't wanted to fall apart like that. It was just that fear was gnawing holes in his resolve. "Thanks."

She lifted her shoulder and let it fall, blocking his simple gratitude. "C'mon, you don't want to be late." She forced what passed for a smile to her lips, though it felt pasted into place.

She desperately wanted to hate him, to cocoon herself in that overpowering emotion and be invulnerable to any and all feelings that were attempting to break through her ramparts. But hatred wouldn't come, wouldn't rise up no matter how much she attempted to summon it.

She couldn't hate, couldn't love. She felt lost and confused.

With ambivalent feelings slamming into each other

like children piloting bumper cars within her, Sara just shut down emotionally. She walked into the living room, then turned to look at him. "Where's your suitcase?"

"By the door." He indicated the small valise. "I've been ready for hours." He picked it up. Sara moved to take the suitcase from him, then at the last moment decided to give him his dignity.

Raymond looked at his daughter for a long moment, saying things with his eyes he couldn't find the courage to say with his tongue. "Let's get this over with."

She nodded, then opened the front door. Stepping aside, she waited for him to pass first. A tiny bit of his cologne wafted by her. He still used the same brand. Old Spice. The name popped into her mind automatically and she thought of the old tuneful commercial. The smile she forced this time came a little more easily.

"It'll be all right," she promised softly, shutting the door behind her.

He seemed to brighten at her words, even though there was no way that she could guarantee anything. Neither of them could.

"Are you expecting a phone call?"

Antonio's voice penetrated the thick fog of thought that seemed to be clogging his brain this morning. Pinching the bridge of his nose as if that helped to gather his thoughts together, Nik looked at the man. "No, why?"

Antonio pointed toward the clock with the cleaver he was using on the row of guinea hens that were lined up before him on the worktable.

"You have been looking at the clock every five

minutes. It is not like you." A thought struck Antonio and he suddenly smiled knowingly. "Did she call in?"

The back doors opened. Two large, wiry men walked in, each carrying a large crate of fresh fish. There were four more crates coming to complete the order. Nik nodded at one of the men. "Who?" he asked Antonio absently.

Antonio waited until Nik turned his attention to him again before continuing. He saw the line of impatience creasing Nik's brow, but it wasn't the first time Nik had been annoyed with him and it wouldn't be the last. With a snap of his wrist he cleaved another hen in half.

"That pretty girl you had coffee with last night. The Italian one." He said it with such gusto that there was no missing Antonio's stamp of approval.

Nik crossed to the men who were bringing in the crates. The taller one handed him a receipt mounted on a clipboard to sign. Nik opened the first crate and gave it a cursory look. He'd been dealing with the same market for ten years and was confident of their product. Nodding, he scribbled his name on the form.

"See you Friday," he murmured as the man took back his clipboard.

When Nik turned around, Antonio was standing at his elbow, waiting for an answer. "No." He fairly huffed out the word at the older man.

That only meant one thing. "You made her quit already?" Antonio shook his head, distressed. "Where have I gone wrong with you, Nikolas?"

Nik waved over two of the busboys and indicated the crates. "Take these into the walk-in and unpack them." He looked over his shoulder at Antonio. The man was following him around, conducting an interview for "The Dating Game" while there were chickens waiting to be boned and orders to be filled. He knew Antonio well enough to know that the man wasn't going to go back to work until he had his answer.

"She didn't quit. She's taking her father in to the hospital for surgery today."

Antonio nodded gravely as he took the information in. Returning to his worktable, he resumed cleaving chickens. "Maybe she needs someone to hold her hand."

Aware that the conversation was attracting attention, Nik moved closer to Antonio. "I offered. She said she didn't."

Antonio looked at Nik as if the man had just announced that he had bought a controlling share in the Golden Gate Bridge from a street peddler. "And you believed her?" He shook his head and laughed.

"Why shouldn't I?" Annoyance began to infiltrate Nik's voice, partially because he was carrying on the same debate silently in his head that Antonio was insisting on dragging out into the open.

"Because all women need to have a man to lean on no matter what they say." Antonio smiled, thinking of his wife and the years they had shared, both turbulent and calm. He would have been lost without her. "And all men like to have a woman in their lives to turn to." He looked at Nik meaningfully.

He could just hear what Sara would have to say about the first part of Antonio's comment. "She's not exactly like other women."

Finished, Antonio set his cleaver down and picked up a boning knife. "That is exactly my whole point, my friend. You deserve someone who is extraordinary."

Nik raised his voice as someone switched on the mashed-potato machine and the low hum pulsated through the area. "I have you, Antonio. I figure that's about all the extraordinary that I can handle."

A loud gasp brought both men's attention around to the stove in the rear of the kitchen. A high yellow-blue flame had suddenly leapt up, surrounding both sides of a pan that Chris was handling.

Stifling an oath, Nik hurried over to the stove, with Antonio on his heels. Chris pulled down the fire extinguisher and aimed the nozzle at the flame as Nik quickly removed the pan. Nik switched off the burner. Chris let out a deep sigh and let the nozzle fall limply to the side of the metal canister.

"Not quite so high next time, Chris," Nik instructed evenly. "The customer asked for stir-fried vegetables with lamb, not charcoal chips."

Chris ran a jerky hand through his hair as he nodded. He replaced the extinguisher and offered Nik a rueful smile. "Sorry, Nik," he murmured as he took over again.

"Why don't you go to her?" Antonio coaxed as he followed Nik to the worktable.

"Are you still on that?" When Antonio nodded, Nik sighed. "I'm not sure where she'll be."

It didn't sound like such an insurmountable obstacle to Antonio. "You can have her paged. But she is bound to be in the waiting area."

That was what Nik would have liked to believe, but Sara had made it sound as if she was indifferent to the outcome of the procedure. Nik raised a brow as he looked down at Antonio. "How do you know?"

Antonio spread his hands wide, as if it was obvious to anyone who bothered to look. "I look in her eyes, I know. Go. Call." He gestured around the kitchen. "There is nothing here I cannot take care of and that I have not taken care of before you knew the difference between a carving knife and a potato peeler.''

A protest rose to his lips and faded silently away. Nik debated for a moment, then surrendered to his impulse. The hospital was only five miles away. He was going to see if he could find her.

All morning he'd been vicariously reliving the time his parents had died. The memory brought with it a sharp ache. Both his parents had died more than ten years ago, yet there were times when he missed them so much that he could hardly bear it. From the very beginning, family ties had been important to him.

Maybe Antonio was right. Maybe it was just all talk with her, all bravado. Maybe she did need someone's hand to hold and was just too proud to say anything. Nik remembered how much he had needed to lean on someone. He couldn't because he was the oldest, the ''strong one.'' There had been his sisters to care for and no one to confide in. If he had let on to Julia and Jennifer how unnerved and afraid he had been at times, it would have made them feel insecure. Their world had been shaken up enough without his adding to it. So he had gone on, silently dealing with his fears, feeling alone.

He didn't think anyone should have to go through what he had by themselves.

Nik untied his apron. There was a phone in the kitchen, but he opted for the privacy of the office. Jennifer was out on a catering call and Katie was down for a nap.

As he walked off he thought he heard Antonio utter a triumphant noise behind him. But when he turned, the old man looked inordinately busy boning the chickens.

*   *   *

There were twelve magazines spread out across the shiny black lacquered coffee table in front of her in the lounge. Agitated, Sara had arranged and rearranged them into piles, straightened them until the edges all appeared to be marching down the edge of the table. She couldn't concentrate long enough to even read the names that were written across the front covers.

Damn him, she wasn't supposed to care. After the way he had abandoned her, she had every right in the world just to drop him off at the front door and keep going. She shouldn't even *be* here.

And yet, she was.

She had had every intention in the world of bringing her father to the hospital admissions desk and then just leaving the premises. But at the last moment she couldn't bring herself to do it. It wasn't even that her father had asked her to stay. Not verbally, at least. But the set of his shoulders had.

And her own concerns got in her way.

Why couldn't she just divorce herself from her father the way he had from her?

She slapped a magazine angrily on the table. Tears gathered in her eyes as she knotted her hands helplessly in her lap.

Damn, it wasn't fair. Why did she have to care?

"How is he?"

Sara literally jumped at the sound of the softly spoken question. She had been so engrossed in the internal war she was conducting she hadn't even realized that there was someone standing over her. She looked up and saw the last person in the world she expected to see.

Nik.

She shifted on the oatmeal-colored sofa. The soft vinyl molded to her body, making her feel as if she was sinking in. "What are you doing here?"

If he concentrated, he could actually see her defense mechanism activating. "Offering a shoulder."

She lifted her chin defiantly, a smile playing on her lips. It didn't reach her eyes. "I don't need a shoulder. I have two of my own." She rotated first one, then the other, like a gymnast warming up. "See?"

Yes, he saw. "And a damn stubborn head in between, it seems."

The smile faded. "You're not paying me enough to listen to you talk to me like that."

Under normal circumstances her retort would have been enough to make him turn and walk away. He didn't need to put up with some woman's flippant attitude. But he'd watched Sara for a few moments before he had spoken to her. He'd seen the way she fidgeted with the magazines, the way she twisted her fingers together as if she was trying to braid them. He'd seen the unconscious concern on her face and knew that everything she was saying now was a sham, a facade she was throwing up for the world.

But why, was the question. To protect herself? From what? Curiosity made him want to find out.

"I'm not talking to you as your boss," Nik answered quietly, his eyes intent on hers.

Nerves jangled within her, but she couldn't draw her eyes away. "What other position are you applying for?" she challenged.

"Friend."

The single word made her feel ashamed of herself. Sara lifted a shoulder and let it drop, embarrassed. She offered him an apologetic smile.

"I guess friends snap at friends sometimes. Want to

sit down?'' Sara indicated the seat next to her with her eyes.

Nik sat beside her. Her nerves, he knew, had to be raw right about now. His had been, he remembered. Except that each time he'd been in this hospital, waiting in this very same lounge, the news, when it arrived, had not been good.

''It would be dull otherwise,'' he agreed. ''And I've a feeling that you're anything but dull.''

She laughed a little then, the way he'd hoped. ''You've been talking to Brom.''

''No, but maybe I will.'' Maybe Brom had some information that would shed light on this mercurial woman who pretended not to have a care in the world for reasons Nik didn't understand. Yet.

''So.'' Nik looked down the hall that led to the operating room. ''Any news?''

She shook her head. Her hands felt icy as she pressed them into her lap. She tried to think of something else besides what was happening in a room a few feet away from her.

''How did you know that I'd be here?''

Antonio had been right, Nik thought, looking at Sara. There was concern in her eyes. ''I called the number on your application form first. There was no answer.''

Why was he putting himself out like this? She was nothing to him. Sara resented his very presence here.

And yet—

Now that he *was* here, she realized that she was glad he was. But she still didn't understand why he had come. ''I said I'd be shopping.''

Nik smiled as he sat back on the sofa. It was new. They'd changed the color scheme in the lounge since he'd been here. And the furniture. But the room still made him tense. He couldn't get away from what being in the room represented.

"Antonio said you'd be here. I've known Antonio a lot longer than I've known you. I went with a sure thing." He glanced at his watch. "The hospital said your father went into surgery over an hour ago." Sara's eyes narrowed as she looked at him in surprise. "I checked first before I came over."

She nodded vaguely at his explanation. Her eyes drifted toward the doorway. Why hadn't the doctor come out to talk to her? Had something gone wrong? The coil within her stomach tightened again. "It's only a forty-five-minute procedure."

Her voice was whispery, as if it was a slender thread that would break if she raised it even a decibel louder. His heart went out to her, even though he knew she'd probably jump all over him if he offered her sympathy. "Sometimes it takes longer than they expected."

Sara nodded. "So I've heard."

It was a stupid thing to say. She hadn't heard. She didn't know why she even said that. Didn't know why her nerves were jumping now like tiny frogs leaping over one another.

A doctor dressed in the green livery habitual to operating rooms stepped into the lounge. Seeing him, Nik placed his hand over Sara's.

Without realizing it, she curled her fingers around it and clutched, hard.

# Chapter 6

Untying his green surgical mask, the doctor approached the sofa in slow, measured steps. There was no one else in the small lounge. His eyes were kind but tired as he looked down at Sara.

"Ms. Santangelo?"

Sara shot to her feet. She had to stand. There was this feeling coursing through her that she would be crushed by the weight of any bad news if she was sitting down. Belatedly she realized that her hand was still in Nik's. It tethered her. Sara pulled it free. She was vaguely aware of Nik rising beside her.

Quickly she scanned the doctor's face, trying to discern a glimmer of information from his expression. All she could see was that the man looked exhausted.

"Yes?" Tension pulsed in the single word.

"I'm Dr. Brice." The surgeon shook her hand, then glanced curiously at Nik as he wiped his brow. "You're her husband?"

"No." Sara's quick, emphatic denial left absolutely no room for speculation as to the nature of their relationship. There wasn't any.

Nik shook the doctor's hand, offering an amiable smile. "Family friend." His tone smoothed over the jagged edge that Sara's renunciation had left behind.

The doctor's smile was automatic, if a little worn. "We had a close call halfway through the surgery. The vein we were working on collapsed and I thought we were going to have to do an immediate coronary bypass. We always have an operating team standing by during these procedures," Dr. Brice assured Sara. His smile was warm, genuine. "Luckily they didn't have to step in. I managed to get the vein reopened. Your father's doing fine now."

She had heard a commotion down the hall earlier and seen several green-clad people rushing to the operating room. She'd been afraid to inquire what was going on.

"Fine?" she echoed. Sara scrutinized the man's face to see if there was any hesitation in his pronouncement. She found none.

"Fine," he repeated. "I can't make any promises, of course." The doctor slipped his cap off and wadded it in his hand. This sort of thing never failed to humble him. "The next seventy-two hours will tell us if the surgery took. And I'll want to see him in my office two weeks after that for an EKG. A treadmill test would be better, but he'll be in no condition for that for a while." Dr. Brice leaned over toward Sara. "Don't tell him I said so," he advised. "He's crusty about his pride."

Weren't they all? Nik thought, glancing at Sara.

Sara nodded. The numbness temporarily refused to drain out of her limbs. He'd made it. "So—" she took a deep breath "—what happens now?"

"He'll be taken to recovery, then to the Coronary Care Unit for two of the three days he's to be here. He'll be monitored continuously." The doctor smiled at her again. "I wouldn't worry if I were you."

Sara drew herself up. Now that the worst was over, she could return behind the walls she'd carefully built. "I'm not."

The doctor nodded. "Good. If you have any questions, feel free to call my office." He inclined his head to both of them. "Good day."

Nik waited until the doctor was gone. He'd been studying Sara as she received the news, watching the different emotions play over her eyes. Watching the line in her jaw grow rigid and then slack. For someone who pretended not to care, she was a cauldron of tension. He had no trouble identifying with that. He'd gone through it himself.

Sara didn't trust her voice for a moment. The relief she felt vibrating within her was too overwhelming. She hadn't thought that she would feel like this, but she did. It was as if a wave had dashed over her, washing away all the grit on her body.

She stared down the hallway. At the end was the operating room. "We're not out of the woods yet," she murmured.

True, but the doctor's words had been encouraging. "You don't strike me as a pessimist."

"I'm not a pessimist. I'm a realist." Sara turned away from the hall and looked at Nik. He was analyzing her again. She liked it even less the second time than she had the first. A tall man and a woman entered the lounge. Sara lowered her voice. "And you strike me as a man who doesn't normally abandon ship for no reason at all."

Nik crossed his arms in front of his chest, but made no attempt to answer her.

"Well?" she pressed.

The woman gave a new spin to the word *exasperating*. But somehow, Nik sensed that she needed him to ride out the storm. "I'm waiting for the subtitles to kick in. Right now I haven't the vaguest idea what you're talking about."

"You left the restaurant," she pointed out.

His eyes teased her, but he maintained a straight expression. "Apparently."

She moved, stepping into the hall, glad to be out of the lounge, knowing he was right behind her. "From what Julia told me before I came here, you practically have to be dynamited out of there."

When she turned to look at him, she found that they were standing too close to one another in the small hallway. She took a step back and felt her shoulder touch a wall. "There was really no reason for you to come."

A nurse hurried past them. Nik moved over and brushed up against Sara. Something warm and fluid coursed through his veins. He saw her expression tighten just a little.

"I already told you, I thought you needed a friend." He grew serious. "Look, my parents died within seven months of each other...."

She hadn't known. For a moment empathy flowed between them, unguarded. "I'm sorry."

"Yeah, so am I." They were standing almost directly in front of the gift shop entrance. Nik took her arm and moved her aside as two women emerged from the shop. "But what I'm trying to say is that I had to face that on my own."

She didn't quite understand. "But your sisters—"

"—Were little more than kids themselves." At sixteen and eighteen there was little else he could think of them as. "They needed to have someone to turn to, not someone to dump on them."

He couldn't have been that much older than they were at the time. He surprised her with the depth of his understanding. "No grandparents?"

Nik shook his head. "No anybody." They had been entirely on their own after their parents' deaths. On their own with next to no money to fall back on. Thank God the house had been paid off. "The point I'm trying to make is that I understand what it's like to suddenly find yourself facing the fact that your parents are mortal. I know how frightening that can be."

Sara managed to steel herself against his sympathy. She didn't need it, she told herself. She was doing just fine.

"I'm sure you do, but you don't have to concern yourself about me, or my feelings. They're quite unfazed, thank you." She saw Nik's brows draw together in a question. Maybe she owed him the smallest of explanations for putting himself out, even though she hadn't asked him to. Or maybe she just wanted to say it out loud for once. "My father gave up the title of parent, with all the associated rights that are tied to it, fourteen years ago."

She believed that, he realized. Or thought she did. "Then why are you here?" he prodded quietly.

Sara squared her shoulders. "I keep asking myself the same question."

Nik thought he already knew the answer to that. "I think it's because you care, Sara."

Sara's face grew somber and her eyes became dark. "Don't transfer your own philosophy onto me." Her mouth twisted cynically. "Not everyone is as noble as you are, Nik Sinclair."

He refused to believe she was devoid of feelings. "Nobility has nothing to do with it. Being human does."

"Oh, I'm human enough." She gave a short laugh, looking away. "Human enough to remember, even if he doesn't." She realized that she was saying too much. "See?" She turned her eyes toward Nik. "I didn't need that shoulder to lean on, after all."

Directly behind her, in the window of the gift shop, was a white negligee arranged amid boxes of candy and stuffed baby toys. Nik couldn't help wondering what Sara would look like in it. The vibrations she gave off were laced with passion that was seeking a release.

He forced his mind back on the conversation. "That's not how I see it."

She didn't want to argue and she knew that, in his own way, Nik was trying to be kind, even if he had no right to put his two cents in. Her mouth curved. "You're a typical man, you know."

Had she seen him looking at the negligee and guessed what had passed through his mind? He lifted a brow. "How's that?"

She smiled then, guilelessly. It made her seem almost beautiful. "You always think you're right."

"Oh, and you don't." Amusement highlighted Nik's expression.

His question struck her as a little ambiguous. "Think you're right? No. Think I'm right? Yes."

Nik shook his head. He shouldn't have expected anything else from her. "Hospital coffee's pretty poor as I remember it, but if you're game, I'll spring for a cup in the cafeteria."

Because there was something about his kindness that made her want to lose herself in it, Sara resisted. She knew where giving her trust to someone led. To a dead-end street. "Your good deed is over, Sinclair."

"The way I see it—" Nik took her hand and led a semi-unwilling Sara down the hallway to the bank of elevators in the rear of the hospital "—it might just be beginning." The elevator door opened and he gently herded her into the elevator. The car was empty.

Sara looked at him defiantly as the doors closed again. "Let's get something straight. I don't like people meddling in my life."

The cafeteria was located in the basement. Nik leaned around Sara to press the button marked *B*. "I'm not meddling," he told her innocently. "I'm buying two cups of coffee."

Sara sighed and leaned against the elevator wall, feeling suddenly very drained. Maybe coffee would help chase away the feeling.

Nik noted the way she seemed to just collapse, like a balloon whose air had just whooshed out. "What's the matter?"

"Nothing." Self-conscious, Sara straightened again just as the doors opened. Arrows pointed the way to the cafeteria. "I'm storing up energy for round two."

He thought about taking her hand again and decided against it. He wasn't about to play tug-of-war with her. She could follow on her own if she chose. "This isn't a fight."

Sara fell into step next to him. "Maybe not, but you're crowding me."

Nik stopped just short of the entrance and looked at her, stifling his annoyance. "Lady, do you always snap at a hand that's being offered to you in friendship?"

Their eyes met and held. The man behind them walked around them in order to enter the the cafeteria. "Until I know what's up their sleeve."

"Hair," he said. "Light brown." He pushed his sleeve up to show her. "Any more questions?"

She laughed then. The light sound dissolved the tension hanging between them. She followed Nik into the food service area. "No, not at the moment."

"Good." He picked up a tray, then indicated the various desserts that were spread out on the ice behind the glass. "Now, do you want anything to eat with your coffee?"

Sara gave the display a cursory glance. She wasn't really hungry. Nerves had sopped up her appetite like bread absorbing the last drops of gravy on a plate. She shrugged. "Surprise me."

"Get us a table," Nik instructed, going toward the coffee urn.

Sara sat at the first empty table she came to. Her legs felt oddly hollow. Maybe she'd been subjected to more tension than she'd initially realized, waiting for the doctor to come and speak to her. Now that this hurdle had been surmounted, things could go back to the way they had been. She and her father would return to their separate camps, their separate lives.

Maybe she'd go to Hawaii next, she mused, her eyes drifting closed. She had always wanted to live in Hawaii. At least for a while.

The sound of a tray being laid on the table had Sara opening her eyes.

Nik was just placing an ice-cream sundae dripping with multicolored sprinkles before her. Sara looked up at him in surprise as he slid into the seat opposite her. "You look like the ice cream type."

The observation brought a smile to her lips. "I am." The appetite that hadn't been there a moment ago suddenly materialized, full grown. She drew the dish closer and picked up the spoon Nik had brought her. He seemed oddly intuitive, especially for a man. "How could you tell?"

He grinned as he watched her dig in. A certain gusto had returned to her face. "It wasn't that hard to deduce. Your eyes took on a sensuous light when you looked at the whipped cream Antonio had put on the mocha mint coffee the other night."

Sara loved all ice cream, high-quality and bargain-priced brands alike. It was her one indulgence. She considered coffee a necessity of life, so that didn't count. "Very observant of you."

She had downed three ice-cream-laden spoonfuls before she noticed that Nik had nothing more than half a cup of coffee before him. And he wasn't drinking it. "Aren't you having anything?"

Nik tasted the coffee. It was weak and tasteless. "Chefs don't sample other people's food."

She'd noticed his physique the first time they'd met. Muscular, he was broad shouldered, with slender hips and an incredibly flat stomach. She was beginning to understand why.

"Jennifer says you don't sample much of your own, either." She let another spoonful slide down. "What *do* you eat?"

He thought for a second. "Vegetables and fruit mostly, usually on the run."

Sara grinned slyly. She had caught him in a contradiction. "I thought you said food was supposed to be savored."

He knew she'd remember that. Sara struck him as the

kind of person who would catalog almost everything in order to save it as future ammunition.

"Don't throw my own axioms back at me." He pushed aside the coffee. It was hopeless. "That's for other people, not me."

She nodded knowingly. "Oh, I see. An exceptional man."

He grinned to himself.

She'd unintentionally managed to feed his ego, she thought. "What, you accept the homage?"

"No." He let her in on the private joke. "It's just that Antonio referred to you as an extraordinary woman today."

Actually, he had been the one to make the reference, but Nik didn't think he should mention that to her. In her present frame of mind she might think he was coming on to her. And he didn't want her thinking that, although, he realized, his eyes slowly drifting over her face, he wouldn't mind doing exactly that. There was something about Sara that attracted him, sharp tongue and all. He dragged a hand through his hair. Maybe he'd been spending too much time with his pots and pans, after all.

Sara accepted his remark at face value. "Antonio's a good judge of character."

The sundae was almost gone. Sara concentrated on it, blocking everything else from her mind. It was easier that way. And a great deal simpler.

Nik folded his hands before him on the table and just watched her in silence.

His eyes made her feel fidgety, as if she was swimming in calm waters but anticipating a shark attack. She swam for shore and familiar ground. "I should have your system all caught up within two weeks."

Nik nodded. That was a lot faster than he could have managed the job. Forever was a lot faster than he could have managed it, he admitted ruefully to himself. "Sounds good."

She kept her eyes on the quickly disappearing dessert, wishing there was more, if only to keep her occupied. "And then I want to transfer it."

He looked at her uncertainly. "To what?"

"Another software program." She didn't think that the name of the program she intended to use would mean anything to him. From everything Jennifer had told her, Nik wasn't software oriented by any stretch of the imagination. Even if he had been, this was strictly an accounting program. "I worked with it when I was doing accounting for TruBlu."

"The jewelry company?" The name was familiar, even to him. TruBlu was second in reputation only to Cartier's and Tiffany's. She had been employed by them? Then what was she doing here?

Sara nodded. "They were using this cumbersome accounting method when I came to work for them. I made a few minor suggestions and they let me streamline the program for them."

Nik leaned back, studying her. The more he knew about Sara, the more amazing she became. And the more enigmatic. "Why aren't you still with them?" He imagined that TruBlu paid quite well.

"I got itchy." Her spoon met the bottom of the dish and she sighed, retiring it. Raising her eyes, she saw that Nik was watching her. She realized that he was waiting for more. Sara shifted a little in her seat. "I don't like to stay in any one place too long."

It was something he would have expected a man to say. He supposed that was prejudiced of him, but he'd always pictured women as wanting commitment and roots. He had always believed that to be one of the better qualities of the gender.

"Why?"

She placed the empty dish on the tray. "Because there are so many other places to see, so many other things to do."

She said it so vehemently, and yet somehow it didn't seem to ring true. "Don't you ever think about settling down?"

"No."

The single word left no room for further discussion. Her coffee was cold. Sara drank it, anyway, just to have something to do. When the cup was empty she looked at her watch.

"My father should be out of recovery by now." She rose. "I'll check with the nurse to see if he's there and then we can leave."

Nik quickly bused the tray, laying it on the conveyor belt that snaked its way into the kitchen. He hurried after Sara. "Aren't you going to go see him?"

Why did he have to keep prodding at her? Hadn't she done enough? How much more was she supposed to give? Until it hurt all over again? "Why? I remember what he looks like from this morning."

For reasons that weren't altogether clear to him yet, Nik didn't want her making a mistake. And that was where this was leading. "That's pretty harsh, Sara."

He had no right to chastise her. He didn't know what she'd gone through. He had no idea what it felt like to be fourteen and think your father hated you. He didn't know what it was like to lie in bed at night, trying to understand what it was that you'd done wrong. "Maybe he deserves it."

The misery he saw flicker in Sara's eyes had him reining in his assessment. There were things going on he didn't understand. But it didn't change his basic gut feelings. "Maybe he deserves a second chance, too."

Anger flared. "What are you, his lawyer?"

Nik took hold of her shoulders. She tried to shrug him off, but he wouldn't let her. "Sara, family ties are important, even to someone who likes to flutter from place to place."

Now he was sitting in judgment of her. Who the hell did he think he was? Sara pulled free of his grasp.

"I don't 'flutter' and family ties are fine for people who have families. What I have are broken pieces of what *used* to be a family." She lowered her voice as an orderly walked by them in the hallway. "My mother made it perfectly clear to me that I was in the way when she remarried. We exchange Christmas cards once a year and little else. My father hasn't sent me a Christmas card in fourteen years, and now—" she gestured impotently in the air "—all of a sudden I'm supposed to forgive and forget and be daddy's little girl again?" Her eyes grew hard. "It doesn't work like that, I'm afraid."

Nik didn't know where to begin. He only knew that he had to. She was in too much pain. "Sara, maybe it's not my place—"

Sara seized on his words. "No, it's not your place. Thank you very much for your concern, but it's not your place to butt in to my life and tell me what I'm supposed to feel and how I'm supposed to act."

Fed up, he surrendered and turned away.

Guilt clawed at her as she watched him go. For a second she remained where she was, then, with an angry huff, she ran after him. "Where are you going?"

He jabbed at the elevator button without bothering to look at her. Hurt or not, he couldn't fathom her behavior. "To the Coronary Care Unit."

The elevator arrived and she stepped into it without thinking, her eyes on Nik. "Why?" Her father was a stranger to him. *She* was a stranger to him. Why was he behaving as if he cared about either of them?

"To let you know how he's doing in case you decide that you want to know," he said evenly.

She still didn't understand. "He's my father, not yours."

Nik looked at her, his expression solemn. "Exactly."

She sighed as the elevator doors closed. "You're not married, are you?"

He wondered what brought that on. "No."

"I didn't think so." He looked at her quizzically as he pressed for the first floor. "If you were married, your wife would have probably killed you by now."

Then he wouldn't be standing here, talking to her. "Isn't that rather convoluted reasoning?"

Sara let out a breath. Maybe it was. She didn't know. His talking was jumbling up everything inside her. "I don't care if you *are* here for the best of intentions, I have to say this." She looked at him. "Shut up, Sinclair."

He merely chuckled to himself. It was amazing that just when he wanted to strangle her she'd say something in the next breath that made him laugh. Life with her would undoubtedly be no bed of roses, but a constant challenge.

Belatedly she realized that he had pressed for the first floor. Had he decided to leave, after all? "Changed your mind about playing devil's advocate?" She pointed to the button he had pressed.

"CCU is on the first floor."

It seemed an odd piece of information for him to have at his fingertips. "How do you know that?"

Nik looked straight ahead at the gunmetal-gray doors. "It's where my father died."

"Oh."

It was all she could say as the elevator doors opened. That he was willing to do this for her after what being here reminded him of left Sara speechless. She silently followed him through doors that sprang open automatically as they approached. Nik led her to a desk where a squadron of nurses sat watching monitors, each tuned to a different patient.

Nik stopped by the first nurse. "Has Mr. Santangelo been brought in yet from recovery?"

The young woman paused only for a moment to read a roster before nodding. "Room twelve." Her face was compassionate as she looked from Nik to Sara. She rose to show them the way. "But you can only stay five minutes."

"That's fine," Nik replied.

When he took her hand again, Sara didn't resist. She welcomed the warmth and silent support, even though she knew she shouldn't.

The rooms were really only glass-partitioned cubicles with a myriad of machines circling a single hospital bed like an army of metal soldiers. And in the midst of the platoon lay her father, asleep and pale, with so many tubes running through his body it was as if a child had scribbled loops upon the drawing of a man.

She wanted to cry.

He looked so frail, this man who had once picked her up and tossed her toward the sky each night when he returned from work.

Nik's hand tightened on hers. Sara realized that he was reliving a memory of his own. Perhaps he had seen his own father in a bed like this. She felt ashamed for having given him such a hard time. If only he hadn't interfered. He didn't know what had transpired in her family. He had no right to impose his own beliefs on her. No right to make her feel guilty.

She was doing a damn fine job of that herself.

Sara blinked hard to keep from crying. She'd promised herself no tears and she meant to keep that promise. Just because he looked like a broken old man was no reason to forget fourteen years of no phone calls, no contact.

She was aware that Nik had retreated, letting her have a moment alone. She couldn't even touch her father, she thought. There were too many tubes in the way.

His hand looked almost translucent where the IV was attached. She reached out and barely brushed her fingertips along his.

"Certainly don't look like Clint Eastwood now, do you?" she whispered.

She could have sworn that she saw her father's eyes flutter ever so slightly and try to open. It was just her imagination, she told herself.

She'd been so sure that after all that had gone before, she had distanced herself sufficiently so that this wasn't going to bother her. She'd been wrong.

Sara pressed her lips together, wishing she hadn't come.

She stepped back, as if to deny what she was seeing. That failing, she desperately attempted to harden her heart to it.

Zero for two.

Turning away before she broke down, Sara saw that

Nik had gone back to the nurses' desk. Now what was he doing? As she approached, she heard him talking to the nurse. ''Will he be all right?''

The nurse briefly scanned the information available to her on the monitor transmitting from room twelve.

''All his vital signs appear to be A-okay.'' The young woman gave Nik an encouraging smile. ''He should be just fine. Is there a number where we can reach you if a problem does arise?''

Sara opened her mouth to respond, trying to recall the telephone number at her father's house. To her surprise, Nik gave the nurse his number before she could say anything.

## Chapter 7

As angry as she was at Nik's presumption, Sara still didn't want to cause a scene in the middle of the hospital. She waited until they were outside the Coronary Care Unit before saying anything to him.

"Boy, you really take this friend role to heart, don't you?"

They were on the cusp of another argument, Nik thought. It fascinated him how Sara's temperament seemed to go in waves, first up, then down, then up again. Nik didn't even bother to try to figure out what it was she was talking about now. He asked.

"What do you mean?"

How could he play dumb? He was interfering in her life, stomping smack in the middle of it with both feet. And no one had invited him in. Nothing she had done could even remotely be construed as encouragement to meddle.

She struggled to keep her voice from rising as they

walked through the winding hallway toward the lobby. "What's the idea of giving that nurse your number instead of mine?"

So that's what this was about. Nik shook his head. Sara was being territorial again. "It wasn't mine," he informed her tersely. "It was the restaurant's phone number. You're going to be working there, aren't you?"

She wanted to shout at him that that wasn't the point, but of course it was. She was going to spend the better part of each day at work. It was only logical that they would contact her at the restaurant.

But she still didn't want Nik taking charge like that. He was taking matters out of her hands as if she was some helpless dolt he had to take care of. She'd been on her own too long to feel comfortable about someone else exercising that kind of control over her.

"Yes," Sara ground out the answer between clenched teeth.

Nik stopped abruptly. He felt he needed to have both feet on the floor at the same time in order to deal with her. Ignoring him, Sara continued walking. She was marching ahead like a soldier heading straight into battle. Nik laid a hand heavily on her shoulder to keep her in place. "So what's your problem?"

Did she have to hit him over the head with a two-by-four before he backed off? She shrugged away his hand. "My problem is that you keep butting in where you have no business being."

For two cents—

Nik suppressed the urge to clip her one on that pretty little chin she insisted on sticking up at him. He shoved his hands into his pockets. And to think he'd felt sorry for her, believing that she was going through the same thing he had. Right. That would give her credit for feelings.

His eyes narrowed as he looked at Sara. "You know, you'd be a damn sight more attractive if you stopped looking for a fight every couple of seconds."

This was all his fault, not hers. "I am not looking for a fight."

Typical woman, always twisting things around. The next time Antonio urged him to hold Sara's hand he was going to lock the old man up in the walk-in refrigerator and leave him there until he came to his senses. "Then what do you call it?"

That was easy. "Protecting my own space."

His green eyes darkened and then went flat. "If you're not careful you're not going to *have* a space." With that, he walked out of the building.

Incensed, Sara hurried after him before the electronic doors had a chance to close again. "And what's that supposed to mean?"

He didn't bother turning around as he scanned the sea of cars just beyond the entrance, looking for his Mustang. "Ever hear the old saying about cutting off your nose to spite your face?"

She set her mouth hard. She hated being lectured to. "I despise trivial sayings."

He looked over his shoulder at her. "Then stop proving that they're true."

Sara didn't bother answering him. Instead, she stormed past him down to the circular path that led into the hospital parking lot. When she stopped to look around, he was right behind her.

Enough was enough. "Are you going to follow me all the way home and tuck me into bed, too?"

Her words created a momentary image in his head

that surprised him with its intensity. He managed to maintain an unfathomable expression.

"It's too early for that."

The way he said it left a lot of room for interpretation. She studied him for a second. Was he coming on to her in the middle of an argument? She couldn't be sure. She thought of giving him a dressing-down, just in case. Yet, as much as she refused to admit it, there was something about the possibility that stirred her.

"I'm going to my car." He pointed to it. The dark blue vehicle was three lanes over from Sara's. "It's parked right over there."

Sara suddenly felt very stupid. And maybe just a shade unjustified in her waspishness. But he *had* brought it all down on his own head.

"Oh." Sara bit her lip, choosing her words. "Sorry." She took a deep breath as she turned toward him. "Look, Nik, I'm sorry if I came across like a wounded bear."

He had to laugh. *"If?"*

What was the use? The man was hopeless. Sara threw up her hands. "I was going to apologize, but never mind. I'll see you in the morning." She rounded the side of a black van. "Oh, damn."

Nik had already begun walking away, but her oath had him turning back, though he had a feeling he'd probably regret it. "What?"

The black van had pulled in after she had parked her car. The driver had used up more than his own share of space. The van's right side was all but blocking her access to the driver's side. Sara gestured at it impatiently, rechanneling all her anger and frustration to the owner of the van.

"Just look at that. I hate people who park at an angle

like that as if they own the road. There's hardly any room for me to get in."

To prove her point, Sara attempted to open the door wide enough to accommodate her small frame. There was barely enough space. Annoyed, Sara moved back and managed to accidentally step on Nik's foot.

Surprised, she swung around. Her body brushed up against his. Again. Electricity swirled through her like lightning down a rod. Unwanted, it was still difficult to ignore.

"Sorry." The apology was scarcely more than a whisper as her voice backed up in her lungs. "You seem to keep getting underfoot one way or another."

She was standing toe-to-toe with him with nowhere to go. Escape was blocked on both sides by either her car or the van. Her door was still open, so backing away from him was out of the question. That left only one way to move. Into his arms.

She looked up at Nik, her eyes large with wonder at the sensations telegraphing through her. Her lips formed a perfect circle. "Oh."

Nik gazed down at her face, as surprised as she was by the mutual jolt. He knew it was mutual by the look in her eyes. For one thing, she wasn't snapping at him. Just resisting.

He realized that he had been unsuccessfully dodging something right from the start. Her. It was time to discover if the sexual tension humming between them was as powerful as it seemed.

Nik wove his fingers through her soft dark hair, framing her face with his palms. "Yeah. Oh."

There didn't seem to be any point in putting this off any longer. He felt the pull within his body, the pull that drew him toward her. Like floodwaters flowing toward the ocean, all his churning emotions had been heading toward this since he had seen her in his kitchen.

"Nik—"

Sara couldn't seem to manage to utter more of a protest than that. Her hands cupped over his, but rather than try to pull them away, she pressed them against his skin. As if to reinforce the contact Nik had initiated.

She had to be losing her mind.

"There you go again," he admonished softly. "Opening your mouth."

It felt as if there was honey in her veins, and she hadn't the strength to pull away from him. From the inevitable. She had no strength at all.

Like a lemming going off to the sea, she thought ruefully, she still had to find out where this was leading her.

Nik lowered his mouth to hers and made a huge discovery.

He didn't know a damn thing about kissing.

First kisses had always been tentative explorations in uncharted territories for him. They were, by turns, interesting, sweet and uncomplicated. What they weren't was explosive. They didn't cause an outpouring of a cornucopia of sensations, tastes, feelings. They didn't involve a complete loss of his sense of direction. And they definitely didn't cause an inversion of the ground with the sky.

All bets were off. He wasn't in Kansas anymore. He was in Oz.

Nik slid his hands away from her face and slipped them around her back. He pressed Sara to him, more to anchor himself to something than for the heavenly sensation the outline of her body created as it fit against his. That was only an added bonus.

Dear God, he'd sampled Harvey Wallbangers that had less of a kick than the taste of her mouth.

She was vulnerable, that was it. There was no other explanation for why she was hurtling through space with the speed of a bullet being fired out of the chamber of a .357 Magnum. From the first moment she saw him, she had thought that Nik was sexy. But that was no reason to feel as if she was a plate of ice cream left out on the porch in the early afternoon.

Sara dug her fingers into his hair, desperately needing to feel something real. This wasn't real, it wasn't happening. It couldn't be happening. His kiss had created a world that was as close to a hallucination as she could imagine it to be.

What had he put into that hospital coffee?

He was glad now that she hadn't listened to him, that she hadn't closed her mouth. The tastes that rose up were sensually arousing as his tongue touched hers. He felt her body dip into his as she moaned.

The sound of her own moan caused a shock wave to vibrate through her body. Sara pulled back, afraid that she would completely lose her identity in the next moment if she didn't.

She realized that she probably looked dazed and wild-eyed to Nik as she shakily drew air back into her lungs.

"Did we just have an earthquake?" she mumbled.

He was reluctant to let her go, but he did. "Felt like it to me."

Sara dragged her hand through her hair, trying to pull herself together. The depth of the passion she'd felt a moment ago utterly unnerved her. Both his and hers. There had been a number of men in her life, but none whom she had ever allowed to matter.

And none had ever kissed her like this.

She'd never experienced anything like it. She'd never longed before, never yearned before where every fiber of her body wanted it to continue, wanted to be taken. Her relationships were always completely superficial, like a drawing on a page. No strings, ever, to tie her down or reel her in. Instinctively she knew that if she ever became involved with a man, really involved, it would be asking for trouble. Relationships hurt. She had learned that from her parents.

The only way to avoid pain was to avoid any sort of actual relationships. And yet here she was, standing hip-deep in trouble.

Sara groped for the feel of the car door behind her. Her fingers slid around the frame.

"I'd better go—"

"Sara—"

Something had happened here just now. God only knew what. Sex, chemistry, attraction, something. Nik didn't want it, or her, just slipping through his fingers before he explored the sensations that had been born in the wake of her kiss. He didn't want her just running off, not yet.

But one look at Sara's face and he knew that there was no way of talking to her now. Something in her eyes reminded him of a wary, frightened child. Maybe it was for the best if they both had a little breathing space, at least for now.

Sara was already getting into her car. Slamming her door, she jabbed her key into the ignition. The car growled to life. She threw it into reverse, her hand shaking.

"You'd better move, Sinclair, unless you want me

backing up over you.'' She hoped that sounded as flippant as she was trying to make it.

Nik had little doubt, as he stepped to the side, that Sara would be as good as her word.

She blasted music all the way to her father's house. She didn't hear a note. It took Sara fifteen minutes to stop trembling. She felt as if her insides were all the consistency of watered-down Jell-O.

Damn that man, she thought. As if she didn't have enough turmoil in her life already.

By morning Sara had calmed down and had reverted back to her blasé self. She had convinced herself that the reason Nik's kiss had electrified her was that she'd been completely, emotionally overwrought. If it hadn't been for the doubly charged situations she had found herself in, first being summoned by the father who had abandoned her and then having to wait out the results of his surgery, Nik's kiss would have left her completely cold.

Well, maybe not completely, but it wouldn't have felt as if there had been a total upheaval in her body composition.

It was the emotional gauntlet she had just gone through that had contributed to her feeling weak-kneed and palpitating as if she had just dived off a high cliff into ice-cold waters, not the man himself.

It was a good working theory, she thought, getting into her car. And she intended to make it work.

Still, as a precaution, she made certain that she didn't arrive at Sinclair's before the rest of the crew came on duty. Better safe than sorry, at least until she regained her bearings.

She held her breath as she knocked on the back door,

and only let it out when she saw that it was Jennifer who opened it.

Katie was trailing after her mother. The ribbon in her hair was slightly askew and drooping.

"Good morning." Sara dropped to her knees and fixed Katie's bow. The child looked like a miniature version of her mother, she thought. Brushing her hand along the little girl's cheek, Sara rose again and headed toward the office. There was a ton of work to do and she was aching to leap into it.

"Boy, you're certainly cheerful this morning," Jennifer commented, following Sara in. "I hear your father's surgery went well. I'm very glad."

Sara dropped her purse into the desk's bottom drawer, then shut it with her foot. She wanted a cup of coffee, and wondered what her first encounter with Nik would be like. She intended to play it very casually, as if yesterday's incident in the parking lot had all been very commonplace in her life.

"Did Nik tell you that?" What else had he shared with his sister? she wondered.

Probably nothing, she decided. She had to give him his due. He didn't seem like the type of man who was driven to talk about his private life.

Jennifer cleared her scattered notes from the desk. "No, actually, Kane did." She saw Sara's puzzled look. "He stopped by to see your father on his way home last night. Did you know Kane and your father work out of the same precinct?"

There had been a lot more that Kane had shared with her last night, things that had Jennifer's heart going out to both father and daughter. But she sensed that Sara wasn't the type who took sympathy easily.

"Small world," Sara murmured. She turned in time to see Nik pass by the doorway. Their eyes met for a moment before he continued walking. "Maybe a little too small," she added under her breath, settling in.

Nik had almost walked into the office, then had changed his mind at the last moment. No sense pushing anything. What would be would be. The philosophy arose from an old song his mother used to sing to him when he was a child.

Part of him still believed in it.

"Hey, Sinclair, any chance of getting a terrific cup of coffee?" Sara called out just as he reached the kitchen.

He stopped, waiting for her to catch up. He smiled easily. So, she was going to play it cool. Well, so could he. "Sure. I'll show you to the coffee urns."

It wasn't in Sara's nature to hide when things made her nervous. The best way to conquer fear of riding was to climb back on the horse that had thrown her. Of course, this time she'd kissed the horse instead of falling off him, but the basic philosophy was the same. If she attempted to stay out of his way, it would only manage to make things worse and blow them out of proportion for her.

Besides, Nik had said that he wanted to be her friend, so that was what they were going to be. Friends. Maybe even good friends. There was room in her life for that. But that was where it would end.

"What happened to my personalized service?" she asked. Nik noted that mischief had replaced the wariness he had seen yesterday in her eyes.

He played along with her mood. "That's for new employees."

Sara fisted her hands at her waist and looked at him, amused. "Well?"

"This is day number two." He held up two fingers. "You're not new anymore."

"Ah, *signorina,* you are here!" As Antonio greeted her, he took Sara's hand and kissed it. His mustache lightly tickled her skin. "I thought perhaps he had scared you away." He nodded toward Nik.

Sara glanced at Nik as he crossed to one of the stoves. "He tried." Nik raised a brow in her direction. Damn, she'd said too much again. "At least someone appreciates me," she quipped flippantly.

"Do some work. I'll appreciate you." Nik turned away. But he was smiling to himself. Neither Antonio nor Jennifer, who had walked into the kitchen just at that moment, missed the expression.

It was three o'clock. The lunch crowd had thinned out and the early dinner crowd was still two hours off. The tempo in the kitchen had slowed considerably. It was as good a time as any, Jennifer thought. She walked into the kitchen.

Nik was experimenting with a new recipe he'd been working on. It wasn't quite going the way he wanted it to. She could tell by his expression. Jennifer debated saving her question for another time, then thought better of it. She loved Nik, but the man needed dynamite lit under him to see things that other people were aware of immediately.

She picked up a packet of saltine crackers from a carton on the worktable as she crossed to her brother. Her stomach was queasy, reminding her of the tiny soul that was forming beneath her heart. "Okay, what's up?"

Another dash of garlic wasn't the answer, Nik decided, staring at the pan before him. It didn't have the taste he was looking for.

Nik looked up at Jennifer, impatient at being interrupted. "In what way? Are you referring to the menu, to the work schedule, to the catering business, to this damn mess that doesn't want to rise up out of the realm of the mundane—what? Be specific, Jennifer, I'm a busy person."

She pulled the red tape off the packet and slipped out a cracker. "You're busy dodging."

Nik moved the pan onto a dormant burner, temporarily surrendering. He pinned Jennifer with a look. "You know, I am strongly becoming convinced that the theory that men and women originated on different planets is absolutely true. What are you talking about?"

She finished the small cracker and twirled the second one in her fingers, her mind on her brother and not the fact that her stomach was lurching. There really wasn't much she could do about the latter, but there might be about the former. "Let me put it in plainer language for you. What's going on between you and Sara?" She punctuated her question with a crunch as she bit into the next cracker.

Nik looked around. The closest pair of ears belonged to Chris and he was busy flirting with Ginger by the exit.

"I'm her boss, she's my employee." Nik decided that he needed something to occupy his mind other than the conversation, and returned the pan to the burner. "At the end of the week a paycheck will pass between us."

Jennifer studied her brother. It wasn't like Nik to deny something that was true. Nik was always forthright, facing everything head-on. Of course, this was probably new to him. She grinned, pleased. ''That's not all that's passing between you.''

His eyes were not altogether friendly as he looked at his sister. ''Meaning?''

Jennifer had watched the two of them the first day Sara had come to work, as well as this morning. Each time they were within several feet of each other there was an underlying current of tension beneath the surface that cut through all the words that flew between them.

''That there's enough electricity going back and forth between you to keep Vegas running for a week.''

He kept his expression bland. ''I didn't know that hallucinations went along with pregnancy.''

''They don't.'' He wasn't going to talk his way out of this. She cared too much. ''You know I don't generally pry into your business—''

''Ha.'' He reached for the cayenne pepper on the spice rack above the stove.

Jennifer placed her hand on the container, stopping him. ''Nik, Julia does that, not me. Give me my due.''

He knew she was only being concerned, but he didn't want to be prodded about this, even by family. ''All right. So why start now?''

She withdrew her hand. ''Because I care.'' For a second she watched him season the sautéed chicken slices in silence. ''Are you going to ask her out?''

He was about to drizzle a handful of finely chopped walnut pieces over the mixture. They fell from his hand in a cluster. ''You mean like on a date?''

It was an outdated word for what she had in mind, but for lack of a better start, it would have to do. ''Yes.''

Nik stirred quickly, attempting to distribute the walnuts evenly. He slanted a look at his sister. "Are you crazy?"

She laughed softly. "You'll have to take that matter up with Kane. Are you?"

He stopped sparring with her. Maybe if she had the truth, she'd understand and leave him alone. A date with Sara was a ridiculous idea, even if the woman's kiss had preyed on his mind all night.

"Every time I make overtures of friendship, she wants to have me castrated. This is not a woman a man takes out on a date."

She'd consumed the last cracker and her stomach was still in revolt. Jennifer crossed to the worktable and picked up another packet. "Brom tells me that she's had a rough time of it."

Nik stopped stirring for a second, considering. It was still no excuse. "That doesn't mean she has to give back in kind."

Jennifer thought about how gentle Nik could be, how supportive. He'd always been there for all of them. The man had a lot of love to give. "I figure you're the one to teach her that lesson." She squeezed his arm.

"I'll think about it."

"Think hard, Nik," she urged softly. "Life is ticking by."

He glanced up at the clock. He was going to have to start getting ready for the dinner crowd soon. "So I noticed."

Jennifer refused to be put off. "I don't want you missing out on what I have. On what Julia has."

He gave the creation in the pan one last stir, placed a lid on top of it and then set it aside to simmer. "Fine, you send Kane and Brom around. We'll go out and do something together."

Jennifer laughed. Nik was hopelessly stubborn when he wanted to be. But he would come around. Or, at least, she hoped so. "You know what I mean. You're the one who taught us all about the importance of family ties, Nik. Go make some of your own."

He thought of Sara and the way she had almost bolted out of the hospital parking lot after he'd kissed her. "The only tie I could manage with Sara is if I bound her up like one of those steers at a rodeo." He walked over to the walk-in freezer to check on the seafood order he had received earlier today.

Jennifer was right behind him. "Maybe she'll surprise you." She stopped short of the refrigerator, waiting for Nik to emerge. "I've been working with her for two days now and I like what I see."

Mentally Nik checked off the amount of seafood he expected to use tonight. "Fine, you go out on a date with her. I'll make your explanations to Kane."

Jennifer grinned.

He slammed the door shut again and looked at her. "What?"

"I don't think you stand a chance."

What were she and Julia plotting? He was sure Julia was the instigator. Jennifer had always been too mild-mannered to push so hard. "Against you?"

She shook her head. "Nope. Against you. I can see it in your eyes, big brother. You like the lady."

Maybe he did, but there was no point in going into that one way or the other. "I also like the Angels. That's not a winning pick, either."

"You'll find a way," she promised. She patted his cheek teasingly, knowing he hated that. "You always do."

He didn't have time for any more games. "Did you

come in here for any other reason other than to harass me? Because if you didn't..."

For the time being, she supposed she'd said enough. Nik would undoubtedly take it from here at his own pace. She just didn't want to see him missing out. "Actually, I did want to tell you that the DeCarlo party called to add fifty more guests to their wedding for next month."

Nik nodded, glad to be back on familiar ground again. "The more the merrier."

"The only problem is Sara says we need more money up front before we can go ahead and—"

He raised his hand to stop her before she got any further. "Sara says?" he echoed. Jennifer nodded her head, aware that she had finally lit a fuse. "Since when does Sara dictate terms for anything?"

Jennifer looked up at him innocently. "Well, she is our accountant now—"

"Our *temporary* accountant," he emphasized. "And I don't want anyone from Accountants 'R' Us to suddenly start dictating our restaurant policy. Is she in the office?"

He was already striding past Jennifer, heading toward the hallway.

"Yes. Now, Nik, don't yell," Jennifer warned, hurrying to keep up. "I don't want Katie to think her uncle's gone berserk."

"Then I'd advise you to take her out for a walk. It's time she got some air."

He might have known that if he gave her an inch she'd take out an entire claim. Just because he'd tentatively agreed yesterday to let her utilize a new program—and even that hadn't been a definite yes—that in no way gave her the green light to get any further involved in restaurant policies. She was working for him, not the other way around, and he was going to take great pleasure in pointing that out.

"Sara," Nik announced, "I'd like a word with you."

Sara had just returned from visiting her father in the hospital. It had been a quick, five-minute visit to check on his condition and to assuage her conscience. Five minutes, after all, was all the nurse had originally said was allowed. Sara clung to that. If she stayed too long, things might get said that she had no intentions of saying.

Agitated, confused, Sara was the perfect candidate for a fight. She glanced toward the doorway and saw Nik standing there. Anger creased his brow. He made her think of Thor just before the Norse god let loose with one of his thunderbolts.

Ah, the perfect recipient for a fight.

She smiled at him sweetly. "Something wrong, Sinclair?" she asked.

He crossed the threshold, struggling to keep his temper in check. He lost. "You bet there is."

Thunderstorm, no doubt about it, Sara thought, girding up.

Jennifer took her daughter's hand and led her toward the doorway.

"C'mon, Katie, time to get some fresh air. Uncle Nik is going to make nice with Aunt Sara." As she moved past him, she saw Nik's brow rise. "It's just an expression, Nik," she explained soothingly. But she grinned knowingly as she said it, as if the title she had bestowed on Sara was a prophecy.

Jennifer left Nik and Sara looking at one another like two roosters laying claim to the same barnyard.

# Chapter 8

Nik glanced over his shoulder to make certain that Jennifer and Katie were out of earshot. Satisfied, he turned his full attention to Sara. But first he had to shut out impulses that had him responding to her on a very different, very basic level. They had no place in this conversation, perhaps no place in their lives at all.

"Just what do you mean by setting up rules for the restaurant?"

Sara drew her brows together, trying to guess what had set him off like this. Offhand she couldn't think of a thing that she had done that would make him come charging in like a steer on the streets of Pamplona during the annual running of the bulls.

"Excuse me?"

He could almost believe that childlike, innocent expression on her face—if he didn't know better. "Jennifer tells me that *you* don't think we should proceed with catering arrangements for the DeCarlo wedding unless we get more money up front.''

''And?'' she prompted, waiting. So far, she didn't see what the problem was.

*And?* Was she being purposely dense, or just baiting him? Either way, it didn't improve his mood. ''Where do you get off, dictating what we can or can't do in running our restaurant?''

There was something almost magnetically attractive about Nik when his expression looked so dark and foreboding. And it was exactly that attraction that made Sara break out in a cold sweat. Defense alarms went off.

''I'd hardly call common sense 'dictating.''' She raised her eyes and smiled sweetly. Poetic justice was alive and well. ''Careful, Nik, or someone's going to accuse you of protecting your own space.''

She was taunting him with what he had lectured her about yesterday. He should have realized that she would, the first chance she got. But she was still wrong. ''That's different.''

The look in her eyes was gently mocking. She was beginning to enjoy this argument. It was tipping in her favor. ''Is it?''

The woman was evoking a mixed bag of emotions from him. He felt like shaking her and knocking some reason into her head. Most of all, he felt like kissing her until they were both senseless instead of just her. ''You know it is.''

Sara spread her arms wide. ''I don't know anything of the kind. Besides—'' her eyes held his again as she referred to something else he'd mentioned ''—I'm only trying to help.''

The hell she was. She was taking yesterday and reversing their roles. "Déjà vu," he said sarcastically.

Sara grinned. "Maybe it is," she agreed pleasantly. "As your accountant—temporary accountant," she amended quickly before he had the chance, though the distinction was more for her own benefit than for his, "I have to call it the way I see it."

She leaned back and assumed what she hoped Nik would regard as a somber attitude. She placed the tips of her fingers together and rocked in the swivel chair. Her eyes never left his.

God, he had beautiful eyes.

She forced her mind back to the little drama she was sketching for him. "Now, the DeCarlos are probably really terrific, trustworthy people who don't even owe interest on their charge cards and pay every bill when it's due. *But*—" she held up one finger in the air "—there are people in this world who will attempt to conveniently 'forget' to pay on time. Or at all. Too many of those and you're overextended. It can happen to anyone, Sinclair. Just read the papers." She gestured toward a folded newspaper Jennifer had left on the file cabinet.

He wondered if she would still be able to talk if someone held on to her hands. She gestured to punctuate almost every statement.

"Don't patronize me, Sara. I'm not a child," he said evenly. "I know that."

"Good." She turned her back to him as she resumed her work. Or tried to. With Nik in the room, it was difficult for her to concentrate on anything. Especially after yesterday.

Sara could feel him standing there, studying her back.

It took all she had not to shift restlessly. "Then there's no reason for this argument."

"Except maybe," Nik began, moving around to the front of the desk so that he could face her, "that I don't like hearing criticism—or advice—" he added when she raised a warning brow "—coming from anyone." He decided to be completely honest. "I suppose I don't like being told how to run things even if it does make sense."

There was silence in the room for a moment. Only the low hum of the computer disturbed it. And then somewhere off in the kitchen someone dropped a pan. A few choice words in Italian followed the incident.

"Then we have that in common, don't we?" She lowered her eyes to the screen.

Nik raised his hand, wanting to touch her shoulder. Wanting to touch her. If he did, she'd probably come out swinging. He let his hand fall to his side. "Sara, about yesterday…"

She didn't want to discuss yesterday. At least, not the part of the day that needed to be discussed.

"I appreciate you coming to the hospital and all the noble intentions that brought you there." Her words had come out in a rush. She stopped and looked up at him. "Maybe I overreacted—about everything."

He knew what she was telling him. That what they both thought was in the kiss hadn't been there at all. But he knew what he'd felt. And he believed he knew what she'd felt, as well. She had responded to him far more than just casually. Still, her denial stung.

His eyes darkened. "Maybe we both did."

Why did that hurt? He was only agreeing with what she had said. Sara set her mouth firmly.

"Good." Her fingers flew over the keyboard, typing

gibberish. She hoped he wouldn't look over her shoulder when he left. "Another point of agreement. We're progressing, Sinclair."

If that was the case, why did he have the distinct feeling that they were going backward? And why did she sound so brittle, like a drill sergeant complimenting recruits newly liberated from boot camp?

He had no answers, but at least they'd stopped arguing for the moment. Nik decided to quit while there was a truce in force. He had too many details to see to in the kitchen. They were unveiling a new item on the evening menu and he wanted to be sure everything was ready. A new food critic was coming around to the restaurant at the end of next week. Nik didn't have time for personal matters that went beyond his immediate family.

He certainly didn't have the time to wet-nurse a small woman with a very large chip on her shoulder and eyes the color of melted dark chocolate. Even if she did make his blood run hot.

He crossed to the doorway, and then stopped. "Had lunch yet?"

"No. I—" She was about to tell him that she hadn't had a chance to eat because she had gone to the hospital during her lunch break. But she caught herself in time. The less personal details she shared, however minor, the better. "I haven't."

His eyes swept over her. She was wearing a green-and-white-striped tank top and a skirt that was, in his estimation, not that much wider than a headband. It showed off legs that were longer than a person of her stature had a right to have. Legs that made his pulse rate go up far faster than the house wine did.

"Get some. You're too thin."

And too damn attractive.

She raised her coffee cup. Inclining her head, she toasted Nik. "My, but you do have a golden tongue, Sinclair."

She was getting under his skin again in more ways than one. Their truce was in danger of going up in flames. "People come here for my cooking, not my rhetoric."

She laughed as she took a sip of coffee. "And aren't you grateful for that one?"

He started to retort. He knew that things would only escalate again, but he seemed unable to help himself. It was almost as if he had no say in the matter. Worse, it was as if he thrived on this constant conflict that was pulsating between them.

But Sara had already turned away from him and toward the screen. She was hastily deleting something, but he couldn't see what.

Nik thought of the reason he had come charging into the office to begin with. They hadn't actually resolved that. At least, he hadn't.

"I'll have Jennifer call Mrs. DeCarlo and ask for another advance," Nik muttered as he walked out of the office.

Sara smiled to herself as she completed deleting the gibberish she had previously typed in.

"You know, for someone claiming to be such a free spirit, you're just as much of a workaholic as people accuse me of being."

Sara glanced up to see Nik looking into the office. She hadn't seen him since he'd ordered her to have lunch. But she had anticipated him.

She stretched and focused on her watch. It was almost

ten. It was hard to believe she'd been in the office by herself for almost five hours. When Kane had come by to collect Jennifer and Katie, Sara had meant to stay only a few extra minutes.

A few minutes had stretched into hours. Though it was just past the summer solstice, the sun had long since retreated from the office like a servant backing out of a queen's room. Sara had absently switched on the desk lamp and kept going.

Just a little longer. She smiled ruefully to herself.

Leaning back in the chair, she arched her back and ran her fingers through her hair, as if that would help clear away the cobwebs on her brain. She saw the flicker of interest in Nik's eyes and it flattered her even though she tried not to let it.

"This is like a good mystery." She gestured toward the files. The pile on the floor now exceeded the pile on her desk. She was making real progress now that she understood Nik's unique method of record keeping. "I want to see how it turns out.

"Besides—" Sara moved the chair around so that she could face him "—I'm *not* a workaholic. It's just that I'm not going to be here that long. I thought I'd work ahead a little so that you'd feel that you'd gotten your money's worth out of me."

It was a lie, but so what? The simple truth was that she liked accounting and right now there wasn't anything else she had to do. But he didn't have to know that. If he knew, it would undoubtedly make him think that he was right.

He'd gotten more than his money's worth all right. And a hell of a lot more than he had bargained for, to boot. She was arguing with him now just for form's sake, he was sure of it.

Nik leaned a hip against the desk, crossing his arms. "You know, I have a strong suspicion that if I said 'day,' you'd say 'night' just because you don't want to agree with me." He did a quick mental check over the past three days. "I don't think we've really agreed on anything since you arrived."

"That's not true." The protest came automatically. And then Sara grinned ruefully as he eyed her. "Well, not entirely, anyway." She lifted her shoulders and let them fall. The tank top moved with her like a second skin and stirred Nik's imagination. He shoved his hands into his pockets to soothe the sudden itch that arose. "Besides, a little antagonism's good for the soul."

And a lot tended to wear it out. "I'm sure you're the reigning authority on that. "

Sara cocked her head. Her eyes were amused. "Trying to start another fight?"

He shook his head. "Trying to agree with something you said."

She laughed, then began to press a sequence of buttons that would store the last batch of data. "Don't start being agreeable now, Sinclair. It'll ruin that carefully honed image of yours."

Maybe talking to her was an exercise in futility. He picked up the newspaper Jennifer had left for him. He wanted to peruse the food section before going to bed tonight. He liked keeping up on the competition.

Nik started to leave, then changed his mind. He didn't want to go straight home tonight. He wanted to look at Sara in the moonlight.

Perhaps someone had substituted peyote for the cayenne pepper, he mused, retracing his steps. God knows he wasn't acting sensibly. A sensible man would have retreated, glad to escape with his skin intact.

Sara looked over her shoulder at him in surprise. "Forget something?"

*Yes, you.*

"You know, when I first bought this place," he began conversationally, as if they hadn't just been at odds a moment ago, "I didn't realize how really great the location was."

She raised a brow, wondering what he was getting at. Most people were aware of location before they even inquired about the price of a store or restaurant, unless they were stupid, of course. Nik Sinclair wasn't stupid.

"Scenically, I mean." He nodded toward his left and the back entrance. "The beach is less than half a mile away from the rear parking lot, just beyond the houses. People like to come here for dinner and then top it off with a stroll along the beach."

She felt uneasy as she resumed storing her material. She had a feeling she knew where he was going with this. And she wanted to go with him, which was what frightened her. She wanted to go *too* much.

Sara didn't look at him. "At some of the prices I've seen on the menu, that's probably all they can afford to do afterward."

She was blocking every attempt he made to get by her barriers. Like a well-trained volleyball player, she was slamming the ball over the net every time it threatened to land in her court. Why was she resisting so hard?

"How long have you been a cynic, Sara?"

Her eyes grew distant as she remembered. "Since I was fourteen."

He didn't believe her. He thought she was just being flippant. But he would have liked to have met her before she had become so disillusioned. "What were you like then?"

She roused herself. He was prodding again. Didn't the man ever give up? "A lot younger."

He laughed and shook his head. "Would you have been game to go for a walk on the beach then?"

Sara switched off the machine and ignored the fact that her heart had gone into an accelerated mode. "I'm game now, if someone would ask me."

He took her hand as she reached for the computer's plastic dustcover. She raised her eyes to his. She was trying to be brazen, but she was failing, he thought.

"I'm asking."

She was twenty-eight, for God's sake. Why was her mouth going dry because a man was asking her to take a walk with him along the beach? It only involved sand and water, not a lifelong commitment. Her mouth stayed dry. "What about the restaurant?"

"Antonio'll handle it. He keeps trying to shove me out of the kitchen every night, anyway. Says he'll lock up." A fond smile creased his mouth and Sara suddenly remembered the way it had tasted. "Personally, I think he's stealing the silverware and selling it off to fund his retirement plan. But I haven't the heart to tell him to go home." He sighed. "He likes to think he runs the restaurant."

And Nik let him, she thought. He took umbrage with her when he thought she was challenging his authority, but he let an old man have illusions and order him around. She liked him for it even though she knew she shouldn't.

"Very understanding of you. ' Nik looked at her in surprise. Her voice had grown soft, silky. "It might be a whole new light to see you in."

He took her hand again and drew her from her chair. "So, are you game?"

Too game. And too chicken. Maybe it went hand in hand, she thought. "You were serious? About the walk?"

"I was serious. About the walk," he echoed with a gentle smile.

*And, I think, about you, God help me.*

Sara was very quiet for a second. She'd promised herself not to become emotionally involved with Nik, no matter how tempting the situation might be. And she always kept her promises to herself.

A smile spread on her face as a fresh wave of confidence came from somewhere. She couldn't deny that, though he was a pigheaded son of a gun, she did want to be alone with him. She found him attractive and stimulating, stimulating on more levels than any other man she had ever met before.

What was she afraid of? She had always handled herself before. And she wasn't going to start running now. "Okay, take me to your beach."

Nik kept her hand in his as Sara retrieved her purse from the drawer.

She waited for him while he gave Antonio a few final instructions for the day. It reminded her of a parent briefing a baby-sitter before going out for the evening. And the restaurant was his baby.

He'd probably make a good parent, Sara judged. She'd observed him with Katie. The man who was all business when he donned his apron became all softness and putty in the little girl's hand.

A lot like her own father had been.

The recollection brought with it a painful stab that was sharp.

"You're frowning," Nik noted as he took Sara's arm.

She didn't want him probing into her mind, didn't want him getting any more of a foothold in her life than he had right at this moment. Even that was too much.

"No, I'm not. My face was just relaxing for a second." She patted his cheek. "Like yours does all the time."

He wasn't going to let her bait him. It was clear to Nik that Sara had been thinking of something. Something that obviously bothered her. He wanted to ask her about it, but knew that it would undoubtedly lead to a confrontation. He wasn't up to engaging in another battle of wits with her. All he wanted was to walk along the beach. And, perhaps, to hold her. Nothing more. It seemed like a simple enough desire.

"Don't start," he warned her, holding the rear door open.

"Wouldn't dream of it."

And fish don't swim, he thought.

He led her down a sleepy little residential street that quietly wound its way to the beach. There were single-story houses on either side, little more than cottages, actually. Bathed in the moonlight, even the most faded house looked quaint and appealing. They stood lined up like sleeping doves resting on a branch.

The beach lay just beyond.

The sea was calm, as if it was asleep, as well. It was desolate. There were only the two of them. A sprinkling of anticipation began to filter through Sara's body.

The full moon cast its light on the tranquil waters. The beams danced along the glasslike surface, forming a silvery path that looked as if it would lead straight up toward the moon.

Nik felt relaxed for the first time that day. Perhaps

for the first time in a week. They walked along in silence for a few minutes, and he smiled to himself as he looked at her profile. Silence. And Sara. It was a completely new experience.

He began talking because it seemed right. "Sometimes I come here after the restaurant closes just to pull my thoughts together. I like the beach much better at night. It's beautiful and peaceful then. Nobody's yelling or fighting. No stray balls flying by to hit you."

"It looks lonely." She couldn't stop the shiver that slipped over her.

It was natural for him to put his arm around her. He didn't even have to think about it. It just happened. Surprised, Sara looked at him. He kept his arm where it was. They continued walking.

"I might have known you'd disagree." But there was a smile playing on his lips as he said it.

"I'm not disagreeing," she contradicted. "It *is* beautiful. But beautiful things can be lonely."

The sadness in her voice was almost tangible. What was she thinking about? "Are you?"

Sara stared straight ahead. How was it that he always made her say more than she meant to?

"I wasn't talking about me. Besides—" she shrugged carelessly and the strap on her tank top slipped off her shoulder "—I'm not beautiful."

He stopped walking and turned her to face him. Gently he laid his hands on her shoulders. His thumb coaxed the strap back into place. Her skin tingled as if he had stripped her nude. Sara struggled to refrain from trembling. "We're disagreeing again."

A small smile quirked her mouth. "Why does that keep happening?"

His hands remained on her shoulders. Her skin felt

soft. He wanted to touch her all over. "Because you're usually wrong."

Even in the moonlight Nik could see the fire reenter her eyes. "I'm—?"

"All right," he conceded, lifting his hands in surrender. There was laughter in his eyes. "Fifty percent of the time you're wrong. The other fifty percent of the time I'm right. Fair enough?"

She began to laugh. He was incorrigible.

When she laughed, when she smiled like that, she took his breath away.

"Better," he whispered, lowering his mouth just a little until his breath was on her face, stirring her emotions, making suddenly tense nerves knit together like fingers laced in prayer. "Much better."

She licked lips that were suddenly parched. This wasn't a good idea. Subconsciously she'd known that even as she agreed to come here with him. Yet she *had* agreed. Was it because she'd been longing to be alone with him, with no one to see them except the moon?

Why was she walking out on a tightrope when she knew there was no net under her, nothing to catch her if she fell? *When* she fell.

Desperate, Sara sought salvation in humor as she took a step back. She felt her heels sinking into the sand. "Does this come under the heading of fringe benefits?"

Gently he brushed his thumb along her cheek and watched desire bloom in her eyes, even as she fought to hold her ground. "Depends on whose you're talking about."

"Mine?" she guessed. It would be the typical male response.

He moved his head slowly from side to side. "Mine."

And then there was no more space between them and no more words to create artificial barriers. His mouth covered hers. The cornucopia burst open instantly, showering him with an even greater spectrum of emotions and sensation than the first time.

He welcomed them all.

Nik pulled Sara to him, locking her in an embrace that was at once fierce and tender at the same time. His blood rushed and pounded through him like the surf during the height of a storm.

Sara didn't even attempt to fight what was happening. She had no strength to do anything but let herself be swept away by the heat of his mouth, by the power of his kiss. Later, when she was back in battle form, when she had her wits about her, she'd do what she could to repair the damage being done right at this instant.

But for now, she reveled in the excitement that seized her as his mouth took hers over and over again, draining her of her very will. She didn't know who or what she was, only that she wanted this sensation to continue. Forever. Longer, if possible.

She could feel the length of his body as it imprinted itself on hers. People weren't supposed to come unraveled just by kissing, she knew that. But she felt like a ball of yarn being batted around by a kitten, unraveling at a prodigious rate.

This wasn't safe, Nik thought. He was on the brink of something, tottering on the very edge. And he was going to fall in.

He had always known that he wasn't the type to do things in half measures. And he wanted her. But more than for just a night. More than for just a week. Commitment was a very real word to him, one he believed in wholeheartedly. Sara had made it abundantly clear that she was only passing through. It would be stupid to allow anything to develop between them.

And yet it seemed, even after such a short while, that he had no say in the matter. Something was happening with or without his consent. And he could only hang on for the ride and hope to be in one piece when it came to its end.

Sara braced her hands on his shoulders, wanting to push Nik away. But somehow she wound up grasping his shirt instead, twisting her fingers into the material as Nik pulled her even closer to him. His long fingers played along her spine until every inch of her vibrated with needs.

Her heart was pounding so hard that it hurt. Her very breath was gone. As his mouth trailed along the column of her throat she felt herself falling in deeper. She was drowning in a bottomless pool of sensations swimming into one another.

Though she didn't want to, Sara struggled to draw back. Stalling for time, attempting to steady her breathing, she leaned her head against his chest. She heard his heart pounding. At least she wasn't alone in this. But it was a small comfort.

This had been even more powerful than the last time. She'd barely recovered before. How was she going to manage to do it again?

She closed her eyes and looked for strength. She didn't find any. Sara couldn't even muster the strength to lift her head.

"So," she managed in a husky whisper, "are you relaxed?"

"No."

Desire and anticipation hummed all through her, begging her to continue. She knew it was impossible.

"Neither am I. I guess that blows your theory about the beach all to hell."

He stroked her hair. In the moonlight it looked almost pitch-black.

"For now." His pulse had stopped doing triple time. Nik ran his fingertips along her arms and felt the slight tremble in response.

*Oh, God, if you only knew what you do to me, woman.*

For a moment he enjoyed the feel of just standing there with her in his arms. "Sara?"

He felt her breath against his chest as she answered. "Yes?"

He took a chance. If they didn't go forward, they'd go backward. She wasn't the type to stand still. "Come home with me."

He felt her stiffen against him. He was losing her.

"More fringe benefits?"

He moved back so he could look at her face. "Sara, I'm serious."

Her eyes clouded over. "Don't be. Not about me." Sara pulled away from him. "I'm telling you from the start, it won't work."

The wariness had returned. Why, damn it, why? He didn't want to push her, but he couldn't just back away, either. "How do you know unless we try?"

She turned away from him and ran her hands up and down her arms. The night was sultry, but she was suddenly cold. "Because I don't want to try, all right?" Failure only lay at the end of the road.

In his heart he knew it wasn't true. "I thought you were the type who was so unorthodox. Who liked to take risks."

When he reached for her, she moved aside. If he

touched her again, she'd give in. And she couldn't. Wouldn't.

"I'll go bungee jumping with you, Nik. Anytime you want. But I won't go to bed with you."

He let out an exasperated breath. He wanted to reason with her, but her resistance made no sense to him. "There's something happening between us, Sara."

"That's *why* I won't go to bed with you. Because there is something between us." Weakening, she spun around and touched his face. He covered her hand with his own and pressed a kiss to her palm.

Sara felt tears forming as she moved away from him. "Leave it alone, Nik."

"Why?" he demanded. "Why?"

She shook her head. "I couldn't begin to explain it to you."

Sara turned and walked slowly back to the restaurant, her shoulders braced like those of a soldier who had been forced to ride into the heart of a battle.

Nik watched her go, then turned and walked in the opposite direction. He had no idea for how long.

She was right. This time walking along the beach didn't soothe him.

It just made him feel lonely.

# Chapter 9

The office felt eerily quiet. Jennifer had taken the day off for a long-overdue outing with Kane and Katie. Today there was no constant stream of waitresses stopping by to look in on the baby or to exchange a few words with Jennifer. Rather than enjoy it, for some reason the silence made Sara feel restless.

She missed Jennifer. The woman was incredibly even-tempered. Unlike her brother, Sara thought with a smile. It was odd how you could know a person for only a few short days and feel as if you'd known them forever.

She felt that way about Jennifer. She had no idea how she felt about Nik, other than hopelessly confused. She opened another folder and started typing.

She knew Nik was standing there before she even turned around. She could feel him looking at her. She didn't even try to explore why she knew. She just did.

"Hi." She tossed the greeting in his direction without looking up from her work.

Feeling a little self-conscious that she had caught him staring at her, Nik walked into the office. "I came to see how you were doing."

Actually, that was stretching the truth a little. He had stopped by just to see her. Period.

Sara looked up just as he reached her desk. There was an interesting-looking blue streak running along the length of his apron. She couldn't begin to guess as to its origin. Cooking was as much of a mystery to her as he was.

"Fine, although I miss Katie's chatter." She'd lost her place, and gave up for a moment. "I've gotten kind of used to it."

"She does grow on you." The silence hung awkwardly between them. Nik dragged his hand through his hair. "Well, if everything's all right…"

He began to leave. He felt like an awkward teenager when he was around her. No, that wasn't right, he amended. Even as a teenager he had never felt this way. He'd been a high school jock who'd enjoyed a full and active social life. Conversations with the opposite sex had never been a problem.

Until now.

Sara seemed to knock out all the known parameters of his world as if they were only rotting pieces of wood. So why did he keep coming back for more?

Nik forced himself to stop in the doorway. "Isn't your father scheduled to be released soon?"

"Tomorrow." Her hand hovered over the keyboard as she turned to look at him. "How did you know?"

"I was there when the doctor talked to you, remember?"

He crossed to her again and this time sat down in the chair next to the desk, making himself as comfortable as he could around her.

"What *is* that?" she finally asked, skimming her fingertip along the blue streak. Her hand came in contact with his thigh. Marginally, but it was enough to affect them both.

Nik shifted slightly, suddenly feeling restless. "Blueberry sauce. Chris spilled some prying the lid off a jar. I had the misfortune of being caught in the cross fire." Nik shook his head. "He's got promise, but a *long* way to go." Not unlike he himself had been ten years ago, Nik supposed.

Leaning his elbows on the arms of the chair, he folded his hands together and studied her face. "Need any help bringing him home?" When she raised her eyes to his face quizzically, he added, "Your father."

An amused smile lifted the corners of her mouth. The man never gave up, did he? "I don't intend to sling him over my shoulder and carry him back to his house."

Nik picked up a folder and pretended to thumb through it. The inventory list of last month's condiment order slipped out. "A simple yes or no would work better in this case, Sara." He bent over to pick up the list from the floor and then dropped it on the desk. "Preferably a yes."

"Why?"

Nik stretched his long legs out. He had exactly ten minutes before he had to get back. Chris was about to attempt making a soufflé on his own. "He's probably weak. Getting your father out of the car into the house might not be as easy as it sounds." He paused. "Even for a woman who can do everything."

She didn't have to look at him to know there was a

sarcastic smile on his face. Maybe she had been laying it on too thickly. "I guess you think I deserve that."

Nik rocked slightly in the chair, his eyes on hers. "Yes, I do."

She blew out a breath and decided to abandon the pretense of being able to concentrate on anything while Nik was only a foot away from her. "If I'm so irritating, why are you always here, volunteering to help me?"

He liked the slight pink hue that rose to her cheeks when she became annoyed. No cosmetic could begin to approximate the glow.

"Haven't you heard?" he asked mildly. "Some of us are trying to earn our wings earlier these days. No waiting until the last minute or until Jimmy Stewart is about to leap off the bridge."

She stared at him as if he had lost his mind. How did a matinee idol from the fifties get into this discussion? "What are you talking about?"

He wondered if she had ever watched old movies as a child. His father had been an old-movies buff who periodically took Nik and his sisters to revivals and old film festivals when they were growing up, as well as any musical that might have been playing within a fifty-mile radius. It made for a well-rounded childhood.

"A classic Christmas movie. You should rent it sometime and watch." He grinned, leaning forward. "How does it feel?"

"How does *what* feel?" She wished Jennifer was here to take the focus away from her. She wasn't doing well at all, despite her efforts to the contrary. He had completely upended her not once but twice and she was having the worst time getting back on an even keel.

Nik thought of all the times Sara had taken him on

a verbal game of hide-and-seek. "To be confused when someone's talking?"

"Not too terrific."

She shrugged, looking for a way to save a shred of pride, of dignity, of sanity. Something. At this point she wasn't sure of anything except that every time she was within spitting distance of Nik, she did. She spat and hissed like a cat that was being cornered. Right about now she felt as if she was standing on emotional quicksand.

She opened another folder and stared at the first page, not making sense of any of it. "It's not my fault if you can't keep up."

"Ditto."

Okay, maybe she had that coming to her. Sara sighed, getting serious. "Really, why are you offering to help me? This is going beyond merit badges and wings."

She really wished he wouldn't try to help. Every time he helped, every time he kissed her, he wedged his way a little farther into her life. And she knew she couldn't afford to have him do that. Reflexively, she fought it. There was a battle raging within her. Part of her wanted what he apparently was offering, but that part was being held prisoner by a steely defense mechanism that was intended to keep her safe.

"Maybe, just maybe, the reason might be," he hypothesized, spreading his hands, "although God only knows why, that I like you, Saratoga Santangelo." She winced.

She should never have filled out her full name on the employee form. "If you really like me, you won't use that name."

"Why? I think it's unique. Like you." He grinned. "Saratoga. It suits you."

She looked away. There was something about his eyes that held her captive. And she wanted to be free. "It reminds me of something I don't want to be reminded of."

He placed his hand over hers. "What?"

Sara extracted her hand, then laid both of them over the keyboard. But she didn't type. "If I talk about it, then I'll be reminded, right?"

Nik shook his head. She was definitely in a class by herself. "For a woman who talks a lot, you're awfully close-mouthed."

Sara just smiled triumphantly. "All part of the mystique."

"All part of the irritation," Nik corrected, but he didn't look annoyed, only bemused, like someone facing a six-hundred piece jigsaw puzzle of Samoyed puppies lost in a blizzard.

His irritation she could easily handle. It was the other part that she couldn't. The part where he told her that he liked her. He wasn't talking about friendship, that much she could see in his eyes.

"Then why—"

Nik framed her face, his long fingers curving about her cheeks. "Because I *do* like you, Sara. A great deal. I don't completely understand what's going on here myself. When I figure it out, I'll let you know. But *until* I do, I intend to go on exploring it. That means I'm going to be seeing you a lot."

She felt her pulse throbbing in her throat like a butterfly caught in a hunter's net. She wasn't sure how she managed to get any words past it. "Lucky me."

"Maybe." He leaned over more. Gently his lips just barely brushed against hers. It felt like brushing against heaven, she thought. "Or maybe we'll both get lucky."

The resistance that had been so strong only a moment ago felt as lax as overcooked spaghetti now. Sara sighed deeply. "All right, I guess I could use some help tomorrow." She glanced at the date that was on the bottom right corner of the computer screen. Something occurred to her. "Don't you work on Saturdays?"

He'd been working seven days a week for a long time. It was time to let go a little. Starting now. If nothing else, if he burned out he'd lose his creative edge, and running Sinclair's meant constant change, constant revamping of menus and alteration of tried-and-true recipes.

"I'm learning to be flexible. Jennifer says it's good for my health and for business." Nik rose to his feet. Time to get back before Chris started another fire in the kitchen. "What time do you want me to pick you up tomorrow?"

She thought for a moment. "Eleven, I guess. He's supposed to be discharged before noon." She looked up at Nik, still uncertain about the wisdom of being around him any more than she had to. "Are you sure…?"

He looked down into her eyes. The pull was there, hard and strong. There was no use denying it. "I'm sure."

Sara felt her stomach flipping over and tying itself in a knot all over again.

Afraid that he'd see more than she wanted him to, Sara turned her chair back to the computer screen.

"Don't say I didn't warn you," she murmured under her breath.

But he heard her.

She was agitated. He could tell by the way she was sitting next to him in the car. Perched as if she expected the seat to explode under her at any moment. But, for a change, he didn't think her state had anything to do with him. She'd been friendly when he'd arrived and their conversation had been pleasant enough, revolving around work, Jennifer and Brom.

Yet there was something in her manner that convinced him she was edgy. She didn't want to be doing this, Nik thought. She didn't want to be going to the hospital to pick up her father.

He realized that, in all this time, she hadn't said all that much about the man. Nik made up his mind to give Brom a call and find out some of the missing pieces to this puzzle.

But he didn't want to wait until tonight. He wanted Sara to tell him. He wanted Sara to trust him. "Do you and your father get along?" Nik saw her shoulders stiffen just a little.

Sara stared straight ahead as they took the off ramp from the freeway. She could see the hospital looming on the horizon just ahead. "I haven't been around him long enough to get along."

Nik eased down on the brake as they came to a red light. Renovating construction was going on to the right, giving the old streets a new face.

He raised his voice to be heard above the jackhammer. "Why's that?"

Sara shot him a look. "You're prying again," she shouted.

He shifted his foot to the gas pedal as the light turned green. "Yes, I am."

She should have gone by herself, as she had first intended. It was just that she'd suddenly wanted a buffer between her and her father on the ride home. This was what she got for being a coward.

"Look, just because you're driving me to the hospital doesn't mean that I have to answer all your questions."

He was definitely calling Brom tonight. "Settle down." To reinforce his words, he placed a gentling hand on her arm, the way he would with an animal that had been spooked. "I'm just curious."

She wished he'd stop touching her. Her skin felt warm just beneath his fingers and she could feel herself wanting things she knew were bad for her. Bad because they would lead to other wants, other desires that couldn't be fulfilled.

She shifted, moving closer to the window. "You know what they said about the cat...."

Nik shrugged as he turned right at the light. "That means I've got nine lives to work with." He glanced at her and grinned. "I'll risk it." His voice grew serious. "After you were out on your own, why didn't you visit your father?"

Sara held on to her purse and stared straight ahead, like a hostile witness on the stand. "I never go where I'm not wanted."

"He said that?" Entering the hospital grounds, Nik guided the car slowly toward the admissions and discharge area. He felt incensed on her behalf. "He told you that you weren't welcome?"

No, he'd never said anything at all. That was the trouble. In all those years he'd never sought her out to talk. "Words aren't everything, Nik."

"Then how did you know he didn't want to see you?"

"I don't want to talk about it anymore, okay?" Talking only aggravated the situation and brought back the pain she had never managed to put to rest or work through. Only lock away.

Nik parked the car near the entrance in a space reserved for compact cars. For a moment Sara didn't move. She sat as if she was bracing herself to face down a demon. Maybe she was, he thought.

Sara turned to look at him. "Do you want to stay here and think of more ways to analyze me while I go—"

He wasn't about to let her face this alone, not the way she felt.

"We'll both go." Nik got out, then rounded the hood and waited for her to join him. "I have a feeling that you need the moral support."

She shrugged indifferently, but inside, she was rebelling against his words. She didn't want or need anyone's help. The day she admitted that she did, she knew she would be in trouble. Because no one stayed for the duration. Her father had proved that to her.

"If it helps you to fill out some good deed requirement list, you can come along to give me moral support. But I can manage perfectly well on my own, so don't think—"

"Sara?" His tone cut through the sea of words like a shark's fin gliding through the crowded waters off a beach.

"That you have to—what?" she demanded finally.

Nik pointed toward the hospital's electronic glass doors. "Shut up and walk."

He made her so mad that she *could* spit. "You know, just because you pay my salary doesn't mean that you can just order me around like that."

"My paying your salary has nothing to do with it. Ever think of running for the Senate? They say that filibusters are really popular there."

She said nothing as she passed him and walked into

the hospital lobby. But he could guess what she was thinking.

Nik grinned to himself.

Raymond was sitting on the edge of his bed, dressed and waiting for her when Sara arrived. His room was small and neatly arranged, a carbon copy of twenty more just like it on the floor. Sara had barely even noticed it in her two previous visits. Each time she had left almost as soon as she had arrived, murmuring that she was on her lunch break and had to be getting back.

Coming to see him had assuaged her conscience. Leaving quickly had helped her cope.

Her father looked almost skeletal in his street clothes. Could four days make that much of a difference in a man's appearance? He looked worn and even more shrunken than he had before the operation. For one unguarded moment her heart ached to see him like this. And then she was resurrecting her barriers, shoring up her heart against all breaches.

"I packed," Raymond told her by way of a greeting. His smile looked as if it required more effort than he had to spare. His eyes, mirror images of Sara's, shifted to Nik. A question rose in them.

Nik moved forward and took the man's hand in his. Raymond did his best to grip it firmly. It was more difficult than he liked.

Nik took in the stubborn set of the jaw, the proud brown eyes. The man was Sara's father, all right. "Hello. I thought I'd help Sara bring you home. I'm Nik Sinclair, Sara's boss."

"He's taken the term to heart," Sara flung over her shoulder.

She looked in the closet to see if her father had left

anything behind. A single wire hanger swayed slightly in the breeze she had created by opening the door. She closed it again.

"It's only temporary, though." She had to keep reminding herself of that before she became too complacent. This was *all* only temporary.

Nik shoved his hands into his pockets as he stood back, out of the way. Caught in the silent cross fire, he tried to understand exactly what was going on between Sara and her father. It was almost as if their roles were reversed. Sara was the angry parent while Raymond behaved like the contrite child.

She felt Nik's eyes on her. He was doing it again, she thought, annoyed. He was analyzing her. She turned toward her father. "Has the doctor been here to see you yet?"

Raymond held up a bulging envelope that was lying on the bed next to him.

"He came by an hour ago to give me my discharge papers." Because it was less painful to look at Nik, Raymond addressed his words to the other man. "I'm a free man." He handed the envelope to Sara. "The nurse said to ring for her when you got here so that she could bring a wheelchair."

Sara looked up sharply, the envelope hovering over the mouth of her purse. Her eyes shifted to her father's legs. "Wheelchair? You can't walk?"

"Sure I can walk." He waved a disparaging hand in the air, annoyed at what he considered the entire dehumanizing process of being in a hospital. "It's some damned hospital policy to take away our dignity. Just like with those drafty hospital gowns they make you wear. Slit straight up the back to rob you of your privacy."

Nik straightened. He jerked a thumb toward the door. "I'll go get the nurse."

"No." Sara placed her hand on Nik's arm, stopping him. "I will."

His first impression was that she just didn't want him doing anything for her. But one look at her face made him realize that the reason she was racing out into the hall ahead of him was that she didn't want to be alone with her father. The realization hit him. That was why she had agreed to his coming along with her in the first place. She didn't want to be alone with the man.

Sara hurried out of the room. Nik looked after her and shook his head.

"Have you known my Sara long?"

Raymond's question had Nik turning away from the door. My Sara. Nik wondered what Sara would have had to say about that.

He felt sorry for the man.

Nik sat in the single chair next to the bed. "No, my brother-in-law recommended her. Brom Culhane," Nik explained.

Raymond's gaunt face stretched into a smile. "Brom." He repeated the name fondly. "How's he doing these days?" Sara's father nodded toward the closed door. "Sara didn't say very much about him." He shrugged self-consciously, his eyes bright. "I've kind of lost touch with everyone over the years."

The man looked so eager for news Nik didn't have the heart to brush him off with a few token words. He searched his mind for something he could tell him. It turned out to be a great deal more than he had realized. They were still talking when Sara returned.

She reentered the room with a nurse's aide directly behind her. Holding the door open as the young woman pushed in the wheelchair, Sara was surprised by the sound of voices. Her father and Nik were talking as if they were old friends exchanging anecdotes. Her father was actually laughing. Sara pressed her lips together.

She didn't know exactly why hearing Nik talk with her father annoyed her, but it did. Ruefully she realized that, in her own way, she had wanted Nik to be on her side. And there were sides drawn in this, very clear-cut sides. She was on one and her father was on the other. And there were never going to be any peace talks.

"Wheelchair's here," she announced needlessly. Nik rose from his seat as the aide lined up the wheelchair next to the bed.

Raymond turned to look at Sara. "You didn't tell me that Nik was related to Kane."

*I didn't tell you a lot of things, because you never asked.*

"I didn't think you'd be interested." Her voice was polite, but completely devoid of feeling. "I have no idea what you're interested in anymore."

Sara picked up her father's suitcase, her mouth grimly set.

Nik glanced at Sara as he helped Raymond into the wheelchair. Raymond seemed like a basically decent man. Just what the hell was Sara's problem? Nik knew he was going to have to find out before they could make any headway themselves.

When they arrived at the house, Nik found himself just taking over. For once, Sara let him.

As Nik helped her father into the house and then into the bedroom, Sara busied herself in the kitchen making coffee. She took an inordinately long time measuring out the crystals and pouring cups of water into the urn.

If she couldn't keep her mind busy, at least her hands were occupied.

She wished she had never come here. Why couldn't she have just made up an excuse, told her father that she couldn't get away? Why had she come all this way just to put herself through all this again?

Because part of her had never gotten over his rejection. She had buried it, but not forgotten it. She'd loved him dearly once and there was a part of her that yearned to reestablish their old relationship. To do that she needed to do the impossible. She needed to forgive him.

Maybe subconsciously that was why she had come, to find a way to forgive him. But she wanted him to know how much he had hurt her, wanted him to squirm for what he had done. Most of all, she wanted her father to apologize. Because she wanted him to tell her why he had walked away from her the way he had.

*Grow up, Sara. Not everything has a happy ending.*

"You're making a mistake, you know."

Startled, Sara dropped the measuring cup, and a shower of dark crystals spilled on the colorless vinyl floor. Muttering, she picked up a sponge from the sink and began wiping up the mess. She looked up at Nik, her eyes just the slightest shade dangerous. "No, I don't know, but I'm sure that you'll tell me."

He took the sponge from her hand and rinsed it, then squeezed out the water. He envisioned her neck in his hand in place of the yellow sponge. "What's going on between you and your father?"

"Nothing." She added the last measuring cup of coffee crystals into the receptacle. "Absolutely nothing."

She said the words with such finality it should have been the end of the conversation. But it wasn't. She might have known that it wouldn't be. Nik didn't seem to respect boundaries or privacy.

"No, it's definitely something." When she wouldn't turn around to face him, he laid his hands on her shoulders and turned her toward him. "Sara, he's sorry for what he did."

Sara lifted her chin. A stubborn look entered her eyes. "I don't really care."

She might be fooling herself, but she wasn't fooling him. "Oh, yes, you do." She struggled to shrug him off, but he wouldn't let her go so easily. He had to get through to her somehow before it was too late. For all of them. "You really care. Otherwise, you wouldn't be acting like a spoiled brat."

The dark look in her eyes would have warned off a lesser man. "You're going a little too far, Sinclair, don't you think?"

"No, I don't think I've gone far enough." He nodded toward the rear of the house. "There's an old man in there who needs you. He's just come face-to-face with his own mortality and he's scared."

Nik wasn't saying anything to her that she hadn't already thought of. But it didn't change anything. "There's nothing I can do about that."

"Maybe not," he conceded. "But you can show him that you care."

Where did he get off, lecturing her? She yanked her arms free. With the kitchen counter at her back, her eyes blazed as she faced Nik. "For your information, that old man who needs all this loving you're talking about ripped my heart out when I needed him. I can't just come skipping back to him and say everything's fine and dandy."

Nik slowly measured out his words. Didn't she see

how counterproductive her feelings were? How destructive? "So where's it going to end?"

She set her mouth firmly. "It already ended."

She didn't believe that, he decided, studying her. "I don't think so. You're still here," Nik pointed out. She began to answer, but he wouldn't let her. "I think you just don't know how to take the first step back."

Her expression was entirely impassive. He had no idea what she was thinking. "And if I never do?"

His eyes met hers. "I don't think you're that stubborn. Or that cruel." She let out a small huff of breath. "It's easy, Sara. All you do is put your foot down on the path, just one at a time." He cupped her cheek so softly, tears nearly welled up in her eyes. "He needs you, Sara."

Her voice was hoarse when she answered him. "I don't need a guilt trip, Sinclair."

She wasn't going to put him off. "You need something, Sara. Something has to break up that dam you've built inside of you or you'll never be free."

She didn't like him making it sound as if she was in some sort of bondage. "Free to do what?"

His eyes were caressing her face. She could almost feel his touch along her skin. "To love anybody again."

"You, I suppose," she whispered.

A smile played on his lips. "Doesn't sound all that bad to me." His fingertips curved along her face. "This schism between you and your father is eating you up inside. You've got to get rid of it, clear it out."

He had to make her understand. Otherwise, when it was too late, she'd never forgive herself.

"Look, Sara, life's short, shorter than we think. I thought my parents would be around forever. They weren't." Regret filled his voice. "There were things I said to them, things I did that I wished I could have taken back after it was too late—''

''You?'' She looked at him incredulously. ''The choirboy?''

He laughed at the label. He was light-years away from that. Especially back then. ''I don't have those wings yet.''

He kissed her forehead lightly. Sara couldn't help thinking she had never felt anything so sweet. Damn him for being sweet. She liked it better when they were arguing. She knew how to handle herself then.

''I know what I'm talking about. Don't waste time being angry or hurt. Talk to him,'' he urged. ''Tell him what you feel.''

Sara dug in stubbornly. ''I don't feel anything.''

''Then tell him that, too.'' He had to be getting back. Nik crossed to the living room. ''But work it out. I'll see you on Monday.''

Sara followed him to the front door. A flutter of panic began forming in her stomach. She didn't want to be alone with her father. Nik had dredged up fresh emotions, disarming her. How was she supposed to cope with this situation? ''You're leaving?''

Was that sorrow? He would take anything he could get. ''I have to.'' He ran a finger along her lips. ''Miss me a little bit. It might be good for us.'' His eyes looked over her head toward the back of the house. ''But right now, you need to be alone with him.''

He closed the door behind him.

Bewildered, confused, Sara slowly walked to her father's room. She stood in the hall for a long time, debating with herself. Finally she knocked lightly on his door.

''Dad?''

He was lying so still on the bed that for a moment, she thought he was asleep. But then he turned his face in her direction, his eyes only half open.

"Can I get you anything?"

He smiled and slowly shook his head. "No, but thanks for asking."

Sara nodded as she slipped out of the room again. "Sure."

Maybe she'd taken the first step after all, she thought, closing the bedroom door behind her. But she was still going to need time for the others. A great deal of time.

"Damn you, Nik Sinclair, for messing me up all over again," she whispered as she went back to the kitchen. She needed a strong cup of coffee. Badly.

# Chapter 10

The telephone rang three times before Sara finally realized that there was no one in the office to answer it. Engrossed in her work, Sara had forgotten that Jennifer was out catering a party. One of the waitresses had taken Katie out for a walk, so the room was empty except for her.

She let it ring again, but no one at the front desk picked it up. Apparently there wasn't anyone there, either, she thought, irritated. The shrill noise wouldn't let her concentrate.

Didn't this thing ring in the kitchen as well? Where *was* everybody?

Sighing, Sara marked her place with her fingertip on the column of numbers she was inputting, and leaned over to pick up the receiver. Her hoop earring clanked against the earpiece as she cradled the telephone against her shoulder.

"Sinclair's," she murmured absently. "How may I help you?"

There was a momentary pause on the other end of the line. Then a deep male voice asked, "Sara?"

"Yes." She frowned. It didn't sound like her father. Who would be calling her here? "Who's this?"

The laugh was resonant. He hadn't called to talk to her, but now that she was on the phone, Brom was delighted. "Your favorite cousin, last time I checked."

"Brom." Sara sat up, the long column of numbers temporarily forgotten. She grasped the receiver in her hand again as she pictured her cousin sitting in his office. "How are you?"

"I'm fine. The more important question is, how are you doing?"

Idly she ran her finger along the bottom of the monitor. She thought of her father. "As well as can be expected." Her mind shifted to Nik and took on a completely different tone. "You didn't tell me that your brother-in-law was pigheaded."

So Jennifer had been right about the situation when she'd called Julia yesterday. Something *was* up between the two. He smiled to himself. Couldn't have happened to a nicer pair.

"I thought I'd leave that as a surprise. Besides, as I remember it, you're pretty damn stubborn yourself. I figured you'd hold your own against him."

Yes, but it wasn't easy. She didn't feel like admitting that, even to Brom, with whom she had shared all her girlhood secrets. She began keying in another set of numbers. "I always do."

He was going to have to leave for the casino shortly. Brom decided to get to the point of the call. "Is he around?"

"Nik? Probably." She hit the Enter key and smiled as another screen materialized. "He's never far off from his pots." She moved her chair away from the desk. "I'll get him for you."

"Thanks." Brom realized he hadn't asked Sara about her father's condition. He was slipping. "Wait, how's your father doing? Did the surgery go well?"

Things felt a little less awkward between her and her father, but still no less painful. She twisted the cord around her finger. "Perfectly. He came through the operation with flying colors."

Brom heard things in her voice that weren't being said. There had been a time when he had known Sara very well. "And you?"

She laughed cryptically. "I've got some colors of my own." Scars, mostly, she thought, but there was no point in dragging Brom into it. She'd cried on his shoulder enough as it was, all those years ago.

He knew how sensitive she was beneath the banter and the ready wit. "Hang in there, Sara."

Sara felt a little self-conscious. "Don't waste time worrying about me. I'm completely resilient." She hurried on before he could ask anything further. "I'll get Nik for you."

She laid the receiver down on the desk and went in search of Nik.

Sara pushed open the door to the kitchen and looked around. Antonio and Chris were conferring by the worktable. "Anyone seen Nik?"

Antonio jerked a thumb toward the walk-in refrigerator. "In there. He's talking to the vegetables."

"Of course," she murmured under her breath.

Sara stopped at the entrance of the huge refrigerator. Nik was standing inside, muttering to himself as he scanned the selection of vegetables on the shelves before him. He exhaled and she could almost see his breath forming.

"Damn."

He wrinkled his nose when he was angry, she noticed. It took the edge off. An amused smile lifted the corners of her lips. "What's the matter?"

He half turned, surprised to see her there. He gestured at the shelves. "I distinctly remember ordering kohlrabi."

Sara wouldn't have known kohlrabi from a cold rabbit, but she assumed that it wasn't there.

"Throw extra parsley on the plate. Nobody'll miss it." She heard Chris trying to stifle a laugh behind her.

But Nik didn't appear to be amused. He leveled a steely look at her. "It's pretty easy to be cavalier with something you know nothing about."

His statement only served to make her look triumphant. "I hope you're listening to yourself and taking notes."

He'd have to substitute Swiss chard until he could get a delivery, he thought. It wasn't the biggest tragedy. Running out of lobster would have taken that prize. At least this week.

When he looked up she was still there. "Why are you standing in the refrigerator doorway, annoying me?"

She nodded toward the hall. "Because Brom's on the phone. He says he wants to talk to you, although why is beyond me."

Nik walked out of the refrigerator and shut the heavy steel door behind him. "Why didn't you just say so in the first place?"

"I kind of liked listening to you curse at the vegetables." She grinned as she moved aside to let him pass. "It's nice to see you get annoyed with something else besides me, even if they are inanimate objects."

He filed away the look on her face. There was no tension evident, merely humor. It seemed that the only way they were going to carry on a conversation where she wasn't freezing up on him or retreating was if she was needling him, Nik thought.

He could put up with that. For the time being.

Nik crossed to the desk in the office and picked up the telephone. "Hello, Brom? What's up?"

Brom had begun to wonder if anyone was ever returning to the phone. His impatience evaporated at the sound of Nik's voice. "I'm calling your bluff."

Nik had no idea what Brom was referring to. "What bluff is that?"

"You promised to come up here and give the restaurant a proper once-over now that the new staff is finally in place, remember?"

Nik moved aside to let Sara sit down at the desk. He watched absently as she began to type in numbers that aligned themselves into columns on the blue screen. "Yeah, I—"

"Did," Brom concluded for him. "A.J's asking when her Uncle Nik is coming up to see her. It's been a while, you know."

Nik cradled the phone between his neck and shoulder as he picked up a list for next week's meat and poultry order. He began to leaf through it. "A.J's six months old. She can't talk yet."

Brom's laugh contradicted Nik's assumption. "She's a miniature Sinclair woman. She'll be talking by the time you get up here."

"Probably," Nik agreed.

Nik looked at Sara, toying with a thought. Maybe she'd be more relaxed at Tahoe, around Brom. Antonio wasn't going on vacation for another three weeks and Chris was coming along well, albeit slowly. Perhaps a break this weekend wouldn't be such a bad idea, after all.

"Just a second," he said into the receiver.

He leaned over Sara and pulled the desk calendar to him. He flipped two pages, scanning each intently. There was nothing special planned on either date. No large parties booked. Nothing out of the ordinary. Antonio could handle it without any difficulty.

Nik replaced the calendar, sliding it next to Sara's elbow. "Okay, Brom, you're on for this weekend."

"Good. I was thinking in terms of having everyone come up," Brom elaborated now that the first part of his plan was falling into place. "Think you can drag your sister and that husband of hers up?"

He knew Jennifer didn't need an excuse. Unlike him, she wasn't wedded to the restaurant. Hers was a fuller life. He glanced at Sara.

"I'm very persuasive when I have to be." Sara made a face at him as if to contradict his statement. "Besides, they'll want to see the baby."

So far, so good, Brom thought. Now for the most important part. "And Nik—"

"Yeah?"

"See if you can get Sara to come up with all of you, as well. It's kind of tough for her, being around her father, dealing with old wounds. I think she really needs to get away."

"My sentiments exactly." Nik remembered the questions he wanted to ask Brom about Sara. He hadn't had time to call him before, but he couldn't do it now, with

Sara sitting right here. He made a mental note to talk to Brom once he arrived in Tahoe.

He looked directly at Sara as he made his promise. "Consider it done."

Brom smiled to himself. He knew he could count on Nik. "Good, I'll have a car come around to pick you up at the airport. Just call me back when you know what flight you'll be taking."

"Will do. 'Bye." Nik replaced the receiver on the cradle and then rotated his neck to get rid of the stiffness.

Sara had pretended to be busy working during the call, but she had listened. They both knew she would.

"Consider what done?" she wanted to know. The look he had given her when he'd said it warned her that something was up.

He dropped the list on the desk. "Brom wants me to bring you with us when we visit."

She didn't think she particularly cared for his wording. "You make me sound like a box of candy you're supposed to pick up at the airport."

He lifted a brow. "Not at all. Candy's sweet. A box of dynamite might be more appropriate a comparison," he corrected. "Will you come with us?"

She shrugged. She certainly wouldn't mind seeing Brom again, but she didn't care for being backed into a corner. "I might be busy."

Nik cupped her chin in his hand and turned her head until she was looking up at him. His eyes searched for a different response.

"Will you come?" he repeated.

Why did she have this feeling that her whole life might change if she agreed? It was just a weekend. A weekend with a whole entourage of people. And Brom. She had always felt safe around Brom.

So what was the problem?

Nik, a small voice whispered in reply.

She blocked the voice out. Sara leaned back in the chair and dragged her hand through her hair.

"Why not?" she agreed gamely. "I always like seeing Brom."

"Good. Unless something unforeseen happens between now and the weekend, we'll be leaving Saturday morning." He began to walk out of the room, then hesitated in the doorway, suddenly realizing that there might be an obstacle. "Is your father up to being left alone?"

Sara nodded. Raymond Santangelo was a hard man to keep down. He had already been up and about for short periods of time.

"He can spend a couple of days by himself." She looked at Nik pointedly, just so that he remembered. "He'll have to soon enough, anyway."

Nik nodded, but made no comment as he walked out of the room. Sara thought she saw him frowning, but she might have been mistaken. At any rate, it wouldn't have changed anything. As soon as she felt her father was well enough, she was leaving. She had to.


True to his word, Brom had the limousine waiting for them right at the airport. When his chauffeur, Harold, opened the rear door, Sara was surprised to see that Brom and Julia were seated inside. The baby, drooling and animated, was between them, sitting in her car seat.

Julia laughed, pleased at Sara's expression. "Surprise."

Nik was directly behind Sara, and gently urged her

into the car, his hands on her hips. Sara tried not to think about how much she liked having his hands on her. The feelings she was experiencing right now were all wrong. They weren't going to lead anyplace. She couldn't let them.

"Julia couldn't wait for you to arrive," Brom explained to them, "so she decided to hold the reunion in the limo."

Holding Katie's hand, Jennifer followed Nik into the car. "Goodness, she's grown so much," Jennifer cried, looking at the baby. She tickled A.J.'s toes. The infant wiggled them and giggled as Jennifer scooted over to let Kane climb in.

"And you haven't," Julia commented as she looked Jennifer over for telltale signs of her pregnancy. Jennifer was still as slender as she ever was.

"Soon," Jennifer promised, mechanically glancing down at her waist. "All too soon I won't be able to see my feet. Only my stomach."

Julia sighed wistfully. "I'd give anything for that sort of view." But she had A.J., thanks to Jennifer's selflessness, and she would forever be grateful to her sister.

Katie sidled up to Brom. "Got candy, Uncle B'om?" She looked up at him hopefully.

A charmer, just like her aunt and her mother, Brom thought. "For you, always." Brom dug into his pocket and presented her with a multicolored sucker. Katie accepted it with the same sort of awe that a woman displayed upon receiving her first bouquet of flowers.

Kane watched his daughter eagerly rip off the cellophane wrapper. He took it from her and shoved the sticky wrapper into his pocket.

"She'll get your car dirty," he warned Brom.

Brom wasn't about to let something so mundane as

worrying about his car being dirtied interfere with Katie's pleasure.

"So, we'll clean it." Brom ruffled Katie's hair and she grinned up at him, her lips already outlined in bright, sticky pink. "As long as the lady's happy."

The baby squealed and Katie went on licking loudly. Voices melded like an orchestra tuning up for a performance as questions flew back and forth in the car.

Sara suddenly felt overwhelmed by what she felt were the natural sounds of family surrounding her. It took her back across the years, when family outings were a regular event for her family. Any given Sunday a large number of them would converge in someone's backyard, or at a park. Uncles and aunts and numerous cousins as far as the eye could see. Or so it had seemed at the time.

Nostalgia brought with it a pang that tightened around her heart.

Sara looked at Brom. She could see by the look in his eyes that he knew what she was thinking. He gave her a reassuring smile and leaned forward in order to be heard better. "Good to see you again, Sara."

An amused smile creased her lips. "You saw me two weeks ago. I've only been in Newport Beach for twelve days."

"Is that all?" Nik asked incredulously. Sara gave him a dirty look that only egged him on. "Feels like forever to me."

Sara poked Nik in the ribs with her elbow. Nik had the good grace to wince as everyone else laughed.

"Everybody in?" Brom scanned both sides of the stretch limo. Jennifer and Katie were on his side, while Kane, Nik and Sara sat opposite him.

"Unless you're expecting someone else," Kane answered. He tested the door next to him to make sure it was properly closed.

Brom turned and tapped on the glass partition that separated the chauffeur from the passengers. When the man turned, Brom gave the signal. "Okay, Harold, take her back to the house."

"House?" Nik raised a brow quizzically as he looked at Brom. "I thought you said we were going to tour the restaurant."

"All in good time, Nik, all in good time," Brom assured his brother-in-law. He grinned secretively as he exchanged looks with Julia. "I've got a surprise for you."

Nik eyed Brom suspiciously. He wondered if there was something wrong at the restaurant that Brom was trying to break to him slowly. After all, Sinclair's/Tahoe was part his.

"I'm not sure I like surprises."

"You'll like this one," Julia promised him as she strapped A.J. securely into her car seat.

"All right, what's the surprise?" Nik asked Brom as he walked into the sprawling ranch house.

"I've got a baseball game lined up for us to play." He checked his watch. "In about half an hour. You'd better hustle."

"Baseball?" Nik echoed in disbelief. The sport, once so important to him, was the farthest thing from his mind these days.

Brom grinned at the stunned look on Nik's face. Nik had probably forgotten that they shared a passion for the game. "I told you that I get together with a bunch of guys regularly." He narrowed his brows comically. "We play some very serious ball."

Julia walked in behind them, carrying the baby. "Very serious." Julia echoed, lowering her voice to approximate Brom's. Her whimsical expression told Nik that she was humoring Brom.

A fondness sprouted within Nik as he remembered his college games. Still, he was more than a little rusty. "I haven't played in years." There had just never been enough time.

Nik's protest failed to impress Brom. "Good, then you can play on the other team." Brom grinned broadly, as if he was anticipating the outcome of the game. "I told you to pack old clothes," he reminded Nik as Jennifer and Kane entered the house.

The instruction had seemed a little odd at the time. "I thought maybe you wanted us to do some cleaning," Nik cracked.

"Maybe later, after you lose. Now change your clothes. They're probably all waiting for us on the field now. Addison Park, remember?" Brom asked Sara.

Sara remembered. She nodded her head as a bittersweet feeling wound its way all through her again. That was the site of the last family outing she'd ever attended with her parents.

Nik looked uncertain as he stood, debating. "I don't know about this."

"Yes, you do," Julia assured her brother. She placed her hand on his back and shoved him toward one of the guest rooms. Brom followed behind her, bringing Sara's suitcase as well as Nik's. "Once a jock, always a jock."

Nik shrugged and let himself be pushed along.

"Your room's right next to his." Brom placed Sara's suitcase inside the door.

She merely nodded as she entered. She was trying to brace herself for the event ahead. It would seem odd if she didn't go along and yet, going to the park, remembering happier times wasn't going to be easy for her.

She wished Brom had picked out another place.

"And this is your room. Now hurry up," Brom instructed. "C'mon, you, too, Kane."

Kane raised a brow. He'd been following with their two suitcases and was caught completely unaware by this new twist. "I don't play baseball."

"You'll learn," Brom promised. "We're one man short."

Nik grinned as he closed the door. There was no arguing with the man. And maybe he didn't really want to. Once, before reality had chewed away at his dreams with sharp, pointy teeth, he had entertained thoughts of trying out for a professional ball club. He had a pretty distinguished record behind him both in high school and college.

But once his parents had died, he'd put aside his dreams and shut them out of his life. There were his sisters to care for and responsibilities to live up to. Baseball was a dream others could go on to pursue, not him.

He grinned to himself. It would be good to have the feel of a bat in his hands again.

As per Brom's instruction, Nik had packed the oldest shirt he owned, a jersey that had two small holes bitten out of it, courtesy of an overactive washing machine. He pulled it on now. The jeans he took out of the suitcase were equally worn, with one knee threatening to break through the thin webbing of white threads at any moment.

When Nik walked out into the hallway again, he almost collided with Sara. She looked like a teenager in her white shorts and hot pink T-shirt. All she needed was a ponytail.

His eyes swept over her legs. He'd hate to see them dirtied, sliding into home plate. "Are you playing?"

All through school Sara had been hopelessly inept when it came to team sports. She shook her head emphatically as she leaned against the wall. "Nope. Your sisters and I are strictly the cheering section."

Nik braced one hand against the wall as he looked down at her. There was a skylight directly overhead and it bathed her in sunlight. He began to think of a different sport than baseball.

"Which side are you cheering for?"

Her eyes were mischievous as she raised her chin. "I haven't made up my mind yet. Let me see how well you play, first."

Jennifer emerged from her room down the hall. "The coach at college thought that Nik was the team's most valuable player." Glancing first at Sara, Jennifer gave her brother a very supportive wink as she passed them and went on.

Nik knew Jennifer had something on her mind other than the game. And so did he.

Sara shrugged, unimpressed. "Must have been a pretty poor team."

The light played on her lips and he wondered if there was going to be any more through traffic in the hallway to interrupt him. "UC Irvine had a very good baseball team that year."

She smirked, her dark eyes teasing him. "If you say so."

He braced his other hand on the wall, bracketing her. Sara's eyes held his, waiting. "Did I ever tell you that you have an irritating smirk?"

"Probably." She raised herself up on her toes, teasing him with the nearness of her mouth. "A ballplayer with something to prove always plays a lot better."

He could feel her breath on his face, on his mouth. His hands flattened on the wall and he inched a little closer to her. "And since when did you start coaching?"

She could feel the heat from his body. She tried not to let it affect her. Or at least not show him how much it did.

"Since now. I've decided that you need someone in your corner, since everyone else will probably be rooting for Brom's team."

"Oh?"

His mouth looked incredibly tempting and she wanted nothing more than to touch her lips to it. Sara mentally groped for a lifeline and found none.

"Sure. It's his house." Feeling oddly light-headed, she gestured vaguely toward the front of the house, where she assumed Brom was waiting. "Let's see what you've got, Sinclair."

He looked into her eyes. "All right, but I want you to remember that you were the one who asked."

Her throat tightened, almost cutting off all available air. Sara refused to surrender to the jittery little hum that traveled through her like a precursor to an earthquake.

"I remember everything. It's both the gift and the curse of having a photographic memory. Now stop talking and let's see some action."

She was going to add "out on the field" but she never had the opportunity. Nik was already touching off an explosion within her as he lowered his mouth to hers.

There was no immunity. Unlike inoculation, there

was no way she could protect herself from him by having kissed him before. No tolerance had been formed, no antibodies filled her to take the edge off what was happening to her. What happened each time he kissed her.

The world flipped over. Day became night and she was catapulted light-years away from a ranch house in Tahoe to a world of fire and heat. Mardi Gras in outer space, she thought, clinging to Nik's shirt.

It took everything she had not to let herself drift through the region permanently. With her head spinning, she pulled back. It was only a small consolation that Nik was breathing as hard as she was.

"God, if you can play baseball only half as well as you can kiss, I don't think that Brom's team has a prayer of winning."

Nik ran his thumb along her bottom lip and had the pleasure of feeling her shiver against him. "Is that a compliment?"

Sara shrugged. "I always call them as I see them." Nik pinned her with a scrutinizing look that drew out the lie like a magnet pulling out a pin. "Well, *almost* always." She placed both her hands on his chest and pushed him away. "Now get out there and play ball."

Once at the park, Sara settled in beside Julia and the baby. Exercising supreme effort, she purposely shut out the barrage of splintered memories that were trying to break through. This was Nik's day to relax and she wasn't going to spoil it, or insult Brom's hospitality by allowing the sadness to get the better of her.

Sara glanced around at the wives and children who'd come to join in the recreation. Blankets were scattered all over the perimeter of the playing field like so many multicolored lily pads floating on a lake.

Brom had thought of everything, right down to providing hot dogs, sodas and popcorn. And right afterward, there would be a picnic lunch.

Jennifer dropped down next to them on the grass. Katie made a beeline for the hot dogs.

"He goes all out, doesn't he?" Jennifer asked her sister.

Julia nodded, but it was Sara who answered. "Brom never did things in half measures. It was always all or nothing." She squinted as she looked for him out in the field. Brom was playing shortstop this inning. "Brom likes to bring passion to everything he does."

Julia only smiled to herself, silently agreeing.

Nik was the third man up to the plate. Sara cringed a little, hoping that he wouldn't do too badly. Maybe a bunt or a walk to get him on base. She didn't want to see him strike out his first time up.

Without realizing it she crossed her fingers and tensed, watching his every movement.

The pitcher threw once, and then again. Each time Nik swung, he came in contact with air as the ball whizzed by him into the crouching catcher's mitt as if it contained some sort of homing device.

Sara shut her eyes.

Jennifer nudged her. "You can't see that way."

"That's the whole point," Sara murmured, opening one eye hesitantly.

And then suddenly Sara jumped to her feet, stunned. Belatedly, she began cheering as the third time the pitcher threw to Nik the ball connected with the bat. A resounding smack splintered the sultry afternoon air and the ball was launched into a huge arc that flew far beyond the outfielder's raised glove.

Julia was applauding madly. She and Jennifer exchanged looks, remembering other games played in professional-looking stadiums. Julia cupped her hands around her mouth. "You've still got the magic, Nik!"

Yes, Sara thought, remembering the interlude in Brom's hallway, he did.

# Chapter 11

The baseball game ran a full nine innings, spanning what seemed to Sara an endless two and a half hours. By the end of it, both sides were more than willing to call it quits.

Brom took the towel Julia offered him, wiping his face as he sank onto the grass. He was the last to join them at the picnic. Julia had packed a huge red-and-white tablecloth that looked as if it could have covered a mess-hall table. It easily accommodated them all.

Brom eyed Nik good-naturedly. Nik had homered twice during the game, the second one a grand slam in the bottom of the eighth.

"And to think I invited this guy up to play." Brom shook his head.

Kane lay sprawled out on the grass, his head cradled in his laced hands. He felt exhausted and extremely grateful that the game was over. "C'mon, Brom, a gambler's supposed to lose gracefully."

Brom never frequented his own tables for purposes other than social. Success in business was all that he asked of Lady Luck. He'd never longed for her to blow on his dice.

"In case you've all forgotten, I never gamble on anything other than a sure thing." Dropping the towel to the grass behind him, Brom reached for Julia's hand and curved his fingers around it. Words weren't necessary between them.

Or for Sara, who looked on, a touch of envy slipping through her like thread through the eye of a needle.

Brom nodded toward Nik as he addressed his case to the others. "I thought I was asking an old, out-of-shape ex-jock for a friendly game of baseball. I had no idea I was getting Hank Aaron."

Jennifer laughed as she dug through the ice chest and found Kane's favorite brand of beer. She tossed him the can. He caught it easily.

"Now you make a catch," Brom complained. Kane had missed an all-important ball that had helped the other side score.

Kane shrugged, pulling the tab. "You should have been throwing beer cans, not balls."

"It wasn't that bad," Jennifer soothed.

Brom shifted over toward the ice chest. "Not bad?" He helped himself to a beer. "You call losing fifteen to six not bad?"

Julia never understood what the fuss was over sports. She shrugged. "It's not like you lost a hundred and twelve to three."

A red rubber ball plopped directly before Nik's feet. He looked around and saw a blond boy, no more than four, running eagerly toward him, his arms outstretched.

Nik tossed the ball to him. He was pumped, he realized, and he loved it.

"That's basketball," Nik pointed out. Julia merely lifted a shoulder, unconcerned about specifics.

Brom thought the matter over. "You don't play that, too, do you?" he asked Nik.

"Nope." In college he'd always been too wrapped up in baseball to go in for any of the other sports.

"Good." Brom nodded, pleased. A glint entered his eyes. "Next time you come up, we play basketball."

"Hey, this is Tahoe. Don't you guys believe in a friendly game of poker?" Kane protested, spreading his hands wide. A little foam emerged from the can and he drank it quickly before it spilled on the grass. He was a lot better at cards than he was at running around and sweating.

"If all else fails," Brom conceded. "How's your game?"

"Fair to middling," Kane answered easily.

"Uh-huh, famous last words." Brom knew confidence when he saw it. "I think we'll stick to basketball as our next game of choice."

Nik closed his eyes as he stretched out on the grass. "We'll talk." Jennifer's voice had him opening his eyes again quickly.

"Katie!" Jennifer rose to her knees, calling after her daughter. Katie had scampered away, chasing after a white butterfly that refused to accommodate her by getting caught. "Come back here. I don't want you wandering off."

Katie looked over her shoulder at Jennifer, as if weighing her mother's words against the allure of the butterfly. The butterfly won.

Jennifer scrambled to her feet. "That girl. You have to keep your eye on her all the time."

"Like her mother," Kane said fondly. "Sit, I'll get her." He handed Jennifer his beer before going to retrieve his pint-sized would-be entomologist.

Jennifer pressed the cold can against her throat as she watched Kane chase after Katie. Seeing her father coming toward her, the little girl squealed and began to run in the opposite direction. Kane snatched her up in his arms and then swung her around until it seemed as if her giggles filled the air.

The others understood Jennifer's immediate concern and shared it. She flushed slightly as she looked at Sara. "I guess ever since the kidnapping, we've all been a little edgy about Katie, even in a place like this."

Sara nodded. No explanation was necessary. Brom had filled her in when she had stopped by to visit before arriving in Newport. He had told her how Jennifer's daughter had been kidnapped from the hospital when she was only three days old. Kane had been the police detective assigned to the case. Touched by Jennifer's plight, Kane had broken police department regulations by allowing her to come with him as he tracked Katie down.

And along the way he had broken a few rules of his own. By the time the trail had led them to Brom's door, Kane, who had lived his entire life in shadows, had stepped into the light and fallen in love with Jennifer.

Sara thought that Brom's story was no less dramatic. When his first wife had been unable to conceive, Brom and Alexis had decided to adopt. Ultimately they had gone a private route when the more conventional method kept stonewalling them. The man handling the private adoption, a once-trusted friend, had turned out to be part of a ring that stole babies from hospitals around the country. Alexis had died suddenly of ovarian cancer just a few weeks before Katie was placed in Brom's arms.

Instantly in love with the infant, Brom had made up his mind to go through with the adoption. His plans had changed abruptly when Jennifer and Kane had shown up to claim the baby. Because she could see how much he loved Katie, Jennifer had invited Brom to visit them anytime he wanted.

It was in the hushed, romantic atmosphere of Sinclair's that he had first met Julia. A few breathtakingly turbulent months later he had married her.

And where was her story? Sara wondered with an envious pang she was ashamed of. Her cousin's story, as well as Jennifer's and Kane's, had almost fairy-tale qualities to their endings. Both couples appeared to be living happily ever after.

Appeared.

But appearances or not, Sara knew that it wasn't going to happen to her. There were no happy endings, real or imagined, in her future. She wasn't made for a relationship. She was afraid to even consider undertaking one. Afraid of the consequences.

Because of what she had seen and what she had lived with.

To discover that her parents' happy marriage, something she had wholeheartedly believed in, was all only an illusion perpetrated for her benefit had made Sara lose faith in her own abilities to perceive things, to see things as they really were and not the way she wanted them to be. She didn't trust her own judgment. And she didn't want to repeat her mother's mistakes.

And yet, she wanted…

This wasn't the time, she upbraided herself.

Sara took a thick roast beef sandwich out of the hamper and began eating slowly, trying to block out her thoughts.

The park was alive with noise. Everyone whom Brom had invited had come prepared for a picnic after the game. There were children playing, parents laughing....

Like the old days, she thought, when she believed happiness was everlasting.

No matter how hard she tried to evade them, her memories continued to find her, a determined little army with pointed lances aimed at her heart.

Sara raised her eyes from her sandwich as Kane returned with Katie in tow. He plopped the girl down next to her mother and flanked her with his long legs as he sat down.

Turning, Sara was aware that Nik was studying her again. And he looked as if he could read her thoughts.

"This is good," she told Julia suddenly, holding up her sandwich. "What kind of dressing did you use?" She didn't know blue cheese from ranch, but it was something to say.

"I didn't make it," Julia answered.

"It's from the restaurant," Brom informed his cousin. "House secret." He winked at Nik.

A challenge. This he was more than up to. "I bet I can guess." Sitting up, Nik moved closer to Sara. He slid his fingers down along her wrist to hold her hand steady and then took a bite of her sandwich. He felt her pulse race beneath his thumb.

Who would ever have thought that having someone mooch her food could turn into an erotic experience? Little quivers of excitement went hurtling into her stomach from all directions.

She needed a cold shower, Sara thought restlessly. And another cold dose of reality wouldn't hurt the situation, either. She needed both and more, because all she could think about was running her hands along Nik's smooth, muscular back and kissing him again. Never mind that the man had just played a hard game of baseball in eighty-five-degree weather and was undoubtedly sweaty as hell.

It didn't change a thing. She still wanted him. Wanted to touch him. Wanted to make love with him the way she had never wanted anything else before.

Sara cleared her throat, wishing she could rid herself of her feelings as well. Her hand dropped limply to her lap, the sandwich forgotten. She looked at Julia. "Got anything cold to drink?"

Julia handed Sara a soda out of the ice chest. The lady had it bad for her brother, Julia thought. She wondered what she could do to help things along.

Nik would have gone on eating out of Sara's hand if no one else had been present. Eating out of her hand and progressing on to sample the taste of her skin, the flavor of her lips.

But there would be another time, and soon, he promised himself. For now, he'd enjoy the company of his family. If nothing else, it seemed to set Sara at ease, and that was an accomplishment.

Nik looked at Brom confidently. "You're using Russian dressing with a light cream substitute, a sprinkling of cayenne pepper and a pinch of garlic for taste."

Kane shook his head, refusing to believe Nik was serious. "You're bluffing." He unwrapped a sandwich himself and took a bite. It was flavorful, but nothing telegraphed itself to his palate. "Nobody's that good."

"Brom?" Nik waited for his brother-in-law to vindicate him.

Brom shrugged, mystified at Nik's ability. "I don't know. I'm going to have to check with Josef, but it sure sounds right."

Jennifer didn't need any verification from a third party. "Never mess with Nik when it comes to ingredients and food," she told Brom and Kane. "The man knows no equal."

Julia unscrewed a jar of apple sauce for A.J. She dipped a spoon into it and, bracing herself, raised the spoon to the baby's mouth. A.J. stuck her tongue out and did battle with the spoon.

"Or so he likes to think," Julia put in.

Nik laughed and shook his head as he took his own sandwich from the hamper. "Same old Julia."

Sara took a bite out of her sandwich, her mouth covering where Nik's had been only minutes before. It wasn't possible for her to taste his lips on the bread. So why did she think she did?

"I think I really like your sister," Sara decided out loud.

"You would. You're two of a kind." Both women seemed to get a perverse pleasure out of needling him, Nik thought.

Sara raised her sandwich in a silent toast to Julia as the latter turned to look at her.

Julia thought she saw something in Sara's eyes that she recognized. A wariness. The same sort of wariness that had once been a part of her own world until Brom had slain her dragons and made the nightmares go away. She wondered what Sara's demons were and if Nik was the one who could make them die.

She'd seen the way her brother looked at Sara. Perhaps he didn't even know it yet himself, but he was taken with the woman. More than taken. If she didn't miss her guess, Nik was halfway in love with Sara.

Julia mentally reviewed the sleeping arrangements and smiled to herself as she coaxed another spoonful of apple sauce between her daughter's messy lips. She was glad she had placed Nik and Sara next door to each other. Proximity always helped move things along.

She only hoped that Nik wouldn't be slow on the uptake.

The picnic went on for another two hours and then, as if by mutual consent, the party broke up. The other men on Brom's baseball team and their families took their leave. Within fifteen minutes the park was quiet. Sara looked around and shivered.

"Are you cold?" Nik asked, surprised. The sun was hot.

"No, I was just thinking."

"About what?" he coaxed.

Behind him, Kane was helping Jennifer fold the tablecloth while Katie dashed back and forth beneath the canopy they had temporarily formed. Brom was taking the basket back to the car as Julia changed yet another diaper. Despite all the activity, he and Sara might have been alone for all the attention Nik paid to the rest of them.

Sara ran her hands along her arms, remembering. "What a great park this used to be."

"Used to be?" He looked around. The park was clean and well kept. He could see the lake just beyond a stately row of trees. There were barbecue pits strategically scattered about to the left of the playing field. "Looks pretty good to me now."

She blinked and then smiled. Turning to him, she nodded. "Yes, I guess you're right. It still is." She started walking toward the car, determined to shake off her mood. "I had no idea you played that well."

Nik laughed as he slipped an arm around her. "Neither did I."

They stayed at Brom's house long enough to shower and then change. Leaving the children with the housekeeper, Brom took everyone to Casino Camelot. There they had dinner in the restaurant that Julia had designed, and then took in a show afterward.

Kane settled back comfortably in the limousine and draped his arm around Jennifer's shoulders. He wondered how he had managed to live all those years without her. He knew he couldn't do it now. She was as much a part of him as his soul. The soul she had helped him find.

He looked at his brother-in-law. "I'll give you one thing, Brom. You certainly know how to entertain your guests."

"It's my business." Brom smiled expansively, content that everyone he cared about had enjoyed themselves tonight. He had a thriving business, a beautiful, loving wife, a daughter he adored and a family he could always count on. Life, he decided, didn't get much better than this.

He gathered Julia closer to him as he looked at his cousin. Sara sat opposite him, beside Nik. She didn't look entirely comfortable. Brom detected the slight tension outlining her body, as if she was fighting some internal battle with herself.

*Stop fighting, Sara. You'll only lose if you win,* he thought.

Brom smiled at her encouragingly. He didn't want Sara to miss out on all this. This was the kind of life she was meant for, not the nomadic one she had adhered to. He wanted her to experience that sense of belonging that he had because of Julia and the baby. But he knew he couldn't show Sara the way. She was going to have to find it on her own.

Brom glanced at Nik. Maybe they could find the way together. If he didn't miss his guess, Nik and Sara would make an excellent pair.

Harold brought the limousine up the winding path to Brom's front door. Brom took Julia's hand as he got out and helped her from the car. The others followed close behind. "Thank you, Harold. I won't be needing you any longer tonight."

Brom pressed a series of numbers on the keypad at the front door, then unlocked it. He stepped aside and let everyone file by.

"It's been a long day and I've got more planned for us tomorrow." He looked at Jennifer and Kane. "Why don't we call it a night and turn in?"

"Sounds good to me," Kane agreed. He laced his fingers through Jennifer's. Katie was safely tucked away in the nursery with A.J. That meant that the rest of the night was theirs. He was looking forward to it.

Sara felt restless, as if she was a Thoroughbred standing at the starting gate, waiting for the gate to open. Except that the end of the race was a foregone conclusion. She knew she'd never get to sleep feeling like this.

"I think I'll raid your refrigerator if you don't mind." She looked from Julia to Brom. Julia nodded her permission. "I don't feel much like sleeping just yet."

Brom gestured toward the kitchen. "Help yourself. My house is yours."

Sara flashed a grateful grin. "At least that hasn't changed." Raised next door to one another, they had practically lived in each other's houses while they were growing up, until Sara moved. "Night, everyone. See you in the morning."

She avoided looking at Nik as she passed him.

"Nik, can I see you a minute?" Kane drew Nik aside in the living room. "I'll be there in a minute, Jennifer," Kane promised his wife.

He waited until everyone else had left the room.

"What's wrong?" Nik perched on the edge of one of the sofa's arms, waiting.

"Nothing. I couldn't help noticing the signals going on between you and Sara."

"You mean like walk and don't run?" Nik quipped. "Mostly don't walk," he added.

"Exactly." Kane felt a little awkward. It wasn't his style to butt in to other people's business. His personal inclination had always been to guard his own privacy. But living within a family, a real family, had taught him that there were times when interfering was necessary. If you cared.

"I don't know if this means anything to you but, working as a detective, sometimes I stumble across information that becomes useful later, like the piece of a puzzle you can fit in only after other pieces are in place."

Nik looked at him, confused. "Are you trying to tell me something about Sara?"

"Maybe, in a way." Kane stumbled along the unfamiliar terrain. "This is actually about her father, Raymond."

Nik nodded. "I've met him." He crossed his arms in front of him. "Go on, I'm listening."

Kane shoved his hands into his back pockets and began to pace around the room as he spoke. "Raymond Santangelo's a hell of a guy. I've known him for about three years and you couldn't ask for a better cop. But he's got this gambling problem. Had, actually," Kane amended. "From what I know, he hasn't bet a penny in almost a year. Up until then, he played the horses whenever he could. Blew everything he had at the track. That's why his second wife left him."

"Second wife?" Nik hadn't realized that Sara's father had been remarried. Or divorced.

Kane nodded. "The one he married after Sara's mother. Anyway, one night, while we were on a stakeout, he talked a little more than he probably would have under normal circumstances—stakeouts can get awfully boring."

Nik had little doubt that no matter how bored he became, Kane would never divulge anything personal unless he fully meant to.

"Santangelo told me that he left his first wife because he didn't want his daughter finding out about his gambling problem. He didn't want to look like a weakling in her eyes. When he couldn't seem to lick his problem, he thought that it was best to sever all contact with her under the circumstances rather than to have her find out."

Nik blew out a breath. So she had no idea why her father had disappeared. That would explain Sara's hostility toward the man. "Obviously Sara didn't agree."

"He had no way of knowing that. He did what he thought was best." Kane shrugged, looking at his brother-in-law. "I don't know if that helps you any—"

Nik rose from the sofa. "What do you mean, helps?"

"Nik, I *am* a detective." Kane's chiseled features

softened as he grinned. "And a man. I've been there before myself, standing in your shoes, confused as hell about a woman because she tied me up in knots inside." He thought of Jennifer, waiting for him in bed. He moved toward the doorway. "Only difference was, I didn't think I was good enough for her." He laid his hand on Nik's shoulder. "That's not your problem. But we've all got hurdles to leap over before we can reach the finish line." He dropped his hand and crossed the threshold. "She's a hell of a prize if you can win her. Night."

"Night." Nik nodded vaguely in Kane's direction, his mind already on Sara. "And thanks."

"Don't mention it."

They parted company in the hall, Kane going to his bedroom and Jennifer, Nik toward his room and restless sleep. As he turned in the hall, he glanced toward his left. There was light coming from the kitchen.

Sara.

Nik debated. Maybe he felt like conducting his own late-night raid on the refrigerator. Or on the raider.

He walked into the kitchen and found that she had opened the French doors that led out onto the patio. Julia had told him that it was her favorite place to have breakfast. In the distance he could see the lake. Beams of moonlight strummed long, slender fingers along the black waters, flirting with them.

Sara was sitting at a glass-top table, twisting the stem of a wine goblet in her fingers. Nik couldn't remember seeing anyone look so sad before.

Sara looked up, sensing his presence a moment before Nik walked out on the patio. "Can't keep away from the kitchen, can you?"

"Occupational habit." He dropped into the seat next

to hers. "Actually—" his voice softened "—it wasn't the kitchen that lured me."

She smiled over the rim of her goblet. "Very sexy line."

He laid his hand over hers. "I don't do lines, Sara. Life's too short for that."

She sighed, closing her eyes. Suddenly she felt very tired. Maybe it was the wine, although she'd only had a few sips. Or maybe it was the tension, finally taking its toll on her.

"Oh, I don't know. Sometimes, when you take it one day at a time, life starts to feel like some sort of an endless entity, stretched out before you."

He wanted to understand her. "I thought you had a good time today."

"I did." She smiled sadly, catching the moonlight in her glass. "Maybe too good."

Nik sighed, feeling like a man in a foreign country without any maps, any road signs. "I'm back to needing subtitles again."

Sara bit her lower lip. Maybe she owed him an explanation, before he thought she was completely crazy. "It reminded me a lot of the picnics I went on as a kid. Especially since Brom was there." A faraway look entered her eyes. "It reminded me of how wonderful I thought life was."

"It still can be."

His voice was warm, coaxing. Maybe he still believed that, she thought. But she didn't. She shook her head as she cupped the goblet between her hands. "No."

"How can you be so certain of that?

"I grew up."

Nik leaned forward, searching for answers in her eyes. "What's that supposed to mean?"

She felt her defense mechanism activating, but she couldn't stop it. "It means that I know good things don't last, no matter how much you think they will or how much you want them to."

Nik refused to accept that. More, he refused to let her accept it. "Look at Brom and Julia, or Kane and Jennifer." He gestured toward the house impatiently, struggling to keep his voice low. "It doesn't look as if it's going to end for them, does it?"

"No, but..."

Her voice trailed off as she lifted her shoulders and let them drop again helplessly. He didn't understand, she thought, and she couldn't make him understand. There were times she couldn't completely understand it herself. But she couldn't shake the feeling that failure waited for most relationships at the end of the road.

So with all this going against it, why did she want to be involved with Nik? It didn't make any sense. She pressed her hand to her head. She felt as if she was going crazy.

He had to find a way to break down her resistance. "My parents were happy until the day they died."

The look on her face was envious. "Mine weren't. I just thought they were."

They were at an impasse, but he wasn't about to surrender. "So what are we looking at?" His eyes probed hers. "Never trying to grab at happiness because there's one failure in the way?"

She rose, leaving her goblet on the table. She walked to the edge of the patio and looked out. Her hands curled around the white wrought-iron fence that surrounded it. "You don't understand."

Her eyes fluttered shut for a moment, absorbing his nearness, his scent, wishing she wasn't emotionally shackled the way she was. "How can I when I don't understand it myself? I just know I'm afraid, too afraid to take the step."

"Don't be afraid." Gently he turned her around to face him. His eyes caressed her face, weakening her resolve. "I won't hurt you, Sara."

She shook her head, trying to resist him. Trying to resist herself. "That's what you say now, but—"

He wouldn't let her finish. "That's what I *mean* now. They're not just words, Sara." Slowly he trailed his fingers along her bare arms. Needs sprang up within her to mark his path.

She closed her eyes, absorbing his touch. "I know, but—"

He laid his fingers against her lips. "No, there is no 'but.'" He dropped his hand. "Trust me, Sara. Trust yourself."

She shook her head, fear licking red-hot tongues through her as if she was standing in the center of a veritable inferno. "You don't know what you're asking me to do."

"Yes, I do." His voice was soft, gentle, soothing, even as his touch inflamed her. "I'm asking you to take a chance. The same chance I'm taking." He searched her eyes for understanding. "I'm not asking you to do anything that I'm not asking myself."

She tried to pull away, but found she had no strength. "You're confusing me. I can't think."

He smiled. "Good. Maybe if you stop thinking you'll give yourself a chance to feel." He took her hand and placed it over his heart. "What do you feel, Sara?"

"Your heart. It's got a good beat. You're very healthy," she quipped, desperately trying for humor.

He wouldn't let her talk her way out of this. It was too important to both of them.

"There it is, Sara—my heart. In the palm of your hand. What are you going to do about it? Are you just going to walk away from it? From me?"

He was undermining her resolve like acid eating through a thin layer of tissue paper. "Did you major in philosophy, as well?"

"No, Sara." Nik pulled her into his arms, fitting her against him. "Just life."

And then he kissed her. Kissed her the way she had been waiting for him to do all afternoon. And skyrockets went off, right on cue.

She was lost.

# Chapter 12

Sara had no time to rally against him. No time to build up her armaments. No time and no will.

She felt as if she was melting against Nik like heated mercury even while she knew that she should be pulling away from him.

Running away.

Yes, running. She had absolutely no defenses within her grasp to fight this hot onslaught of his mouth on hers, this plundering of her very soul.

She didn't want to fight it.

His body twisted against hers, absorbing the full measure of her frame as it pressed along the length of his. Nik was hard and rigid against her. Desperate, she searched for indignation, for anger, for something, damn it, that would help.

There was no help.

His mouth was tangy and sweet and overpowering,

reducing the structure of her barricades to rubble. They crumbled pitifully.

She couldn't get enough of him. She knew she had to stop. If this was just good sex, then maybe she could accept it. But it wasn't. There was so much more to it. And she knew she couldn't handle it.

Sara thought she was losing her sanity.

Drowning in him, going under for the third time, she somehow managed to drag her head back. Her pulse was breaking the sound barrier as it throbbed all through her body, demanding satisfaction.

"Wait," she implored. She pressed her palms against his chest. They felt as forceful as twigs trying to keep back the wind. "We shouldn't be doing this here." She looked over her shoulder at the darkened house. "What if someone sees?"

He thought of Julia and Jennifer. They had their fingers crossed so hard, hoping something would happen between Sara and him, that he was surprised they could dress themselves in the morning. Brom had made it clear that he hoped Nik could fill the void he felt was in Sara's life. As for Kane, even he had tried to help things along by telling him about Sara's father.

Nik ran the back of his hand along her cheek, exciting them both. "If they do, they'll probably throw a party and have us married before morning."

"No!" Sara snapped out the word, pushing him from her as she took a step away. The wrought-iron rail at her back prevented any further escape.

She was really frightened. Why? What did she see when she looked at him? He had to understand.

"Don't worry, I won't let them bring a preacher around." Nik slipped his hand over hers. His strong fingers rubbed her skin slowly, sensuously. He saw passion struggling to break through in her eyes. "Come on, I know just the place to escape from prying eyes."

She didn't want to escape from prying eyes. She wanted to escape from him. And herself. Sara shook her head. "No—"

Suddenly she was airborne, effortlessly swept into his arms. Surprised, she could only stare at him. She tried to find her voice in order to demand her release. The words wouldn't come. Her arms betrayed her as they slipped around his neck for support. Struggle though she did, she *wanted* this.

"What are you doing?"

Nik grinned, walking into the kitchen. He pulled the terrace doors closed after them. "If the mountain won't come to Mohammed, Mohammed is just going to have to carry the mountain to where he wants it to be." Still holding her, he left the kitchen.

"And where's that?" Sara's throat was dry, tight as she asked the question. Her body hummed, yearning. She felt desire growing at a prodigious pace.

"My room."

His bed. Heaven.

What was the use of fighting? She knew that she was destined to end up there. She'd known when she had boarded the plane this morning. Perhaps she'd known since she had seen him in the kitchen, a rugged, gorgeous-looking man communing with something in a copper pot.

With a sigh that bordered on surrender, Sara laid her head against his chest. She felt Nik's heart beneath her cheek. She knew it was silly, but it made her feel secure. Warm. Safe. She hadn't felt that way in years.

Nik only smiled to himself as he crossed into the darkened hallway.

Sara prayed everyone in the house was asleep and that no one would see them. There was no strength left in her to resist. Not against him. Not against herself. And certainly not against the inevitable.

The door to his bedroom stood open. Nik crossed the threshold and then eased the door closed with his elbow. It clicked into place as the latch bolt slid into the strike plate.

The soft, almost imperceptible sound reverberated in Sara's head, echoing like the sound of a cell door being closed.

Suddenly she came to life, squirming in his arms. "Put me down, Sinclair." She cloaked herself in a few precious shreds of anger. It was a desperate attempt to deny the almost violent needs racking her body. "I'm not a sack of meal you can just carry off at will."

*Too late,* Nik thought as he set her down. *It's too late for both of us.*

Wariness rimmed with panic entered her eyes. "Sara." His hands whispered along her arms. "There's nowhere to run."

And nowhere to hide.

She knew that. That's what made it all so frightening. She couldn't escape this. It was as if she was glued to the hardwood floor. "You're really making this hard for me."

"Yes, I know." There wasn't a speck of remorse in Nik's voice.

She felt like a prisoner. And he was the jailer. Him and those eyes of his that saw through her. "Damn hard."

He began to coax her mouth open with his own. His lips were firm, seeking. His tongue outlined her lips. A flurry of small, teasing kisses just barely touched her mouth, like butterflies flirting with the tips of the summer grass. He heard her sigh as she wound her arms around his neck. Her body adhered to his.

She searched his eyes. He knew, damn him. He knew. "I want you, Nik. God help me, but I do."

His hold tightened around her. His smile was gentle. "I never say no to a beautiful lady."

A frenzy spun through her. If this was to happen, it had to happen quickly, so she could outrun her thoughts, her fears. She tugged at his shirt, pulling it free from the waistband. Anxious, her fingers fumbled.

Nik captured her hands in his and pulled them aside. She looked at him, confused. Didn't he want this?

"Slowly, Sara, slowly," he cautioned. "Savor it, like a gourmet meal."

For a fleeting moment passion was tempered with humor in her eyes. You could take a man out of the kitchen, but never the kitchen out of the man. "Is that how you think of yourself? As a gourmet meal that you've graciously consented to serve to me?"

She didn't understand yet. He shook his head as he crooked a finger beneath her chin and lifted it so that her eyes met his.

"No, that's how I think of *us* and what there is between us. Something special. Something really out of the ordinary."

There were explosions going on inside him, coupled with an urgency he'd never known before. But as much as he wanted to take her this instant, he knew that he had to go slowly, or not at all.

Tonight was something he wanted her to remember. Always. Tonight would be the cornerstone of the foundation he intended to lay for them. The memory would be something for Sara to cling to when she began fearing that nothing lasted.

This would last.

But he had to convince her, and that took time.

Nik lifted her hands to his lips and softly kissed each one in turn. He watched her eyes change and darken until they were almost black, like deep, rich Swiss chocolate.

Releasing her, he slid his hands along her sides and then slowly inched his palms along the swell of her breasts until he reached her shoulder blades. And the zipper that ran the length of her dress.

Sara sucked in her breath as she felt the zipper begin to part along her bare back. Deftly, Nik guided it down slowly. He pressed only the tip of his finger against the tab, moving it lightly down the delicate slope of her spine. Heat flashed along her skin, marking the path. She shivered as the zipper separated completely.

Needs slammed through him as Nik brought his mouth down on hers again. He molded her body to him, attempting to absorb the sensations that were skimming over her.

The thin shoulder straps drooped in submission, slipping down her warmed skin. Nik's hands wove a spell over her as he caressed her back. His own heart hammering, he skimmed his lips over the hollow of her throat. Then his mouth, hot and moist, moved from one shoulder to another.

Sara arched against him, desperate to draw in every last shred of sensation that Nik was creating for her. Her body felt like a blazing inferno, the very core of a steam engine. She was going to explode at any moment unless he took her.

"Now," she cried hoarsely against his mouth. He

swallowed the word and tasted the desire in it. Sara's fingers dug into his shoulders, frantic for the feel of him. "Now."

Nik cupped the back of her head in his hand, tilting it away. Her mouth was mussed from the imprint of his. His stomach knotted. "Shh."

He stepped back and her dress floated away from her torso. She was nude from the waist up. Reverently, as if he was worshiping at the altar of a goddess, Nik molded his hands around her breasts. His thumbs teased the pink edges until they hardened, rigid with desire.

Unable to bear the separation, Sara moved against him. Passion flared in his eyes, spurring her on. Only half lucid, she undid the buttons of his shirt and then peeled it from his body. She wanted to feel him against her. Like a creature needy for warmth, she wanted to feel the heat radiating from his body to hers.

Again he stopped her. She was moving too fast and he could only restrain himself for so long. Exercising the patience he had inbred into his life to the limit, Nik laid Sara on the bed and buried his head at her breast. His tongue moved quickly from one peak to the other as she gasped and twisted, her hands grasping for him.

Her skin shone, damp with moisture as she pulled him to her. He loomed above, a fraction out of reach, trying to memorize her face the way it was now, at this instant. Her eyes were almost wild, dazed. There was no wariness, no barriers.

For now, she was his.

Later they would work on forever, he thought. This moment, he had now. Wanting to rip the last barriers away, Nik forced himself to go slowly. He pulled her dress down the long, tantalizing length of her legs, dragging her panties along with it. It all fell in a colorful heap at the foot of the bed.

Her skin was golden, her limbs supple and graceful as she tangled them around him, eager, wanton. Sensations pleaded for release.

"You're still dressed," Sara protested in frustration.

"Not for long."

Nik undid the belt and pulled off his trousers quickly, never daring to take his eyes from hers. She might disappear if he did.

Completely nude, they tumbled onto the bed together, lost in one another.

Her mouth was hot on his, searching for things that had no name, feelings that had no form. She only knew she wanted to continue to lose herself in him. To take and be taken until there were no coherent thoughts left in her mind, no protest left in her soul.

Anticipation had Sara spiraling upward to the first climax. He needed only a little to drive her over. The slightest touch to her core did it.

Nik watched in fascinated awe as she bucked and twisted, digging strong fingers into his back.

She tried not to scratch him as she literally scrambled back over the edge. Her breathing was short, labored as pleasure dashed over her like the pounding surf during a typhoon.

Sara sighed long and hard as she sank, limp, farther into the bed. It felt as if she had fallen for miles, when she hadn't even moved.

Opening her eyes, Sara saw Nik smiling just above her face. She looked at him, a half question forming in her eyes.

He was energized by her very reaction. "Lady," he promised, "you ain't seen nothing yet."

The journey began again with a jolt. His hands were clever as they lightly slid along her moistened core, teasing, promising, then moving back until she whimpered. And then he plunged his fingers inside to work her up into a frenzy again.

Stars exploded in her head as she was thrown into the center of the hurricane. Agony and ecstasy entwined eternal hands and held her captive together.

She wanted it to stop.

She wanted to die this way and never have it end.

She was magnificent, he thought, watching her. And he was only human.

His first goal had been to pleasure her, to show her what could be. To make her understand how important she was to him. But he could only hold himself back for so long. He wanted desperately to be inside her, to join with her and be one.

Ever so gently Nik rolled over onto her, then propped himself up on his elbows. He felt her part her legs for him and then arch against him in mute supplication.

He didn't need any more.

Nik drove himself into her. A moan echoed in his throat as she sheathed him eagerly, desperately, her hips cradling against his. Framing her face as he kissed her, Nik moved his hips, coaxing a mirror rhythm from hers.

Together they began a ride that neither of them was destined ever to forget.

Weakened, humbled, stunned and very, very content, Nik crumpled onto Sara, too exhausted to do anything else. He felt her heart beating wildly, like the wings of a hummingbird, against his chest.

From somewhere he found the strength to brush a kiss along her hair. It drained him. It was another moment before he could ask, "Am I too heavy for you?"

"No." She murmured the word and it rippled against his shoulder, stirring excitement within him even as he lay in a state of total collapse. Too much would never begin to be enough.

"Good," he muttered. "Because I can't move."

"Neither can I." She liked the feel of his weight on her. Sara allowed her hands to play softly along his back. It felt every bit as strong and muscular as she had fantasized it would be. "If there's an earthquake now," she mused aloud, "they'll find us like this."

He tried to lift his head, and decided against it. Not yet. He wanted to stay this way just a little longer. "I've got no problems with that."

She smiled, and he could feel her lips curving. It tickled his skin. A warm feeling began to spread through him again.

"They could bury us in the same coffin," Nik proposed, as if considering the matter. "It'd be a lot cheaper that way."

It was so absurd she laughed. "You're macabre."

The slight movement of her belly as she laughed excited him. Nik felt his strength suddenly, miraculously returning.

"No, just practical." He raised himself on his elbow to look at her. "Sometimes."

Light from the single lamp in the room played along his face, leaving half in shadow. It made him seem a little unreal.

Just like this feeling inside her.

"But not now," she guessed.

"Most especially now."

She didn't understand. "And what's practical about this?"

He maintained a straight face, but his eyes gave him

away. "Well, it *was* the only practical solution. If we hadn't made love tonight they would have had to come and lock me up by morning."

She felt herself smiling. "And why would they have locked you up?" She tried to tug a sheet up over her breasts. Nik held on to it firmly, foiling her as he grinned as mischievously as any boy.

"Because I would have gone completely insane from wanting you."

She doubted that very much. "Oh, it's been that hard for you."

Nik traced the slight dimple in her cheek that formed with her arch smile.

"It's been that hard for me." He was smiling, but there was something very serious in his tone. And then the look shifted again and his eyes were completely roguish. "Speaking of which…"

She could read his mind. Perhaps because it echoed her own. She could feel desire beginning to swell and fill her veins again. Still, she couldn't give in so easily.

"Isn't this about where you have a cigarette and then roll over and go to sleep?"

He shook his head. "Not my style. First of all, I don't smoke."

Nik gathered her to him so that there was absolutely no space between their bodies. He felt her stirring in latent anticipation and his own body responding.

"And second, I'm definitely not sleepy." His fingers drifted along the swell of her hips, lingering, caressing, inspiring. "That only leaves us with one thing to do."

She found that she could still tease, still give as good as she got. The knowledge pleased her. "Whip up a new recipe?"

*Start with one man, one woman, add in spice, lace,*

*with love and hot, sultry sex. Simmer for an hour. Serves two for a lifetime.*

A smile lifted the corners of his mouth as he thought of this particular recipe finding its way into a cookbook. "In a manner of speaking."

"Speaking," she repeated solemnly, as she raised her head and then brushed a fleeting kiss over his lips. "You want to talk?"

He was already balancing himself over her, anticipating the feel of her body, soft and giving, hot and demanding, beneath his. He slowly moved his head from side to side. "The farthest thing from my mind."

Sara felt herself melting, and struggled to keep her mind from falling into the same burning abyss. "What is on your mind?"

"You, Sara."

Nik kissed her lips once, then again, a little more deeply. He felt her responding instantly. It was almost as if they had always been like this, reading each other's needs, responding to each other's desires.

And perhaps, in some other time and place, they had been. Soul mates, predestined for one another.

"You," he repeated just before his mouth took hers in earnest.

Sara parted her lips, eagerly admitting his tongue, suddenly hungrier than she had been the first time. She cinched her arms around his neck, eager to return in kind what he was giving her.

The minutest glimmer of a thought, before all thought dissolved again, had her knowing that this couldn't possibly last.

Nothing good ever lasted.

But for tonight, just for tonight, she could pretend that it did.

And for tonight she could love him the way she wanted to be loved. The way she had wanted to be loved all of her life. Everlastingly. Tonight she could pretend that the word *forever* had a meaning.

Liquid quicksilver turned to molten lava in her veins as Sara ignited beneath his touch. She inflamed them both.

Before dawn nudged aside the darkness with strong fingers of light, Nik knew that whatever came, whatever else lay out there waiting for him, he was never letting Sara out of his life again.

# *Chapter 13*

Fourteen years had gone into forming who and what she was. Fourteen long years. Sara couldn't just change all that overnight, even though part of her fervently wished that she could. She couldn't just open herself up to the relationship, to Nik.

But she could treasure what had happened for its own sake.

It had been an incredible night. One that she knew she would remember forever. She stirred against Nik, wondering if he was awake yet. Light was flooding the room through the filmy white curtains. It had to be at least seven, if not later. It was time to get up and go back to her room before anyone saw her.

She didn't want to move.

Just a few minutes more.

Sara slipped her hand over Nik's chest. Her fingers drifted over the light sprinkling of sandy brown hair even as pointed daggers of fear began to slowly rip along the edges of her mind, depriving her of peace.

She sighed.

Nik felt her breath swish along his skin. He'd been awake for a while now. Perhaps he hadn't actually slept at all, just dozed a little. He hadn't wanted to disturb her by moving. The feel of her body against his was something he cherished far more than comfort.

Now that she was awake, Nik shifted so that he could look at her. He studied her face for telltale signs. "Regrets?"

She nodded slowly. "Two." She held up an index finger. "That we did it." A second finger joined the first. "That we didn't do it sooner."

Maybe it was the early-morning fog on his brain. "Isn't that two different sides of the same coin?"

His assessment was truer than he thought. The smile on her face was tinged with a sadness she wasn't fully aware of exposing.

"Yes, but it's the same coin." She realized that she was being too serious and giving away too much. Her tone lightened. "I never claimed to be an easy woman to understand."

And that sentence would get his vote for the understatement of the year.

"That you didn't. " He positioned himself farther up on the bed until he was leaning against the headboard. "But then, I don't make hamburgers. I work with sirloin."

Some of the sadness melted as she laughed: "Is everything a food metaphor with you?"

He considered her question seriously. "Basically. For instance." His green eyes darkened slightly as he trailed his fingers along the plane just above her breasts. "Your skin's like fresh whipped cream."

His voice was low, seductive. She felt herself slipping into it as if it was a tub of scented bathwater.

"Whipped cream topping off a cup of hot chocolate on a cold winter's day. To be savored while curled up in front of a roaring fire at a ski lodge."

She managed to rouse herself, and then smiled at him. "Sounds good."

His eyes made love to her. "Tastes even better."

Nik pressed a kiss to her arm and languidly worked his way up her shoulder. Sara's head fell back as she drank in the exciting rush he created within her. But the sensation was dueling with her reborn fears. The match between them was almost even.

Almost.

The scale began tipping in Nik's favor.

Sara struggled to keep her mind clear. She couldn't be found in his room like this. "Nik, it's almost time to get up."

Nik raised his head until their eyes met. "Exactly what I was thinking."

The man was impossible. What was worse, he was destroying her resolve. She wanted to stay here with him like this. Forever. Sara tried to push him back but there seemed to be no strength in her hands. "Everyone else'll be up, too."

Nik concentrated on her ear. It was small and delicate and tempted him to nibble on it, like a perfectly designed hors d'oeuvre.

"They're an inventive group. They'll find something to do."

With a sudden burst of willpower Sara sat up, though she would have far preferred sliding down onto the bed with him. She grasped the sheet and pulled it around her breasts.

"I have to get back to my room," she insisted.

She was right. He couldn't rush this just because he knew, in his heart, that it was right for both of them.

Nik leaned back on his elbows. "Spoilsport."

He was teasing her now, but she couldn't lead him on. "Nik, I'm not any good at relationships."

Distress tinged her features. Nik pretended not to see in hopes that it would disappear again. "Could have fooled me."

He wasn't taking this seriously. "No, I mean really. I always mess things up somehow."

He didn't want to hear about a string of former lovers. If he didn't know about them, they didn't exist. What mattered most was now. And the future. And them.

"Past history." He waved it away as if it were a mere fly buzzing about his head. "Clean slate. Fresh start. With me." He took her hand and held it firmly though she tried to pull it away. "With me, Sara," he repeated. "We've already got a head start. Let's just see where this'll go."

*Nowhere,* she thought, but refrained from saying anything. He'd find that out for himself soon enough.

When he released her hand Sara rose, still wrapped in his sheet. Sara dragged her hand through her hair and wished he wouldn't look at her. She could probably haunt houses right about now. "I need a shower."

He glanced over toward the bathroom. The idea of soaping her body sounded pretty good from where he sat. "We could save time by doing it together."

She was busy gathering her clothes together. "We wouldn't save anything if we did it together."

She gasped in surprise as he grabbed her waist and pulled her to him. Nik kissed her hard, reminding her of what the night had been all about. "Except maybe, my sanity."

Why did he keep insisting on turning her knees to rubber like that? She drew her body away. She couldn't think when he held her so close. "We already saved that last night, remember?"

He shrugged, unfazed by the reminder. "My sanity's very fragile."

She gathered the pile of clothing into her arms again, this time maintaining her distance from him.

"It'll have to fend for itself." She crossed to the door, the ends of the Roman toga she had fashioned out of the sheet trailing after her on the floor. "See you in an hour, Sinclair."

Nik sighed dramatically as he fell back on the bed. "If they haven't locked me up by then."

It was all too tempting to lie down next to him and recreate last night. But she held her ground. "I'll chance it."

Opening the door, Sara looked furtively around the hall. She felt like a teenager trying to sneak back into her house after curfew.

Satisfied that the hallway was empty, she slipped out of Nik's room and into her own.

It felt as if the weekend had just raced by. More than that, Sara thought as the plane taxied down the runway, it felt as if this weekend had happened to someone else, not to her. The events had been too idyllic, too wonderful. The aura that had been created by it all, the baseball game, the picnic, the night of passion followed by the brunch party Brom had surprised them with, just couldn't last. She could already feel it beginning to fade.

Only pain lasted. Happiness dissolved like soap bubbles blown into the air. Bright and shiny rainbows one minute, gone the next.

When the plane finally came to a halt in the Newport Beach airport, Sara knew the adventure was over. She had to regain control of herself. It was time to take a tight rein over her emotions again before things got way out of hand.

If they hadn't already.

Her father was going to recuperate soon. When he did, she would leave, Nik or no Nik. It was a pattern she had followed all of her adult life. She always knew when to leave. When things looked as if they were getting too serious. Too much for her to handle.

They deplaned and entered the terminal. Sara was barely aware of what Jennifer was saying to her. Something about work. Katie was being cranky and whimpering, interfering with the conversation Sara wasn't really paying attention to.

Kane picked his daughter up and she curled against him. It was hours past her bedtime.

"See you in the morning," Jennifer said over her shoulder as she hurried out with Kane to the parking lot. Home for them was only a couple of miles away.

Sara picked up her suitcase.

Nik reached for it, his hand covering hers. Sara wouldn't relinquish her hold. Nik let go. He knew that they had taken another step backward. "I'll take you home, Sara."

They walked through the electronic doors that had eased open as they approached. "No, that's okay." She looked toward the line of taxis that stood waiting for fares, even at this hour. "I'll just grab a cab."

Stubborn to the end, he thought. "When I was a kid, my mother always taught me to return anything I took and put it in the exact same place where I found it. If I didn't, she read me the riot act."

Sara gave him an irritated look. Why couldn't he just let her retreat? "Your mother's not here, you're not a little kid anymore and I'm not a thing you have to return to its proper place."

Nik tugged on the suitcase. "Humor me." A glint entered his eyes. "Or would you rather I reverted to food metaphors again?"

Sara released the suitcase, raising her hands in surrender. "Heaven forbid."

What was the harm? So he'd drive her home. So she'd be alone with him in a small space for a little while. What was the big deal? She could more than handle herself.

At least, she had before.

"Okay." She nodded as she began to walk toward the parking lot where they had left his car. "You can take me home."

How did she always manage to sound like a queen commanding her subjects? "I can die a happy man. My wishes have all come true." With his suitcase beneath his arm and hers in his hand, Nik took Sara by the arm as they walked. In his opinion, it was well worth the juggling act.

It was dark and there weren't that many people around. Sara began to regret her capitulation. "I said okay to a ride, not sarcasm served up hot."

He saw his Mustang and motioned her toward it. "All right, no sarcasm served up hot." He stopped next to his car, setting the suitcases down. His eyes washed over her, making her yearn for last night. "What would you like served up hot?"

*You.* Sara looked away as he opened the trunk. "Nothing."

Nik deposited the suitcases and shut the trunk. The smile on his face told her that he had read her mind. But at least he had the good grace not to say anything.

Accepting a ride home from him *was* a big deal. She realized it almost the moment she sat in the car next to him. Once the car door was closed, the space between them felt nominal. Intimate.

She didn't need this, she thought, staring at the road ahead. Her insides felt jittery, as if she were a child anticipating her first recital. Except that there wasn't going to be a recital. There wasn't going to be anything and she knew it. The weekend had been an aberration. This was what her life was supposed to be like. Singular. She had made the choice to spend it alone a long time ago.

She didn't want her mother's sorrow to become her own. No man was ever going to walk out on her. No man was ever going to break her heart.

That meant no surrendering to longings or desire. Nik represented both.

She'd been much too quiet on the way home. He was afraid to guess what she was thinking. Nik turned down a dark residential street. Streetlights and an occasional porch light illuminated his way.

He glanced toward her. "When can I see you again?"

Her fingers knotted together in her lap. She held on so tightly the tips began turning white. "Tomorrow, at work, I'll be there bright and early, as usual."

Nik had trouble controlling his anger. They'd come

too far to begin playing games again. "That's not what I meant and you know it."

She searched for ways to put him off. Her own survival depended on it. If she allowed herself to get in any deeper, she wouldn't be able to pull herself out. He didn't understand. No one did. He was already getting annoyed with her. It was always like this. Next, the arguments would come. And then the tears. It was better to be alone. No pain, no gain didn't pertain to relationships.

Sara's voice hardened. "You mean for another tussle in bed?"

Nik's hands grasped the steering wheel hard. He pretended it was her throat. How could she reduce last night to those terms? "Was that what it was to you?"

"Yes." She looked down at her fingers and slowly unknotted them. "No."

When she raised her head again, the look in her eyes was defensive. It wasn't as if she hadn't warned him. He knew what he was getting into. "Look, I told you I wasn't any good at relationships."

He took another turn, this time to the left. There was contained fury in his voice. "Why are you trying so hard to prove it?"

"So I won't—so you won't get hurt," she amended quickly, cursing herself for the slip. She slanted a look at him.

They both knew she was afraid of being hurt, but Nik played along. "My hide's a good deal thicker than you think."

"Impossible," she muttered, trying to sound flippant.

"And I won't hurt you." The promise was soft but nonetheless binding.

She smiled ruefully in the dark. "You already are," she said quietly.

By causing fissures in her walls, by making her break her own rules, by making her feel something for him, he was already causing her pain.

She pointed to the left, anxious to get away. "We're here." She unfastened her seat belt and wound the purse strap around her hand. "You don't have to stop at the house. I can get out right here on the corner."

She was acting like an idiot. "Why don't I just push you out as I drive by and throw your suitcase out after you? That way I won't have to come to a stop at all." He couldn't remember a recipe, no matter how difficult, ever trying his patience the way she was.

He pulled the car up to the curb before her father's house and got out. Wordlessly, struggling to keep his temper in check, he rounded the back. Unlocking the trunk, Nik took out her suitcase.

There were a hundred different things he wanted to say to her. He wanted to ask why she was jeopardizing their future together. He wanted to lash out at her for her stubbornness and her determination to kill what was flowering between them. He wanted to demand to know what the hell she was so afraid of.

But he said nothing. He merely handed her the suitcase.

Nik slammed the trunk closed. "I'll see you in the morning."

She nodded, taking the case. Sara avoided his eyes. "Right." She began to walk away.

Nik stood looking after her. "Love doesn't have to hurt, Sara."

She stopped, her shoulders stiffening. She didn't turn

around. "It doesn't have to," she agreed. "But it does."

And then she walked away.

It wasn't until she heard his engine start up again and then fade away that she played back his last words in her head.

*Love doesn't have to hurt.*

Love? Had he just told her that he loved her? No, it wasn't possible. Love didn't happen like a flash fire in a pan. It—

Had, she thought. Sara let her barriers down long enough to admit it to herself. Love had happened just that fast, just that overwhelmingly. If not for him, it had for her.

Oh, God, she was in trouble.

She felt numb and confused as she put her key into the lock and let herself into the house.

It took her a moment to realize that the lights were on in the living room. Her father was sitting in the beige-and-brown recliner, looking through the magazine section of the Sunday paper. He let it drop when he saw her come in. "Have fun?"

She crossed to him quickly. "Are you all right? Is something wrong?" She tried to remember where she had put away the surgeon's phone number.

Raymond smiled at her display of concern. "I'm just fine, Sara."

She let out a sigh of relief, her adrenaline draining from her. Her eyes narrowed. It was almost eleven o'clock. Her father had always been a firm believer in going to bed early. "What are you doing up?"

He moved the lever on the recliner. The footrest disappeared as he sat up. "Waiting for my daughter to get in. You said you'd be back tonight," he reminded her.

She frowned. He needed his rest. "You shouldn't have stayed up."

Having her fuss over him was something new. He let himself enjoy it for a moment. "I liked staying up waiting for you." Raymond thought of his daughter's teen years. "I missed out on doing that."

*Not tonight, Dad, I can't handle this tonight.* Restlessly Sara shifted the suitcase to her other hand. "You missed out on a lot of things."

"Yes, I know." He wanted to take her hand, to ask forgiveness, but he didn't know how. He was just beginning to learn how to forgive himself. "And you have no idea how sorry I am about that."

Sara's expression grew distant. "No, I don't. I haven't the faintest idea how sorry you are." She remembered how she had finally come to terms with it all, how she had hardened her heart. Or tried to. "I didn't think you were sorry at all."

"Then you thought wrong."

Sara turned from him. Raymond reached for her hand, stopping her. She was surprised at how much strength there was in his grip. He had always held her so gently when she was a child. Now it felt as if he was holding on for his very life.

His eyes implored her to believe him. "Not a day went by when I didn't miss you. I have always, *always* loved you, Sara."

Her eyes were cold, but she could feel them misting. Damn, she didn't want to cry now. Not now. "You had a very funny way of showing it."

He smiled disparagingly. "I thought I was showing it the only way I could."

She pulled her hand away. Her anger flared red-hot. "By deserting me?" How could he insult her by talking such nonsense? "By making me feel that my father, the man I loved more than anyone else in the world, didn't care about me anymore?"

Raymond shook his head. He suddenly felt very old. "That wasn't the way it was."

"Then how was it, Dad?" she demanded, her voice rising. "How was it for you? For me it was lousy." Tears began to fall. "Other kids had fathers they could spend time with. Fathers to talk to. Fathers to give cards to on Father's Day."

Sara wiped away the tears angrily with the heel of her hand. She didn't want her father thinking that she was crying over him.

"I didn't even have an address." She looked at him accusingly. "I didn't even know where you were. Just somewhere in California."

"I was right here all the time. I sent child support checks every month." That much money he always put by. Despite his obsession, he would never have cheated Sara of her due.

Sara shrugged, annoyed with herself for letting loose like that, letting her emotions free. "I found that out later. But Mother said you moved without a forwarding address. She said the envelopes the checks came in had a different postmark on them every month."

Raymond offered her his handkerchief, but she refused it, sniffing instead.

The pain refused to remain buried any longer. "The first year you disappeared out of my life, I called information, hoping to track you down by your phone number. I was going to call and yell at you for leaving, but you weren't listed anywhere." She bit her lip to stem the flow of fresh tears that threatened to come. Sara remembered sitting in her room with a road atlas she had bought. "I called information in every city in Southern California that I could find."

His conscience shot steely arrows of guilt through him. "I'm a cop, Sara. We like to stay unlisted. You remember."

She swallowed. The lump in her throat was huge. "Yeah, I remember."

He didn't know what to say. He only knew he had to say something. He was losing her. "Sara…"

There was no use in going around and around about this. The past was behind them, leaving an inky black mark in its place. Nothing her father could say would change what he had done to her. He had shut her completely out of his life for his own selfish reasons. Because he wanted to start a new life without her. That was what her mother had told her when Sara had asked.

And what Sara believed, because there was no reason not to.

Sara shrugged indifferently, dismissing the conversation. "I'm tired, Dad. I'd like to go to bed now. And you should, too," she added as an afterthought.

He had let silence plead his case for too long. Raymond caught her by the arm, imploring her to stay. "No, I have to explain."

She'd fought too many emotional battles today to remain polite. Her resolve broke.

"Explain what?" she lashed out. "That I was a reminder to you of your mistake, just like I was to Mom? I don't want to hear it." She tried to pull away, but he wouldn't let her.

She had to hear the truth, no matter how painful it would be for both of them.

"No." Raymond raised his voice. "You're going to listen."

She yanked her hand free, accidentally knocking over the suitcase. She hardly noticed it. "You can't talk to me like that. You haven't the right to play father now after all these years."

"Maybe you're right." Raymond let his hands hang at his sides, but his eyes held her in place. "Then listen to me because you're fair."

She sighed as she dragged her hand through her hair. She was crazy for letting him talk her into this. "All right. Talk."

Raymond began to pace, agitation fueling his steps. Now that she was listening, he wasn't certain he had the right words at his disposal.

"I didn't break off contact with you because you reminded me of a mistake I had made." He laughed softly to himself at the irony of her accusation. "Hell, Sara, you were the only thing about my life that was good and clean. I stopped seeing you because I thought it was for your own good—"

"My own good?" she echoed incredulously. "How can you *say* that?"

He shrugged, looking away. "Vanity, I guess. I didn't want you to know what a weakling your old man was."

He had completely lost her. "I don't understand."

Raymond looked at her then and she found herself pitying him. She tried to lock the sentiment out, but it seeped through. "Maybe I should start by explaining your name."

He had told her about that. Time and again. It had been her favorite bedtime story. Didn't he remember? "You named me after the place where you met Mom."

"Yes, but it wasn't Saratoga the city. It was the racetrack."

Just the way the kids at school had always teased her. "Go on," she said quietly.

He drew a long breath. His mouth felt dry, but he pressed on. "We met when she was standing in line in front of me at the two-dollar window at Saratoga. We were both betting on the same horse." He smiled ruefully. "The horse won. I told your mother she brought me luck. She confessed that she had never placed a bet before. She had come with her girlfriend on a lark." Shame entered his eyes. "For me, betting wasn't a lark, it was an obsession."

Sara could see that the admission was difficult for him. He stuck his hands in his pockets and pressed on like a tired mountain climber trying to reach the summit.

"I managed to get it under control for a while. But then I started playing again. Nothing big at first. It still got the better of me. I won big a few times and then I was hooked all over again. I started betting more and more, until I was betting money I didn't have." He sighed heavily. "We had to sell the house."

Sara could only stare at her father, stunned. Everything was falling apart. Just as it had then. "That's why we moved? You said you wanted to go to a different neighborhood."

"I would have said anything to keep you from finding out the truth. For a while I honestly thought I could get my betting under control, but it was controlling me. Underneath it all was always that hope, that dream that I could get all the money back that I had lost and set us up for life."

He turned and stared out the window, unable to face her any longer. He was afraid of what he would see in Sara's eyes.

"One day your mother said that I loved gambling more than I loved her. That if I did love her more, I would have stopped gambling when she asked me to. She didn't understand that I couldn't.'' A streetlight cast a pool of light on his front lawn. He stared at it, remembering the pain his decision had cost him. "I didn't want to leave her trapped in a marriage where she felt unloved. I agreed to get a divorce on the condition that she would never tell you about my gambling.''

Sara thought back over the years. So many things made sense now that had seemed odd at the time. How could she have been so stupid, so blind?

He looked at her reflection in the window. "For a year I fought it, hoping that we could get back together again, become a family. But there didn't seem to be any use. I couldn't stop going to the track. So I dropped out of your life. I didn't want you to be disillusioned about me.''

She wasn't the only one who had been blind. "Don't you see? Your turning your back on me was what disillusioned me. So, you have a problem—''

"Had,'' he corrected firmly, finally turning around. There was pride in his voice. "I joined Gamblers Anonymous. I've stayed away from the racetrack and betting for almost a year now.'' A familiar smile quirked his lips. Sara recognized it as her own. "I don't even allow myself to watch "Mr. Ed'' reruns on cable.''

Sara didn't know whether to laugh or to cry. All those years of blaming herself, of lying awake at night, trying to figure out what it was that she had done wrong to make him leave. They had all been wasted. It hadn't been her fault at all.

Hesitating, Sara forced herself to make contact. She laid a hand on her father's shoulder. He covered it with his own. When he looked at her there was gratitude in his eyes.

She was still angry at him, angry about the years that he had allowed to be cast away. Years neither one of them could ever get back.

Raymond searched her face and saw the beginning of forgiveness there. He felt like crying himself.

"It wasn't you I pushed away, Sara. It was myself."

Nothing would ever remove the sadness from his eyes, Sara realized. He had been hurt just as much as she had by all those empty years.

"But I've paid for it." Raymond opened his arms to her, but made no move, still afraid. "And I'm not pushing anymore."

Sara moved into his arms, embracing him. And this time she let the tears flow freely.

# Chapter 14

Nik drove up to the curb and shut off the engine. For a moment he just sat in the car looking at the house bathed in the light of the late-afternoon sun. Sara's car was in the driveway. That meant she was home. Good. He hadn't called ahead because he was afraid she'd leave.

Nik unbuckled his seat belt.

It had been an exceedingly hectic week. He'd hardly had time to draw two breaths in succession. There had certainly been no time for any meaningful dialogue between himself and Sara. Any words they might have exchanged on the subject of last Saturday night would probably have deteriorated into a shouting match, given his harried state and Sara's wariness. For a whole week, when he did have any time to talk to her, Sara had quipped and bantered, keeping him at bay. Like a circus animal trainer who cracked her whip and held up a chair

between herself and the lion, Sara had been warding
him off with her sharp tongue.

It was as if their night of love and discovery hadn't
even happened.

But it had, and he was resolved to make her face it.
Face it with him. Whatever there was standing in their
way, keeping her from him, Nik intended to blow it out
of the water. He wouldn't have come as far as he had
in his own life if he had meekly accepted the inevitable,
or bowed readily to defeat when the first shot was fired.

If anything, he thrived on adversity. And Sara was as
adversarial as they came.

Nik pocketed his keys, still watching the house for
some sign of her. "This is war, Saratoga Santangelo,
and I'm about to fire another salvo at that sweet little
broadside of yours."

Determined, Nik intended to fight any way he could
to get through to Sara. Dirty if necessary. His first line
of offense involved food and Sara's father.

Nik got out of the car and circled to the trunk. It was
filled with food—entrées, desserts, everything that was
necessary to prepare the type of feast that would bring
tears to the eyes of the most hardened critic of Italian
food. Kane had mentioned to him that Raymond had a
weakness for Italian food, and Nik had gone to work.

Nik decided to begin the battle slowly. Carrying a
covered dish of cannelloni, he walked up to the front
door and rang the bell.

He rang twice before the door finally opened. Sara
stood in the doorway. She was barefoot, wearing a
baggy T-shirt and frayed cutoff shorts that were cut so
high on one thigh it had him tightening his grip on the
handles of the serving dish.

Sara was annoyed at the instant flutter that went

through her at the sight of Nik on her doorstep. There wasn't anything she could do about it. But she could manage to maintain a cool, flippant expression even though her pulse had accelerated like an adolescent's at the sight of her first crush.

Sara leaned one hand against the doorjamb, blocking his way. She glanced at the covered dish and raised a questioning brow. "I already gave at the office."

Nik had seen the momentary flicker of desire in her eyes. It was all the encouragement he needed. "The office decided to give something back."

Stubbornly she remained fixed in the doorway. "Why aren't you at the restaurant, Sinclair? It's only six-thirty."

Nik nudged her aside with his shoulder. Sara reluctantly stepped back and let him walk in. "It's Saturday."

That wasn't an answer. Jennifer had told her that Nik worked six days a week and half days on Sunday most of the time.

She fisted her hands at her waist, challenging him. "You took last Saturday off."

"I'm becoming decadent." Nik looked around the room, but didn't see Raymond. He nodded toward the right, taking a guess. "The kitchen this way?"

"Yes, but—"

Nik was already leaving her behind. She picked up speed, reaching the kitchen at the same time he did.

Why was he bringing her food? "We're not a charity case, Sinclair."

He ignored the antagonistic tone of her voice. For some reason Sara was afraid of him. He intended to find out why.

"You told me about the extent of your cooking, remember?'' He placed the casserole on the counter and mentally cleared off space for the rest of the things he had brought with him that were still in the car. Sara was going to have to move the blender and the toaster, but that was about all. ''I figured your father must be starving right about now.''

Pompous ass, they were doing just great without him. Who did he think he was, barging into her house—her father's house, she amended quickly, realizing her slip—and—and—

Raymond walked into the room behind them. ''Sara, who was—'' He stopped as he realized that Sara had company. He looked at Nik's face. Recognition was immediate, but the name lagged a minute behind. ''Nik, isn't it?''

Crossing to him, Nik took Raymond's hand, shaking it. The older man looked a great deal healthier now than he had the last time Nik had seen him. Maybe Sara wasn't as bad a cook as she claimed.

''Yes. How are you?'' Nik asked.

Sara couldn't get over the fact that the two men were acting as if they were old friends instead of practically strangers. What gave Nik the right to just waltz into her private life like this?

''Fine.'' Raymond's leathery cheeks spread in a warm smile as he glanced at his daughter. ''Sara's been taking good care of me.''

Sara shifted in place, uncomfortable with the compliment. They'd made headway since last Sunday, but there were still some things between her father and her that had to be worked through. It took time to mend breaches, even under the best of circumstances and intentions. It didn't help to have matters announced to the whole world. Or to Nik.

"Nik thinks I'm starving you to death." Sara gestured at the casserole dish. "He's obviously brought you a care package."

The tolerant smile on Nik's face fanned her temper. Just as he knew it would. He liked her better when she was angry. She tended to act on impulse then. And he could work with that.

"She told me that the extent of her cooking abilities was to burn things. I figured she was keeping you alive on those little frozen food packages you boil and serve." He nodded toward the refrigerator.

Defensive, Sara moved over and leaned against the refrigerator. Any minute, the man would start taking inventory. She didn't feel like being subjected to any criticism.

Damn, it was bad enough having to deal with her own edginess when she was around him at the restaurant. Why did he have to bring that tension here? Wasn't she going to have any peace from him?

Sara raised her chin, her eyes narrowing. She was spoiling for a fight. "And if I was?"

Nik viewed frozen food in the same light that he thought of fast food. Unfit for human consumption. "It's a good way to become malnutritioned."

Raymond knew a fight in the making when he saw one. He quickly crossed to the counter. "Let's see what Nik brought us, Sara."

"His nose, which he's sticking into things again." Sara folded her arms in front of her chest as she turned away from both of them.

Raymond flushed slightly as he looked at Nik, then took care to tread very cautiously. This was harder than maneuvering through a booby-trapped minefield.

"You'll have to forgive my daughter, Nik. I'm afraid

that being cooped up all day with me is making her a little testy.''

Sara gave her father a sharp look. ''I can make my own apologies, Dad.''

Nik's expression was agreeable as he waited. Sara remained silent. ''Well?'' he prodded her expectantly.

She gave him a saccharine smile. ''When I think an apology is necessary, you'll hear one.''

Raymond sighed as he moved toward Nik. ''She always did have a stubborn streak,'' he confided.

Any minute now he was going to pull out baby pictures of her, Sara thought, her fuse dangerously low.

Nik nodded. ''I kind of suspected that.'' He moved toward the doorway. Confronted with Sara and her microshorts, he'd forgotten all about the rest of the food in the trunk.

Sara raised her hand like a student in class and waved it before both men. ''I'm standing in the same room with you, gentlemen. There's no reason to talk about me as if I were dead.''

''Dead people are docile,'' Nik pointed out. ''No one can ever accuse you of being that.'' He nodded toward the front door. ''Want to help me?''

''Leave?'' she suggested, bringing a touch of eagerness to her voice.

''No.'' His voice was mild, patient. It had an inverse effect on her temper. ''I've got more food in the car.''

He glanced over his shoulder to see that Raymond had let curiosity get the better of him and was lifting the lid on the serving dish. The older man looked as if he had suddenly fallen in love.

''Cannelloni,'' Raymond whispered with a reverence that was usually reserved for the interior of churches.

Kane had been right, Nik thought.

He grinned, pleased. "I always enjoy cooking for an appreciative audience." Nik turned to Sara and took her arm, ushering her out. "I have eggplant parmesan, manicotti and cannolis in the trunk of my car, plus an assortment of vegetables."

"Cannolis?" Raymond's eyes shone as he replaced the lid on the dish.

"Two dozen, freshly made," Nik promised as he walked out of the kitchen. He discovered that he didn't have to drag Sara with him. She was bearing down on him of her own volition.

Her hand on his shoulder, she pulled him around to look at her once they were outside the house. Her eyes were like two dark arrows, aimed straight for his heart. There was no mistaking them for Cupid's arrows, he thought. They were more along the lines of poison-tipped darts.

"Are you out of your mind?"

"Possibly," he conceded. A sane man would have retreated by now.

She didn't have the patience for word play today. He was crowding her, and she lashed out.

"Why are you trying to kill my father?" she demanded. "The man just had an angioplasty. In case you don't know what that is, that's a procedure intended to rectify a heart blockage caused by too much fat buildup. Fat, as in what you're offering to feed him."

He unlocked the trunk. It popped open, giving Sara a clear view of the interior. There was enough in there to feed three people for a week. The man was moving in!

"I know what an angioplasty is," he said mildly. They were going to need to make two trips, he decided. He didn't want to drop anything.

Nik was obviously two tacos short of a combination plate. Sara gestured at the trunk, anger seeping from her very fingertips. She hadn't traveled all this way and gone through emotional hell just to indulge her father and see him back in the hospital in six months or less.

"If you know what an angioplasty is, how can you bring him all this in good conscience?" He was using her father to get to her, that's why. "Or don't you have one?"

His smile hardened around the edges. "My conscience is alive and well, Sara." He moved several things aside, arranging them to facilitate removal. "I'm not a short-order cook, Sara. I'm someone who's studied the art of preparing meals. The key word here," he emphasized, "is *art*."

She was far from convinced. "The key word here is annoying."

He didn't have time to stand and argue with her all day. Though it was the tail end of the afternoon, it was still hot and the food would spoil if he didn't get it into the house. "I know how to prepare Italian food using low-fat products."

She shivered, thinking of her last experience with something bearing that label. She eyed the contents of his trunk dubiously. "And still make it taste like something other than rubber?"

Nik removed a large box from the trunk and handed it to Sara. The box felt surprisingly light in her hands. Sliding the lid aside, she looked in to see four rows of cannoli neatly arranged. Chocolate-sprinkled cream peered invitingly out of both ends. She felt her mouth watering despite herself.

"And still make it taste like something other than rubber," Nik assured her.

She shut the lid again. "This I have to see."

Nik took out a large pot and hefted it toward the front door. "I was counting on it." His words drifted over his shoulder.

Sara followed him into the house. She just bet he was, she thought.

Nik took over the kitchen like a liberating World War II general marching into formerly enemy-occupied territory. Sara and the sauce both simmered as, for the next hour, Nik reheated the main dishes and prepared the pasta salad and vegetables he had brought with him.

The man was everywhere. Everywhere she didn't want him to be.

Sara finally occupied herself by setting the table. She looked at Nik grudgingly as he pronounced his manicotti "perfection." No wonder he never wore a chef's hat. He probably couldn't find one that was big enough to fit his head.

With a clang, Sara laid down the knife she was holding. "You have a way of taking over, don't you?"

He glanced in her direction, amused. "Only familiar territory."

Placing the fork on the other side, she turned and looked at him. "That would apply to the kitchen and the food."

What was she getting at? "Right," he agreed slowly. He added a dash of oregano to the sauce, then tasted it. Good.

She was tired of shadowboxing. "So what are you doing, butting in to my life?"

He replaced the lid on the pot and checked on the spaghetti he was preparing as a side dish. He intended to give Raymond a smorgasbord of food to choose from. The rest would be leftovers to be eaten over the course of the week. "I don't follow."

She didn't like talking to the back of his head. Abandoning the table, she walked over to him by the stove. "That's unfamiliar territory."

Now they were getting to it, he thought. Still, he went on as if the conversation only marginally held his attention rather than completely, the way it actually did. "Not entirely. I just thought I'd keep you from making any mistakes you'll regret later."

She thought of last week. It should never have been allowed to happen. It had made her too vulnerable. "I already have."

Knowing the way her mind worked, anticipating her answer, hearing it shouldn't have hurt. But it did.

Nik maintained an impassive expression. "I was referring to you shutting your father out of your life. Last time I looked, you seemed pretty intent on doing that."

Unable to deal with the way he was looking at her, Sara went back to setting the table. It was amazing how much mileage she could milk out of something so simple. "Well, we've come to an understanding since then."

Now that Nik thought of it, Raymond had looked a little more at ease. And the air hadn't been charged with the same degree of tension as when he'd brought Raymond home from the hospital.

If anything, it seemed as if that tension had shifted completely so that it now surrounded him and Sara. "I'm glad to hear that." Nik sprinkled grated cheese into the sauce.

She yanked the refrigerator door opened and took out a small bottle of wine. "Which is more than you and I have come to, it seems.'' She slammed the refrigerator door shut again.

Nik looked up from the dish of eggplant he was arranging. His eyes seemed to touch hers. ''I'm working on it, Sara. I'm working on it.''

*And undoing me.* She looked away. ''We're working at cross-purposes.''

''Maybe,'' he agreed. For a moment he abandoned what he was doing and crossed to her. ''I have a solution.''

Sara moved to the other side of the table as she folded another napkin and slid it next to a plate. She chewed on her lower lip. ''What?''

He wanted to nibble along her lip the way she was doing. The taste of her mouth returned to him in vivid waves. ''Come and join my side.''

She raised her eyes just for a moment. ''You're overbearing.''

He grinned, making no move to return to what he'd been doing. ''When I have to be.'' He moved in front of her again. ''Some people call that tenacity.''

Sara set down the last knife and fork. There was hostility in her eyes. He had invaded and wasn't leaving. ''I call it a royal pain.''

Somehow, she wasn't exactly sure how, Nik had managed to back her up against the counter. Suddenly the kitchen seemed a lot smaller to her, and he was filling every available space.

Nik lifted his hand and lightly swept it over her hair. It was hard to believe that he could be so gentle one moment, so infuriatingly abrasive the next. ''Then let me make the pain go away, Sara.''

She licked her lips. The very sheen tempted him.

''*Then* you'll be leaving?'' Her voice was so shaky

she was ashamed of herself. It reflected what was happening to her internally.

"Not on your life." Nik searched her face for a moment, looking for something that insisted on remaining hidden. With a sigh he stepped back, giving her room. "Tell your father dinner's ready."

Sara walked out of the room, though she wasn't completely sure how. Her insides were vibrating like a tuning fork. All systems were screaming Mayday. And the plane was going down.

Because he had embraced discipline as a way of life, Raymond ate in moderation. But he sampled everything. His abundant appreciation was evident in every bite he took and savored.

He looked at Nik, seated across the table from him. "This is wonderful." Raymond took the smallest sip of wine to wash down the last of the tetrazzini. With harnessed gusto he turned to the cannoli. "I thought that food like this was out of my life forever."

Raymond sighed as he let the dessert melt on his tongue. "If you were a woman, Nik, I think I'd be proposing right now."

If he were a woman, she wouldn't be hip-deep in trouble right now, Sara thought belligerently.

Feeling that anything she said would only be used to serve Nik's purpose somehow, Sara had elected to eat in silence. It seemed as if Nik and her father hardly noticed her verbal withdrawal. They talked all through the meal. They'd found common ground in the fact that they both knew Kane, and had gone on from there to cover baseball, cooking and police work.

She hadn't seen her father this animated since she

was a child. No doubt about it, she thought grudgingly. Nik was good for her father.

Just bad for her.

As was his habit with things he prepared, Nik had eaten very little. "No need for anything as drastic as marriage," he said with a laugh, then nodded at the counter behind him. "There are plenty of leftovers for you, and I'll give you all the recipes." He wasn't normally so generous with his original recipes, but he made an exception this time. "I promise that your doctor will approve of every single one."

Raymond eyed the plate of cannoli, but knew that one had to be his limit. With a heavy sigh he laid down his fork.

"Recipes won't do me much good," Raymond confessed ruefully. "I'm not very handy in the kitchen. And Sara—" He glanced toward his daughter and his smile was reminiscent of the ones she had once been so used to. Approving and loving. "Well, Sara has other attributes."

Nik raised his glass to his lips, his eyes on hers. "Yes, I know."

Sara looked down at her cannoli, debating whether to eat it or throw it. He had no right to do this to her, to invade her life and make her feel as if everything was being turned upside down.

The suggestion in his voice had her muscles contracting. In the past week she'd worked so hard at severing the tie that had been formed that one night. She'd almost deluded herself into thinking she could do it. Now here he was, reigniting the bonfire within her even as he was stoking her anger.

Raymond pushed himself away from the table. His chair scraped along the vinyl floor. "Well, all this good food has made me feel really sleepy. I'm afraid a tired old man is going to have to withdraw."

He began to rise, but Sara reached over and caught his hand.

"No." Damn, did that sound as panicky as she suddenly felt?

Leaning, Nik picked up Raymond's plate and set it on top of his own. "Sara," he reproved mildly, "your father knows what's best for him."

Sara saw traces of the smile Nik was struggling not to let show. She bit her lip to refrain from saying something in front of her father she might regret. She'd have to wait until they were alone to give Nik Sinclair the dressing down he deserved.

Raymond rose to his feet and shook Nik's hand. "I can't tell you how wonderful all this was for me. Really wonderful," he echoed.

"You can stop by the restaurant any time," Nik told him.

Raymond had approached each new dish with almost equal gusto. But Nik had paid close attention and noted that the man had favored one slightly above the others, taking seconds of the small portions he had allowed himself.

"I'll whip up another plate of tetrazzini for you," Nik promised as he stood. "On the house."

"Thanks, I might just take you up on that." Raymond stretched, then crossed to the doorway. Nik was gathering silverware together. "Don't worry about making too much noise—washing the dishes, I mean," he added with a transparent grin Sara could have killed him for. Sold out by her own father. "I sleep like a rock once I'm in my bed."

Sara, still seated, shut her eyes. She felt as if her

father had just placed a For Sale sign on her body and waved it at Nik. At least he hadn't offered a dowry, she thought cynically.

Raymond looked from Nik to his daughter. He could only hope. "Well, good night." He withdrew.

"Night," she muttered darkly without looking in his direction.

"You know," Nik mused out loud, stacking plates on top of one another, "this might be a whole new way to go at the restaurant." He rolled the idea over in his head seriously. "We could have a separate menu for people who have to watch their fat intake." He looked at Sara. "As my accountant, what do you think?"

Sara grabbed the plates and all but sent them crashing as she set them in the sink with a thud. "As your *temporary* accountant, I think that you're overextending yourself by a hell of a margin."

He was actually considering doing it. Her meaning eluded him. "Do you think so? Seems to me that the restaurant—"

She swung around to look at him. "Here," she said fiercely. She enunciated every word, in case he somehow still missed her meaning. "I think you're overextending yourself by being here like this."

The hell with cleaning up the kitchen. He could do it later. Right now there were other things that needed cleaning up a lot more.

Something in his eyes when he looked at her told Sara she should be running for higher ground. The floodwaters were definitely coming.

She stood nailed to the floor.

Throwing the dish towel down, he pulled her to him so suddenly the air whooshed out of her lungs as their bodies made sizzling contact.

"You think that's overextension?" The look in his eyes was half amused and half threatening in the promise they held. "You ain't seen nothing yet."

Sara tried to push him away. Damn, she wasn't a weakling. Why did her arms feel like useless rubber bands now?

"The last time you said that—" she began and then got no further.

He sure as hell hoped that old man slept as soundly as he claimed, because he knew that there was no turning back from this point.

"Yes?"

Words were sticking to her mouth again. And she couldn't force herself to look away from his eyes. It was as if they held her very soul captive.

"You took me to bed."

He cupped her cheek with his hand and gently brushed his fingers along the skin. "There's something about familiarity that breeds a feeling of security."

Panic, cold and hard, seized her. Panic that he would make love to her here and now. Panic that he wouldn't. "But not for me."

"Then we won't make it all that familiar," he told Sara.

Each time they made love, Nik promised himself, it would be different. An exploration to find something new in territory that was well-known and well loved.

What was she doing? How could she just capitulate this way? Sara scrambled to regain ground.

"But—"

Whatever else she was going to say melted away like snowflakes on a hot stove as he put his hands on her. Nothing more, just that. His hands on her shoulders and his eyes on hers.

And she was his.

She knew it was weak and that she would live to regret it. But she had already made up her mind to leave within a week. Her father's doctor's appointment was on Friday. He was recovering rapidly. She could see it. There was no excuse to remain any longer after that.

This one last time, she let herself give in to what she'd been yearning for all week. This madness of the blood that was no good for her.

He pressed a kiss to her neck. Shards of pleasure slashed recklessly all through her.

"Where's your room?" he whispered against her throat.

"In the back." He felt her words vibrate along his mouth, exciting him.

Her father's room was off the living room and faced the front of the house. "Then we won't be disturbing your father." It wasn't a question.

She could only shake her head mutely. The only one he would be disturbing, ultimately, was her.

## Chapter 15

He'd thought that the first time would be the most important and that nothing else could ever compare to it. He was wrong. Each time he made love with Sara would be just as precious, if not more so, than the last, no matter how long he lived.

No matter how many times he made love with her.

Nik wanted to give her the world, wrapped up in shiny paper and bound in bright ribbons.

He had only himself.

It didn't seem nearly enough. He wanted to give her something special, to somehow wipe away the sadness, the tinge of distrustfulness in her eyes that always lingered there, even when passion shone, full bloom.

He wanted to make her his. Forever.

Nik closed Sara's bedroom door behind him. He didn't bother turning around. He couldn't take his eyes off Sara.

He could hear her breath catch when he touched her face. It was impossibly erotic.

Softly, as if she would melt at the slightest contact, he brought his lips down to hers. Her sigh of acceptance had his blood surging through his veins like the end of the *1812 Overture.*

Urgency battered him like waves against the shore, demanding satisfaction.

But he managed to maintain control. He swore to himself that she would never know anything but kindness from him. Someone had obviously hurt her. He was never going to chance Sara confusing him with that man, even for a moment. He'd leave her rather than risk that ever happening.

Where was the strength that she was so proud of? Where in heaven's name was her resilience? Why did everything dissolve to liquid when he touched her? Why did she silently vow to relinquish everything she believed in, everything she knew to be true, just so that he would touch her again?

She was betraying herself for the price of a kiss.

Sara had no answers. And the questions were fading. All she wanted was for Nik to make love to her, to make love *with* her. To completely surround her until he was her walls, her ceiling, her floor.

Sara almost cried with joy as she felt his hands move over her body, caressing her, revering her. Making her burst into flame as he gathered her to him.

If she was any closer she'd be through him, and yet, it wasn't close enough.

It would never be close enough.

She dug her hands into his shoulders, trying to absorb him as his mouth laid siege to hers with an abandonment she reveled in.

Nik cupped her head and drew her away. He looked at her, his own breathing ragged and echoing in the silent room. The rise and fall of her breasts against his chest was driving him crazy.

"Oh, God, Sara, this was all I could think about all week. Just being with you again like this."

Sara vainly sought control. He had it all. "Before or after you seasoned the Stroganoff?"

Nik slid his tongue along her ear and enjoyed the shiver it evoked. From both of them.

"Before," he swore, his breath hot along her skin. "Way before."

Dear God, she was going to make a fool of herself and tear his clothes off right here and now. She wanted him. Wanted to be with him. Joined for all eternity. "No food metaphors?"

Her voice was thick with desire. It matched his own. "None. Nothing but you, Sara." He looked into her eyes and saw his reflection there. He was her prisoner. "Always you."

She would have sold her soul to believe that. But she knew better.

Knew...

She didn't know anything except that she needed him. Now.

Nik slid his hands down her spine. Bunching the hem of her T-shirt in his fingers, he began to lift it from her body. Sara raised her arms for him, her eyes never leaving his. There was such love there, it made her ache.

*It fades, Sara. Love fades. Promises fade.* Her mother's voice echoed in her brain.

Nik tossed aside Sara's shirt. "You're not wearing a bra," he murmured even as he cupped her breasts in his hands.

Her skin tingled, first hot, then cold. "I never seemed to get around to putting it on this morning."

He felt intoxicated by her scent. It was strong and arousing. Her body flowed through his hands, hot, moist, ready. He caressed, coaxed, worshiped. Her shorts snapped open readily beneath his fingers just as she tugged at his jeans.

Hands urgent, seeking, shed clothing quickly. Material fell to the floor and tangled, a silent prophecy.

Both nude, they tumbled onto Sara's bed, arms and legs entwined as their lips were sealed to one another. Hearts made silent promises, beating wildly as they rolled together. Each sought the comforting feel of the other. Each wanted to please and thus be pleased.

His mouth was everywhere, causing tiny earthquakes along her body.

She tasted of desire, dark and alluring. He could have feasted on her for a year and never sated his appetite. He filled himself with her until all that he tasted, smelled and felt was Sara.

She felt his tongue flitter teasingly around her nipple, hardening it instantly. As she moaned, he moved to the other breast. Agony and ecstasy played for control of her, each winning, each taking.

She was almost gasping now as she arched against him. She desperately wanted to do this to him, to make him spiral off into the darkness, searching for the light, just as he did to her.

But he was too quick for her. Too quick and too clever, and she could only hang on to the sides of the roller coaster that had her soaring up and then plunging down.

Her stomach quivered as she felt his mouth trail along her skin. Stars burst through her brain as she felt Nik bring his mouth to her very core. With a muffled cry she felt herself free-falling through space, riding the crest of an explosion. Nik needed only to touch her to set them off.

All he had ever needed to do was touch her, right from the beginning.

Sara grabbed fistfuls of her comforter as Nik wove his magic again. And again. She felt herself hurtling upward and then slowly being let down. She was in a million pieces, bright and glowing like the stars in the sky.

Her arms felt limp. *She* felt limp. It was all she could do to pry her eyes open and look at him. Gravity was fighting her for control of each lid.

It took her a moment before she found the strength to even form words. "Are we still on earth?"

"Just barely."

Nik's body whispered against hers as he slid along the bed until his face was level with hers.

He loved looking at her, loved seeing the different emotions play across her face. Wonder, desire, need. And ecstasy. Ecstasy had to be his favorite. Because he had created it for her, offering it to her like a bouquet of the rarest of roses.

He brushed the hair from her cheek. "The next time," he promised, "we're going to make love someplace where there isn't anyone else around."

*There isn't going to be a next time.*

Sara tried to focus her mind on what he was saying. "Why?"

He rolled on top of her, balancing himself on his elbows. Looking into her eyes. "Because I want to hear you call out my name when I make love with you."

She slid her tongue slowly along her lips. She saw

raw desire flame in his eyes. "Nik." It was barely a whisper. It was all she could manage.

He shook his head, curling his fingers along her cheek. "With more feeling."

She smiled then. It was so genuine, so guileless it took his breath away. "That would require more air in my lungs, and you stole it from me."

"Then we're even."

He laced his hands with hers as he positioned himself over her. Sara parted her legs for him, her heart hammering wildly in anticipation.

His mouth covered hers when he entered her. Nik felt her sharp intake of breath on his tongue, tasted it in his mouth.

It excited him beyond belief.

He couldn't help himself. He'd sworn that he would make love to her slowly, patiently, but he broke his promise to both of them. Passion rose up and seized him so tightly in the palm of its hand that all he could do was give in to it.

The rhythm it evoked took him and he rode her hard. That she met him movement for movement only increased his ardor.

In a final burst over the summit, they found their salvation together.

Exhausted, Nik could only muster enough energy to slide to the side so that he wouldn't crush her. The way he felt right now, his elbows couldn't even begin to support his weight.

*Please, I want this feeling to go on. Please.*

But even as Sara prayed, she could feel the euphoria leaving her, taking with it its protective cloak. The cloak that kept reality away. She shivered.

He could feel her withdrawing even though she hardly moved. *Why, Sara? Why?*

Nik turned his face toward her and managed to keep the concern from his eyes. He pressed a kiss to her forehead. "That was a nice overture. If you give me a minute, the curtain will go up on the main performance."

Their eyes inches apart, Sara stared at him incredulously. She felt as if all of her had been reduced to the consistency of overcooked tapioca pudding. Not being a physical weakling, she'd assumed that he would be in a similar condition.

"You're kidding."

Nik grinned at the unabashed wonder in her voice. He managed to raise himself up on one elbow. The vantage point served to inspire him. He had a better view of her this way. And he would never tire of looking at her.

"There are two things, I promise you, that I will never kid about."

She ran the tip of her finger over his lips. "Food," she guessed as a smile lifted the corners of her mouth.

He barely nodded. "And making love with you." He pressed her fingers to his lips and kissed them with such feeling that desire was instantly reborn in her. "Not necessarily in that order."

He believed it, she thought. At least for now. And for now, so did she.

Tomorrow there would be other truths, the way there were for her parents. The way it was for her mother. But tomorrow was still a long way off. And she still had most of tonight.

Sara slipped her hands around his neck. "Put your money where your mouth is."

He laughed softly, gathering her to him. "I'd rather put my mouth where you are."

She shifted her hands through his hair, memorizing every moment, every texture, every taste, and filing it away. For tomorrow and all the empty tomorrows that would follow. "Nobody's stopping you."

*For now,* she thought silently.

And then Sara ceased thinking at all.


"Pretty good news, eh, Sara?" Feeling like a million dollars, Raymond leaned back in the car and let a sigh of relief escape.

Sara had just spent the past forty-five minutes with her father at his cardiologist's. The doctor had given him a very favorable prognosis. From all indications—after the extensive tests that had been performed both at the hospital and in his office—it appeared, Dr. Brice told them, that Raymond Santangelo would probably outlive him.

Sara grinned. There was no need to feign her relief. "The best."

Raymond watched the scenery pass by with the renewed appreciation of a man who had been given a second chance. When he thought of the years he had wasted...

But all that was in the past. He had the rest of his life to enjoy things.

He turned to Sara. "I don't mind telling you that I was pretty worried back there." He saw concern crease Sara's brow, and he hurried to explain. "I mean, I was feeling okay, but you never know...." His voice drifted off as he thought about it.

"I was feeling pretty much okay before the operation, too. Right up until the last week or so." A self-deprecating smile curved his lips as he remembered. "I guess, looking back, it was a pretty lucky thing I talked to Madigan."

Sara eased her way out of the medical complex and turned onto a main thoroughfare just as the signal turned red. "Kane?"

Raymond turned to see if any policeman was in sight. His daughter's driving methods weren't exactly orthodox. "Yeah. Nik's brother-in-law."

She wondered if it was her imagination or if her father had placed extra emphasis on Nik's name. "What's he got to do with it?"

"Everything," Raymond said emphatically. "He's the one who made me go to the doctor." He laughed dryly. "Gave me the option of going on my own or going on report. He doesn't mince words."

Sara brought the car to a semihalt at the red stop sign, glanced both ways and continued going. Her father frowned at the California stop, but he was feeling too good to reprimand her.

"No, he doesn't," she agreed. "I guess I owe him my thanks."

Raymond laughed as he thought of Kane's receptiveness to that. "His kind doesn't take well to being thanked. Just like Nik." He stole a look at his daughter's profile. "You know, with this clean bill of health the doctor just gave me, maybe we could take Nik up on his offer."

Sara raised a brow in her father's direction as she entered the residential tract. "What offer?"

"You remember," he coaxed. "To stop by the restaurant for some tetrazzini. We're all out." Yesterday he had finished the last of the leftovers from the food that Nik had brought him.

Sara nodded, vividly remembering everything about that evening. She smiled at her father. "You're free to do anything you want, Sergeant Santangelo."

Raymond looked at Sara wistfully. "I thought that maybe we could go as a family."

She felt a touch of guilt for what she was planning. "You and me?"

His response was immediate and eager. "Yeah." *And Nik.* When Sara didn't answer, he sighed. "I guess that's not much of a family."

She wondered if her father was feeling genuine remorse, or if perhaps, just perhaps, he was attempting to manipulate her.

In any event, she answered honestly. "I told you once, Dad, just the two of us would have been more than enough for me." She smiled as she looked at him. She was glad she had come. Glad she had made her peace with him. "It still is."

"Then it's a date?"

Sara shook her head. Her mind was made up and she couldn't allow herself to change it. Or to postpone what what she had to do. It was going to be hard enough as it was. "No."

"But—"

Sara took a deep breath, fortifying herself for what she was going to say. "I said I'd only stay until you were well."

"Um, you know—" he rubbed his chest in small, concentric circles "—there *is* this tightness in my chest that I didn't want to mention."

Sara grinned. "Uh-huh. You're a great cop, but a lousy actor, Dad."

Raymond laid his hand on her arm. Even his touch

implored her. "Stay, Sara." When she turned to look at him, he said, "This isn't acting."

She knew that. And there was an ache in her heart because she had to refuse him. "I can't."

They had made their peace. It wasn't him she was leaving. "Is it Nik?"

Eyes back on the road, Sara nodded solemnly. "Yes."

He didn't understand. Everything he'd witnessed had told him that they cared about one another. He knew Nik cared about Sara. It was evident in the way he looked at her.

"I would think he'd be a reason to stay."

"Maybe," she agreed, trying not to think about Nik at all, "if I were like everyone else."

Sara turned into her father's driveway. She shut off the engine, but neither of them made a move to leave the car.

Touching her cheek, Raymond turned her face until she looked at him. "I've always thought of you as special, Sara," he said gently. "But not stupid."

"And you think leaving Nik is stupid." She wasn't asking. It was a foregone conclusion. She could tell by her father's expression.

"Hell, yes." He couldn't say it emphatically enough. "Men like Nik don't grow on trees."

A smile quirked Sara's mouth as she remembered another conversation, pressed in the pages of time. A conversation that had gone on to form the rest of her life. "That's what Mom once said about you."

Raymond suddenly understood. "Sara, don't let my mistakes mess up your life."

*Too late,* she thought. All she could do was smile in response.

Raymond took both of his daughter's hands in his. He suddenly felt very helpless. "Everyone's different, Sara. Nik isn't me. Nik doesn't have private demons he's a slave to."

It wasn't a demon she was worried about. She could handle flaws, *expected* flaws. It was the inevitable that terrified her. Seeing Nik walk away from her someday would be more than she could bear.

But her father's declaration had her curious. "How do you know?"

Raymond shrugged. "I had him checked out."

Sara looked at him, stunned. "You what?"

It had seemed like a perfectly natural thing for him to do. "Hey, I'm still on the force, with a lot of connections. Kane gave Nik a glowing report, which is saying a lot for Madigan."

He couldn't read her expression, but he couldn't back out now, even if he wanted to. "Maybe I wanted to catch up on playing 'Dad.' I finally got a chance to butt back in to your life, Sara. Don't have me butting out again."

Uncomfortable, Sara opened the car door and got out. "It's a lot more complicated than you think."

Getting out on his side, Raymond looked at his daughter over the roof of the car. "I can't tell you what to do, Sara."

There was no hostility in her voice, only resignation as to what she had to do. "No, you can't." She walked toward the front door.

Raymond followed her. "But there comes a time when people should stop weighing everything and just take a chance. Something like this might not come again."

She could only make the connection to what her father had espoused before. "You mean luck? Gambling?"

"No, I mean love and yes, gambling. In a way." Falling in love with someone was a gamble. He knew that. "One thing I've learned, Sara, and I learned it a little too late—" he placed his arm around her shoulder "—love's the only game in town that's worthwhile."

For a second she enjoyed the feeling, the closeness that existed between her and her father at this moment. But her mind was already made up. Still, she didn't have the heart to tell him yet. Tonight. She would tell him tonight. When she packed.

"I'll think about it."

"Good." He took out his key. "Think really hard." He unlocked the door and crossed the threshold. "Parents don't want to see their kids make the same mistakes that they did."

"Don't worry," she said quietly, "I won't."

The third time he looked up, Nik realized that he was watching the clock on the wall like a nervous apprentice chef babying his first soufflé. Sara had said that she was taking her father to the doctor first thing in the morning. It was now after eleven. How long did "first thing" take?

Had something gone wrong? The phone hadn't rung. Was he hoping for too much, thinking that she'd call if she needed someone to lean on?

Muttering to himself, he picked up a ladle and stirred the bouillabaisse he had simmering on the stove. When he glanced up in the direction of the clock again, he saw Sara walking by the entrance.

Surprised that she didn't stop in the kitchen to talk

to him, his fingers went lax. The ladle slipped into the huge pot.

"Damn!" Nik made a grab for the spoon. The handle was hot. He yanked his hand back. He'd singed it like a novice. It did nothing for his temper.

Antonio looked over Nik's shoulder, amused. "New ingredient?"

Nik wrapped his fingers in the corner of his apron. They stung and throbbed, but his mind was elsewhere. He nodded toward the pot. "Just get it out."

Using a pot holder, Antonio caught the top of the ladle and drew it out of the pot. He laid it on the stove, then looked at Nik's hand. "I would put some ice on my hand if I were you."

"That's not where it hurts." Nik headed toward the hall.

"Then I would marry her," Antonio called after him, "and take care of that pain, too."

*Easier said than done,* Nik thought.

He stopped in the office doorway. Sara sat with her back to him. He could tell by the set of her shoulders that something was wrong. Did her father need to go back in for more surgery? Had the angioplasty not taken?

"Sara, what's wrong?"

She swung around. She wasn't ready, she thought, her pulse quickening. She would never be ready to say these words.

And yet, she had to.

Sara forced a smile to her face. "Oh, Nik, just the person I wanted to see."

Her voice was strange, Nik thought. Strained. As if she was addressing a stranger she didn't want to talk to. Why?

He sat on the edge of the desk and took her hand. Whatever was wrong, they could face it together. "How's your father?"

Sara flexed her fingers and drew her hand away. "He's fine." She looked up at Nik, reminding herself that all this was for the best. For both of them. No broken hearts to mend down the road, because there wouldn't be any road. "He should be back to work in about six weeks." She smiled, but her heart wasn't in it. "Sooner if he has his way."

"That's good." Why was this sudden feeling of panic clawing at him, making him waltz around her with empty chatter? Damn it, *what was wrong?*

Sara ran her hand over the discs that were neatly boxed in a see-through holder on the desk. "I've gotten all your records brought up-to-date."

He watched her face, waiting for an opening, waiting for a clue. "Congratulations." He measured out the word slowly.

Words began coming in a rush. Sara rose to put distance between them. It felt as if the office was closing in on her. As if her world was closing in on her.

"And I transferred everything to a different program." She twisted her fingers together, hating herself for fidgeting. "It'll make keeping track of the accounting much simpler for you. I've left directions for Jennifer to follow."

Nik didn't move. "You can explain it to her when she comes in tomorrow."

"I'm afraid that's impossible." She said the words to the file cabinet.

"Why?" His voice drew her back around to face him like a woman under a trance.

Sara forced herself to look at him. She owed him that much. "I won't be here tomorrow."

# Chapter 16

Silence hung heavily between them, oppressive and sticky, like an endless Louisiana summer night.

"The day after, then."

His eyes were angry, accusing. She couldn't make herself look away. Guilt warred with fear. "No, I won't be here then, either."

Nik gripped the edge of the desk on either side of him. "Why?"

Each word felt as if it weighed a ton as she forced them from her mouth. She hadn't expected it to be easy, but this was awful, beyond anything she had imagined.

"I'm leaving first thing in the morning. Today's my last day here."

Nik pressed his lips together. His voice was low, tense, like a cat crouching to spring. Sara braced for a verbal attack.

"I see. Just like that?"

How *could* she? he thought. She loved him. He knew

she loved him. He wasn't the type to delude himself, to imagine things that weren't true just to feed his own ego. She *did* love him. How could she just turn away and leave?

The accusation in Nik's voice made Sara defensive. She knew she had to push hard if she was going to push him away. "Look, Nik, I don't like permanency. I thought that was understood. I like moving around, I like change. Frequent change."

She took a deep breath, but she was going to need more than oxygen to fortify herself, to provide the courage to say what she had to say. "You knew that this was just temporary." She waved a hand around the room, taking in the computer, the office. Them. "We both agreed to that."

They had agreed on a lot of things, albeit silently, he thought. He searched her face for a clue as to why she was suddenly fleeing, but there was a shield up, keeping him out.

"That was before things began going so well." He pinned her with a look, daring her to deny it. "Until you came along, I didn't think I could give up control." He allowed just the tips of his fingers to glide along her cheek. He saw the muscle there quiver. "I find that I can. Very easily."

Sara moved aside. She couldn't allow him to touch her again. Her resolve would break if he did. "That's very flattering, but I think it's time for me to get on with my life."

Her words couldn't have hurt more if they'd been tiny sharpened knives. "I thought that was what you *were* doing."

Until she had come into his life, he hadn't thought that he would ever fall in love. But he had. Deeply. He was prepared to beg her to stay if he had to. It wasn't his style, but this was about more than pride. This was about a lifetime. Sara had heaped those words at him for a reason. She was trying to chase him away. He couldn't let her.

Coming up behind her, he placed his hands on her arms. "Sara, I want you to stay."

She closed her eyes and told herself she wasn't going to cry. "I can't."

His voice was hard when he spoke again. "Can't? Or won't?"

She shrugged out of his hold, but couldn't force herself to look at him. Her voice was cool. It was the performance of her life. "The bottom line is the same. I'll be gone."

The door slammed behind her. She hadn't realized that the sound could be so jarring. Or that her decision would cause her such pain.

Sara crumbled into the chair like a marionette whose strings had been cut. Forcing herself to move, to do *something*, she switched on the computer. There was still some last-minute work to finish up. Pride wouldn't let her leave before that was done. She never left things unfinished.

Except her own life.

The words she had spoken to Nik had tasted raw, foul in her mouth when she'd uttered them. But they had to be said. She had to get away, now, before she couldn't at all. Before it was too late.

The screen before her opened, waiting for a command. Tears made her lashes heavy, blinding her. Sara blinked them back, then rubbed her streaked face with the heel of her hand. Focusing on only her work, going on automatic pilot, she hit a combination of keys. The message on the screen asked her to please wait.

"I can't," she whispered. "I can't."

It wasn't easy this time, picking up and going. Not like all the other times. She'd never been this entangled before.

She'd never been in love before.

Sara leaned her elbows on the desk and covered her mouth with her fingers, holding back a sob that threatened to escape.

Maybe just this once, she could—

*No.*

Her fear that their relationship would progress to its natural conclusion outweighed everything else. Above all else, she didn't want to experience the pain she had seen in her mother's eyes.

It had been bad enough to endure her parents' divorce as a child. To watch her own marriage disintegrate, as she knew it inevitably would, would totally destroy her. She couldn't risk it. Sure, she could hope that it wouldn't end up the way so many other marriages had, but all the hope in the world wouldn't insulate her heart, wouldn't keep it from breaking, if Nik left her.

Her hands felt icy. It was as if all the blood, all the life had drained out of her. She rubbed her hands on her jeans, trying to get the circulation moving.

But what would get circulation moving again in her heart?

This was for the best. It was, she insisted adamantly. She had made up her mind a long time ago that it was better to do without love than know what it was to love someone, to be loved by someone and then be deprived of it. Sara knew that she couldn't have coped with Nik

walking away from her. If he looked at her someday
and said he didn't love her anymore.

It was better *this* way.

So if she was doing the right thing, why did it feel
so wrong?

The message on the screen read Error, Try Again.

"A lot you know," she whispered, her throat raw
with tears she was holding back.


Nik had avoided her all day.

Sara had seen him only once today, and he had
looked the other way. A part of her, a small, childlike
part, had hoped, had wanted him to grab her by the
shoulders and shake her until she changed her decision.

It was all just a fantasy, just like their nights together
had been. If he had tried to talk her out of it, she knew
nothing would have changed. She would still leave at
the end of the day. She had to.

But, oh, God, she wanted to feel that he did love her.

*Better this way, better,* the computer seemed to hum
as Sara typed in the final line.

She stared at it. That was it, she thought. Finished.
Everything was up-to-date and running. She was finished. She'd left clear notes for Jennifer to follow when
she took over. There was no reason for her to linger at
Sinclair's any longer.

No reason at all. Leaning over, Sara switched off the
computer.

*Get up, Sara, it's time to go.*

Sara remained seated in front of the computer.

She cursed Nik's soul for doing this to her. Every
other time when she'd left a job, it was to go to something else. She'd always felt as if another adventure
would be waiting for her on the horizon. A new start.

Anticipation would pump through her veins. She would look forward to whatever lay ahead, always forward. Never back.

Now she felt as if she was fleeing, running *from* rather than running *to*.

There was nothing to run to anymore. Her life was behind her. Nik had brought her face-to-face with the pattern her life had taken on and she didn't like it.

Sara took a deep breath and squared her shoulders. *The man has got you turned inside out. You'll be a basket case inside of a month. Time to hit the road, Sara, girl.*

"You okay, Nikolas?"

Antonio placed his hand on Nik's arm. Concern etched its way into the fine lines about the man's mouth and eyes. He had watched Nik bang pots and snap at people and then apologize all through lunch and dinner. There was just so much pain a man should be required to take.

No, no, he wasn't okay, Nik thought belligerently. He'd lost his temper this morning and then told himself that maybe this was for the best, after all. Let her go. Who the hell wanted to love a crazy woman, anyway? Eight hours later the answer was still the same. He did.

Nik turned angry eyes on Antonio, hardly seeing the man. "Yeah, why?"

Antonio thanked his patron saint that he wasn't the recipient of the harnessed fury he saw in Nik's eyes. He had never seen Nik like this.

"Ginger said that she was leaving today. Sara," Antonio added needlessly. He nodded toward the hall and the office beyond.

Determination made the planes of Nik's face stand out. He knew what he had to do. "She thinks she is."

Nik glanced at his watch, even though he was standing directly in front of the clock. She was still in the office, despite the fact that her workday had ended hours ago. She didn't want to go any more than he wanted her to.

Antonio looked from the doorway to Nik's face. There was a fight brewing. "You want me to lock up?"

Nik stripped his apron off like a retired gunfighter about to put on his holster. His eyes never left the doorway. "Yeah."

Antonio caught the apron Nik tossed aside as he strode out of the kitchen. "The best ones are not gotten easily, Nik."

"Then she must be a hell of a prize." But then, he already knew that.

Nik glanced at Antonio over his shoulder. The other man smiled and held up his thumb in the universal signal of confidence.

"My money is on you, Nik."

*Let's hope that's enough,* Nik thought.

As he approached the office Nik forced himself to calm down. Sara had taught him things about himself he hadn't realized. In arguing against the need for her services in the first place, and then resisting the revamping of his accounting program, he'd finally been forced to see that he'd been too obsessive about controlling all facets of the restaurant. The grasp he had maintained on it had been his way of coping with his parents' death. It was his way of trying to be in control of life in general. The restaurant was his microcosm and he was the ruler.

But it wasn't that easy. Nothing ever was.

He realized that he couldn't control his own fate. But he sure as hell had an option in choosing the path he took through life.

And he wanted it to be with Sara.

It was time to smell a few roses. Nik fully intended to smell them with her at his side.

His temper sufficiently under control, Nik looked in. Sara was still in the office. She was just sitting at her desk, staring at the computer screen. The computer wasn't on.

*Here goes everything.*

Nik walked in. "That was me, four weeks ago." He swept his hand to include both Sara and the dormant computer. "Except at the time, there was this miserable white line running across the screen." He dragged his finger along the monitor to illustrate. "Telling me that I had killed the program."

She had barely refrained from jumping when Nik walked in. She managed to compose herself. She had to.

If she just kept talking about business, she could get through this.

"I don't think you can kill this one. It's geared for the busy executive who doesn't have time to fool around with a lot of steps."

"Nothing like not having to fool around with steps." He eyed her for so long she almost screamed. "You about ready to go?"

Was he going to push her out the door? Had she hurt him that much that he wanted to be rid of her as soon as possible?

Sara searched his face. There wasn't a single trace of hurt evident. Her heart sank even deeper into the abyss it had fallen into.

But there was something there, in his eyes. Something she couldn't quite understand.

Nameless, it made her nervous.

"Yes, as a matter of fact, I am." She pushed away from the desk. "Everything's all here, just the way I found it." She indicated the file cabinet. "Just neater."

Fumbling inwardly, Sara picked up her purse. She clutched it against her like a poultice whose function was to suck out the poison from a wound.

She cleared her throat. "Well, I'd better go tell everyone goodbye."

Sara turned toward the door. Nik caught her arm, stopping her. Sara looked at him quizzically, confused. There were so many signals bouncing within the confines of the room she didn't know which one to believe.

Nik's expression was mild, as if he were talking to a casual acquaintance. "Why don't we take a walk on the beach first?"

It was dark on the beach. Dark and intimate. Just like the first time. Sara knew she should just refuse. "Why?"

Nik shrugged carelessly, glancing over his shoulder at the window. His hand remained on her arm. "It's a nice night."

Sara tried to dig in. She knew being strong was her only hope. She shook her head. "I don't have the time, Nik—"

His fingers moved along her arm, creating tidal waves within her. Resistance began to drown.

"After tonight—" he looked at her meaningfully "—you'll have all the time in the world. We both will."

Maybe he wasn't as unscathed by her leaving as she'd first thought. Panic began erecting building blocks of trepidation within her.

Sara bit her lip uncertainly, torn between common sense and needs. "Nik…"

If nothing else, he still knew how to goad her. "Afraid?"

She raised her head, her eyes narrowing. "No," she lied.

"Good." He ushered her out into the hallway. The faint shuffle of retreating footsteps told Nik that Antonio had eavesdropped on them. He didn't care. Privacy wasn't an issue. Winning Sara was. "Then let's go."

Rather than walk through the restaurant to the front door, Nik led Sara out the back entrance. Maybe privacy *was* an issue, he thought. He didn't want to share her with anyone else.

He wasn't saying anything, just walking. The quiet was making her crazy. She felt like a settler waiting for the Indians to attack at dawn's first light. Nerves were tangling into an intricate web within her.

*Say something, damn you.*

He just continued walking beside her.

Sara swallowed. She shouldn't have come. "I also arranged your files so that it will be easier for you to pull up records when you have to pay taxes."

Nik didn't even look at her. His profile was impassive. "Very efficient of you."

Sara looked down at the sand beneath her feet. Tiny drifts swarmed around her sneakers with each step. "I thought so."

The conversation fell, stillborn, right next to her feet in the sand.

She wanted to hit him. She wanted to run back and get into her car.

She didn't know what she wanted.

The silence hung on as they walked. The sea, mildly

restless, teased the shoreline like a flirtatious Southern belle, lifting skirts of foam before retreating. Somewhere in the distance Sara heard a girl giggle.

She squinted, trying to discern shapes in the moonlight. She saw two teenagers, a boy and a girl, running on the beach some distance from them. The boy was chasing the girl. Laughing, she was no match for him. When he caught her they both tumbled down on the sand, oblivious to everything but each other.

Aching, remembering, Sara looked away.

Moonlight outlined her profile. It had been all he could do not to take her into his arms from the first moment they had been alone. Nik continued walking and stared straight ahead. He'd hoped that some sort of magic words would occur to him to make her change her mind.

But nothing came.

He stopped and turned to her, blocking her way. "Marry me, Sara."

Sara blinked, certain she had misheard. Praying that she had misheard. *Don't make me say no.* "What did you say?"

Uncertainty rippled through him, like the winter wind through the top branches of a tree. She was going to say no. He could feel it. "Marry me, Sara."

Instead of answering him, Sara turned away and began to cry.

Nothing hurt more than the sound of her sobs. Nik forced her around to face him again. Anger and pain mingled in his words. "I asked you to marry me, not jump off a cliff."

She sniffed, desperately trying to brazen her way through. "Same thing."

His eyes swept over her face. *Why?* He didn't understand. And he wasn't going to let her go until he did. "Do I frighten you that much?"

She shook her head, her eyes downcast. "No. *You* don't."

His patience was at an end. "Then—?"

Sara raised her eyes to his face again. "The future does."

Was it just a matter of terminally cold feet? He almost laughed. "Sara, nobody knows what the future holds. But that doesn't mean we can't try to grab a little bit of happiness along the way."

He didn't understand the huge, bottomless fear that existed within her. And she didn't have the words to make him.

"I can't. The consequences are too great."

Nik threw up his hands as his voice rose. "What consequences?" Out of the corner of his eye he saw the two teenagers withdraw.

Lowering his voice, Nik struggled to be understanding. "Sara, if there was someone in your life who hurt you, tell me," he implored. "I need to know who I'm fighting, *what* I'm fighting, because damn it, I *am* going to fight." He took her into his arms. "I'm not letting you leave my life like this."

Sara couldn't talk. Instead, she buried her face against his shoulder. Silent tears wet his shirt. Nik held her close, stroking her hair. "If some man—"

She had to stop this, she upbraided herself. "It wasn't a man. Not entirely."

Nik thought of his sister's date rape. It had taken Julia years to leave the shadow of fear behind her. Nik took Sara by the shoulders and gently drew her away. "Sara, tell me. Who?"

She didn't want to. She had never really gone into

how badly she had been scarred. Not even with Brom. "My father. And my mother."

It made absolutely no sense to him. And then, suddenly, it did. "The divorce?"

She nodded. She tried to pull away, but his hold was firm. Binding. Because she was suddenly so tired she couldn't resist. "I don't want that kind of hurt."

"We're not even married yet and you've already got us divorcing. Was the honeymoon good?" He tried to make light of it, but it was difficult for him. He couldn't understand throwing away everything because of what *might* be. "Sara, one step at a time."

"I can't take that step. I'd rather not travel the road at all than take that last step." She closed her eyes and pressed her lips together, helpless. Just as she had been then. Helpless to ease her mother's pain.

Nik didn't say anything. He just held her. It was all he could do.

"I thought my parents had a great marriage. When it broke up, I guess I kind of went into shock." She felt his hands on her, felt his strength. She drew it to her and continued.

"My father was the greatest guy in the world and he walked out on us, walked out on his promise to love my mother until death did them part. If he couldn't stay, why should you?"

"Sara—"

She shook her head, determined to finish. "My mother went all to pieces for a whole year. There wasn't anything I could do for her, except listen. She'd just sit around and stare into space for hours at a time. She'd talk about how she had watched her love die."

Sara raised her face to Nik. He saw that it was bright with tears. He stroked them away with his thumb.

"She once told me that when she first fell in love with my father, every day felt like Christmas inside of her. That joy, that expectation of being with someone you loved was like Christmas for her."

Sara bit her lip, remembering the look on her mother's face. "And then, slowly, that feeling faded. It wasn't Christmas anymore. When they divorced, she cried in my arms. She said all she wanted was for that feeling to come back. And it never did."

Sara took a deep breath, putting her hands up against Nik's chest. She needed to drive a physical wedge between them. He was filling up all of her space and she hadn't the strength to break free. He had to release her.

"I saw the ache in her eyes, the agony." She had to make him understand. "I don't know what I'd do if I lost you."

It made less than no sense to him. "So instead of losing me, you're throwing me away instead? Sara, don't you see, *that* doesn't make any sense."

She tried to pull away, but he wouldn't let her. Like a trapped animal she railed at him. "I'd rather feel empty than heartbroken."

He cupped her cheek with his hand, looking into her eyes. "And how do you feel now?"

There was no point in lying. She knew he could see the truth in her eyes. "Miserable."

He drove his hands through her hair, framing her face. She was too precious to lose. Pigheaded, but precious. Now that he had taken her into his heart, there was no way he was going to let ghosts from the past steal their happiness. "So what have you gained by running away?"

Defeated, drained, Sara slumped against him, her head resting against his shoulder. "A headache."

Nik smiled to himself in the moonlight as he absorbed her warmth into his body. "Stay, Sara," he whispered into her hair. "Stay."

She wavered, wanting to remain more than she had ever wanted anything else in her life. But fear tugged at her with both hands. "I'm afraid, Nik."

He knew that it was the most difficult admission she had ever made. "It doesn't have to be that way for us. Love doesn't have to die."

"But what if it does?" she persisted, wanting him to find a way to assure her, wanting him to make her fears disappear. "It did for my parents. Can you promise me Christmas every day?"

He could lie, but she would know it wasn't the truth. And if it was going to survive, their relationship had to be built on a solid foundation, not a layer of deceit.

"No, I can't." He took her hands and held them tightly in his. "Because if Christmas was every day, then it wouldn't be Christmas any more. It wouldn't be special." He looked into her eyes to see if she understood what he was trying to say. "Married life is made up of good days and bad days. Besides," he added with a smile, "the Fourth of July and New Year's Eve are pretty terrific, too."

She wanted to believe him with her whole heart and soul. All she needed was a little more…

"Yes, I guess they are."

She was coming around. Nik felt himself back on solid ground. "I promise to love you on Groundhog Day and leap year day and every other day, as well."

His lips feathering along her face, he kissed each lid shut and absorbed her sigh into his heart. His face grew serious. "I won't let you walk out of my life because of something that 'might' happen."

She knew he meant it. That he was willing to fight for her rather than just let her go dissolved the last of her resistance.

"I can't promise you that I won't lose my temper, or be stubborn. Or that there won't be times when I get so totally wrapped up in what I'm doing that I seem to ignore you. And we'll argue." He anticipated her reaction. "Arguing's healthy, Sara," he soothed. "It clears the air. For love."

He looked into her face and fell in love all over again. "What I *can* promise you is that I will always love you, no matter what." He laughed softly. "Hell, I love you now and you're being as stubborn as a mule."

She was crying again. But this time they were tears of happiness. Her mother had been unreasonable to expect that everything would always be perfect. Sara knew that things couldn't ever be perfect, but she also knew that they would be as perfect as humanly possible. With Nik.

She smiled at him through her tears. "I guess I can't ask for more than that."

"Sure you can." He held her closer. "You can ask for me."

"I'm asking."

Sara threw her arms around his neck as she kissed him. The surge within her was instantaneous. She realized with a sigh that she had finally come home.

The surge grew into a burst of joy. The kind, she suddenly remembered, that she used to experience on Christmas when her family was all around her.

For them, she thought, just before his kiss swept her away, Christmas wouldn't be every day. But just sharing every day with him would be enough.

# *Epilogue*

Nik walked through the arched doorway that led from his recently remodeled kitchen into the living room. He grinned as he stopped and allowed himself to drink in one of the more pleasing views of his wife. Sara was standing on the top step of the three-tiered step stool, her posterior directly at Nik's eye level.

Standing on her toes, she was precariously leaning into their ten-foot Christmas tree, adjusting one of the numerous tiny lights that decorated it like a swarm of brightly colored fireflies.

Going with his impulse, Nik slowly slid his hands up along her hips until he grasped her waist. It occurred to him that she felt just the tiniest bit thicker here. But it didn't matter. It just meant that there was more of her to love.

As if he could possibly love her any more than he already did.

Sara looked over her shoulder. She tried to sound stern, but her heart wasn't in it. She was too happy. "You almost made me fall."

"I'm always here to catch you." Still holding her, he cocked his head and surveyed the tree. They had spent two days decorating it, with Sara issuing orders like a hardened drill sergeant. Nik had begun to wonder if she intended it to become a permanent fixture in their living room. "How long are you going to keep fussing with that thing?"

She frowned as she turned around again. Screwing in a fresh red bulb, she pocketed the dead one. "There was a light out."

Nik laughed. "The tree has over three thousand lights on it, Sara. Trust me, nobody'll notice if one's out."

He lifted her from the step stool and let the length of her body slide over his until her feet touched the floor again.

Sara smiled up at Nik, savoring the sensations he had ignited.

"Mmm, don't start anything we can't finish." Her arms still laced around his neck, Sara angled her wrist to look at her watch. It was later than she thought. "Everyone will be here in a few minutes."

He loved the way her eyes half closed when desire seeped into her body. "We could lock them out and have them stand outside for an hour or so." His fingers ran seductively along her sides. "It's pretty mild out."

Sara brushed a kiss on his lips, then disentangled herself from his arms. "Seriously, I want everything to be just right." She was almost beaming, he thought. "This is my first family Christmas in years."

Jennifer and Julia were both coming for Christmas

Eve with their families. And Sara's father had promised to join them. The house was going to be full of people and noise any moment now.

Nik cherished the quiet. And her. "Have I told you lately that I love you?"

Sara smiled, anticipating Nik's reaction to the surprise she had for him. The one she had barely managed to keep to herself. "Not today. Are you taking me for granted?"

The room echoed with his laugh. "After what I had to go through to win you over? Not in a million years."

Unable to wait any longer, Sara picked up a small package from under the Christmas tree. It was wrapped with shiny blue foil that had whimsical angels dancing over it. Curly blue ribbon streamed down from both sides. She handed the package to Nik.

"Would you like to open one of your gifts a little early?"

He took the box in his hands, but his eyes were on her. "You?"

Sara laughed. He was so dear to her. The electric lights from the tree took his image and splashed it over the surface of the multicolored balls until there were dozens of Niks all over. She could never get enough of him.

"That's later," she promised. She touched the box. "I meant this."

Old habit had him shaking the box. It didn't make a single telltale sound. "That's cheating." He said the words solemnly, then grinned like a small boy with a secret. "Maybe I'll make an exception this once."

Sara held her breath as his fingers tangled in the ribbon.

The doorbell rang. "Foiled again." Nik handed the box back to her. "I'll go see who it is."

Swallowing her disappointment, Sara let the box drop to the cream sofa as she followed him to the door. "As if we didn't know."

Nik threw open the front door. The simple action set off a chain reaction. Seven people came trooping in, one at a time. Packages, greetings and warm embraces all mixed together in a swirl of affection and holiday cheer.

Surprised, Sara hugged her father. "Dad, I thought you were coming later." She took his heavy sheepskin jacket and folded it over her arm.

"So did I." He nodded at Kane as he placed his contributions to the holiday loot beneath the tree. "But the detective outranks me."

Kane added to the booty spilling out from under the tree as Jennifer helped Katie off with her coat.

"We decided to save your father from having to drive by himself, and picked him up," Jennifer explained. She shrugged out of her sweater and handed both it and Katie's coat to Sara.

For the moment Sara left all the outerwear she'd collected on the sofa. She looked at Jennifer with concern, empathizing. The baby was due any time now. "Can I get you anything?"

Jennifer shook her head. This was her third time around and she had become a veteran. She knew what to expect. "An extra cup of energy would be nice, but thanks, I'm fine."

"She tried to do everything herself. Again," Kane complained, giving Sara a quick kiss hello.

Jennifer winked at her sister-in-law. "It was a ploy

to get him more involved with decorating the tree and the house.''

"She refuses to believe that I'm all thumbs when it comes to things like that." Kane held up his hands as if that was conclusive evidence.

Julia and Brom were dividing their time equally between Jennifer's house and Nik's during their stay in California. Julia laughed, placing a finely manicured hand on Kane's arm. She looked at Sara. "The house is a veritable winter carnival," she confided. "For a man who's all thumbs, I'd say Handsome's coming along just fine."

Brom edged his way to Sara through the crowd. "And how are you?"

He took Sara's hands in his, pleased at the transformation he had witnessed in his cousin in the past six months. She had bloomed and become the Sara he remembered.

She squeezed his hands. "Never better, Brom." Sara looked over her shoulder at Nik. "Never better."

Brom nodded, releasing her. He stepped over toward Nik, who was down on the floor indulging in a huge hug being bestowed upon him by Katie. "So, married life agrees with you."

Nik rose to his feet. "Yeah." He indicated Sara. "Too bad she doesn't very often." It had taken him a while to convince Sara that arguments between a husband and wife were natural and didn't signal the beginning of the end, but he had finally gotten the point across. Now she argued with relish and abandonment.

Sara smiled confidentially. "I like to keep him on his toes."

"That she does," Jennifer testified, thinking of some of the heated debates that took place at the restaurant.

Nik brought in the tray he had carefully prepared. A variety of hors d'oeuvres covered every inch of it. "Anyone want anything to eat?"

Brom was the first in line. He chose two different hors d'oeuvres, his mouth watering on cue. "Why do you think we came all this way? It certainly wasn't to see your ugly puss again."

Popping the second hors d'oeuvre into his mouth, he made a quick grab for A.J. before she managed to pull the lowest branch of the tree in her effort to steady herself. A.J. had taken her first steps at exactly one week prior to her eleventh month. And all semblance of peace had been forever lost.

Julia rescued her husband and took A.J. into her arms. A.J. protested, squirming. "Hush, honey. Aunt Sara doesn't want to see her ten-foot tree sprawled out all over the floor."

Nik laid his arm around Sara's shoulders as he watched the ebb and flow of family in the room. *His* family. This, he thought, was what life was all about.

"Happy?" He whispered the question against Sara's temple.

She sighed as his warmth rippled through her. "Do you have to ask?" She bent to retrieve the gift he had abandoned when the doorbell rang, and offered it to him again.

She was certainly persistent. Nik studied the package, intrigued. "What is *in* this thing?"

Sara mustered the most innocent look she was capable of. "Only one way to find out. Open it."

The conversation around them mellowed. All eyes turned toward Nik. Sara had made everyone curious.

"Okay." Nik made short work of the ribbons, tossing them to the side.

Katie scooped them up. "Can I wear this, Uncle Nik?" Her tiny brows disappeared beneath the dark bangs. She had the ribbon twined around her fingers.

Nik paused to give his niece's shoulder a tiny squeeze. "I'll have you decked out in ribbons before the night's out," he promised.

Aware that Sara and everyone else was watching him intently, Nik turned his attention to the gift. He sent angels scattering as he tore off the paper. Eager now, he opened the lid. Inside the square box, lying in the center of a bed of red tissue paper, was a white envelope.

"Tickets," he guessed as he plucked the envelope out. He had promised Sara a real honeymoon once they got the time, instead of the weekend they had spent at the Hilton hotel. "Okay, where is it you want to go?"

"Harris Memorial Hospital," Sara couldn't resist saying. "In about six months." She had known for a month now. Suspected for longer. It had been all she could do not to tell him. She had wanted it to be her Christmas present to him.

"What?" Confused, he opened the envelope.

Julia and Jennifer didn't need to see what was in the envelope. They sprang to their feet simultaneously, ready to hug their sister-in-law. Each was patiently restrained by her husband.

Kane and Brom exchanged looks. Both men knew that the moment belonged exclusively to Nik and Sara. They remembered their own good news.

Nik forced himself to focus on the single line of script on the white paper. "Merry Christmas. You're going to be a daddy. Twice. It's twins!" He stared at it for a moment in silence, afraid to believe.

Sara bit her lip. Had she guessed wrong? Was he disappointed? Or worse, angry for some reason? They hadn't really discussed having children. She had just assumed, after watching him with his nieces, that he wanted children of his own.

The next minute the look on Nik's face answered her questions.

He turned to her, awed. "Oh, God, Sara, is it true?"

She breathed a sigh of relief. That was joy in his eyes, not anger. "I never put anything in writing that isn't true."

"Twins?"

*"Twins?"* Raymond cried incredulously, a wide grin slashing his thin face.

She nodded toward both men. "That's what the doctor said."

"Well, you've outdone me," Jennifer said with a laugh.

Elated, Nik swept Sara into his arms, holding her close. "You're not taking the tree down," he warned. From now on she was going to take it easy even if he had to tie her up.

"Are you planning on keeping it up?" She laughed, nodding at the tree.

"Maybe." Nik looked into her eyes. "So that it can be Christmas every day. Officially."

She cupped his face, touched that he had remembered. She looked down at the sheet that he was still holding in his hand. "I guess that's about the best gift I could have given you."

"No."

She looked at him, puzzled.

"The best gift," he said softly, "was you." Nik held up the paper. "But this is a pretty close second."

And then, as the rest of the family looked on, Nik kissed the mother-to-be of his children.

\* \* \* \* \*

Dear Reader,

Few things strike greater terror in a writer's heart than being asked what inspired them to write a particular book, especially a book they wrote ten years ago. I mean, I can barely remember what I had for lunch yesterday and now I'm supposed to remember where I got an idea a decade ago? But in this case, it wasn't a problem and any movie buff who reads *A Very Convenient Marriage* will immediately recognize my inspiration. In *Father Goose*, Cary Grant is the quintessential very, very reluctant hero and Leslie Caron is the just as quintessential uptight schoolteacher. They loathe each other on sight but circumstances force them together and they're soon exchanging insults, slaps and then kisses. They are Goody Two-Shoes and The Filthy Beast, one of the most romantic couples every to grace the silver screen.

Sam and Nikki follow in their footsteps. They hate each other on sight and, as any romance reader knows, that's the surest first step to true love.

I hope you enjoy reading the book half as much as I enjoyed writing it!

*Dallas Schulze*

# A VERY
# CONVENIENT MARRIAGE
## Dallas Schulze

# *Chapter 1*

"Let me get this straight. You're suggesting that it's a good idea for me to marry a woman I've never laid eyes on?" Sam Walker leaned back in the big leather chair and gave the man sitting behind the desk a look that questioned his sanity. "You're kidding, right?"

"Do I look like I'm kidding?" Max Devlin braced his elbows on his desk and leaned forward, his dark eyes intent. "This is the perfect solution to both problems."

"Perfect solution?" Sam raised one eyebrow. "Marrying a woman I've never met? I think you've been spending too many hours reading legal briefs and not enough time in the real world. In the real world, people do not marry people they don't know."

"You might be surprised. When they get divorced, it turns out that they didn't really know each other as well as they thought."

"Don't get philosophical on me. You know what I mean. I've never even *seen* this woman."

"What difference does that make?" Max asked impatiently. "I'm suggesting you marry her, not put her in your will."

"There speaks the lawyer." Sam's grin revealed deep dimples that creased both cheeks. "It's okay to marry her as long as I don't leave her my estate." The grin faded abruptly. "If I had anything worth leaving to anyone, I'd sell it. And then I wouldn't be sitting here listening to this crazy suggestion of yours."

"Wouldn't do you any good to sell anything, anyway. Cole wouldn't take the money, and you and I both know it." Max spoke with the confidence of someone who'd known Sam since third grade when they'd bloodied each other's noses and then become the best of friends.

"He'd take it." Sam's tone held grim promise.

"No, he wouldn't. He's as stubborn as the rest of you."

"He'd take it because it's for Mary. He'd do damn near anything to see her well. We all would." Sam's face softened at the thought of his niece.

"I know."

Max was more than a little fond of five-year-old Mary Walker himself, which was one of the reasons he'd come up with this scheme. It would solve problems for two people who were more friends than clients. If he could just persuade the two of them to do what was good for them. He picked up a slim black-and-gold fountain pen and twisted it between his fingers, deciding on a small shift in tactics.

"I know Keefe has put his ranch on the market, but real estate is in pretty bad shape in Southern California right now. It could take him months to sell it, and Cole is going to hate taking the money even if Keefe can sell.'' He made his voice thoughtful and carefully free of any hint of pressure.

Sam winced. When Max got that reasonable tone, he knew he was in trouble. It meant Max was convinced that whatever he had in mind was best for whoever he was talking to. And once that happened, it was damned near impossible to get him to turn the idea loose.

''Tell me this brilliant plan again.'' Sam stood up and walked across the room to the coffeepot that sat on one end of the elegant wet bar. He topped off his cup and then turned to look at his friend. ''Tell me in short, simple sentences. I was on stakeout all night, and about the only thing keeping me upright at the moment is caffeine.''

''Where was this stakeout? The bottom of a sewer?'' Max eyed Sam's scruffy clothing with exaggerated distaste.

''Too real world for you, Counselor?'' Sam grinned.

''Let me put it this way—it's a good thing it's so early in the morning. Having someone who looks like you in my office is probably a violation of my lease.''

''I could have a word with the landlord, show him my badge.''

''He'd probably think you stole it.'' Since Max *was* the landlord, the conversation was nonsensical. It was simply a continuation of an ongoing joke between the two of them, contrasting Sam's working-class background with the world of wealth and privilege into which Max had been born.

Sam carried his coffee back across the room and sank down into the comfortable leather chair. It took a conscious effort to resist the urge to lay his head back and doze off. After spending most of the night sitting on a pile of garbage in an alley, he was more than ready for sleep—caffeine or no caffeine. But if Max had a way for him to get the money for his niece's surgery, no matter how crazy it was, he'd listen.

"Okay," Sam repeated, "tell me again about this brilliant plan."

"It's simple." Max dropped the pen and leaned forward, fixing Sam with the same intent look he used to sway judges to his point of view. "You need money for Mary's surgery. A lot of money. Nikki has a lot of money but she needs a husband to collect it. The two of you get married. Nikki gets her inheritance. You get the money for Mary's surgery. Everyone lives happily ever after."

"Yeah, right. And the moon really is made of green cheese." Sam shook his head. "All these years and I never knew there was any insanity in your family."

"What's wrong with the plan?" Max refused to let himself be drawn into an exchange of insults.

"What's *not* wrong with it?" Sam leaned forward and set his cup on the desk. "It sounds like something out of a movie or a book, Max. We're talking marriage here."

"We're talking about a perfectly reasonable business arrangement between two consenting adults," Max corrected. "Just because a marriage certificate is part of the bargain is no reason to turn it down."

"There's the lawyer again." Sam rubbed one hand over his face, wishing he'd had a chance to get some sleep. He was sure there were any number of logical objections to this crazy idea—he was just too damned tired to think of them. "I don't want to get married again."

Sam's wife, Sara, had died almost five years before. He'd never imagined himself marrying again. Certainly not under these circumstances.

"This wouldn't be a real marriage." Sensing victory, Max leaned forward. "You and Nikki would have to share a house for a year but that's all."

"That's *all?* You're suggesting I move in with some strange woman for a year and you say *that's all?*" Sam glared at him through eyes red-rimmed from lack of sleep. "What about her? Doesn't she have any problem with this?"

"She wants her inheritance, and the way her grandfather's will leaves things, she has to be married before her twenty-seventh birthday and stay married for a full year in order to get it."

"So she wouldn't have any money for a year," Sam said, pouncing on the obvious weak spot. "Which means Mary would have to wait a year for her surgery."

"Nikki can give you the money up front." Max's smile was smug as he eliminated that objection. "She has money of her own. Besides, it's my understanding that the doctors don't have any plans to do surgery in the next year. Possibly not in the year after that. So, even if you had to wait until the end of the year for the money, it wouldn't really make any difference, would it?"

Max was right but Sam didn't plan to admit as much, at least not out loud.

"If she's already got money to burn, then why does she care about the money from her grandfather? Or does she just figure that you can't ever have too much?"

"Nikki has her reasons for giving in to her grandfather's request."

"What reasons?"

"If she wants you to know, she'll tell you," Max said, suddenly very much the lawyer.

Sam gave him a sour look. "Is this part of some lawyer code? It's okay to marry your clients off but not to talk about their money?"

"Something like that. Look, just meet her. Talk to her. Then make up your mind."

Sam was silent for a moment and then shrugged and reached for his coffee cup. "What the hell, I can always say no. Set up a meeting."

Max cleared his throat. "Actually, I already have. She should be here any minute."

Sam choked on a mouthful of coffee. Once he'd stopped coughing, he glared at his friend. "Confident, aren't you?"

"I knew you'd see reason," Max said imperturbably. "Since timing is somewhat critical for both of you, I didn't see any reason to waste time."

*Or to give either of them a chance to change their minds.* But Max didn't say that out loud. It would have been easier to persuade Saddam Hussein to have tea with Mother Teresa than it had been to convince Sam and Nikki to consider his plan for solving both of their problems. Now all he had to do was hope that they didn't hate each other on sight.

It was a vain hope.

Five minutes later, Nicole Beauvisage walked into the office, smelling of Chanel and luxury. Sam's blue eyes swept over her, from the smooth twist of her pale gold hair, across the elegant perfection of her peach silk suit, to the Italian leather of the matching pumps with their three-inch heels. His gaze rose, lingering on a pair of legs good enough to cause accidents, taking in the trim lines of her figure, before settling on the perfect oval of her face.

For her part, Nikki paused just inside the door, her gaze widening a little as she looked at the man Max had suggested she marry.

*"I've known Sam Walker since we were kids,"* Max had said. *"He's a great guy. You'll like him and you'll like his family. The Walkers are a close-knit bunch, a Norman Rockwell kind of family. Besides, he's a cop. How can you go wrong?"*

Nikki considered the answer to that question as she looked at Sam Walker, great guy, police officer and member of a Norman Rockwell kind of family. Funny, she didn't recall ever seeing a Rockwell painting with anyone who looked like him in it.

Shaggy dark blond hair, worn too long for her taste, a square-jawed face that couldn't quite be called handsome but she had to admit was arresting. There was a cleft in the middle of his chin that she refused to find attractive.

His shoulders were broad, and she guessed they were solid muscle, but it was difficult to tell beneath the layers of ragged coat, filthy sweater and torn shirt. The jeans he wore looked as if they hadn't seen a washer in at least a year of steady wear. He wore heavy boots that laced up the front, but the sole of one flapped loose, revealing a sock of indeterminate color.

Her green eyes widened in shock before meeting the cool blue of Sam's and reading his assessment of her.

*Rich ice princess,* his look said.

*Filthy pig,* hers responded.

It was instant antipathy.

Max nearly groaned aloud with frustration.

"Nikki. Come on in." He came around the desk to

take her arm, ignoring her slight resistance as he led her
toward Sam. "This is Sam Walker. Sam, this is Nikki
Beauvisage."

"Mr. Walker." Her voice had the cool sound of ice
tinkling in a glass. There was an almost imperceptible
pause before she extended her hand.

"Nikki." Sam grasped her hand firmly, taking pleasure in her faint shudder as he leaned toward her. He
knew exactly how bad he looked, not to mention
smelled. It had taken considerable effort to achieve just
the right look, and he wanted to be sure Ms. Nicole
Beauvisage got the full effect.

"Max has told me so much about you," he said,
giving her hand a hearty shake.

"I don't think he told me nearly enough about you."
The look Nikki cast at Max held more than a trace of
annoyance. She pulled her hand free and Sam noticed
that while her manners were too good to allow her to
look and see if any of his dirt had migrated to her, she
was careful to hold her hand away from the pastel elegance of her suit. "I thought you said Mr. Walker was
a police officer, Maxwell."

Max winced, recognizing the anger behind that coolly
polite inquiry. He shot Sam a warning look with little
hope that it would be heeded. Damn the pair of them,
anyway.

"Sam was on a stakeout all night, Nikki."

"If I'd known I was going to be meeting you, I'd
have swung by my apartment and changed into my best
Armani suit."

"Not on my account, I hope. If it would make you
more comfortable, I could ask Max for a few pieces of
rotten fruit to put in my pockets," she offered sweetly.
"Or possibly a bottle of cheap wine would be more

appropriate.'' Her nose wrinkled subtly at the smell of stale wine wafting from his clothes.

"Sorry. I was out of Dom Pérignon.'' Sam's smile held an edge sharp enough to cut.

"Stop it, you two.'' Max stepped between them, physically as well as verbally. "Sit down, both of you. The cleaning service charges extra for getting blood out of the carpet.''

He saw Nikki seated before turning to look at Sam. Sam hesitated a moment before sitting back down. Only when the combatants had retreated to their respective corners did Max step out from between them.

Nikki crossed one leg over the other and fixed her gaze on the tip of her pump.

Sam studied the grain of the wood on the desk, pretending not to notice the truly riveting length of leg she displayed.

Max looked at the pair of them and wondered if maybe Sam hadn't been right about the insanity in his family.

"So, I know the two of you must have questions to ask each other.''

They both looked at him.

Nikki raised one shoulder in a delicate half shrug.

Sam rolled his eyes.

Max reached for a package of antacids. "We could start out slow. How about the weather? The weather report said it might rain.''

"It's that time of year,'' Sam said.

"Actually, it's rather early for rain,'' Nikki corrected.

They both fell silent.

Max popped an antacid and chewed furiously. "Okay, we'll skip the small talk. What do you think of my idea?''

"It's nuts."

"It's insane."

The responses came one on top of the other.

Max smiled. "Well, at least you agree on something." His smile faded and he fixed them both with his best stern, lawyerly look. "Look, this meeting is for your benefit, not mine. You've both got problems. I came up with a solution. If you don't want to take it, it's not my problem. I've got better things to do with my time than play referee for the two of you. Are you going to get married or not?"

Sam looked at Nikki.

Nikki glanced out the corner of her eye at Sam.

He frowned.

She shrugged.

And Max wondered how many years he'd get for killing two clients.

"The idea is nuts," Sam said finally.

"Completely crazy," Nikki agreed firmly.

"Do either of you have a better solution?"

"No."

"Not at the moment."

"The moment is all you've got," Max pointed out. "You're both in somewhat time-critical situations."

Sam shifted uneasily beneath his look, thinking of his niece's surgery, of his family's worry.

Nikki frowned, reminded that she was running out of time to comply with the terms of her grandfather's will.

"It might work," Sam offered grudgingly.

"Of course it will work." Max's smile reflected his relief at having gotten a marginally positive response. "What's not to work? You just have to get married, live together for a year, and then you part company with no hard feelings."

"It's the living together that disturbs me," Nikki said, casting Sam's large frame an uneasy look.

"I can't say I'm all that crazy about it either," he threw back.

"Living together is one of the terms of the will," Max reminded them. "Nikki's house is big enough that you won't even have to see each other. It shouldn't be a problem."

Sam's mouth tightened at the reminder of her wealth. "Maybe I'd prefer that we live in my apartment."

Since he lived in a studio apartment in a rough area of Hollywood, it was a ridiculous suggestion. Max, who knew where he lived, gave him a disbelieving look. Nikki, who didn't, looked at him coolly.

"I have no intention of moving out of my home, Mr. Walker."

"Maybe I don't want to move out of mine, *Ms.* Beauvisage." He ignored Max's astonished look. "Not everyone wants to live in a mansion in Beverly Hills."

"Pasadena. It's a mansion in Pasadena," she corrected sweetly. "And unless you have room for a housekeeper and a maid in your apartment, it seems more logical that you should move into my home, rather than the other way around."

*Housekeeper? Maid?* Sam choked on the image of himself living in a house with servants. "I suppose you've got half a dozen gardeners and a chauffeur, too."

"One gardener and some part-time help. I drive my own car."

"Should I be impressed?"

"I really don't care one way or another. As long as it's understood that *if* we were to get married, we'd be living in *my* house."

Their gazes clashed, and it occurred to Sam that he'd never seen eyes of such a clear, deep green. It also occurred to him that he was making a production out of nothing. He really didn't give a damn where they lived.

"I guess I could sublet my apartment," he conceded grudgingly. He ignored Max's snort of laughter at the idea of subletting the scruffy one-room studio.

"So you'll live at Nikki's house," Max said cheerfully.

"There is one thing I want to make perfectly clear," Nikki said. A hint of color tinted her pale skin, but her eyes were steady on Sam. "You do understand, Mr. Walker, that this is to be strictly a marriage in name only. I don't want any question about that."

Sam's eyes chilled to an icy blue. He let his glance go over her, from head to toe and then back again to meet her look. "You don't have to worry, Ms. Beauvisage. I don't think I'll have any trouble controlling my animal lust around you."

His tone made it clear that he didn't find her in the least attractive. Nikki's flush deepened, but she nodded as if satisfied with his response. "Good."

Sam returned his attention to the desk.

Nikki studied the tip of her shoe some more.

Max resisted the urge to tear his hair out.

"So, is it settled? Are you going to get married?"

"I want the money up front," Sam said abruptly.

"You'll get it. *I'll* have to insist on a prenuptial agreement."

"If you don't, I will," he snapped. His pride was already stung by the necessity of taking any money from her. "Other than the money agreed on, you don't have *anything* I want."

"Other than your name on a marriage license, you don't have anything *I* want, either. Isn't it nice that we can agree on something?" she purred.

Max chewed another antacid and considered another line of work. Something with less stress. Air-traffic controller at LAX, maybe.

"A prenup is a given," he told them. "To protect both of you. I can have one drawn up by tomorrow afternoon. It should be pretty straightforward. I'll specify that, aside from the agreed-upon sum of money, you both give up all claims to each other's property."

"Fine with me," Sam said, wondering what the odds were that Ms. Nicole Beauvisage would try to lay claim to his five-year-old Bronco or his collection of baseball cards, the only items of any particular value he owned. Somehow, he doubted either one would hold much appeal.

"There is one other thing that concerns me," Nikki said slowly.

"I promise not to play basketball in the ballroom or leave my dirty socks lying on the Louis XV," Sam offered facetiously.

"That's quite a relief." Her smile was as icy as her eyes. "But my concern is more basic, Mr. Walker. Once you have your money, what guarantee do I have that you'll stick around for a year?"

"You have my word."

"I don't know you, Mr. Walker. I hope you'll understand my hesitation at staking my financial future on your word."

He did understand. And if it had been anyone else, he wouldn't have been offended. But there was something about this woman that got under his skin and made him react in ways he wouldn't have normally.

"Sam's word is good," Max said hastily, reading the anger in his friend's face.

"Draw up a contract," Sam snapped without looking away from Nikki. "She's paying me in advance for a year of my time. Make sure it's nice and legal and binding. You can do that, can't you, Max?"

"Sure. But it's really not—"

"I wouldn't want Ms. Beauvisage to have any doubts about getting her money's worth." Sam's voice was smooth as silk and sharp enough to draw blood.

"Thank you," Nikki said calmly.

"You're welcome."

The deadly politeness had Max reaching for another antacid. Maybe he should buy stock in the company, he thought, studying the wrapper. The silence stretched.

Nikki waited for Sam to speak.

Sam waited for Nikki to break the silence.

Max waited for the antacids to settle his stomach.

None of them knew how much time passed before the sound of Max's secretary settling in at her desk in the outer office finally broke the stillness.

"Well, are you going to do it or aren't you?" Max demanded, no longer trying to hide his exasperation.

There was a brief silence.

Sam spoke first. "I want it understood that no one is to know this isn't a real marriage."

If he actually went through with this insane idea, he didn't want Cole to know what he'd done. It would be hard enough to get his younger brother to take the check without him knowing the full circumstances of how Sam had acquired the money.

"As I'm sure Max told you, one of the provisions of the will is that this should be a genuine marriage." Since Nikki was very carefully not looking at Sam, she missed the sharp look he shot in Max's direction, a look that made it clear that he had not been informed of this particular fact. "Of course, in our case, it would only have the *appearance* of being genuine," she continued, "even if the will didn't require it, I'm not particularly eager for the world to know I had to get married in order to receive my inheritance."

"That includes my family," Sam said. "As far as they are concerned, we'd have to appear to be a normal couple."

*A Norman Rockwell kind of family.* Nikki remembered Max's description and wondered if it was possible that the hostile, scruffy, irritating man in front of her really came from that kind of family.

"I think I could manage that," she said. "If you can manage to convince my friends and family that you married me for something other than my money."

The reminder stung, making Sam's response sharper than it should have been. "I think my acting ability will stretch that far," he said smoothly.

The color that tinted her cheeks made him regret the words. He *was* marrying her for her money, dammit. It shouldn't be so aggravating to be reminded of that fact.

"I hope so" was all she said.

"So you're agreed that the marriage is to appear real," Max said.

"I haven't agreed to a marriage," Nikki pointed out sharply.

"Neither have I."

Max reached for another antacid and chewed furiously. "Look, I'm not a white slaver. I'm not going to force you two to get married. But as your attorney, I'm going to point out that this is the perfect solution to both sets of problems and that I think you're a pair of fools if you walk away from this opportunity. And as your friend, I'm going to tell you that you're acting like a couple of idiots. Now, are you going to get married or aren't you?''

There was a long silence.

"I don't like him," Nikki said without looking at Sam.

"I'm not wild about you either, honey."

Max threw up his hands. "You don't have to like each other. You just have to get married! Are you going to or not?''

There was another pause.

Sam shrugged. "I'm game if she is."

Nikki nodded slowly. "I can't believe I'm saying this but, all right, I'll marry him."

"Don't act like you're doing me a favor, honey," Sam snapped.

"I *am* doing you a favor. And don't call me 'honey.'''

"You're doing each other favors," Max said, verbally stepping between them again. "You need each other, and for the next year, you're going to be living together. You might as well get used to the idea."

Sam glared at Nikki, thinking he'd never met a woman he disliked more. Or one with better legs.

Nikki glared at Sam, thinking it was a shame Max couldn't have found her someone a little less overwhelmingly male. And wasn't it a good thing she didn't find him in the least bit attractive?

Max looked at the pair of them and wondered if his own sanity would survive the next year.

# Chapter 2

Once an agreement, however grudging, was reached, it didn't take long to work out the details of the arrangement. Aside from the fact that the bride and groom detested each other, the only possible barrier to the upcoming nuptials was the necessity of convincing Nikki's grandfather's attorney that they were getting married for the usual reasons.

Lymon Beauvisage had foreseen the possibility that his granddaughter might make a marriage of convenience in order to get her inheritance and had done his best to circumvent the possibility. As the final proviso in an already complicated bequest, he'd left his friend and lawyer, Jason Drummond, the final say in whether or not Nikki received her inheritance. If he believed the marriage was real, he'd release the money at the end of the year. If he didn't, the money went to Nikki's older brother, Alan, who'd already received—and squandered—his half of their grandfather's estate.

"You just have to convince Jason Drummond that you're in love with each other," Max said.

"Unless he's deaf, dumb and blind, that may not be so easy," Sam said, looking as if he were starting to reconsider the whole idea.

"All it takes is a little acting," Max coaxed.

"There's a limit to my acting ability," Sam muttered. Out the corner of his eye, he saw Nikki stiffen and realized that his comment could be taken as a slap in her direction, which wasn't what he'd intended.

"I'm surprised, Mr. Walker." Her voice was sweet enough to send chills down his spine. "You're so convincing as a rude, filthy wino." She paused and her delicate brows drew together in a small frown. When she continued, her tone was one of concern. "Perhaps that isn't as much of a stretch as convincing Uncle Jason that I might actually want to marry you."

Sam winced in acknowledgment of the hit, but restrained the urge to respond in kind. The last thing he wanted was to prolong this meeting, not even for the pleasure of continuing the verbal warfare with the woman he'd just agreed to marry. He wanted to go home, wash off the smell of that alley and get some sleep. Maybe when he woke up, this idea would seem as logical as Max claimed it was and not the insanity it looked to be at the moment.

"Uncle Jason?" he questioned.

"My grandfather's attorney is also a family friend."

"That should make him fairly willing to be convinced," Max put in optimistically.

"Less strain on your acting ability, Mr. Walker," Nikki pointed out with a saccharine smile.

"Thanks."

It was agreed that Nikki would contact Jason Drummond and arrange for him to meet Sam as soon as possible.

"The sooner you get his approval, the sooner you can get married," Max said.

"A thrilling thought," Nikki said as she rose, preparatory to leaving.

Sam, who'd been about to gather his energy to rise, a courtesy his mother had drummed into him, relaxed back into his chair. He was damned if he was going to waste his time on polite forms with this stuck-up little ice princess.

"I'll let Max know when I've arranged a meeting with Uncle Jason."

"You do that."

Max started to suggest that it would be easier if she contacted Sam directly, but immediately thought better of it. The way things stood right now, it was probably safer if the bride and groom had as little contact with each other as possible before the wedding.

"I'll be in touch," she said to Max. She glanced at Sam and gave him a cool little nod. "Mr. Walker."

"Ms. Beauvisage." He returned the nod, his tone mocking her formality.

Nikki's mouth tightened, and he saw fire flare in her green eyes. He waited for the explosion, but it didn't come. She turned and walked out of the office without another word. Sam watched her leave, surprised to realize that he actually felt a twinge of regret at her restraint.

He let his eyes drift down her narrow back to her legs. She had the disposition of a pit viper. It was too bad she also had legs like an angel. It didn't take much imagination on his part to picture those legs sliding into the expensive car she undoubtedly drove.

Or between a set of black silk sheets.

\* \* \*

Nikki heard the rapid tap of her heels against the tile entryway of the office building and realized she was almost running. She forced herself to slow down as she exited the building and stepped out into the bright sunshine.

She *wasn't* running, she told herself as she pulled open her car door and slid onto the genuine imitation sheepskin-covered seat. Sam Walker might be a bit larger than life, and some women—susceptible women—might even find him wildly attractive, but she herself hardly noticed such things, and they certainly wouldn't send her fleeing from her lawyer's office.

She had an appointment with her mother, that was all. The fact that she wasn't meeting Marilee for three hours and that Marilee would probably not arrive for another forty-five minutes after that was irrelevant. She'd concluded her business here and she was leaving. Nothing odd about that.

Nikki's hands weren't quite steady as she put the car into gear and pulled away from the curb. She'd done it. She'd actually agreed to marry a man she'd just met. A man she didn't know and wouldn't like if she did. Her mind reeled at the thought.

When Max had suggested the idea as a way to get her inheritance, he'd made it sound so simple, so businesslike that she'd had no hesitation in agreeing to meet with his friend. But she hadn't been expecting Sam Walker and she hadn't been prepared for the jolt of awareness she'd felt when they shook hands. What had sounded like a simple business arrangement suddenly seemed much more complex.

Nikki turned the car onto the Glendale Freeway and

headed north. She'd planned to do some shopping before meeting her mother for lunch, but that was before she'd met Sam Walker, before she'd agreed to marry him. Right now, she needed to talk to someone she could trust, someone who had no ax to grind.

Twenty minutes later, she parked the scruffy ten-year-old Chevy in front of a neat little house on a street lined with other neat little houses. The front door opened as she walked up the driveway and a short, thin man of about thirty came out. Bill Davis had married Nikki's best friend four years ago, right after Liz graduated from UC Santa Barbara. They had little money, a house made chaotic by a toddler and all the attendant problems of raising a family, but they loved each other deeply. Nikki was unabashedly envious of their happiness.

"Hello, Bill."

"Nikki." His plain face creased in a smile when he saw her. "Isn't it a little early for the idle rich to be out slumming?" he asked as he hugged her.

"I like to get started early. Slumming, properly done, takes more time than most people realize. Is Liz around?"

"In the kitchen, feeding the holy terror."

"Don't call my godchild a terror. He's adorable."

"You don't have to live with him," he said darkly. "When I left, Michael had just tried to put the goldfish in his oatmeal and Liz was trying to convince him that Oscar didn't need a hot breakfast."

"And you fled in the midst of that?"

"Like a coward," he admitted cheerfully. "I've got cars stacked up like cordwood, waiting for work."

"Nice to be busy." Bill was manager and chief mechanic at an auto repair shop in Montrose. He and Liz were saving money in hopes of buying the business when the current owner retired in a couple of years.

"Bring that junk heap by and I'll take a look at it," he said, nodding toward her car. "I still think you ought to sell it for scrap and buy a real car."

"Barney *is* a real car," she protested. "It had been Bill's four-year-old son who'd named Nikki's car, thinking the faded purple paint job was reminiscent of the dinosaur he watched every day on television.

They spoke a moment longer before Bill left for work. Nikki let herself in the house with the familiarity of an old friend. She called out Liz's name and received a frazzled-sounding response from the kitchen. Picking her way across the mine field of toys strewn across the living room floor, she could hear Liz telling Michael firmly that Oscar did not want his fishbowl filled with milk, any more than he wanted to swim in Michael's oatmeal.

"Aunt Nikki!" Michael's greeting was enthusiastic as only a four-year-old's could be. He scrambled off his chair and hurled himself at her, oblivious to his mother's command not to touch anything until his face and hands were washed. An instant later, Nikki had an armful of four-year-old boy and smudges of oatmeal and jelly on her silk suit.

"You have to learn to dodge," Liz said as Nikki stood.

"I don't want to dodge. The suit will clean." Nikki grinned down at the little boy, who was rifling through her cavernous purse, looking for the small treat she never failed to bring him. Today it was a palm-size dump truck, and Michael immediately began scooting it across the kitchen floor, making engine noises.

"You spoil him."

"He's too sweet natured to be really spoiled," Nikki said.

"Sweet natured?" Liz repeated disbelievingly. "Ask Oscar how sweet natured he is."

Nikki followed her gesture to the goldfish bowl perched on top of the refrigerator beyond the reach of four-year-old fingers. Oscar swam lazily around his small home, undisturbed by his close encounter with Michael's breakfast.

"Oscar looks none the worse for wear. I can't say the same about you, though." She gave her friend a critical look as Liz collapsed into a chair. Liz's hair stood out from her head in springy carrot-red curls and her hazel eyes held the dazed look of a disaster survivor.

"Michael woke us up at four-thirty. Then the toilet stopped up. Bill spent half an hour working on it and finally pulled out one of Michael's action figures. Apparently Michael wanted to send him on a diving mission. The remains were so mangled, there wasn't even enough left for a decent burial. I didn't get to the laundry yesterday, so the only clean underwear Bill could find is a pair of tiger-striped bikinis I bought him as a joke. He's convinced he'll be in some kind of accident and be rushed to the emergency room where the doctors will find him wearing kinky shorts. The bread was moldy, there was only one egg, which I cooked for Bill, and Michael has spent the morning trying to introduce Oscar to the joys of breakfast."

Nikki let a few moments go by at the end of Liz's recital of the morning's disasters and then lifted her brows in surprise. "Is that all?"

"Get out." Liz threw a paper napkin in her direction, watching as it drifted into Michael's half-eaten bowl of oatmeal. "If I had the energy, I'd throw something more lethal. Worse, I'd send the holy terror home with you.''

Grinning, Nikki lifted the kettle off the stove and carried it to the sink. ''A cup of tea will restore your energy. And anytime you want a couple of days off, you know I'd love to have Michael.'' She set the kettle on the stove.

''Friendship only goes so far,'' Liz said broodingly as she watched her son crawling across the floor with his new truck. ''I may hit you up for enough money to run away from home instead.''

''Yeah, right.'' Nikki found the tea bags and two cups. ''You wouldn't give up your life for anything, and you and I both know it.''

''This morning I'd sell it for a wooden nickel and consider myself lucky.''

''Liar.'' Nikki poured the water over the tea bags before carrying the cups to the table. She sat down across from Liz. ''You adore Bill and Michael.''

''Maybe.'' Cradling her hands around the mug of tea, Liz looked as if she might be getting her second wind after her hectic morning. ''Enough about my miserable existence. What's up with you?''

Nikki took a sip of tea and considered possible responses to that question. In the end, she chose the simplest and most direct. ''I'm getting married.''

The stark announcement brought Liz's head up so fast Nikki had visions of whiplash. ''You're what?''

''I said I'm getting married.'' Repeating the words didn't make them sound any more real. ''In a few days,'' she added, feeling a flutter of panic at the thought.

''Who?'' Liz looked bewildered. ''I didn't know you were even dating anyone.''

"I'm not."

"But you're getting married?"

"Yes."

Liz stared at her, and then her eyes widened in understanding. "Your grandfather's will? You're getting married because of that?"

Nikki nodded. "Max set it up. It's a friend of his. A police officer."

"Have you met the guy?" Liz's tea was forgotten as she leaned forward, her eyes bright with interest.

"This morning." Nikki shifted uncomfortably, remembering that meeting. "In Max's office."

"What's he like?"

What was he like? Sam Walker's image sprang into Nikki's mind, far more vivid than she would have liked. Why couldn't Max have found her the kind of guy you forgot as soon as they were out of sight?

"He's tall," she said slowly.

"How tall?"

"I don't know. Six-one, six-two. I didn't have a tape measure with me."

"Skinny, fat, somewhere in between?" Liz asked briskly.

"Somewhere in between." The lackluster description hardly did justice to Sam Walker's broad shoulders and narrow hips, but it was close enough.

"Is he handsome?"

"No. Yes. Sort of." Nikki flushed as her friend's eyebrows rose.

"Nice to hear you sounding so decisive," she commented.

"If I'd known you were going to be so interested, I'd have taken a snapshot." Nikki winced at the defensive sound of her own voice. She had to get a grip. "He has…dents in his face."

Liz choked on a mouthful of tea, coughed briefly and then stared at her friend. "Dents? You mean a birth defect or scars of some kind?"

"No." Nikki waved one hand to dismiss that idea. As far as she could see, Sam Walker was as close to perfect as it was possible for a man to be. If you liked that type, anyway. She'd never really seen the appeal of shaggy dark blond hair, blue eyes, a smile to die for and muscles like a Greek god. No appeal at all. "He's got a cleft chin and creases when he smiles," she said, aware that Liz was still waiting for her to explain what she'd meant by dents.

"Creases?" Liz frowned. "Dimples? You mean the guy has dimples?"

"Yes." She didn't want to think of them that way. Dimples sounded…attractive, and she didn't want to find anything about Sam Walker attractive. Not his dimples, not anything.

"So, is he good-looking or not?" Liz asked, her frustration clear in her voice.

"What difference does it make? I don't care if he looks the way Danny DeVito did in *Batman Returns*. All I need is a husband for the next year so I can get my hands on my money."

"That's true. Still, if you have to spend a year married to some guy, it wouldn't hurt if he was attractive and pleasant to be around. Is he nice?"

"Nice? I guess." *Nice* wasn't the word she would have used, but she supposed he hadn't exactly been un-nice. Or, at least, no more un-nice than she herself had been.

"And the two of you hit it off?" Liz pursued anxiously.

"Well enough," Nikki temporized. There was no reason to mention that they'd hit it off about as well as oil and water. "Since this is just a business arrangement, we don't have to be bosom pals."

"True." Liz took a sip of her tea, her expression thoughtful. Michael was scooting his new toy up and down the wall, making engine noises more suited to a 747 than a three-inch-long dump truck. "It's ridiculous that you should have to go to these lengths to get your inheritance. Your grandfather didn't make your brother get married before he got his money."

"Grandfather didn't think much of women and their ability to manage money." Nikki got up and refilled the teakettle, more for something to do than out of a desire for more tea. "I gather Grandmother had feathers for brains, and I can't say Mother is much better."

"There's nothing wrong with your mother's ability to manage money. Every time she starts running out, she marries someone rich. Efficiency itself."

Nikki snorted with laughter at this blunt summation of her mother's money management techniques. They'd known each other long enough and well enough for Liz to speak her mind without fear of offending.

"I don't think Grandfather had your appreciation for Marilee's methods." Nikki glanced at her watch. "I'm supposed to be having lunch with her today. She's on her way to Europe tomorrow to look for husband number five. Or is it six? If I'm lucky, she'll marry another count or earl or something and stay in Europe for the next year. If I'm really lucky, I can be divorced before she even knows I'm married. Let's face it, my mother is a ditz, my grandmother was a ditz. Ergo, according to my grandfather, *I* must be a ditz. He figured he was protecting me by forcing me to get married because everyone knows men are better at managing money.'' There was more resignation than anger in her voice.

''Yeah, right. Bill couldn't balance a checkbook if his life depended on it. And look at your brother. He ran through the money your grandfather left him in a couple of years. Why didn't Alan have to get married to inherit his half of the money? I know, I know.'' Liz waved one hand, forestalling Nikki's response. ''We've had this discussion before. Alan's a man and the last of the Beauvisage name. Therefore, he gets his inheritance up front instead of being forced into marrying some total stranger.''

''I don't *have* to get married,'' Nikki said as she poured fresh hot water into both of their cups. ''I could just let the money go to Alan, which it will do if I'm not married by the time I'm twenty-seven. I do have a trust fund that's mine whether I marry or not. It's not like I'll starve without it.''

''No, but you couldn't afford to keep your house.''

''It's too big for one person anyway.'' Nikki tried to sound as if the thought of losing the house she'd grown up in didn't bother her. But in reality she loved the big old house and hated the thought of letting it go.

''And you couldn't afford to keep the Rainbow Place going,'' Liz finished, playing the trump card.

Nikki was silent for a moment, thinking about the day-care center she funded in a low-income area. She'd started it four years ago when she'd graduated from college and realized that a degree in American history didn't do much to prepare her for a job in the real world. Not that she'd needed a job, but she had needed something to occupy her time, something to make her feel as if she were making some contribution to the world.

She not only provided the operating capital, she also worked there three days a week. It had become a vital part of her life and it would leave a real hole if she had to give it up. But far more important was the impact it would have on the mothers and children who'd come to depend on Rainbow Place. Without safe day care available, many of the women would have to quit their jobs to stay home with their children. Many of them would end up on welfare.

No, she couldn't let the center close. With the money she'd inherit when she got married, she could afford to keep it open. Without that money, the center's future was in serious jeopardy. She sighed.

"How'd you like to come to a wedding?"

"You and the guy with the dents in his face?" Liz's hazel eyes sparkled with laughter.

"Me and Sam Walker," Nikki confirmed. She picked up her cup and cradled it between her hands, staring down into the amber-colored tea. "Of course, we still have to get Uncle Jason's approval," she added, not sure whether she hoped to get it or prayed that they didn't.

## Chapter 3

Nikki adjusted the cuff of her kelly-green suit jacket, using the motion as a cover for a discreet glance at her watch. It was almost one-thirty and the message she'd given Max had been for Sam Walker to be here at one o'clock.

He was late and she was going to kill him with her bare hands.

He knew how important this meeting was, knew they had to have her uncle's approval in order for her to get her inheritance. But he couldn't even bother to show up on time. This was probably some macho attempt to show her that he didn't have to take orders from her. Not that she'd given him any orders. She'd simply left a message with Max stating the time and place of the meeting she'd arranged.

Perhaps she had been a bit peremptory, but Max would have softened that when he passed the message on to Sam. Which meant that there was no excuse for him being late at all. Except to annoy her, and he was certainly succeeding in that. She became aware that Jason was speaking and forced her attention away from plans for Sam Walker's demise.

"...so I drew out my sword and ran him through, which was an unconventional way to win a trial but effective nonetheless."

"What?" She stared at Jason in bewilderment, wondering just what it was she'd missed. "What are you talking about? Who did you run through?"

"The opposing attorney, of course." He seemed surprised that she had to ask. "A very annoying man with an irritating habit of rubbing his hands together like Uriah Heep gloating over his coins. I never could stand him, and neither could anyone else, which is probably why the judge cited me for contempt of court rather than murder."

His blue eyes, only slightly faded by his sixty-five years of living, twinkled at her through the lenses of his neat horn-rimmed glasses. "You missed all the best parts, Nicole. It was a very good extemporaneous effort on my part, if I do say so myself."

"I'm sorry, Uncle Jason." Nikki's smile was both regretful and affectionate. "I guess I faded out on you."

"That's quite all right, my dear. Worried about your young man, are you?"

"Just a little." She nearly choked on hearing Sam referred to as *her* young man. "It's not like him to be late." She didn't have any idea whether it was like him or not. For all she knew, Sam Walker was always late for incredibly important appointments.

"Would you like to call and find out what's delaying him?"

"No, that's all right. I'm sure he'll be here any minute.'' She could hardly admit that she didn't know where to call. All she knew was that Sam was a cop; she didn't have the slightest idea what city he worked for.

Luckily, before her nerves were completely shot, Jason's secretary ushered Sam into the office.

''Mr. Walker.'' Jason rose and went to greet him, which was just as well because Nikki was momentarily paralyzed by her first sight of her husband-to-be.

She'd wondered what he'd look like cleaned up and wearing decent clothes. Even covered with several layers of dirt and rags, he'd had a definite impact on her senses, but that was nothing compared to what she felt now.

Not that he looked all that different, it was just that he looked…different. Taller, even broader through the shoulders, lean hipped and with a long, rangy walk that bespoke confidence and maybe just a touch of arrogance. His dark blond hair was neatly combed and considerably cleaner than it had been the first time they met, but there was still something a little untamed about the way it curled against the back of his collar.

He wore a well-tailored gray suit and a white shirt. Paired with this conservative attire was a fuchsia-and-black tie, patterned with indescribable swirls and dots. Just looking at it made her dizzy.

Or was it looking at Sam Walker that made her light-headed?

''Mr. Drummond. I'm sorry I'm late. I had to testify at a hearing this morning and the proceedings were delayed.''

''I understand. The legal system is many things, but timely it's not.''

The two men shook hands. ''I think Nicole was beginning to get a little worried, though,'' Jason continued, turning toward her with a fond smile. "I thought she was going to wear out her watch, she looked at it so many times."

"I'm sorry you were worried, darling. I should have thought to call from the courthouse." Sam's smile was a masterpiece of concerned affection.

"Darling" stared at him, barely managing to keep her mouth from gaping. *This* was the unwashed, unkempt, uncivil man she'd met less than a week ago? This attractive, well-dressed man looking at her as if he adored her?

She realized that Jason was watching them, waiting for her response, and she managed to force a smile that she hoped looked more natural than it felt. "That's all right. I knew it had to be something important that kept you." She stood up so that she wouldn't feel at quite such a disadvantage.

"Next time, I'll be sure to call and let you know I'm running late."

He crossed the room to where she stood and reached toward her. Momentarily confused, Nikki half extended her hand, thinking he meant to shake it. But that wasn't what he had in mind. He did take her hand, but only to use it to draw her toward him.

The wicked glint in his eyes dispelled the illusion of loving affection and gave Nikki warning of his intention. She turned her head slightly and the kiss aimed at her mouth landed on her cheek instead. Even that small contact had more impact than she liked. He was too close, too large and too male. She could smell the subtle, woodsy scent of his cologne, feel the faint, masculine roughness of his chin. She didn't like him being so close, forcing her to be so aware of him.

Sam lifted his head and looked down at her with every appearance of adoration. "I'm sorry I worried you, sweetheart, but I'm glad you care enough to worry."

Nikki guessed there were women who would have been charmed by his boyishly wicked smile. Foolish women who might actually enjoy this little game he was playing. If they'd been alone, she would have shoved him away and probably planted her fist in his face. But with Jason looking on, she couldn't do either. A quick glance told her that the other man was standing behind his desk, watching them with an indulgent expression.

"That's all right, darling."

Her smile was enough to chill Sam's blood but there was no time to avoid the spike heel that was planted squarely on the toe of his soft leather dress shoe and then slowly ground down. Pain sliced across the top of his foot.

If they'd been alone, he wouldn't have bet money on his ability to resist the urge to shake her until her perfect white teeth rattled. Probably caps, he thought uncharitably. His hands tightened on her shoulders and their eyes did battle.

She was a spoiled, rich little brat and the next year stretched ahead of him like an eternity.

He was an overbearing, obnoxious, mercenary male and the next year was going to be absolute hell.

"You two will have time for that later," Jason said, smiling at the pair of them. "Why don't you have a seat, Sam. I hope you don't mind if I call you Sam. I don't see any need for formality, do you?"

"Not at all." Sam released Nikki's shoulders and swallowed a sigh of relief as she removed her heel from his foot. He resisted the urge to check for blood. From the feel of his foot, she must have sharpened the heel of the damned shoe into a stiletto.

He sat down in the chair beside Nikki's and tried not to notice the subtle floral scent of her perfume, which was like a summer breeze wafting across a bed of roses. An ounce of the stuff probably cost as much as he made in a week, he reminded himself.

"Nikki told me that she'd explained the situation with her grandfather's will to you and the necessity for this interview," Jason said. "She tells me that you'd just as soon walk away from this inheritance rather than rush her into marriage."

The look Sam shot Nikki held grudging approval. He'd wondered how he was supposed to convince her grandfather's attorney that he wasn't marrying Nikki for her money. She'd done a perfect job of smoothing the path.

"I don't want her to feel as if she has to make any decisions in a hurry. It's not like I'm marrying her for the money," he added, with a smile. Which was more or less true, since *his* money, the money for Mary's surgery, was coming out of what she already had. One thing he'd learned from doing undercover work was that it was always best to stick as close to the truth as possible.

"I'm glad to hear it." Behind the smile in Jason's eyes was a shrewdness that warned Sam that it would be foolish to underestimate him. He steepled his hands together on the desk. "Nikki hasn't really told me much about the two of you. Where did you meet?"

"Meet?" Sam looked at Nikki. He cocked one eyebrow, as if to suggest that she should answer the question. She swallowed and searched her suddenly blank mind for a reasonable response. God, why hadn't they worked out these kind of details ahead of time?

When the panic in her eyes made it clear that she didn't have a clever response handy, Sam answered Jason's question himself. "We were intoduced by a mutual friend, actually. After everything Max told me, I knew even before I met her that Nikki was the perfect woman for me."

Nikki was torn between gratitude and anger. There was nothing in what he'd said that could arouse Jason's suspicions but she was not blind to the double meaning behind his words. "After everything Max told him," indeed. All Max had had to say was that she was rich.

"Max?" Jason asked. "Didn't I meet him at your house, Nicole?"

"Yes. We've been friends for years."

"A lawyer, isn't he?"

Nikki swallowed. He couldn't possibly suspect the truth just because Max was a lawyer, could he? "Yes, he is."

"Seems like there are a lot of us around," Jason said casually. He leaned back in his desk chair and studied the two of them for a moment. "Nikki tells me that the two of you haven't known each other long."

"Not long," Sam admitted. "But I knew exactly how I felt about Nikki from the first moment I saw her." He threw a loving glance at Nikki, who fumed under the laughter in his eyes.

"Love at first sight, hmm?" Jason's smile was indulgent.

"Something like that."

Nikki would have given a great deal to have planted her fist smack dab in the middle of Sam's smiling mouth. She could only hope that Jason would take her blush for one of modesty rather than rage.

"I didn't approve of the way Lyman drew up his will and I made no secret of that. But he was a stubborn man." He peered at Sam from under bushy gray eyebrows. "You might be warned that stubbornness is a family trait," he added, smiling.

"I'll keep that in mind." Sam glanced at Nikki, hoping he looked fond rather than irritated.

"I couldn't persuade him to change his mind, so I drew up the will as he'd requested and agreed to be executor. And neither my disapproval of the provisions of the will nor my fondness for Nicole can be allowed to color my judgment," Jason said firmly. "Lyman may have been stubborn and, I think, misguided in this, but he did love Nicole and he honestly felt he was doing what was best for her. As his friend, as well as his attorney, I must do my best to carry out his wishes."

There was a moment of silence while the potential bride and groom considered the import of his words. Obviously, Jason was not averse to approving their marriage, as long as he was convinced that they were getting married for the right reasons.

An image of Mary's small face flashed through Sam's mind and his jaw tightened. He'd walk through fire to get her the help she needed. But, while walking through fire might be easier than spending the next year with Nikki Beauvisage, it wouldn't do Mary any good.

Without taking his eyes from Jason Drummond, he reached for Nikki's hand, which lay on the arm of her chair. She jumped in surprise and automatically tried to pull away, but he tightened his hold ruthlessly.

"I understand your concern," he said to Jason. "And I appreciate it. Nikki is a very...special woman. She certainly deserves the very best.'' His shrug was self-deprecating. ''I don't know if I'm that, but I can tell you that marrying Nikki means more to me than anything else in the world.''

He threw Nikki a look that held both warning and command. The next few minutes were critical. A five-year-old's health hung on whether or not Jason believed they were in love.

Jason nodded as he leaned back in his chair. He let his eyes drift from the couple in front of him, focusing instead on the swath of smoggy sky visible out the window. Sam and Nikki waited, unaware that they were still holding hands, unconsciously drawing support from the contact.

The silence seemed to stretch forever, but in actuality, it couldn't have been more than a few minutes before it was broken. Jason slowly looked away from the window, his faded blue eyes drifting from Nikki's face to Sam's before settling on their linked hands.

''The two of you are very sure this is what you want? That you really *want* to marry each other?''

''More than anything, Uncle Jason.'' There was so much sincerity in her voice that Nikki almost believed herself.

''Absolutely, sir.'' Sam was startled by the fervor of his own response. But he *did* want to marry her, just not for the reasons Jason Drummond thought he did.

Jason pinched his lower lip between thumb and forefinger, looking at the pair of them with eyes that seemed able to penetrate the suddenly flimsy-seeming fabric of their charade. They waited, hands clasped, neither of them breathing. Once again, Jason's gaze dropped to those linked fingers and his expression took on a pensive air.

After a moment that seemed an hour long, he nodded slowly. "All right. You have my blessing."

His acceptance, when it came, was so simple that it took a moment for it to register. When it did, Sam's hand tightened over Nikki's fingers until she squeaked a protest. With a quick apology, he released her.

He had it. The money for Mary's surgery was all but in his hands. So what if he had to spend the next year living with the ice princess. It was worth it.

Nikki flexed her fingers absently after Sam released them. It was done. She'd be able to keep the Rainbow Place open without spending her time begging money from other sources. The price was steep: twelve months of sharing her house with a man she couldn't stand. But she could survive that.

She glanced at Sam. At least, she was fairly sure she could.

# Chapter 4

With only a little effort, the bride and groom were able to avoid seeing each other again before the wedding. The few communications necessary were filtered through Max, who also made the wedding arrangements.

It was Sam's suggestion that they simply go to Las Vegas and, as he put it, get it over with. Nikki's response to this, via Max, was that no one who knew her would ever believe that she'd get married in such a tacky place.

Sam, taking this, quite rightly, as a comment on his good taste or lack thereof, responded that she could do whatever she wanted as long as she didn't expect him to dress up in a powder-blue tuxedo and ruffled shirt. Or at least that was the portion of his message Max chose to pass on, deeming it unnecessary to get too literal. His suggestion that he make the arrangements was gratefully accepted by the engaged couple.

He found a small chapel in Burbank for the ceremony, traditional enough to allay any suspicions anyone might have about the authenticity of the marriage, but simple enough to satisfy the bride and groom.

Liz and Bill brought Nikki, and the four of them—Michael included—arrived a few minutes early and waited outside for Sam and Max to arrive. They could have waited inside, but the woman who was to marry them had shown a definite tendency to wax sentimental and Nikki wasn't in the mood for hearing homilies about the joys of wedded bliss.

Aside from Max and the Davises, the only other guest was to be Jason Drummond. When she'd refused Sam's suggestion of a Vegas wedding, Nikki hadn't stopped to consider that Jason might not have come to an out-of-town wedding. As it was, having him in attendance meant that they'd have to keep up the facade of being a happy couple, which wasn't easy when she'd rather have had a root canal without anesthetic than marry Sam Walker.

"He's late." Bill glanced at his watch and then scowled at the quiet street. He'd made no secret of his dislike of the whole idea. When he'd heard of Nikki's plan, he'd said bluntly that it was crazy. He'd agreed to attend the wedding, but Nikki knew it was as much to vet Sam as it was to offer her support.

"Less than five minutes." Liz gave her husband an exasperated look. It wasn't often that he put on his protective male attitude, but when he did, he did a thorough job of it.

"If the guy is so anxious to get married, you'd think he'd show up on time."

"You were thirty minutes late for our wedding." Liz

reached out to grab Michael's hand, pulling him away from the brick planter he'd begun to dig in.

"I got caught in traffic," Bill said defensively. "That was different."

"My mother didn't think it was different. She spent the entire half hour telling me that if you loved me, you'd have left plenty of time to get to the church."

"Only your mother could translate being late into not loving you," he groused, but he shut up about the groom not having arrived.

Nikki barely heard the exchange. She was too busy trying to convince herself that this was a good idea, that she shouldn't turn and run as far and as fast as she could. A week ago, it had seemed like her only choice. Now, standing outside the plain stucco facade of the chapel, waiting for her groom to arrive, the idea of marrying a man she'd only met twice seemed absolutely insane.

There had to be another way. She could sell the house and use that money to keep the Rainbow Place open for a while. And she could do fund-raising once that money ran out. Other people managed to keep worthwhile projects going without marrying complete strangers. Why couldn't she do the same?

"There's Max." Liz's announcement brought Nikki's head up. She stared at the approaching men, feeling like a doe watching the approach of a hunter.

"*That's* Sam Walker?" Liz's incredulous question broke Nikki's paralysis.

"Yes." The single word was all she could get past the sudden lump of panic that clogged her throat.

"Dents?" Liz hissed in her ear. "Dents? You're marrying a guy who looks like this and all you can tell your best friend is that he has dents in his face? He's gorgeous!''

Max and Sam reached them just then, saving Nikki the necessity of finding a reply. She really didn't need Liz to point out Sam's attractiveness. It was bad enough that she was marrying him; it was an added source of irritation to be forced to admit that the man was a bona fide hunk. He was wearing the same gray suit he'd worn to the meeting with Jason, paired with a plain white shirt. She'd thought the crazy tie he'd worn then might have been a quirk, but the one he had on today was an indescribable concoction of turquoise and hot pink on a dark gray background.

She let Max make the introductions, grateful for the small delay before she had to speak to Sam. But she still wasn't ready when he turned those deep blue eyes in her direction. She lifted her chin and met his look, hoping she looked as cool and unemotional as he did.

Sam had spent a week telling himself that Nikki Beauvisage couldn't be half as beautiful as he remembered. But seeing her, he knew he'd been lying to himself. Bathed in the ruthless glare of the afternoon sun, she was every bit as beautiful as she had been in kinder indoor light.

Her pale gold hair was pulled back from her face and twisted in some kind of knot at the back of her head. It was the kind of style that made a man's fingers itch to pull out the pins that held it. Her eyes were an even more vivid green than he'd remembered, contrasting with the milky paleness of her skin. If it hadn't been for the lush fullness of her lower lip, she could have been a painting of an angel. But he didn't think angels had mouths that made men think of smooth sheets and smoother skin.

Not to mention a body that curved in all the right places. Those curves were nicely displayed in an ivory-colored suit, worn with a green shell that echoed the color of her eyes. Sam didn't need to look at the labels to know that both items were pure silk. He was vaguely aware that the others had moved away a little, giving him and his soon-to-be bride at least the illusion of privacy.

"Mr. Walker." Nikki's greeting was as cool as her image. If it hadn't been for the slightly panicked look he'd seen in her eyes as he and Max approached, and the nervous tightness of her fingers on the tiny leather purse she carried, Sam might have believed that she was completely unmoved by what they were about to do.

"Call me Sam. I've never been crazy about husbands and wives calling each other Mr. and Mrs. It's cumbersome." He could have stopped there. He *should* have stopped there but some demon made him add: "Especially in the bedroom."

Nikki stiffened as if someone had just shoved a pole down the back of her tailored jacket. "That hardly matters in our case."

If her eyes got any colder, he was likely to have icicles hanging off his chin, Sam thought. "No family?" he asked, ignoring her comment. "I'd think you'd want them here to witness the happy event."

"My mother and my brother are both in Europe." Not that it was any of his business, Nikki thought, immediately sorry that she'd given him an answer. "I don't see your family in attendance. I guess you don't want them to know you're marrying for money?" She was unreasonably pleased when the sweetly asked question made Sam's mouth tighten.

"No. But you already knew that."

Tit for tat. A great way to start a marriage, Nikki thought, even one that wasn't really a marriage. Less than five minutes and already he'd managed to get under her skin in a way she couldn't remember anyone else ever having done. How was she going to survive an entire year married to this man?

"Drummond is here." Max stepped forward, his words both warning and announcement.

Sam slid his hand through Nikki's arm, his tight-lipped expression relaxing into a fond smile. Only Nikki was close enough to see that the smile stopped short of his eyes. "Smile, darling. It's show time."

Nikki tensed as Max's look swung from Sam to her, his expression questioning. "Ready?"

This was her last chance to back out of this whole crazy arrangement. She could walk away right now, kiss her inheritance goodbye and never have to see Sam Walker again. But she'd also be saying goodbye to the needs of a lot of people who depended on her, not to mention her own hopes and dreams for expanding the center, maybe even opening another one.

Over Max's shoulder she could see Jason approaching and she knew that the final moment of decision had arrived. She could say she'd changed her mind and never have to see Sam Walker again. Or she could marry him and start counting down the next three hundred and sixty-five days to freedom.

Her hand tightened unconsciously on Sam's arm, feeling the hard strength of muscle under the fabric of his sleeve. For one crazy moment, she had the urge to bury her face in his shoulder and hide from the world. The idea was so ridiculous that her shoulders stiffened and she took a quick step away from him. She'd been standing on her own two feet for a long time. And if the time ever came that she needed someone to lean on, it certainly wouldn't be Sam Walker.

"I'm ready," she said, aware that she'd never felt less ready for anything in her life.

Afterward, Nikki remembered her wedding in bits and pieces, like images caught in a photographer's flash.

Sam being introduced to Michael, shaking his hand with a grave courtesy that made the four-year-old's eyes widen in wonder.

Then the chapel itself, with the sun slanting through the lattice-and-ivy roof, casting dappled shadows across the stone floor.

Jason's loving smile as he watched the two of them in front of the altar.

The sound of a soft female voice reading the marriage vows, which Nikki couldn't hear through the humming in her ears.

And Sam Walker.

His image was the clearest of all. His big frame standing so close to hers, his face expressionless as he listened to the words meant to link two people who loved each other, meant to create ties that would last a lifetime.

Nikki jumped when he reached out and took her hand in his. Her eyes locked on his face. As if in a dream, she heard him repeating his vows, promising to love, honor and cherish her. Till death do us part. *Or until she inherits her money,* she thought, suppressing a wild urge to giggle hysterically.

And then she felt the cool weight of a ring slide onto her finger. She looked down at the circle of plain gold that sat so snugly at the base of her third finger. A wedding ring. She hadn't even thought about a wedding ring. But Sam had thought of it. And not just for her. Nikki stared blankly at the much larger gold band he pressed into her palm. She could barely hear her own voice as she repeated her vows, making promises she had no intention of keeping, vows she planned to break. Her hands were shaking so badly that she had a difficult time sliding the ring on Sam's finger.

He closed his fingers around hers, holding her hand in a sure, steady grip. Nikki lifted her face to his and he felt something twist in his chest at the look in her eyes. She looked young and vulnerable and just a little frightened. His hand tightened over hers, offering a silent reassurance he wasn't sure was justified. What they were doing was crazy—a devil's bargain made in a house of God.

"You may kiss the bride." The minister's words sounded unnaturally loud.

Liz and Bill looked at the couple standing before the simple altar and wondered if Nikki knew what she'd just done.

Max looked at his clients and friends and wondered if putting them together had been a stroke of genius or an act of madness.

Jason Drummond looked at them and hoped he'd done the right thing when he gave his approval to their marriage.

Sam looked at Nikki and realized that he'd been wondering what her mouth would taste like since the first moment they'd met.

Nikki looked at Sam, feeling a flutter of panic uncurl in her chest, a feeling that, once he kissed her, some indefinable line would have been crossed and there'd be no going back.

Later, she told herself that she might have pulled

back at that moment if it hadn't been for the fact that Sam was still holding her hand. But if she were completely honest, with herself if with no one else, it wasn't his grip on her hand that held her in place. It was a deep, feminine curiosity, a need to feel his mouth on hers, to know his taste and touch.

It was a plain, unadorned kiss, a simple pressing of his lips to hers, certainly nothing to justify the sudden quivery feeling of her knees—that had to be nerves. Nor was there anything in his kiss to explain the urge she had to curl her fingers around the edges of his jacket and cling, to burrow against him as if he could shield her from the rest of the world.

Sam lifted his head slowly. There was a dazed look in Nikki's eyes that he could relate to. He felt a little dazed himself. He'd certainly shared more passionate kisses in his time, but he couldn't remember the last time he'd had the urge to gather a woman close and hold her, to protect her from harm. Or maybe he could remember. He'd had a similar feeling when he held Sara.

The thought of his first wife made him drop Nikki's hand and step back. He'd loved Sara. That was why they'd married. His marriage to Nikki was an entirely different story, purely a business proposition. He had no intention of forgetting that.

Nikki saw the barriers come up in Sam's eyes as he released her hand and moved away. Her spine stiffened. If he hadn't stepped back, she would have.

It had only been a kiss, she reminded herself. It was a momentary delusion that made it seem as if she could feel it all the way to her toes. She was tired and stressed. That's what was causing this slightly weak feeling in the knees. It certainly wasn't caused by a simple kiss from a man she didn't even like.

This was a business arrangement. That was probably the only kiss they'd ever share.

And she refused to admit to even a twinge of regret at that thought.

The bride and groom left the chapel in separate cars. The only unfortunate thing about the arrangement, as far as they were concerned, was that their destinations weren't also separate. From their terse farewells, it was clear that, given a choice, they'd have parted company at the chapel and never seen each other again. But even if the terms of the will hadn't made that impossible, Jason had been kind enough to make arrangements for the small wedding party to go out to dinner after the ceremony.

"I couldn't let you get married without having a celebration, Nicole," he'd said with an affectionate smile.

The last thing Nikki wanted to do was celebrate her marriage, which already felt like a prison sentence, but she forced what she hoped was a pleased smile and gave the older man a warm thank-you.

Jason was the first to leave the chapel. Nikki had been standing next to Sam, his hand resting on the small of her back, presenting the picture of connubial bliss. The door shut behind Jason, and Sam dropped his hand as if he'd been touching a hot coal. At the same moment, Nikki stepped away, putting distance between them.

"If I'd known he was going to do this, I would have found a way to prevent it," Nikki said, directing her words to no one in particular.

"Things might have been simpler if we'd gone to

Vegas." Sam's comment was aimed directly at his bride.

"Some people might think it's perfectly normal to be married by an Elvis impersonator standing under a flashing neon heart, but no one who knows me would ever believe *I'd* get married that way."

"Since there's no one here but us chickens, I don't see what difference it makes where the damned ceremony is performed. We could have gotten married on top of a flagpole and no one would ever know."

"It's a moot point now," Max said before Nikki could snap out a response. "You're married and Jason has arranged a reception and you're just going to have to make the best of it."

There was a moment's silence while the combatants digested the simple truth of his words. Nikki was the first to speak.

"You're right, Max." She gave him a gracious smile. "We'll just have to make the best of it. Why don't I go with Liz and Bill and show them the way to the restaurant? Perhaps you can do the same for him?"

She nodded her head in the direction of "him" without taking her eyes from Max. In some indefinable way, she managed to imply that Sam would probably need considerable guidance in order to find the restaurant.

Sam ground his teeth together but refrained from comment. He might as well start practicing restraint now. Over the course of the next year, he had the feeling he was going to need a great deal of it.

"If I don't throttle her by the end of the first month, it will be a miracle," Sam said without taking his eyes off the road.

"After tonight, you'll probably barely see each

other,'' Max said soothingly. ''Besides, she isn't that bad.''

Sam gave him a sour look. ''Not if you like a woman with a tongue like a pit viper and a temper like a rabid wolverine.''

''You haven't exactly been a picture of sweetness and light,'' Max pointed out. ''I think the two of you are about even at this point.'' Sam's silence was as good as an admission of guilt. ''All you have to do is look happy for a couple more hours and then you two can pretty much go your separate ways for the next year.'' He gave Sam a sideways glance, his bland look giving way to one of gentle malice. ''Besides, a wedding deserves a celebration.''

The look Sam shot him made it clear that he wasn't in the mood to appreciate the humor in that remark. ''The only thing I'm looking forward to celebrating is my divorce a year from now. I do *not* see any reason to celebrate this farce of a marriage.''

Seeing their exit coming up, he flipped on the turn signal, putting so much force into the simple gesture that Max wouldn't have been surprised to see the lever snap off in his hand. He hid a smile. It wasn't often that he saw Sam Walker with his feathers ruffled.

''Then look at it as a celebration of the fact that Mary will be able to have her surgery.''

''Yeah.'' Sam rolled that thought around as he guided the Bronco off the freeway. Max was right. He should be thinking of his niece and his brother, of what this marriage would mean to both of them. The fact that he and his new wife got along about as well as the Gingham Dog and the Calico Cat faded into insignificance beside the thought of Mary being able to run and play like other five-year-olds.

"That's something worth celebrating," he conceded grudgingly. "But I still think the idea of all of us going out to dinner together is stupid."

"The two of you are going to be living together for the next year."

"Don't remind me."

"You're bound to share a few meals in that time. You might as well start now."

Sam turned into the parking garage near the restaurant. "I married her. That doesn't mean I have to eat with her."

"I can't imagine how I let Max talk me into this," Nikki said, speaking as much to herself as to Liz and Bill.

"I don't remember seeing any bruises from him twisting your arm," Liz pointed out. She was sitting in the back seat where she could keep an eye on her son. Since Michael was busy orchestrating a ferocious battle between two action figures, she was free to give her attention to her friend in the front seat. "You seemed to think marrying Sam was a good idea."

"I was wrong. It's a crazy idea."

"It's a done deal," Bill said. He glanced in the rearview mirror before changing lanes. "Besides, Sam seems like an okay kind of guy. I thought the whole idea was nuts, but I feel better about it after meeting Sam."

"Me, too," Liz agreed.

"I'm glad you both like him." Ridiculous as it was, Nikki felt a little betrayed by their ready acceptance of Sam. "How would you like to have him living with you for the next year?"

"It won't be so bad. In a house the size of yours,

you'll barely know he's there. Besides, you're the one who married him, not me.''

"Don't remind me.'' She was being unreasonable and she knew it. She couldn't blame Liz for not seeing past Sam's ruggedly handsome exterior and charming smile. Not that *she* thought it was charming. At least, not very. Grudgingly, Nikki admitted that he probably seemed like the embodiment of a woman's dreams— *some* women's dreams, anyway. Certainly not hers.

"I can't remember the last time Michael took to someone the way he took to Sam,'' Liz said, determined to point out Sam's attributes. "He really has a way with children.''

"It seems that way.'' Nikki couldn't argue with her there. Sam had developed an immediate rapport with her small godson. Ordinarily, that would have gone a long way to softening her attitude toward the man she'd just married, but she wasn't interested in having her attitude softened. She'd just as soon keep up the mutual dislike they had going. It seemed safer.

"He seems very nice,'' Liz pointed out ruthlessly.

"Mmm.'' Nice wasn't exactly the word Nikki would have used. Pushy, annoying, overbearing, maybe. But not nice. She pretended a fascination with the traffic outside the window, hoping Liz would take the hint. She should have known better.

"You've got to admit he's very attractive.''

She had no intention of admitting any such thing. "If you like that type, I suppose.''

"You mean the tall, blond, blue-eyed, built-like-a-god type? It is a little passé, isn't it?''

"Should I be jealous?'' Bill asked, frowning at his wife in the rearview mirror.

''Just because I happened to notice that Nikki's new husband is a hunk?''

Nikki only half heard the byplay going on between her friends. They'd just driven into the parking lot of the restaurant and she'd seen Sam and Max standing outside, waiting for them so that they all could enter the restaurant together and Jason wouldn't know the bride and groom had parted immediately after the ceremony. The fact that her heart was suddenly beating much too fast was caused by pure dislike. It had nothing to do with Sam Walker's broad shoulders or his craggy good looks. Liz might be impressed by those things, but *she* certainly wasn't. Not even a little bit.

Nikki was grateful for the dimness of the parking garage as Bill pulled the car into it. She didn't want Liz's sharp eyes to see the additional color in her cheeks and question the reason for it. Knowing Liz, she'd put some ridiculous interpretation on it and suggest something like Nikki being attracted to her new husband. Which was obviously absurd. Even if she did happen to notice that he was attractive, it was only on a purely intellectual level and certainly wasn't the cause of the sudden fluttery feeling in her stomach.

And no matter what Liz said, this was all Max's fault. It would be a miracle if she made it through the next couple of hours without wringing his neck. Of course, if she was going to commit murder, Sam Walker might be a better target. Then she wouldn't have to worry about how she was going to get through the next year with him as her husband.

Two hours later, Nikki was no longer worrying about the next twelve months. Her focus had narrowed to the next twelve hours.

Her wedding night.

Throughout dinner, all she'd been able to think about was how much she wished it were over. Sitting in the restaurant, playing at being a happy newlywed, had been sheer torture. She could hardly wait for the meal to be over with so she could go home. It was only when the meal finally ended and everyone was preparing to leave that it hit her that when she went home, she wouldn't be going alone. Liz and Bill had agreed to drive Max home, which meant she was going to be left alone with her new husband.

It had taken considerable effort to refrain from clinging to Liz and begging her friend not to leave her alone with Sam. In the ten minutes since Nikki and her husband had left the restaurant, the silence had reached an almost deafening level. Sam drove with the easy competence she'd expected. She might not like him, but he struck her as the kind of man who did most things well.

She twisted the wedding ring on her finger. The plain gold band felt as if it weighed ten pounds, dragging her hand down. Or was that her conscience feeling the weight of the lies she'd told? Her gaze was compulsively drawn to Sam's hands on the steering wheel of the truck. Light glinted off the wedding ring on his left hand.

"Is the ring too big?"

Nikki jumped. It had been so long since either of them had said anything that the sound of his voice was startling.

"The ring?"

"The one you've been fiddling with ever since we left the restaurant," he clarified.

"No. No, it's fine." She forced her hands to relax. "It just feels odd. I'd forgotten all about rings. I'm glad you thought of them. It would have looked odd if we hadn't had them.''

''Very odd.''

Well, that had been an almost pleasant exchange, she thought. A first for the two of them. It had been very thoughtful of him to provide the rings. She touched her ring and frowned. She didn't have the slightest idea how much a police officer was paid, but she seemed to recall hearing that it wasn't all that much. Could he afford these rings? She cleared her throat. ''It's a nice ring.''

''Glad you like it.'' He didn't take his eyes off the road.

''I think I should pay you for it.''

There was a moment's silence before Sam spoke. ''That's not necessary.''

Something in his tone suggested that it might be wise to drop the subject, but she chose to ignore it. She didn't like the idea of him buying her a ring. It was too reminiscent of a real marriage. And this marriage wasn't real. Not in any way.

''No, really. If you want to pay for your own ring, that's one thing, but there's no reason for you to spend your own money on a wedding ring for me. If you'll tell me how much they were, then I'll pay half. It's only fair.''

''It's not necessary,'' he said again.

''I insist.'' She wasn't sure why this had become so important, but it had. ''There's no reason for you to buy me a ring.''

''You can insist until you turn blue in the face.'' Sam's tone was soft as silk and sharp as a razor. ''I don't want you to pay for the damned ring.''

''But this is a business arrangement, and any expenses incurred should be shared.''

Sam's hands tightened on the wheel as visions of murder and mayhem danced before his eyes. With an effort, he kept his voice level.

"I appreciate the offer, but—"

"Really, it's a simple matter of good business," Nikki interrupted. "I should have provided my own ring, but since I didn't think of it and you did, that doesn't mean I shouldn't pay my fair share."

"If you don't shut up about the damned ring, I'm going to pull off and dump you in the emergency lane and let you walk the rest of the way."

His tone was so calm that it took Nikki a moment to realize what he'd said. Shock was followed almost immediately by indignation and anger.

"That caveman attitude may impress some women, Mr. Walker, but I'm not accustomed to being spoken to like that."

"Too bad. It might have improved your disposition."

"There's nothing wrong with my disposition. You're the one with the personality traits of a—a Neanderthal. I can't believe I let Max convince me that this idea would work. I'd rather live on the street than spend the next year married to you."

"It's not my idea of a really fun time, either, honey."

"Don't call me honey."

"Would you prefer Mrs. Walker?"

"What I'd prefer is for you to take a long walk off a short pier," she snapped. She sat back in her seat and threw him a furious look. "And I will pay for the ring!"

Sam's only response was to glance in the rearview mirror as he flipped on the turn signal. Nikki sat in stunned silence as the truck coasted to a stop in the emergency lane.

"You can't stop here. This is for emergencies." It was a weak protest at best.

Sam unbuckled his seat belt and half turned in the seat so that he faced her. "Are you going to shut up about the ring?"

Wide-eyed, she stared at him, trying to read his expression in the dimly lit cab. She couldn't believe he was acting like this. Just because she wanted to pay for her own ring—a perfectly reasonable thing to do. "You wouldn't dare leave me here."

By way of an answer, he leaned toward her. Nikki gasped as she felt his arm brush against her. She pressed her spine so tight to the seat that she practically melted into the upholstery. But Sam simply grabbed hold of the latch and pushed open the door.

The freeway noise immediately rushed in on them, but Nikki was barely aware of it. Her eyes were locked with Sam's in silent battle. There was no softening in his expression. She looked away and unlatched her seat belt. Picking up her purse, she started to slide out of the truck, intending to call his bluff.

She paused. It was awfully dark out there. A tractor trailer roared by, and the truck rocked in its wake. She considered the three-inch heels on her pumps, not exactly the proper footwear for a stroll along the freeway. Of course, he wouldn't really let her walk.

Would he?

Sam waited, wondering what the hell he was going to do if she actually got out. Obviously, he couldn't let her walk to the nearest emergency phone. She wasn't exactly dressed for strolling along the freeway, and it would be just his luck some maniac would get hold of her and then he'd have her murder on his conscience.

Besides, if anyone was going to have the pleasure of strangling her, it was going to be him.

He shouldn't have threatened to dump her on the freeway. And her offer to pay for the ring shouldn't have made him so angry. It wasn't even an unreasonable suggestion. It was just something about the way she'd said it, as if she thought he couldn't afford to buy a wedding ring. And the fact that it had taken damn near all of his savings to buy the rings didn't make him feel any more cordial toward her. There was just something about her that got under his skin and touched off his temper in a way he couldn't remember anyone else ever doing.

He waited to see what she was going to do.

Nikki waited for him to tell her he was just kidding. That he had no intention of making her walk. But he didn't say anything. She weighed her pride against her safety. It was a tough choice. Another truck roared by and she tried to imagine what it would be like to be standing beside the road when one of those metal behemoths rushed past.

Without a word, she pulled the door shut and faced forward in her seat. If she hadn't been so angry, she might have noticed Sam's almost silent sigh of relief.

They finished the drive to Nikki's house without another word being spoken between them.

# Chapter 5

Sam pushed the restaurant door shut behind him, closing out the cool, damp air. Winter, or what passed for it in Southern California, had arrived abruptly the night before, blowing in with the first storm of the season and drenching the southern half of the state. The rain had tapered off to a miserable drizzle, just enough to make visibility poor and keep the roads slick. Sam spared a moment of gratitude that he wasn't with the highway patrol. Or driving a tow truck.

Brushing the rain from the shoulders of his denim jacket, he looked around. He'd never been in the Wagon Wheel Café but he'd been in places like it. The decor, if you could call it that, was strictly functional. A black-and-white-tile floor that showed signs of age, faded red vinyl booths and a few dusty plastic plants in pots scattered at random throughout the single room. He didn't have to look at a menu to know that the food would be plainly cooked, plentiful and reasonably priced.

"Find yourself a place and light, sugar. We don't stand on formality here." The woman who spoke was in her fifties. Her hair was a shade of red that owed nothing to nature, but her smile was genuine.

"I'm looking for someone."

"He's in the corner booth," she said immediately. "Said he was meeting his brother." She looked Sam up and down. "There any more like you at home? Maybe a few years older?"

"There's four of us, but I'm the oldest."

She sighed. "Ain't that always the way of it? Either too young or married or both."

Sam's smile lingered as he made his way between the rows of booths to the corner one. Keefe looked up as he stopped beside the table. He smiled, but Sam was shocked by the lines of exhaustion etched around his brother's eyes. Keefe was the younger, though by less than two years. At the moment, he looked ten years older.

"Sam." The single word served as a greeting.

"Keefe." Sam had barely slid into the booth when the red-haired waitress arrived. She set a thick white china mug in front of him and filled it with steaming coffee without asking.

"You two want to look at a menu, or should I tell you what's good?" She topped off Keefe's mug as she spoke.

Sam glanced at Keefe who shrugged indifferently. "What's good?" Sam asked.

"The steak and eggs is about the best thing on the menu, but don't ask for the eggs scrambled. Clive, he thinks a scrambled egg ain't done unless it crunches when you bite down."

"We'll take the steak and eggs," Sam told her after

another glance at Keefe, who shrugged again. "Eggs over easy. Steaks rare."

"Comin' right up, sugar."

After she'd left, Sam looked at his brother. "You look like hell."

"Good to see you again, too." Keefe lifted his coffee cup and took a deep swallow. "I've been putting in a lot of hours."

"Including working all night? You look like you haven't slept in a week. I thought ranchers went to bed at sundown. Are you out branding cattle at midnight?"

"Don't pull the big-brother act on me." Keefe's smile was tight around the edges. "The only ranchers who go to bed with the sun are the ones who ranch for a hobby. I'm trying to make a living from the Flying Ace, remember?"

"I remember. How's it going?"

"I'm breaking even this year, which is about as much as I'd hoped. I wouldn't be doing that much if Jace Reno hadn't busted his butt for me this past year."

"He's a good friend."

"And a hell of a rancher. He should have a place of his own." Keefe swallowed the last of his coffee and set the cup on the edge of the table for the waitress to refill. "If I want a lecture on my life-style, I'll go see Mom."

"Sorry." Sam forced back the questions he wanted to ask. "Old habits are hard to break."

"Even bad ones." Keefe grinned and some of the tension seemed to leave his eyes. "You always did act like the nineteen months between us were nineteen years, especially after Dad died."

"I was the oldest. Someone had to keep the rest of you in line."

"You're lucky Gage and Cole and I didn't get together and beat some sense into you."

"I wasn't that bad," Sam protested.

"Worse." Keefe pulled a cigarette pack out of his pocket and tapped it until the end of one came loose. As he lit it, he caught Sam's frown and grinned tiredly. "Like I said, even bad habits are hard to break."

"I thought you quit when you and Dana got married."

The humor instantly disappeared from Keefe's eyes and the lines around his mouth deepened, making Sam regret mentioning Keefe's ex-wife. "Yeah. Well, you may recall that we haven't been married for a while now so if I want to rot my lungs, there's no one around to nag me. Unless I have breakfast with my big brother, of course."

"Sorry." Sam shook his head. "I didn't drive all the way up here to harass you."

"Could have fooled me." But there was no anger in Keefe's response. "Why did you ask me to meet you? Thanksgiving is only a couple of weeks away. I'd be seeing you then."

Sam shifted uncomfortably in the vinyl booth. He'd driven three hours from L.A., leaving before dawn. And Keefe had driven down from his ranch in the Sierra Nevadas. There was so much to say, but now that he was here, he didn't know where to start.

The waitress's arrival with their food gave Sam a moment more to think. When she was gone, he watched Keefe stub out his half-smoked cigarette.

"Have you talked to Mom?" Sam asked finally.

Keefe picked up his knife and fork before glancing across the table at his older brother, his dark eyes shrewd.

"I know you're married, if that's what you're pussy-footing around mentioning."

"A couple of weeks ago." Sam cut a piece off his steak and stared at it.

"Mom says nobody's met her." Keefe chewed and swallowed. "I don't think she was real thrilled about the way you did things—not having any of the family at the wedding and all."

"We were in a hurry," Sam muttered as he reached for his coffee cup.

"She pregnant?"

Sam choked on the coffee.

Keefe waited calmly until he'd stopped coughing. "Is that a yes or a no?"

"No!" Sam gasped the word out, reaching for a glass of water. "God, no."

Keefe's brows rose at Sam's adamant response. "That's the usual reason people get married in a hurry."

"Well, it wasn't our reason," Sam said shortly. He sliced another piece off his steak and chewed it without tasting.

"Okay." Keefe reached for his coffee. "You plan on telling me what the reason was?"

"How's Mary?"

Keefe looked surprised by the abrupt change of topic, but he went along with it.

"About the same, as far as I know. I haven't talked to Cole in a while, but I asked Mom and she said there was no change. She still needs surgery and Cole still doesn't have the money for it. I've got my place listed, but there aren't many people buying ranches these days." His expression was grim. "I guess it's a good thing they're not going to be doing the surgery right away. Gives us a little time to come up with the money."

"Take it off the market."

"I might as well, for all the good it's doing to have it listed."

"You don't need to sell it."

Sam gave up the pretense of eating and looked across the table at his brother. He'd made the long drive to see Keefe because he wanted to tell him the truth. He might be able to convince everyone else that his marriage to Nikki was a real one, but he knew Keefe would never believe it. Of his three brothers, he was closest to Keefe. They'd fought the most when they were young, but they'd still ended up friends.

"I don't have to sell the ranch?" Keefe said slowly. "If you're saying that, then it must mean you've found a way to come up with the money Cole needs." Sam could see the wheels turning in Keefe's head, adding things up and coming to the obvious conclusion. "Does this have something to do with you getting married in such a hurry?"

"It has everything to do with it." Sam's grin was crooked. "I have just made what is called a marriage of convenience, Keefe. And considering the circumstances, it's a *very* convenient marriage. I'll have the money for Mary's surgery by Thanksgiving."

There was a long moment of silence, and then Keefe pushed aside his half-eaten meal and gave all his attention to his brother. "You want to run that by me again?"

"You heard me the first time."

"I heard you, but I don't believe what I heard. You married some woman to get the money for the surgery?"

"That's right."

There was another long silence and then: "Are you nuts?"

"Just desperate. It was Max's idea."

"Max knows about this?" Keefe asked, surprised.

"He set it up. Nikki is a friend of his."

"Nikki? Is that your wife?"

"Yeah." Sam frowned over the description. The word *wife* didn't sound right. Sara was his wife, the only wife he'd had, the only one he'd wanted.

"Maybe you'd better explain this whole thing to me from the beginning," Keefe said. He reached for his cigarettes as if they were a lifeline.

Sam was surprised at how little time it took to tell the whole story. Keefe's cigarette was burned only halfway down when he finished talking. It seemed as if something that had such a cataclysmic effect on two lives should take more than a couple of minutes to describe.

"So she gets her inheritance and you get the money for Mary's surgery," Keefe summed up when Sam was done. "And all you've got to do is stay married for the next year."

"There's only eleven and a half months left now," Sam corrected him.

Keefe's brows rose and one corner of his mouth twisted in humor. "You sound like a prisoner marking off the days to parole on the cell wall."

"That's about how I feel."

"Is she that bad?"

Sam started to say yes but caught himself and shook his head instead. "It's not Nikki. We barely see each other. Which is just as well, because we get along about as well as oil and water."

"She hard to get along with?"

"Yes." Sam's mouth twisted in a self-deprecating smile and he shrugged. "But I probably haven't been much better. On the way home from the wedding, I threatened to dump her out on the freeway and make her walk the rest of the way. She damn near did it, too."

Keefe's eyes narrowed speculatively at the reluctant admiration in his brother's tone. He wondered if Sam was even aware of it.

"She's stubborn as hell," Sam was saying.

"And you're a picture of sweet reason." Keefe's tone was dry as dust.

"That's me." Sam grinned. "Not a stubborn bone in my body."

"Tell that to someone who didn't grow up with you." Keefe shook his head as he stubbed out his cigarette. "I can't believe you actually did this—got married like this, I mean."

"You'd have done the same thing."

"Probably." Keefe reached for his cigarettes, caught Sam's eye and dropped them back in his pocket without taking one. "You're as bad as Mom," he complained without heat. "What does this new wife of yours look like?"

There was that word again. *Wife.* It was technically correct but it made him uneasy to hear it said out loud. He shook off his uneasiness and considered the best way to answer Keefe's question. What did Nikki look like?

An image of her, more vivid than he would have liked, sprang to mind. She was exquisite, like a fine china figurine or a painting by one of the masters. She was golden hair and porcelain pale skin and eyes the color of jade. She made him think of cold winter nights and soft rugs in front of a fireplace. Or hot summer days and cool green grass and the feel of her skin beneath his hands.

"You *do* know what she looks like, don't you?" Keefe's quizzical question made Sam realize that he'd been staring into space as if struck dumb by the question about Nikki's looks.

"Of course I do." He lifted one shoulder in a half shrug and reached for his coffee. "She's about five feet four inches, weight maybe a hundred and twenty pounds. Blond hair, green eyes."

"You sound like you're giving a police report," Keefe said, disgusted by the lack of information. "That description fits just about anyone from Michelle Pfeiffer to Attila the Hun. Details, bro. Details."

"I think Michelle Pfeiffer is taller," Sam muttered.

"So are half the women in the country. What does Mickie look like?"

"Nikki. Her name is Nikki. And she's…attractive." The word hardly did her justice, but if he tried to describe her to Keefe, Keefe was going to end up with the idea that he was attracted to her, and he wasn't. At least, no more than any living, breathing male would be. It was impossible *not* to find her attractive.

"Attractive. That tells me a lot. It's a good thing you're a cop and not a writer. I can see your description of the characters now—the woman pointing the gun at Fosdick was…attractive."

"I never claimed to be Hemingway," Sam pointed out sourly.

"Good thing, too." Keefe lit another cigarette, ignoring Sam's pointed frown this time. "You going to tell the family the truth about this marriage?"

"No." Sam shook his head. "You're the only one

I'm telling. It's going to be hard enough to get Cole to take the money without him knowing how I got hold of it. Gage spends most of his time out of the country. As long as he knows Mary's okay, he won't question the whys and wherefores. And I don't see any point in worrying Mom.''

''You think you and this Nikki can pull off the happy couple act well enough to fool the family?''

''I hope so.'' Sam didn't need his brother's raised eyebrow to tell him that he didn't sound as positive as he might have liked. That was still a big question. Could he and Nikki maintain the facade of loving newlyweds when they could barely be in the same room without going for each other's throats?

Sam was no surer of the answer to that question a few hours later, when he turned onto the narrow street that led to Nikki's home—his home for the past two weeks. In those two weeks, he and Nikki had done a fine job of avoiding each other, which wasn't difficult in the large house. But he didn't doubt that they could have managed to keep a certain distance, even if they'd been sharing a one-room studio apartment.

Luckily, his new residence was far from a studio apartment. The house was nestled in the hills that surrounded the Rose Bowl. Even after having lived there for two weeks, Sam still found himself surprised by it. He'd had a certain image of the place before he married Nikki. He'd been picturing pillars and a veranda, a sort of latter-day Tara. He should have known better. Everything about Nikki Beauvisage—now Walker—spoke of money, but it wasn't flashy money. It was quiet money, the kind that had been around so long that it didn't need to be flashy.

And the house in front of him could be called many things, but flashy wasn't among them. A sprawling, two-story, Spanish style home with off-white stucco walls and clay tile roof, it nestled gracefully into its setting. Three ancient pepper trees, their delicate branches shifting in the slightest breeze, stood near the house, contrasting with the darker green of the oaks that created a ragged line along the edges of the property. The landscaping was beautiful but modest, giving the impression of nature gently curbed.

Sam parked in front of the house, at the end of the long driveway. As soon as he cut off the engine, he was struck by the quiet. Like a lot of other things about his new living arrangements, he still wasn't used to the silence.

He'd grown up in a lower-middle-class neighborhood in Glendale, a place with lots of families, lots of kids and dogs, and not much silence. His own apartment was situated not far from Hollywood and Vine, a fabled corner that had little to recommend it these days, unless one liked taking a chance on getting mugged. The street noise was so prevalent that he'd long since stopped hearing it.

Here he listened to a silence broken only by the sound of a mockingbird working its way through the scales. In the distance, he could hear a subtle rushing noise that was the traffic on the Foothill Freeway, but the sound was far away and unobtrusive. The house was set so far back from the small winding road that he couldn't even hear a car go by.

For no particular reason, the quiet was suddenly irritating, and Sam took some pleasure in slamming the door of the Bronco when he got out. The mockingbird paused, as if shocked by the rude interruption, and then continued with his song, graciously ignoring the ill-mannered human in his territory. Sam glared in the bird's direction. Even the birds were high-class.

The complete irrationality of that thought brought him up short. He was losing it. The stress of this past month had finally gotten to him. He brought his hand up to run his fingers through his hair, but his eyes caught the glint of sunlight on the gold band nestled at the base of his finger and the movement was never finished.

It felt odd to be wearing a wedding ring again. He rubbed his thumb over the band, remembering. He'd worn a ring during his marriage to Sara. It had been buried with her, along with a good part of himself. When he'd bought Nikki's wedding band, he'd hesitated a moment over the matching band for himself, but he knew his family would expect it.

It had been tough enough to spring the news that he was married again, he didn't want to do anything that might make them question the reasons for that marriage. It was important that they all believe this was a real marriage, particularly Cole. His youngest brother had more than his fair share of pride, and knowing the reasons for Sam's marriage would grind that pride into the dust.

He'd have to stress to Nikki that his family was not to know the truth behind their marriage, any more than her family could.

Nikki. His wife.

Sam shook his head in disbelief as he started toward the house. He just couldn't quite connect the words *Nikki* and *wife*. Not his wife, anyway. Maybe by the time the year was up, he'd get used to the idea. He paused to consider that possibility and then shook his head. Nope, Nikki Beauvisage and Sam Walker just didn't go together. Not in a year, not in five years, not in a lifetime.

He glanced at the beat-up old Chevy parked directly in front of the house. It was painted an improbable shade of purple that made him shudder every time he saw it. He still couldn't believe the vehicle belonged to Nikki. It was a long way from the sleek luxury car he'd envisioned her driving. The first time he'd seen it, he'd assumed it was the housekeeper's and thought that if it was the best she could afford, maybe it was time to suggest a raise. But the housekeeper, Lena Sinclair, drove a respectable, late-model sedan and the purple bomb was Nikki's.

Sam shook his head as he passed it, wondering, as he did every time he saw it, why a woman who wore silk suits and Italian leather shoes drove a car that looked—and sounded—as if it were on its last legs.

He pushed open one of the heavy wooden doors and stepped inside. The entryway was all Spanish tile and white stucco. There was a fountain in one corner, and a profusion of potted tropical plants. The stained-glass skylight overhead provided enough light to keep the plants luxuriantly green. The exterior landscaping was the province of the gardener, an elderly Scotsman named McDougal, but the indoor plants were Lena Sinclair's pride and joy.

When Sam entered, she was nipping faded fronds from one of the several ferns that hung from wrought-iron hooks on the wall above the fountain. The thud of the door closing behind him made her turn. She dropped a faded leaf into the basket that hung over her arm as she came to greet him.

"How was your drive?"

"Long and wet," Sam said with a smile. Nikki's housekeeper had proven far more welcoming than Nikki had been, and Sam liked her.

Lena was one of those women who could have been any age from forty to sixty, though Sam thought she was closer to the latter than the former. He guessed that, in her youth, she'd been strikingly beautiful. In late middle age, she was still a handsome woman. She was tall, with a trim figure and a subtle elegance to her carriage that made him think of deposed queens rather than housekeepers.

"Supper's in an hour," she told him.

"Thanks, but I'll probably just get a sandwich later."

They had the same conversation or a variation of it nearly every evening. He wasn't comfortable with the idea of her cooking for him, but, even more than that, he had no desire to share a meal with Nikki. They'd managed to be civil for the past two weeks, a feat that could be attributed, in large part, to the fact that their paths rarely crossed. He didn't see any reason to tempt fate by having a meal with her.

"I've got my best baked chicken in the oven, fresh whole-wheat rolls and an apple pie to die for," Lena coaxed.

Sam felt his stomach stir with interest. Aside from a couple of stale doughnuts in the early hours of the morning, the only thing he'd eaten all day was half of a steak-and-egg breakfast with Keefe. The meal Lena had just described sounded wonderful. On the other hand, the odds of him and Nikki making it through an entire meal without getting into an argument were slim to none.

"Is Nikki home tonight?"

Lena's patrician features tightened with annoyance.

"I swear, the two of you are acting like a pair of children. Nikki going out to dinner and you eating sandwiches in the kitchen like a sneak thief just to avoid sitting down to dinner together."

"I don't think sneak thieves normally take time for a sandwich," Sam pointed out.

She ignored the facetious interruption and continued her scolding lecture. "The two of you agreed to live together for the next year. Do you plan on spending all that time avoiding each other?"

"It's worth a try."

"Well, it won't work. My nerves won't take it, even if yours will. Besides, the holidays are coming up." She waved her pruning shears for emphasis. "Seems to me it's going to look a little odd if you spend them apart."

"We'll work something out," Sam assured her, without the least idea of what that something might be.

"Not if you don't talk to each other."

"We'll talk. And I'll be ready for dinner in an hour. I wouldn't miss your baked chicken for the world." After all, from what she'd said, it sounded like Nikki wasn't home, so there was no sense in wasting a perfectly good chicken dinner.

Lena watched him disappear up the stairs and considered her conscience. She hadn't actually told him that Nikki was going to be out. She could hardly be blamed if he chose to infer that from what she'd said. Her conscience was in fine shape, she decided as she turned back to her plants.

Besides, she was tired of watching the pair of them walk around like a couple of unfriendly cats forced to share a barn. It was time and past that they sat down and actually talked to one another.

\* \* \*

Nikki approached Sam's room with all the enthusiasm of a dental patient anticipating a root canal. At least a dentist gave you novocaine, she thought, stopping in front of his closed door. She could have used an anesthetic to still the butterflies in her stomach.

It was ridiculous to be so nervous at the thought of talking to him. In the two weeks since the wedding, they'd managed several perfectly civil exchanges. Of course, none of those had consisted of much more than hello and goodbye, but they *had* been civil, which was more than could be said about any of their exchanges prior to their marriage. Or after, for that matter. Her mouth tightened at the memory of Sam threatening to put her out on the freeway on their wedding night.

But she wasn't going to think about that now, she reminded herself firmly. She had business to discuss with him. It should only take a moment and, once it was done, he could continue avoiding her. For the moment, she chose to ignore the fact that she'd been doing a considerable amount of avoiding herself.

Nikki smoothed her palms down the sides of her pale grey wool trousers and then adjusted the collar of her jade green silk shirt. Fussing with her clothes was a delaying tactic and she knew it. The truth was, Sam Walker made her just a little nervous. He was large and he was ridiculously male. Worse, she was married to him. It wasn't as easy as she'd hoped to forget that.

She suddenly became aware of the picture she must make, hovering in the hall like a schoolgirl dreading a meeting with the principal. Her soft mouth tightened with irritation. This was *her* house and she wasn't going to stand here getting butterflies in her stomach at the thought of talking to the man she'd married.

Nikki lifted her hand and rapped briskly on the door.

The response she received was muffled but she thought she heard the words *come in*. The sound of that deep voice renewed the tension in her stomach and her hand was not quite steady as she reached for the doorknob. The fact that they were married was irrelevant, she reminded herself. He was practically an employee, if she chose to look at it that way. Not that she could imagine ever hiring Sam Walker for anything. But, husband or employee, he was still just a man, no different from any other man.

On the other hand, maybe there were a few differences.

Nikki stood transfixed in the open doorway. Sam was across the room, his back to her, his attention on the open drawer in front of him.

And he wore not a stitch of clothing.

She forgot how to breathe as her stunned eyes skimmed the muscled width of his back to the tight globes of his buttocks and down the length of his legs.

There were, most definitely, differences between Sam Walker and other men. She'd seen a lot of men in bathing suits that covered little more than the bare necessities, but this was the first time she'd found it hard to breathe. As if compelled by some outside force, her eyes moved upward, tracing every corded muscle on the way.

There was a towel bunched casually in his left hand, held against his hip. From that and the dampness of his hair, she assumed he must have just taken a shower, which explained the fact that he was naked. But it didn't explain him telling her to come in.

She was angry, of course. Or she would be as soon as she caught her breath. How dare he expose himself to her like this, as if…as if they were really married!

There was a jagged white scar across one shoulder and she wondered how he'd gotten it. Would it feel rough in contrast to the smoothness of his skin? What would it feel like to put her hands against the hard muscles of his arms?

Not that she'd want to do that, of course. But the mental denial sounded a little weak. And there was a faint tingling feeling in her fingertips that hinted at a curiosity she had no business feeling.

It seemed as if she stood there forever, but in reality, it was probably less than a minute. Sam reached for something in the open drawer. The simple movement made the muscles ripple across his back and shoulders.

Nikki swallowed hard.

She didn't make a sound, but something must have alerted Sam to the fact that he was no longer alone. He turned suddenly, spinning around in a half crouch, his right hand going across his chest—reaching for a shoulder holster, she realized. Of course it wasn't there.

No shoulder holster. Nothing at all to cover the solid wall of muscle that was his chest. Nikki stared wide-eyed at the mat of dark gold hair that covered his chest, tapering downward across a tautly muscled stomach to—

"What the hell are you doing in here?" Sam's irate demand jerked her eyes upward, but not before she'd seen enough to make her mouth go dry.

"You said to come in," she stammered, thrown momentarily off balance by her own reaction to the generous display of male pulchritude before her.

"I said 'just a minute,'" he snapped. He jerked open the crumpled towel and wrapped it around his hips.

Nikki was surprised and dismayed by the twinge of

regret she felt. What on earth was wrong with her? It wasn't as if she found the man attractive.

The thought was enough to stiffen her spine.

"I distinctly heard you say 'come in.'" She hadn't *distinctly* heard anything, but she certainly couldn't admit that now.

"Then you need your ears cleaned." Sam finished knotting the towel, his jerky movement revealing his irritation. "Why the hell would I say 'come in' when I'm standing here bare beam and buck naked?"

"I have no idea." Nikki had regained her poise, or at least a portion of it. "I thought perhaps you had exhibitionist leanings."

"And maybe the heart of a voyeur beats beneath that prim exterior. Maybe you're sorry I covered up?"

The fact that she *had* felt a twinge of regret added to the color in Nikki's cheeks. "Don't be ridiculous," she snapped.

"Shall I drop the towel?" he asked in a tone that made her want to smack him. "I certainly wouldn't want to spoil your fun."

Though her face felt as if it were on fire, Nikki managed to give him a look of cool indifference. "You don't have anything I haven't seen before." She paused, letting her eyes flick downward. "And in somewhat greater quantity."

Color tinted Sam's cheekbones, but the look in his eyes suggested it was caused more by anger than by any blow she might have dealt his male ego.

"Was there something you wanted? Or did you just barge in here to leer at me?"

"I was invited in," she said through clenched teeth.

"You stick to that story, if you like." He nodded

agreeably, and Nikki's hands clenched against the urge to wipe the bland expression from his face.

"Max called. There are papers you need to sign. *That's* what I came to tell you."

"Thanks. I'll call him."

He didn't look in the least apologetic, damn him. "Next time, I'll slip a note under the door."

"You do that. Now, if you don't mind, I'd like to get dressed."

Nikki stood there for a moment, wishing desperately for a clever response, something that would make it clear just how much she disliked him, how little desire she had to ever speak to him again. And most of all, how little attraction he held for her. But she couldn't come up with the words to convey all those things. Worse, from the gleam in Sam's eyes, she suspected that he knew exactly what was going through her mind and was amused by her frustration.

The only option was to withdraw with as much dignity as possible. Which was what she did. She stepped back into the hall, pulling the door closed with a gentle click, not allowing him the satisfaction of seeing her slam it.

She stood in the hallway, feeling as if steam must be coming out her ears. She'd never in her life met anyone who made her want to commit violent acts. Never—until she'd met Sam Walker.

And she'd had to go and marry him.

She cast a last frustrated glance over her shoulder at the blank door, wishing desperately that she hadn't let Max convince her that this marriage was a good idea, that she'd married someone else, *anyone* else.

But she was stuck with Sam Walker, at least for the next eleven and a half months.

Nikki forced herself away from the door. He was an obnoxious jerk, but she probably wouldn't have to deal with him again for days. With luck, maybe she could stretch it to a week.

# *Chapter 6*

Luck was not smiling in Nikki's direction.

Half an hour after her encounter with Sam, she left her room to go down for dinner. She'd been avoiding eating in the dining room for the last couple of weeks, not wanting to share a meal with Sam. But Lena had expressed considerable annoyance over Nikki's new habit of taking a tray up to her room, asking if she planned to eat her meals in her room for the next year. The idea didn't sound bad to Nikki, not if it meant less time spent in Sam Walker's company.

Lena must have read the answer in Nikki's eyes, because she'd clicked her tongue in exasperation and pointed out that Sam hadn't eaten a single meal in the dining room since he'd moved in. The two of them were acting like a pair of children. She would have continued, but Nikki lifted a hand in surrender and promised to come down to dinner. After all, what were the odds that Sam would choose tonight to eat in the dining room?

Apparently, they were much better than she'd hoped.

She saw him as soon as she entered the room. He was standing in front of the floor-to-ceiling window, looking out into the courtyard that was tucked into the corner of the L-shaped house. The rain was a glistening curtain sliding through the lights that illuminated the naturalistic waterfall and small pool that dominated the center of the courtyard.

It was a beautiful view, and one she'd often admired herself, but Nikki wasn't in the mood to appreciate it. Obviously, Sam had decided to come down to dinner tonight. Equally obvious was the need for an immediate change of plans on her part. The last thing she wanted to do was sit across a dinner table from Sam Walker. Talk about a prescription for indigestion.

She took a step backward, intending to slip out of the room before he saw her. Better to face Lena's wrath than to spend time with her reluctant husband.

But before Nikki could make her escape, Lena came through the door across the room. She was carrying two bowls from which steam was rising. Her dark eyes immediately spotted Nikki, who was poised for departure in the doorway.

"There you are, Nikki. Just in time."

At the sound of Lena's voice, Sam turned and saw Nikki. He was wearing a pair of softly faded jeans and a chambray shirt that echoed the blue of his eyes, but a sudden image of how he'd looked wearing only a towel—and not even that—flashed through Nikki's mind. She could only hope that the light was dim enough to conceal the color that came up in her cheeks.

From Sam's expression, it was clear that he was no more enthused about the idea of sharing a meal than she was. The knowledge carried a perverse sort of pleasure. At least she wasn't the only one who'd be miserable.

"The soup smells wonderful, Lena," she said as she strolled into the room, giving no hint that she'd rather have been walking into a lion's den.

"There's nothing like a good bowl of soup on a chilly night like this," Lena said as she set the bowls down.

Nikki was dismayed to see that she'd arranged the place settings together at one end of the long table, one on either side, so that she and Sam would be staring at each other across the width of polished mahogany.

"Lena said you were eating out tonight," Sam said, making little effort to conceal his displeasure at finding out otherwise.

"Actually, I just said she'd been eating out lately," Lena said serenely. She reached out to straighten a spoon, bringing it into perfect alignment with the fork beside it. "Why don't the two of you start on the soup. I'll bring in the rest of the meal."

There was a moment's silence after her departure. The hiss of the rain outside suddenly seemed very loud. Nikki stared at Sam's hand where it rested on the back of one of the chairs. His hands were large, long fingered and strong. She thought of the corded muscles in his thighs, of the way the muscles in his shoulders rippled beneath his skin.

"I think I'll see if there's anything I can do to help." She was halfway across the room before the sentence was complete. At the moment, she didn't care if he knew she was running. She just wanted to get out of the room before he noticed that she was blushing like a girl in the throes of her first crush.

Lena glanced up as she entered the kitchen. Her sharp

gaze took in Nikki's flushed face and the panic in her eyes. Her smile was subtly smug as she returned her attention to the steamed vegetables she was transferring from pan to bowl.

"If you've come to offer help, I don't need any," she said.

"I've come to ask what you think you're doing." Nikki kept her voice low, not wanting Sam to hear her.

"I'm finishing up dinner." Lena raised her dark brows in surprise.

"You know what I mean. You told me he wouldn't be here tonight." Nikki took the pan Lena handed her and set it in the sink.

"I said he hadn't eaten in the dining room since he'd moved in." Lena shrugged her innocence. "How was I to know he'd choose tonight to do something different?"

"Because you told him *I* wouldn't be here."

"That's not what I said. I just said you hadn't—"

"I heard what you said. And I know perfectly well you were setting the two of us up. What I don't know is *why*."

Lena finished garnishing the vegetables with parsley sprigs and slivers of red pepper before raising her head to meet Nikki's indignant look.

"I set you up," she admitted without the smallest show of guilt. "I told your Sam, and I'll tell you—it's more than past time the two of you sat down and talked."

"I don't want to talk to him. And he's not *my* Sam. He's not *my* anything."

"He's your husband."

"Only for the next year, and I don't know how I'm going to get through it."

"Well, you're not going to get through it by acting like a couple of children. Sneaking around the house to avoid each other. If I hadn't come in when I did, you would have gone back up to your room tonight, wouldn't you?"

"I don't want to eat with him." Nikki flushed at the childish sound of her protest, but it was nothing more than the truth.

"Do you plan on going the whole year without eating a meal together?" Lena demanded.

"If I can manage it, I'll go the whole year without setting eyes on him."

"Well, you can't manage it. You know it, I know it and he knows it. If the pair of you weren't too old for it, I'd smack your heads together to knock some sense into you."

Nikki's eyes shifted away from Lena's. She suddenly felt as if she were five years old again and had just been caught with her hand in the cookie jar. When she was a child, it had always been Lena who'd provided a sense of discipline and stability in her life.

Her father had been killed in a boating accident when she was a baby, and her grandfather had moved her and her mother and brother into his house, making no secret of the fact that he didn't trust Marilee to take care of his grandchildren. It had proved a wise move since Marilee had embarked on a series of affairs and marriages that had spanned the years since. During the marriages, she'd moved out of the big house, but, at her father-in-law's insistence, her children had stayed.

Marilee had flitted in and out of her life like a beautiful butterfly, never quite with them even when she was living in the same house. Nikki's brother, Alan, had been old enough to reject any attempt at filling the gap

Marilee's periodic disappearances left in his life, but Nikki had desperately needed Lena's stable presence in hers. Lena was much more than a housekeeper to her, and her disapproval stung.

"I don't like him," Nikki muttered when the silence had gone on longer than was comfortable.

"You don't know him well enough not to like him. And if you didn't like him, you shouldn't have married him."

"Max didn't exactly provide me with a lot to choose from," Nikki pointed out.

"Well, there's not a thing wrong with the choice you made. And you might find that out if you'd take a minute to get to know him. I don't see what you're complaining about. He's well-spoken, a police officer, and he's a good-looking man. Not like some of the namby-pamby types you've dated these last few years."

Nikki stared at her, horrified. "You're not matchmaking, are you?"

"You're already married to him. Why would I matchmake?" Lena lifted the foil off the chicken and rice she'd just taken out of the oven and transferred the chicken to a platter.

"But it's not a real marriage," Nikki shouted in a whisper.

"You said the words. You signed the papers. And your Sam looks pretty solid to me. I'd say that makes it a real marriage."

"You know what I mean. And he's not *my* Sam."

"What I know is that it's time and past that you met a man who won't lay down and roll over for you or your money." Lena began transferring the rice to a bowl.

"He *married* me for my money," Nikki pointed out, surprised to realize that the thought stung.

"I'm sure he had his reasons," Lena said, undisturbed.

"Like greed," Nikki muttered.

"I don't think so. Your Sam doesn't strike me as a greedy man."

"He married a woman he didn't even know in return for a nice, fat check. Which he demanded up front, by the way. If that's not greed, I don't know what is. And he's *not* my Sam," she added without much hope of being listened to.

"I'd guess he had his reasons," Lena said comfortably. "Besides, you did the same thing—married him for money."

"But it's *my* money."

"No, it's not." Lena shot her a stern look. "It's your grandfather's money and you're cheating to get it."

The criticism stung all the more because Nikki had felt a few guilt pangs over the way she was circumventing her grandfather's intentions.

"Grandfather shouldn't have put such a ridiculous clause in his will," she muttered.

"No, he shouldn't have. And if he hadn't been such a blind, stubborn fool, he'd have realized that you'd do exactly what you have. Heaven knows, you're as stubborn as he was. I don't blame you for doing what you did, but now that you've made your bed, I think you should lie in it with a bit more grace. Both of you," she added, nodding toward the dining room to include Sam in her disapproval. "If you can't share a meal without arguing, then you're going to have a hard time getting through the next year, now aren't you?"

She didn't seem to expect a response, because she nodded to a cloth-covered basket.

"Bring the rolls with you when you come," she ordered as she picked up the platter of meat and vegetables.

Frustrated and confused, Nikki stared after her. Just what she needed—Lena lecturing her on Sam Walker's attributes. Not to mention the possibility that Lena had matchmaking in mind. It was going to be difficult enough to live with him for the next year, without adding Lena's interference to the picture.

But she was right about one thing—they certainly should be able to make it through a meal together without arguing. The question was whether or not they would.

The soft hiss of the rain in the courtyard seemed to thicken the silence inside, making it an almost tangible presence. Neither of the room's occupants had said a word since Lena's departure. The housekeeper had gone home as soon as the meal was served, leaving the newlyweds alone in the big house.

Sam ate with the methodical precision of an assembly-line worker building widgets. And with about as much pleasure.

Nikki picked at her meal, rearranging the food on her plate and forcing down an occasional bite. She was vividly aware of the man sitting across the table from her.

"I think we were set up."

Nikki jumped, startled. The silence between them had been so thick that it was a shock to have it broken. Her eyes jerked to his face.

"Set up?"

"For this meal. I think Lena set us up." There was

a hint of rueful humor in his eyes, and Nikki felt the knot of tension in her stomach ease a little.

"I think so, too," she agreed.

"You'd think I'd recognize a sting when it's staring me in the face, but I fell for it like a rookie."

"I've known her long enough to be suspicious, but I didn't see it coming."

"She's very good. I mean, she didn't actually tell me you weren't eating in tonight. She just held out the bait and I jumped for it." There was real admiration in Sam's tone.

"She did the same thing with me. Said you hadn't been eating here at all."

"She said the same thing about you."

"I haven't been. Not since the…since we…"

"Got married?" Sam said the words she couldn't quite get out.

"Yes." Nikki gave up the pretense of interest in her food and pushed her plate aside. "It seems so incredible, I have a hard time saying it."

"I know what you mean."

Sam pushed his own plate aside and reached for the thermal coffeepot Lena had set on the end of the table. He held it up, lifting one brow questioningly. Nikki nodded and pushed her cup across the table. Sam filled both their cups, nudged the cream and sugar in her direction and then leaned back in his chair, cradling his coffee between his palms. The bone-china cup looked ridiculously small and fragile in his large hands.

Nikki added a spoonful of sugar and a healthy dollop of cream to her coffee. The only sound in the room was the soft rush of the rain outside and the musical chime of her spoon against the delicate porcelain of the cup as she stirred her coffee. But the tension that had characterized the silence only moments before was gone.

"I think this is some kind of record," Sam said.

"What is?"

"We've been together for—" he glanced at his watch "—almost twenty minutes without getting into an argument."

"We didn't speak for seventeen of those twenty minutes," she pointed out dryly.

"And that's another record. Three minutes' conversation without attempted murder on either side."

"Where's Ripley when you need him?"

There was a short, almost companionable silence. Nikki took a sip of coffee and shot a surreptitious look across the table at Sam, wondering if he was as surprised as she was that they were actually managing a civil exchange. From the look in his eyes when they met hers, he was.

"I was out of line this evening when you came to my room," he said. "I'm sorry."

The reminder of the scene—was it only an hour ago?—brought an extra tint of pink into Nikki's cheeks. She looked away from him, trying to banish the image of his nudity. "I really did think you'd said to come in," she said, hoping he wouldn't notice her blush.

"I guess your finishing-school ears just aren't accustomed to my middle-class accent."

Nikki's shoulders stiffened. So much for their brief cease-fire, she thought. He couldn't go more than a few minutes without making snide remarks about the differences in their backgrounds. She was surprised by the depth of her disappointment. The last few minutes had been so pleasant.

She lifted her head, a cutting response hovering on

the tip of her tongue. And she saw the humor in Sam's blue eyes. There was nothing sarcastic or critical in his expression, and Nikki realized she'd misjudged him.

Maybe not for the first time?

It was a novel thought, the idea that she might have misjudged him. Not that she'd been completely wrong. Certainly she hadn't misjudged his determination to dump her on the Ventura Freeway in the middle of the night. But maybe he wasn't quite as hopeless as she'd thought.

"Next time, I'll ask you to repeat yourself," she said. And it was hard to say who was most surprised by the faintly teasing note in her response.

"Maybe I should ask you to repeat what you think you heard." Sam's half smile became a full-fledged grin, and Nikki's heart bumped ever so slightly. He really was a remarkably attractive man, if you liked the type. And wasn't it a very good thing that she didn't?

"Lena thinks we should try to get along," she said abruptly.

"So I gathered." Sam cradled the cup against his palm. "I assume that's why she set us up tonight."

"Yes."

"It would certainly make the next twelve months a little easier."

"True."

There was a brief silence while they both considered just how long a year could be.

"I guess I haven't been the easiest guy in the world to get along with," Sam said finally.

She could have commented that that was the understatement of the year, but she didn't. He'd offered an olive branch and the least she could do was respond in kind. "I haven't been an angel of sweetness and light."

"I'm the one who's been at fault in most of this."

Nikki shook her head. "I can't let you take all the blame. I know my temper's been short."

"I don't blame you. I've been a real s.o.b."

She felt a flash of irritation. Did he have to argue with everything she said? "Really, I'm just as much to blame as you are," she insisted in an aggressively reasonable tone.

Sam's smile tightened subtly and his eyes took on a faint chill. "I launched the hostilities in Max's office the day we met. You're not to blame for responding in kind."

Nikki fought to control her annoyance. Really, he was the most obnoxious man she'd ever met. And wasn't it typical of him to insist on having the final word and taking all the blame—

Suddenly it hit her that they were actually on the verge of quarreling over who was most to blame for their past quarrels. The absurdity of it brought her eyes to Sam's face. The same thought must have struck him, because his eyes reflected her own surprise and disbelief.

"This is ridiculous. I can't even believe we're arguing about this," he muttered.

Neither could Nikki. She wasn't normally an argumentative woman. What was it about the man she'd married that brought out this side of her? And how were they going to dig themselves out of this latest hole?

"You're right, it is ridiculous. If you want to take all the blame, I won't stop you." She nodded her head graciously.

"Gee, that's big of you," Sam said dryly. "Thanks. I think."

"You're welcome."

Nikki saw the laughter in Sam's eyes, and a soft giggle escaped her. Sam chuckled. The moment of shared laughter banished the last of the tension between them.

"Maybe we can blame everything on the situation," Sam suggested. He shook his head as he reached for the coffee pot. "I thought arrangements like this only existed in books and movies."

He raised the coffeepot and gave her a questioning look.

"No, thank you. One cup is my limit."

"You'd never make it as a cop." Sam twisted the lid back onto the thermal pot and picked up his cup.

"Do you have to drink a lot of coffee to be a cop?"

"At least a pot a day," he confirmed solemnly. "We've got to have something to go with all those doughnuts."

"I can imagine." Though from what she'd seen of him—which, come to think of it, was a considerable amount—she doubted that Sam spent much time eating doughnuts. A man didn't end up with all that lean muscle by spending his time at Winchell's.

"Do you think we could manage to maintain this level of civility for more than a few minutes?" he asked, his tone pitiable.

Nikki shot a quick glance across the table, taking in the humor in his eyes, the warmth of his smile and the tousled thickness of his dark blond hair. She was shocked to realize that she didn't think it would be difficult at all.

"Maybe if we worked on it," she conceded.

"I'm willing to try if you are. A year is a long time to be at odds with someone you're living with. We could try and think of each other as roommates. My brother Gage has a woman roommate, and they manage to rub along together fairly well.''

''In a way, I guess that's what we are,'' Nikki said slowly.

''Truce?'' He offered his hand across the table.

Nikki hesitated only a moment before accepting the gesture. She felt an immediate jolt of awareness, the same tingling feeling that she'd had the first time they shook hands in Max's office. She'd had it again, only much stronger, when he'd kissed her in the chapel.

His fingers seemed to swallow her hand, making her very aware of how much larger and stronger he was. The thought should have been frightening. They might share a marriage license, but he was still a stranger. It wasn't fear Nikki felt, though. It was a deep feminine awareness of the masculinity of the man across from her, of the differences between them.

''Truce.'' She heard the breathy tone of her response and hoped Sam would attribute it to the surprise of finding them in agreement. She pulled her hand free.

''Maybe we'll make it through this next year without killing each other after all,'' Sam said, giving her another of those grins that made her pulse jump.

''It just might be possible.''

Somehow, twelve months didn't sound nearly as long as it had a few minutes ago.

''So, how's married life?'' Liz's eyes were bright with curiosity. ''I don't see any wounds, so I assume you and your new hubby haven't come to blows yet.''

Once a month, she and Nikki got together to have lunch, go shopping or catch a movie together. Liz deposited Michael with a baby-sitter and, as she put it, escaped long enough to confirm that the real world still existed. Nikki thought that Liz's husband and son *were* the real world, but she enjoyed a chance to spend a few hours with her friend. This was the first time they'd seen each other since the wedding and Liz was bursting with a curiosity she didn't even try to hide.

"He's not my *hubby* and married life is just fine, especially since it's not really a marriage."

Liz clicked her tongue in disgust at this boring response. "Details. I want details."

"What kind of details are you hoping for?" Nikki asked. She gave her friend a stern look. "As if I didn't know. You're hoping for some lurid tale of passion."

"Lurid tales have gotten a bad rap in recent years. And what's wrong with passion?"

"Nothing. But that's not why I got married. For heaven's sake, Liz, I'm not going to jump into bed with a man I barely know just because we share a marriage license."

"You've thought about it, though, haven't you?" Liz asked wickedly. "I mean, there he is. And there you are. All alone together in that big house."

"I think you've been spending too much time watching soap operas. Things don't work the same way in real life as they do on TV. Maybe we should get together more often so I can give you a reality check," Nikki said, giving her a concerned look. "There's nothing going on between Sam and me."

"If I were living with a man as gorgeous as Sam Walker, I don't think I'd be boasting about the fact that nothing was going on."

The waiter's arrival with their meals gave Nikki a momentary respite, but she knew Liz too well to think the topic would be forgotten. She was right. The moment he was gone, Liz pinned Nikki to the booth with an intense look.

"And you can't tell me that you haven't given some thought to the possibilities inherent in this whole setup."

"I hardly even know he's in the house," Nikki said, lying through her teeth. She gave Liz a quelling look as she reached for the saltshaker. "This is strictly a business arrangement and that's all it's ever going to be. Enough said. Now, can we please change the subject? How is my adorable godchild?"

From Liz's expression, it was obvious that she didn't think there'd been nearly enough said, but she accepted the change of topic. And in a gesture of true friendship, she refrained from bringing up Sam's name for the rest of the afternoon.

Nikki appreciated her restraint. She only wished that he'd stay out of her thoughts as well as the conversation. And she wished she'd been telling the truth when she said that she hardly knew he was in the house. But if she'd told Liz the truth, she'd have had to admit to thinking about her new husband more than she liked.

It had been a week since they'd agreed to a cease-fire. As she'd crawled into bed that night, she'd wondered if it was possible that she and Sam could really get along. From the moment they'd met, they'd struck sparks off one another.

Now, driving home after her time with Liz, she found herself considering the possibility of a whole new kind of sparks between them. She dismissed the idea almost immediately. Even if she were to become attracted to Sam, and assuming the feeling was mutual, it wouldn't make any difference. This was still a business arrangement and, if there was one thing she'd learned from her grandfather, you did not mix your business and your private lives.

"And you forced me to break that rule, Grandfather, when you came up with that ridiculous clause to put in your will," she said out loud as she turned into her driveway. "Because you forced me to mix business with my private life in a major way."

Sam's truck was parked in front of the house. Nikki's heart jumped a little, but that was easily explained. She and Sam might have been getting along this past week, but she still wasn't accustomed to the idea that she no longer lived alone. And it wasn't as if she and Sam had become friends overnight. The overt hostility was gone, but they were still strangers. They'd hardly seen each other this past week, which could be why their truce had held, she thought as she pushed open the front door.

Sam was coming down the stairs as she entered the house, as if he'd been conjured by her thinking about him. He smiled when he saw her, and Nikki was struck by how much more pleasant it was to be on speaking terms. Prior to their truce last week, they'd probably have exchanged little more than a nod.

"Nikki, I'm glad I caught you," he said, taking the last two stairs in one stride.

He was wearing jeans, well-worn and faded, clinging to his long legs in a way that made her aware of the muscles beneath the snug denim, and the light from the chandelier picked out the gold in his dark blond hair. All in all, he looked altogether too attractive. It was too bad Max hadn't come up with a nice, mousy type for her to marry, someone with a plastic pocket protector and safety glasses that slid down his nose—someone who wouldn't have even the slightest effect on her pulse.

With an effort, she forced herself to concentrate on what Sam was saying.

"I was hoping I'd get a chance to talk to you before I left for work."

"I thought you worked today," she said. Walking to the narrow mahogany side table that sat along one side of the entryway, Nikki set her purse down and picked up the stack of mail there before turning back toward Sam. The little bit of extra distance made it easier to breathe.

"No rest for the wicked." His smile couldn't completely banish the tired lines beside his eyes. "Thanksgiving is next week." Sam was shrugging into his jacket as he spoke. "I never thought to ask if your family is coming back from Europe for the holidays."

"My family?"

The questioning tone of her voice made Sam's brows go up. "Your mother and your brother," he clarified. "Are they coming home for Thanksgiving or Christmas?"

"Not that I know of. I think Mother planned to spend the holidays in Monaco. I don't know what Alan will be doing." She shrugged. "We're not really very close." Which was a bit of an understatement, particularly when it came to her brother, whom she hadn't seen since their grandfather's funeral two years before.

"Then there's no conflict," he said with satisfaction.

"Conflict?"

"With your family and mine both expecting us to join them. We can go to Los Olivos." He pulled his keys out of his pocket, apparently satisfied that the decision had been made.

"I can't spend the holiday at your family's home," Nikki protested, horrified at the idea.

"Why not?"

"Because they think we're married."

"We *are* married."

"You know what I mean." Agitated, she set the mail back down and shoved her hands in the pockets of her slacks.

"You mean they're going to expect us to act like a couple." He took the lift of her shoulder as agreement and continued. "You didn't think we could make it a whole year without running into situations where we'd have to pretend we were really married, did you?"

"It's too soon. We could never carry it off. Besides, I was planning on spending the holidays with Jason. Otherwise, he'll be alone." She finished on a note of triumph, confident that she'd solved the question of the holidays.

"Isn't Jason going to think it a bit odd if we spend our first holiday together apart?" Sam's tone was dry. "We're supposed to be madly in love, remember?"

Nikki stared at him. She wanted more than anything to argue with him, but she couldn't. Jason would think it very odd if she spent Thanksgiving with him and left her new husband to go off and join his family.

"Why don't you see if Jason wants to join us?" Sam asked, accepting her tacit agreement that they'd be spending the holidays together. "Thanksgiving is pretty much of an open house and I know he'd be welcome."

"I'll ask," Nikki said, giving in to reality.

"Don't look so glum," Sam chided. "We haven't burned anyone at the stake in at least five or six years."

"That's reassuring."

He grinned at her gloomy tone, lifted his hand in

farewell and disappeared out the door. Nikki stayed where she was, listening to the delicate sound of the fountain in the corner and trying to convince herself that this visit didn't have disaster written all over it.

# Chapter 7

Thanksgiving dawned gray and cloudy, a perfect reflection of Nikki's expectations for the day. She'd had a full week to anticipate meeting Sam's family, a full week in which to consider all the things that could go wrong. The possibilities were awful enough to make her pray the clouds would open up and rain so hard that they'd have to give up the idea of driving north. Unfortunately, by midmorning, the sun was starting to nudge its way through and the radio was announcing that it was going to be a beautiful holiday.

Sam drove to Los Olivos. With a vague idea of having a quick getaway available, Nikki had suggested they take her car. But neither Sam nor Jason made any secret of their doubts about it being able to make the three-hour trip. Nikki's protests that Barney was a great deal more reliable than he looked were ignored. And since Barney's heating and air-conditioning system consisted of opening or closing windows, she didn't pursue the argument.

Besides, she didn't really want to drive. She was better off climbing into the back seat of the Bronco and leaving Sam to carry on the bulk of the conversation with Jason, giving her yet more time to brood about meeting his family.

It would have been difficult enough to meet them if she'd really been his wife, a genuine addition to the family. But the fact that the marriage was simply a business transaction made it even more nerve-racking.

If there was a good time to be introduced to Sam's family, it surely wasn't in the midst of a major holiday. Nikki stared out the window at the passing scenery and wished she'd insisted on meeting the rest of the Walker clan sooner. Never mind the fact that, until two weeks ago, she'd barely been able to exchange a civil word with Sam and that she'd probably rather have had her nose pierced than spend any time with him, let alone meet his family.

The fact was, if they were going to pull off this charade for the next year, she really should have met his family before this. What kind of a daughter-in-law didn't want to meet her in-laws? They'd probably already figured out that it was a sham. And if they hadn't, they undoubtedly soon would. It would have been nice to believe Sam's assurance that they wouldn't be looking for evidence that his marriage was anything less than what it seemed and would, therefore, take it at face value and accept her as his wife. But she couldn't shake the feeling of impending disaster.

They'd take one look at her and know she was a fake. Then they'd tell Jason, and she'd not only lose her inheritance, she'd probably go to jail for fraud of some kind. She'd lose her friends, her money, have to wear ugly clothes and probably spend the rest of her life as the girlfriend of some woman named Bubba.

It was, perhaps, fortunate that lack of sleep caught up with her before Nikki's imagination could paint even more lurid pictures of the disasters that lay ahead. She dozed off shortly after they left the outskirts of Los Angeles behind them, sleeping until Jason reached back to shake her awake minutes before they arrived at the Walker home.

"You should have had Jason wake me sooner," she said, keeping her voice low as Sam opened the back door. She was rummaging through her purse for her brush. "I look like a disaster survivor."

"You look fine."

"If you like the hair-on-end, ruined-makeup look," she snapped in a whisper. She was vividly aware of Jason standing on the other side of the car and of the need to present a happy-couple image to him.

Sam's smile tightened. "You're meeting my family, not filming a shampoo commercial."

"I wouldn't want to meet a dog collector looking like this." She jerked the brush through her hair, smoothing it into a thick gold fall around her shoulders.

"It's a good thing none of my family work for Animal Control, then, isn't it?"

"Problem?" Jason walked around the car, curious about the delay.

"Nikki's worried about how she looks," Sam said, sounding so like an indulgent husband that Nikki almost believed it herself. "I was just telling her she doesn't need to primp. She always looks beautiful."

"That's true," Jason agreed, and Nikki could only

hope that the sun in his eyes prevented him from seeing the hostile look she shot her loving husband.

She slammed the brush back in her purse and jerked the zipper closed. The Walkers would just have to take her as she was, because she wasn't going to sit here, and put on lipstick after she'd just been accused of primping. She would have liked to ignore the hand Sam offered to help her out of the car, but Jason would surely notice. Besides, her left leg was asleep and she didn't want to risk falling face first onto the sidewalk.

"Don't look so nervous," Sam chided, taking her hand to steady her as she got out of the truck. "They're going to love you."

Nikki knew his assurance was given, at least in part, for Jason's benefit, in keeping with Sam's role of loving husband. But she wanted desperately to believe it. Not necessarily that they'd *love* her, but that they wouldn't take one look at her and know her for the phony she was.

She didn't think she could have been any more nervous if she really had been a new bride. Though she knew it was strictly for show and she was still annoyed with him, she found herself grateful for the strength of Sam's fingers around hers as they walked up the slightly erratic brick path.

The house was a simple, one-story stucco, painted white with deep blue trim. The yard was small and beautifully kept. There was a split-rail fence made of cedar that had weathered to a soft gray. Along the street, and set just inside the fence, were rose beds. Roses in every possible color dipped and swayed in the cool breeze. Pansies lined the walkway, their cheerful faces nodding a welcome.

It was a friendly picture, and Nikki found herself insensibly soothed by it. It didn't seem possible that anything bad could happen in a house with such a cheerful yard.

They'd just reached the foot of the steps when the door burst open and a tall, dark-haired man stepped out.

"I'm probably going to have to raid a turkey farm," he was saying over his shoulder. "Wouldn't it be easier just to roast the damned dog?"

It was apparently a rhetorical question, because he pulled the door closed, cutting off any possible reply. He turned, saw Sam, and a smile banished the somewhat intimidating frown on his face. "Sam!"

"Gage! I thought you were in the wilds of Borneo or Brazil." Sam released Nikki's hand and took a quick stride forward, meeting his brother as he stepped off the porch.

"It was Africa. And I was able to wangle six weeks' leave."

Nikki hung back, watching as they hugged, a little surprised by their obvious pleasure at seeing each other. She couldn't remember anyone in her family ever being quite so enthused about getting together. An air kiss next to her cheek was about the most she'd ever gotten from her mother, and her brother had never expressed anything stronger than indifference to her presence.

The family resemblance between the brothers was slight. Both men were tall and broad shouldered, but Gage Walker's hair was a brown so dark it hovered on the edge of black, his features more even than Sam's. But the clear blue of his eyes was familiar, as was the humor in them.

"I understand you've got big news," Gage said, looking past Sam with unconcealed interest. "I hope this isn't your wife. She's too pretty to waste herself on someone like you.''

Nikki flushed at the compliment, but the butterflies in her stomach subsided a bit. At least one member of Sam's family seemed friendly.

"Nikki, this is my brother Gage." Sam turned and caught her hand, drawing her forward. "He spends most of his time in uncivilized parts of the world building bridges and dams and other things for which the natives have no use."

"He's just jealous because he spends all his time writing parking tickets." Gage's hand swallowed hers, and his smile held nothing but welcome.

Nikki dared to draw a shallow breath, listening with half an ear as Sam introduced Jason. One down and heaven knew how many to go.

"What were you saying about robbing a turkey farm?" Sam asked when the introductions were complete.

Gage's dark brows hooked together in a frown, though Nikki thought she saw laughter in his eyes. "You just missed all the uproar. Mom got the turkey out and set it on the counter to baste it. The phone rang, and while she was answering the phone, Hippo stole the turkey off the counter. Mom screamed bloody murder, which scared Hippo, and he took off through the living room, still carrying the turkey, Cole and Keefe and I in hot pursuit. We got the turkey back, but the uproar upset Mouse, and now there are feathers and half-cooked turkey all over the living room."

"You can grin if you want," he told Sam with mock indignation. "But you aren't the one being sent out to find another turkey, with instructions to find one even if I have to drive to L.A."

"Hippo?" Nikki questioned faintly. He didn't mean a *real* hippo. Did he?

"One of the mutts Mom collects," Gage explained. "She usually finds homes for them, but no one was willing to take on an animal the size of a small truck, so Hippo has become a fixture. Cole's little girl named him after she saw him yawn."

"And Mouse isn't a mouse?" *And why didn't Sam tell me he had a niece?*

"A cat," Gage explained, grinning. "She's timid. She was sleeping on an old pillow when Hippo and the turkey made their entrance into the living room. I think she tried to dig her way into the pillow to hide."

"Which explains the feathers," she said, relieved to have a reasonable explanation.

"Which explains the feathers," Gage agreed. "I've got to go see if I can find a turkey, or Mom will wring my neck. Good to meet you, Jason. Welcome to the family, Nikki."

"Thank you." Nikki turned to watch him stride down the walk and slide into the sleek black Corvette parked at the curb. She looked at Sam.

"Maybe we should give your mother time to get things straightened out. We could come back later."

"Don't be ridiculous. Mom won't mind."

Without giving her a chance to argue, he walked up the porch steps, pulling her with him. If Jason hadn't been with them, Nikki might have argued more vehemently. If she and Sam had really been married, she might have insisted that her first introduction to his mother not come in the midst of a domestic crisis. Caught between reality and facade, she said nothing.

The door opened into a small entryway, which opened directly into the living room. The room seemed full of people, but after a moment Nikki was able to sort it out into two men, a woman and a little girl. The woman was kneeling in the middle of the floor, rubbing a damp rag over a spot on the carpet. One of the men was standing in front of a window, trying to pry a large tiger-striped cat loose from the top of the curtain. The other man was scooping feathers off the sofa and dropping them in a brown paper grocery sack. The little girl was picking up an occasional feather, but the bulk of her attention was on the operation at the window.

"Be careful, Uncle Keefe," she instructed now. "Mouse had a bad scare."

"*Mouse* had a bad scare," Keefe muttered under his breath. "Don't forget she went over *me* to get to the top of the drapes. The damn thing has claws eight inches long."

"Don't curse in front of Mary," Rachel Walker ordered without glancing up from the spot she was scrubbing. "If the cat drew blood, I'll put some iodine on the scratches later. Right now, I want this place in some kind of order before Sam and his new wife get here."

"Trying to fool your new daughter-in-law into thinking the place isn't a loony bin, Mom?" Cole asked, dropping another feather in the sack. "It might be better if she knew the truth right off."

"Just pick up those feathers, Cole," Rachel ordered, shifting her attention to another spot.

"Wouldn't it be easier to vacuum them up?"

"Not until your brother gets Mouse off the curtains. She's afraid of the vacuum."

"She's afraid of her own shadow," Keefe muttered in disgust. "I've met rocks with more brains." But Nikki noticed that he was very gentle in prying the frightened animal loose from the curtain.

Sam opened his mouth to announce their arrival, but his niece had seen them and beat him to it. She darted toward them. "Uncle Sam!"

As she jumped to her feet, her arm hit the sack of feathers, which her father had set on the back of the sofa. Cole made a quick grab for it, but succeeded only in bumping it again. The sack tumbled off its perch, trailing feathers in its wake like big, fluffy snowflakes.

Startled by the little girl's shriek, Keefe tightened his hold on the cat he'd just succeeded in prying loose from the curtain. It was too much for Mouse's already traumatized nerves. With a yowl loud enough to wake the dead, she sank four sets of claws into her rescuer's arm. Keefe yelped and dropped her to the floor. She streaked across the carpet like a furry orange missile and disappeared toward the back of the house.

Rachel Walker's head jerked up. Still on her hands and knees, she stared at the new arrivals. Her horrified expression made Nikki's heart sink.

Sam caught his niece up in his arms, balancing her easily on his hip. His greeting broke the momentary stunned silence. "Hi, urchin."

"Oh, no." As first greetings from a new mother-in-law went, it could have been worse, Nikki decided. It could have been "Get out."

"Hi, Mom."

"Oh, Sam. How could you do this to me?" Rachel groaned as she stood up.

"*I* didn't steal the turkey," Sam protested with a grin.

"You were a wretched boy, and you've grown into a wretched man." She glanced down at the rag in her hand and then, with a sigh, let it drop. "Everything was going so well," she muttered, to no one in particular.

"Hippo stoled the turkey," his niece informed him. She leaned forward in his arms and fixed Nikki with big brown eyes. "I'm Mary. Are you my new aunt?"

"I... Yes, I guess I am." This was getting more complicated by the minute, Nikki thought. Now she was lying to small children. "I'm Nikki."

"I had everything organized," Rachel said. Her eyes drifted from the feathers dusted over the sofa to the spots on the rug to the doorway through which the cat had disappeared. "It was the phone," she announced, fixing Nikki with a sudden look. "Everything was going fine until the wretched phone rang."

"I'm sure it was," Nikki agreed hesitantly, wondering if Sam had forgotten to tell her that his mother's mind was starting to go.

"I've never liked phones." Rachel bent down and picked up the damp rag, looked at it a moment and then stuffed it in the pocket of the pink gingham apron she wore over a pair of lavender slacks and a white blouse. "They always ring at the most awkward moments, like when your hands are covered in mud."

"Or when you're basting a turkey," Cole added helpfully.

"I only turned my back for a moment."

"If you didn't insist on keeping that wolf in the house, you'd be able to leave a turkey sit on the counter without posting guard over it," Keefe said. He was dabbing droplets of blood off the series of scratches that decorated the back of his hand.

"It's not poor Hippo's fault." Rachel immediately leapt to the dog's defense. "How was he supposed to know the turkey wasn't for him?"

"Do you normally feed him half-roasted turkeys that

happen to be sitting on the counter?'' Keefe asked, not troubling to conceal his annoyance.

"Of course not. But I didn't explain that it *wasn't* for him, either."

"Most dogs understand that the counters are off-limits without needing to have each specific item of food pointed out to them."

"If you hadn't yelled at the poor thing, he wouldn't have run off with the bird. You scared him."

"Excuse me, but when I see a dog absconding with the Thanksgiving turkey, that seems reason enough to yell."

Nikki felt like a spectator at a tennis match as her eyes followed the conversation back and forth between mother and son. None of her worried imaginings had included a scene quite like this one.

"Welcome to the Walker family, Nikki." Sam's tone was dry and laced with amusement.

"Oh goodness!" Rachel turned a stricken gaze in their direction. "I didn't even say hello, did I?"

"Not exactly," Sam said.

"I'm so sorry, Nikki. You must think you've married into a family of savages." Rachel crossed the room to where they stood and reached out to take Nikki's hands. Her grip was firm and strong, surprisingly so for such a small woman. "I did so want everything to be nice when you arrived." She gestured to the chaos behind her. "This isn't the first impression I'd planned, but welcome to the family, my dear."

Nikki stepped awkwardly into the embrace Rachel offered, her thoughts spinning at the realization that *Rachel* had been nervous about meeting *her*.

"Thank you, Mrs. Walker." Up close, Nikki found it hard to believe that this woman could be the mother of four strapping sons. She didn't look old enough, for one thing. Her soft dark hair was cut stylishly short and framed a face of remarkable sweetness. Any impression Nikki might have had that Sam's mother was a few bricks short of a full load was dispelled by the quick intelligence in her dark eyes.

"Call me Rachel, please. 'Mrs. Walker' always makes me think of my mother-in-law, whom I never liked. And since the feeling was mutual, I don't consider that speaking ill of the dead. I swore I'd never be a mother-in-law of the sort she was, so you don't have to worry about me poking my nose in things that are none of my business."

As if on cue, Mary, who'd been watching and listening from her position in Sam's arms, piped up. "Are you going to have a baby?" she asked, fixing Nikki with a bright, curious gaze.

Instant silence greeted her question. Nikki could feel her smile freezing solid. Her voice came out a little wheezy. "What?"

"Daddy told Uncle Gage that was prob'ly why you and Uncle Sam got married so quick," Mary explained. "'Cause you were going to have a baby."

"My brother, Ann Landers," Sam muttered, shooting Cole a fierce look. "No, Nikki is not going to have a baby."

"Talk about little pitchers," Cole said on a groan. He crossed the room to take his daughter from Sam. "Your ears are entirely too big, you little pest."

"If you don't want me to hear things, then you shouldn't talk so loud," she pointed out, with unarguable, five-year-old logic.

"When you're right, you're right," Sam said, giving

his brother a pointed look, which Cole ignored. He smiled at Nikki.

"Hi, I'm Cole. The one with the overactive imagination. Welcome to the madhouse."

Nikki took the hand he offered. There was a rueful apology in his eyes. The resemblance between him and the little girl he held was marked. Both were fair haired with chocolate brown eyes. But Cole's smile was reminiscent of his brother's, tailor-made for breaking female hearts.

"The one nursing the scratched hand is Keefe," Sam said, completing the introductions as Keefe came to join them.

"I think I'll live," Keefe said dryly. "Glad to meet you, Nikki. It's not always this bad."

"Sometimes it's worse," Cole offered.

"Ignore him," Keefe suggested as he shook her hand. "Aside from a few neurotic pets, we're a fairly normal bunch."

Nikki wondered if it was her imagination that put something watchful in the look he gave her, something more than curiosity. As if he knew something the rest of his family didn't.

Before she could follow that line of thinking any farther, she suddenly remembered Jason, who'd been standing quietly behind her. She turned immediately, slipping her hand under his elbow and drawing him forward to introduce him to her in-laws, relieved to have an excuse to direct attention away from herself.

She'd made it through the initial meeting without anyone pointing a finger and denouncing her as a fake, but there was plenty of time for disaster to strike.

"A Norman Rockwell kind of family" was how Max had described the Walkers. Until now, Nikki hadn't been willing to admit, even to herself, just how much that description had influenced her decision to marry Sam. Her own family had borne little resemblance to the sort of cozy images for which Rockwell was famous.

From the time she was small, the two stable figures in her life had been her grandfather and Lena, and, while she'd never doubted their love for her, she'd always had a wistful longing to be part of a big, close-knit family, the kind common on television and all too rare in real life.

And now, by virtue of a business deal cum marriage, she was part of such a family, at least for the next year. The Walkers bore little resemblance to the Brady Bunch, but there was no mistaking the affection between them.

Rachel, in particular, fascinated her. Her initial impression that her mother-in-law was a little on the vague side turned out to be far from accurate. Though she was barely five feet tall and looked as if a strong breeze might carry her away, it seemed as if Rachel had only to express a wish and one or more of her sons moved to fulfill it.

It was obvious that they adored her. Equally obvious that the feeling was mutual. Nikki tried to remember if Max had said anything about Sam's father, but could come up with nothing beyond the fact that he was dead. She wondered if Rachel had raised her sons alone.

Despite her certainty that disaster lurked around every corner, it was turning out to be the best Thanksgiving she could ever remember having. It took some time for her to dare to relax, even a little. She was vividly aware she was there under false pretenses and afraid of making a verbal slip that would expose the truth about her marriage to Sam. But as no one demanded an explanation for their hasty marriage or asked any questions she couldn't answer, she started to believe that Sam had been right about his family accepting their marriage at face value.

It had probably been ridiculous to worry so much. After all, what sane person would expect to find a genuine marriage of convenience in their own family?

Gage returned in about an hour. He brought a huge turkey, which happened to be frozen solid, two chickens and ten pounds of hamburger. Since it would be days before the turkey could thaw, there was a hasty reshuffling of the dinner menu.

The turkey went in the freezer, the two chickens went in the oven, and Sam and Cole threw coals in the barbecue to cook the hamburger. Within a couple of hours, they sat down to roast chicken and grilled hamburgers with all the traditional Thanksgiving trimmings. Nikki couldn't ever remember enjoying a meal more.

# *Chapter 8*

The remainder of the day passed in a kind of pleasant lethargy. After dinner, everyone helped clear the table. With so many bodies in such a relatively small area, it might have been more efficient if the task had been left to one or two, but no one seemed concerned with efficiency.

Once the table was cleared and the first load of dishes was in the dishwasher, there was a general retreat to the living room. Nikki was amused by the way Jason rose when Rachel entered the room, offering her his chair with an old-fashioned gallantry that brought a delicate flush of color to the older woman's cheeks.

The television was turned to one of the many football games being played. With the score at thirty-five to three, there wasn't much suspense in the competition, but that suited the low-key mood just fine.

Nikki, whose interest in football was about on par with her interest in the sex life of tree frogs, wandered over to the baby grand piano that dominated one corner of the living room. She brushed her fingers soundlessly across the keys.

"Do you play?" Rachel's question startled her, since she hadn't been aware of the other woman's approach.

Nikki shook her head. "I had lessons when I was a child, but I was terrible at it. I could hear the music in my head, but I could never seem to get it from there to my fingers."

"I can't play a note and my singing is so bad that the boys used to cry when I'd sing lullabies to them." Rachel smiled at Nikki's chuckle, but shook her head. "It's true. I can't carry a tune in a bucket. But David, Sam's father, he had a voice like an angel and could play just about any instrument you'd care to name. The boys got what musical talent they have from him."

Nikki's mind boggled at hearing the four large men, currently sprawled on various pieces of furniture, called *boys,* but she supposed it was a mother's privilege to call them that.

"Does Sam play piano?" she asked.

"No. He played guitar when he was in college, but I don't think he kept up with it. I think he just used it to attract girls."

Nikki couldn't imagine that Sam Walker had ever needed any kind of accessory to attract the opposite sex. He came equipped with everything necessary for that, she thought, shooting a quick look at his long body, which was settled comfortably in a big, overstuffed chair. With an effort, she dragged her attention back to what Rachel was saying.

"Cole inherited his father's voice, even sang in the church choir when he was a boy. Gage is the one who plays piano. There was a time when we thought he might make a career of it, but...things changed.'' Something in her tone suggested that whatever it was that had changed, the memories weren't pleasant. Nikki sought to distract her.

''What about Keefe? Does he sing or play an instrument?''

''Only if you're in the mood for torture,'' Cole put in. He was sitting on the sofa. Mary had crawled onto his lap after dinner and was now fast asleep, her tiny body curled against his chest. It was a sweet picture.

''Torture?'' Nikki asked, glancing at Rachel for an explanation. But it was Keefe who answered.

''What Cole is trying to say is that there isn't a musical bone in my body.''

''Actually, dogs have been known to howl in pain when Keefe sings,'' Gage clarified. He grinned as he fended off the pillow Keefe threw in his direction.

''Please, don't anybody mention dogs,'' Cole said.

There was a general mutter of agreement as everyone remembered Hippo's impact on the holiday dinner. But Nikki noticed there didn't seem to be any real rancor behind the complaints. She had yet to meet the canine in question, since he'd been banished to the backyard for his transgressions. She wanted to get at least a glimpse of the fabled creature before they left.

There were half a dozen pictures in a motley assortment of frames sitting on top of the piano. Nikki picked up one to look at it more closely. It was a family portrait, taken when the brothers were in their teens. They were seated on a dark sofa and the four of them stared at the camera with varying degrees of tolerance. Sam couldn't have been more than seventeen or eighteen, but he'd had a look of maturity beyond his years.

It took a conscious effort to drag her gaze to the rest

of the family. She glanced at the three other boys, but her attention settled on the little girl standing in front of them. Four or five years old, with hair that was a rich, deep auburn and thickly lashed, blue eyes, she wore a ruffled pink dress and had a pink ribbon threaded through her curls.

"Who is that?" Nikki asked, thinking it might be a niece or cousin.

There was an almost imperceptible pause before Rachel answered. "That's Shannon. My little girl."

There was old grief in her voice and in her eyes as she reached out to take the picture from Nikki. Her forefinger settled gently on the glass that covered the picture, almost as if she were touching the child's face.

Nikki became aware of the silence around them and realized that Rachel wasn't the only one who'd heard her question. She glanced at Sam, wondering if she should have known who Shannon was, if a real wife would have known. He shook his head slightly, giving her a look that she took as reassurance.

"I'm going to take a walk." It was Gage who broke the tense little silence. Nikki caught a glimpse of his face as he stood up. He looked older than he had moments before, his features hard, his eyes a wintry blue.

"It's raining," Rachel said.

"I won't melt." He gave his mother a quick, tight smile. If it was intended as reassurance, it fell short of the mark, because the worry stayed in Rachel's eyes as she watched him walk out the door.

He left behind him a strained silence. Cole's attention was on his sleeping daughter, his hand stroking over her golden hair. Keefe stared at the television screen as if riveted by the ridiculously unbalanced competition being played out there. Sam looked after his brother, and for a moment Nikki thought he might follow Gage, but if that was his intention, he changed his mind after a glance at his mother's face.

"He'll be all right, Mom."

"I know." Rachel turned to set the picture back down on the piano, her hand not quite steady.

Utterly bewildered by the undercurrents of the past few minutes, Nikki looked at Jason, forgetting for the moment that he might think it odd that she was so completely in the dark. He spoke up immediately.

"I don't know about anyone else, but I think I'm about ready for another slice of pumpkin pie."

"I'll get it for you," Rachel said, obviously grateful to have something to do.

"Coffee would be good right about now," Cole suggested.

"Coffee and pie coming up."

"Perhaps I can help," Jason offered. He rose and followed his hostess into the kitchen.

Nikki looked at Sam, her eyes full of questions. *Later,* he mouthed, shaking his head to indicate that this wasn't the time to discuss the odd little scene that had just passed.

Her shoulders lifted in an almost imperceptible shrug. It was really none of her business. Not the way it would have been if she were truly a member of the family. She started to turn away, but her eyes met Keefe's. There was something in his look that made her feel as if he had read her mind, somehow sensing the distance between herself and Sam.

What would a real wife do after the tense little scene just past? The answer seemed obvious.

Looking as casual as she could, Nikki walked over to Sam's chair and settled herself on the arm of it. Sam shot her a startled look, which she answered with a sweet smile, a fierce glare and a subtle twitch of her head in Keefe's direction.

He glanced past her at his brother. Nikki assumed Keefe was looking at them, which explained Sam's sudden smile as he realized the necessity for keeping up their charade. But it didn't explain the wicked amusement in his eyes when he looked back up at her.

"You don't look comfortable there, sweetheart," he said lovingly.

"I'm fine, honey."

"Well, I'm not. I'll get a crick in my neck looking at you." Before she could guess his intention, he slid his arm around her waist and dragged her off the arm of the chair and into his lap.

Nikki's first impulse was to scramble up and away from him. Her second was to plant her fist in his nose and *then* scramble away. She might—just might—have done it and left Sam to try to explain her actions to his brothers. But her entire inheritance was at stake. Reluctantly, she stayed where she was, shooting Sam a look that promised future retribution.

"Comfortable, sweetheart?" Sam asked.

"Perfectly," she said through clenched teeth. She shifted position and managed to plant her elbow firmly in his midriff. "How about you, honey?"

Sam's response was muffled. Acting in self-defense, he slid his arm around her waist and dragged her close against his chest, leaving her no room to maneuver. Nearly nose to nose with her husband, Nikki glared at him.

"Isn't this cozy?" Sam asked cheerfully.

"Terribly," she agreed without opening her teeth.

This close to him, she was vividly aware of the width

of his chest, of the muscled strength of the arms holding her. His thighs were hard beneath hers. She could smell the faint woodsy scent of his cologne and see the narrow line of dark gray that rimmed the blue of his eyes. She felt surrounded by him, overwhelmed by his sheer masculinity. His mouth was only inches from hers. If she leaned forward just a little...

She jerked her thoughts back from that dangerous path, stiffening her spine as she looked away. Her gaze collided with Keefe's and she was surprised to read something that looked suspiciously like sympathy in his eyes. Again, she had the impression that he knew a great deal more than she might have expected.

Before she had a chance to pursue that thought, Rachel and Jason came back into the room. Keefe got up to clear a small end table so that Jason could set down the tray he was carrying.

"You two look cozy," Rachel said with a glance at the newlyweds.

Nikki forced a smile and murmured something noncommittal. She tried to angle her elbow into Sam's midriff again, but he was holding her too tightly. She felt the amusement in him and promised herself a suitable revenge. Something along the lines of a dip in boiling oil, perhaps.

The doorbell rang just then. Rachel went to answer it, returning with a tall, elderly woman. In the ensuing rush of greetings, Nikki twisted away from Sam's hold and stood, taking care to plant her foot firmly on his as she did so. His grunt of pain put a genuine smile on her face.

Though the newcomer was probably nearing eighty, her spine was ramrod straight and the cane she carried seemed to be more for effect than necessity. Her lined face showed traces of real beauty in the elegant arch of her cheekbones and the still bright blue of her eyes. She was wearing a pair of black wool trousers and a silk blouse of peacock blue. She wore her snow-white hair in a plain chignon and carried herself like a woman accustomed to having the world fall in line with her wishes. But there was a sparkle of humor in her eyes to soften the arrogance. She sat down with the grace of a much younger woman.

"Nikki, this is Molly Thorpe. She's a friend of the family. Molly, this is Sam's new wife, Nikki Walker." She hesitated. "I didn't even think to ask you if you were keeping your maiden name, dear."

"Are you kidding? The only reason I married Sam was so I wouldn't have to keep spelling Beauvisage for the rest of my life."

"Beauvisage?" Molly Thorpe looked at Nikki sharply. "You're too young to be Lyman's daughter. Must be the granddaughter."

"Did you know my grandfather?"

"We'd met a time or two. Heard he died a while back."

"Yes, he did," Nikki confirmed. "I miss him a great deal."

"Then he was a lucky man," Molly said. "Can't ask more out of life than someone to care enough to miss you when you're gone." She looked past Nikki. "Good bloodlines here, Samuel. You'll have fine children. No sense blushing," she added when Nikki's face flamed with color. "I'm too old to mince my words. Don't have enough time left to spend it finding polite phrases to spare people's sensibilities. Ain't pregnant yet, are you?"

"No." Nikki's denial was strangled.

She heard Sam laugh. "Mary already asked her that, Molly. I'm starting to think there's something you're not telling me, sweetheart."

Nikki shot him a look that would have slain a lesser man where he stood. Sam just grinned. She was grateful to Keefe for stepping forward to greet Molly, drawing attention away from her.

"You're incorrigible, Molly."

"I hope so. There's not much else to be at my age." She held out her hand to him, her eyes warm with affection. "Keefe. How are you?"

"Fine." He took her hand and bent to brush a kiss over her cheek. "I won't ask how you are. I can see the answer for myself."

"You could have seen it anytime these past three years if you'd taken the trouble to visit," she told him sharply. She didn't give him time to answer, but continued in a slightly softer tone. "Have you seen my great-niece lately?"

There was an instant of tense silence that told Nikki there was more to the question than what it seemed on the surface. She was aware of several quick glances being shot in Keefe's direction.

"I haven't seen Dana since the divorce," he answered calmly.

The old woman's ebony cane tapped the floor in a gesture of impatience.

"I expected better of you, Keefe Walker. Thought you were smarter than my great-niece," Molly said bluntly. "I was pleased as punch when you two got married. Thought you'd manage to hang on to her, keep her away from that silly goose of a mother and that mental midget of a father of hers."

"Sorry I didn't live up to your faith in me," Keefe

said with a tight smile. He reached in his pocket for a cigarette, caught his mother's eye and thought better of it.

"I am, too. Dana's got a head on her shoulders, even if she don't choose to use it as often as I'd like. And she never will use it if her parents have their way. A more foolish pair I've never encountered." She peered up at him with a roguish smile. "And at my age, I doubt I'll live long enough to encounter a dumber pair."

"I suspect you'll outlive the lot of us, Molly." Keefe might not have wanted to talk about his ex-wife, but he was obviously quite fond of her great-aunt.

"I might at that." Bracing herself on her cane, she got to her feet, waving away Keefe's attempt to help her rise. "Day comes I can't get up on my own, they can take me out in the pasture and shoot me." She tilted her head back until her eyes met Keefe's. "When I was Dana's age, I wasn't stupid enough to let a man like you slip away. Married the only one I met. And if I were forty years younger, I'd give Dana a run for her money."

"I don't think Dana's in the running anymore," Keefe said dryly. "Besides, if you were forty years younger, I doubt I could handle you."

"'Course you couldn't," she snapped. "I'd do the handling. And damned lucky you'd be to get me."

"I don't doubt it. They don't make 'em like you anymore, Molly."

"Good thing, too," she said on a rich chuckle.

Molly didn't stay long. She'd just dropped in to wish the family a happy holiday, she said, refusing an invitation to have coffee and pie. Gage returned as she was leaving. He was soaked to the skin, but the haunted look had faded from his eyes.

It was after eight o'clock when Sam suggested that it was time they started the drive back to L.A. Rachel protested immediately.

"It's pouring rain. And it's such a long drive. You wouldn't be home till nearly midnight. Why don't you spend the night?"

"I don't think so, Mom. We really should be getting home."

"Why? I thought you said you had tomorrow off."

"I do, but—"

"Jason, do you have to go to work tomorrow?" Rachel asked, turning to the older man.

"The offices are closed for the weekend. But I couldn't impose myself on you like that."

"Nonsense. There's plenty of room. And I wouldn't be able to sleep for worrying about the three of you out on the roads in this kind of weather."

"I really would rather get home," Sam said. He glanced at Nikki. "I'm sure Nikki would, too."

"Actually, I'm pretty tired," she contradicted, ignoring the demand in his eyes. Obviously, he wanted her to say that she was anxious to get home, but after his annoying behavior earlier, she wasn't particularly in the mood to oblige him. In fact, she rather enjoyed thwarting him.

Besides, she *was* tired. She stifled a yawn. Her nap in the car hadn't been enough to make up for the week of poor sleep that had preceded it.

"If your mother doesn't mind putting us up, I'd like to stay, honey."

"Honey" looked less than happy, but he didn't pursue the argument. Nikki couldn't suppress the urge to give him a triumphant look. It was time he realized that he wasn't going to win every round. But Sam's response wasn't what she might have expected. Instead of looking annoyed, he looked resigned, and there was a kind of rueful laughter in his eyes which she didn't like at all.

She liked it even less a little while later when she realized why he'd been so adamant about driving back to L.A. and why he'd given her that amused look when she sided with his mother.

"The two of you can have the front room," Rachel was saying as she led the way to the back of the house. "It has its own bathroom."

*The two of us?* Nikki barely managed to swallow back the urge to repeat the phrase out loud. She wouldn't have been able to keep the horror from her voice. *The two of them? As in her and Sam? Together? In the same room? For an entire night?*

"It's only a double bed, but you two haven't been married long enough to mind being cozy," Rachel was saying indulgently as she pushed open the bedroom door. "The sun comes in this window first thing in the morning, so you'll need to draw the blinds if you want to sleep late."

"Oh no, I'm sure we won't want to do that," Nikki said, staring at the bed, which seemed to dominate the room. "I have to be back in L.A. before noon," she lied. "So we'll be leaving fairly early."

It was too bad she couldn't think up a plausible excuse to leave that minute. But no one was likely to buy the idea that she had an appointment in L.A. at midnight.

"If you wouldn't mind helping me make the bed," Rachel said, "then the two of you can call it a night whenever you'd like. I don't have guests very often, so

I don't leave the beds made up. I think it's so much nicer to have fresh sheets. Don't you?''

Nikki murmured an agreement, but she wasn't thinking about sheets, fresh or otherwise. There was that phrase again, *the two of you,* as if she and Sam were a couple. Of course, Rachel had no way of knowing they *weren't* a couple, but it was still disconcerting to hear her refer to them as if they were a single unit, the way they would have been if this were a real marriage.

Rachel got a set of sheets out of the linen closet in the hall while Nikki stripped the bedspread off the mattress.

"I'm so glad the two of you decided to stay over," Rachel said as they eased the bottom sheet into place. "It's been a long time since I had a houseful of family like this. It used to get very crowded when the boys were all married."

Nikki's head popped up. "*All* married?"

"Well, not Gage, of course. I don't know if he'll ever marry. And the way he spends all his time traveling, he's never in one place long enough to get to know anyone. But when the other three were married and they'd all come home for the holidays, this poor house bulged at the seams."

From her smile, it was obvious that she hadn't minded the crowding. She bent to smooth a wrinkle from the crisp white sheet. Nikki was grateful for the chance to cover up her shock. *Sam had been married before?* Why hadn't Max told her? Why hadn't *Sam* told her?

"It was nice having a houseful of people," Rachel said as she straightened. "But then Dana and Keefe split up, and Cole and Roxie. But Cole got custody of Mary, so that certainly could have been worse. The worst of it was when Sara died.''

*Sara? Sam's wife? He was a widower?*

Rachel stared past Nikki, her expression pensive. ''I wasn't sure Sam would ever marry again.'' She was silent for a moment and then seemed to shake herself free of her memories. She focused on Nikki, her smile warm. ''I'm so glad he found you. It's good to see him happy again.''

Nikki flushed and looked away, at a loss for words. The charade that had seemed so simple was getting more complicated all the time. She'd thought of it as affecting only her life and Sam's, but it was becoming obvious that she'd been ridiculously shortsighted.

Here was Sam's mother thanking her for making him happy again. If it hadn't been so painful, it would have been laughable. The only thing she'd done to make Sam happy was write a very large check. And the only other thing he was likely to want from her was her signature on the divorce papers when the year was up.

# Chapter 9

The bedroom door had barely closed behind Sam before Nikki pounced.

"Why didn't you say something?" she demanded.

He didn't pretend not to know what she was talking about. "What should I have said? 'Sorry, Mom, we can't spend the night because we'd have to share a room.' Don't you think it would have looked a bit odd if we had separate bedrooms a month after the wedding?"

"Lots of married couples sleep in separate bedrooms."

"Yeah, but that doesn't mean they'd rather drive three hours in a rainstorm rather than face sharing a bed."

Nikki's spine stiffened and her eyes turned a pure, icy green. "We are *not* sharing a bed."

"If you speak a little louder, maybe the whole house will be able to hear you." The accusation was unfair since she'd been keeping her voice low, but he wasn't particularly concerned with fairness at the moment. It had been a long day. He was tired and not particularly thrilled at the prospect of the night ahead.

"We are not sharing that bed," she repeated.

Sam had never before heard anyone make a whisper sound like a shout. It was a unique talent, but one he was a little too tired to appreciate at the moment. If it hadn't been such a long day, with an even longer night to follow, he might have dragged out the discussion for the sheer pleasure of watching her lay down the law. "You're right. We are not sharing that bed. I'll sleep on the floor."

Nikki was already drawing breath to argue with him when it registered that there was nothing to argue about. She gave him a look of mingled relief and annoyance.

"The floor isn't going to be very comfortable," she said.

"Do you have a better idea?" Sam unbuttoned his shirt cuffs.

"Maybe I should be the one who sleeps on the floor. After all, this is your home...."

"This is my mother's home," he corrected. "And I'm not going to arm-wrestle you for the right to spend a miserable night trying to get comfortable on the cold, hard floor, so unless you're desperate to sleep there, I'd suggest you don't argue. My chivalrous streak isn't very wide."

She stared at him consideringly for a moment. He could almost see the debate going on in her head. Did she protest politely and risk having to sleep on the floor or did she give in and let him have the last word? He should have known she'd find a way to do neither.

"As a strong nineties kind of woman, I should insist on equal-opportunity misery."

Sam's grin was slow. "As a nineties kind of man, I wouldn't dream of standing in your way." He swept one hand out in invitation. "The floor is yours if you insist."

"That's quite all right. It's enough that you respect my right to sleep there. You're welcome to it," she said graciously.

"Gee, thanks."

"Don't mention it."

"I won't," he said dryly. "I'm going to get ready for bed. If your sensibilities would be shocked by the sight of me in my underwear, then I suggest you turn the light out while I'm in the bathroom."

Their eyes met and he knew she was thinking the same thing he was, which was that she'd seen him in considerably less. Nikki looked away first, her cheeks a little flushed.

"Lucky for me that your mother had something I could wear," she said, gesturing to the nightgown she wore.

Sam wished she hadn't mentioned it. He'd really have preferred not to think about her in a nightgown, because that made him think about her in bed, and that didn't bear thinking about. At least his mother hadn't loaned her some silk-and-lace thing designed to drive a man wild. The garment was floor-length white cotton with a pattern of tiny pink roses scattered across it. Long-sleeved, high-necked, modest enough for a nun. And damned if she didn't look sexy as hell in it.

He cleared his throat. "Looks big enough for an entire family to sleep in," he said casually.

She laughed, a soft, husky sound that shivered down

his spine. ''The colors might be a little subdued, but I'm sure there's enough fabric for a circus tent.''

''Gotta be close.'' He looked away and reached for the top button on his shirt. ''I'm beat. I'm going to clean up and try and get some sleep.''

''Okay.'' Nikki turned away and then hesitated, looking back over her shoulder at him. ''Are you sure? About sleeping on the floor, I mean?''

Was she trying to drive him nuts? She was standing there with the light behind her and he could see the shadowy outline of her slender body beneath the prim nightie. The odd juxtaposition of modesty and sensuality was sexier than if she'd been standing in front of him completely nude. Sam was caught off guard by a wave of gut-level hunger.

''I'll be fine on the floor. Unless you want to share the bed,'' he said huskily.

His eyes met hers and saw them widen at the desire he didn't trouble to conceal. Something flickered in her eyes, an awareness that made it clear that he wasn't the only one conscious of the potential explosiveness of the situation. He had a moment to wonder just what he'd do if she said yes, and then she looked away and the moment was gone.

''The floor looks fairly soft,'' she said with a nervous half smile.

''Tell that to my back,'' he grumbled without heat.

He shut the bathroom door without waiting for her to respond. Leaning his hands on the edge of the sink, Sam stared at his reflection in the mirror, searching for signs of incipient insanity. Had he actually just suggested that he and Nikki might sleep together? Wasn't his life complicated enough without adding sleeping with his wife to it?

When he opened the bathroom door ten minutes later, he'd taken the time to give himself a firm talking to. His marriage to Nikki was in name only, which was exactly how he wanted it to stay. It was one thing to be civil. It was even okay to admit that there were moments when he thought he might actually like the woman he'd married. And he'd be a fool to try and deny her attractiveness. But that was as far as it could go. He didn't need the added problems that would come with acting on that attraction.

Nikki had taken his advice and the bedroom was dark. Before he shut off the bathroom light, Sam saw that she'd folded the heavy bedspread and laid it on the floor as a makeshift mattress. A blanket and one of the pillows completed his bed. He flicked out the light and then waited a moment for his eyes to adjust to the darkness before making his way across the bedroom.

He'd slept in more comfortable places, but he'd also slept in much worse, Sam thought as he laid his head on the pillow and pulled the blanket up around his shoulders. Listening to the rain beating against the side of the house, he had to admit that, floor or no, this was certainly nicer than being on a freeway somewhere between here and Los Angeles.

Now if he could manage to forget that a beautiful, sexy woman who just happened to be his wife was lying only a few feet away. If he could convince himself that he was all alone…

"Sam?"

The sound of her voice, pitched low and intimate, did nothing to relax his tense body. Maybe if he didn't say anything, she'd think he fell asleep the instant his head hit the pillow.

"Sam? Are you asleep?"

His eyes popped open and he stared at the ceiling. "I'm awake."

"I think today went pretty well, don't you? I mean, I don't think anyone suspects anything."

"I told you they wouldn't."

"It just seems so obvious to me that we're not really married that it's hard for me to believe it isn't obvious to everyone else. I guess it's just my guilty conscience."

"There's nothing to feel guilty about," he said firmly, ignoring the fact that his own conscience was less than comfortable with the deception they were playing.

"I can't help but feel guilty when your family has been so nice. They've accepted me as if I really was your wife."

"You *are* my wife." Funny how it was getting easier to think of her that way.

"Only on paper."

He heard the covers rustle as she turned over, and he closed his eyes, trying not to think about her in bed, with nothing between her and the sheets but that soft nightgown. Nothing between her and his hands... He opened his eyes and stared up the ceiling again. Maybe she'd go to sleep now. Maybe she'd—

"Sam?"

He closed his eyes in resignation. "Yeah?"

"I didn't mean to upset anyone when I asked about the little girl in the picture."

Sam felt his body tighten. "You couldn't have known it was a problem."

There was another silence from the bed, and he hoped she was going to drop the subject even when he knew it wasn't going to happen.

"Was Shannon your sister?"

It took him so long to respond that Nikki began to think he was going to ignore the question. Maybe she'd overstepped the undefined boundaries of their relationship by asking.

"Shannon is my half sister," Sam said finally.

"Is?" There was surprise in Nikki's voice. "I thought... The way your mother referred to her, I thought..." She let the words trail off.

"That she was dead? She's not." There was a fierceness behind the words, as if saying them could make them true. "A year after my father died, Mom remarried." Sam spoke rapidly, wanting to get the the story over with. He didn't like talking about what had happened. "She was lonely, and I think she had some idea that the four of us needed a father. So she married Seth Hardesty. He was a cop, like my father had been, and she met him through a mutual friend.

"The marriage was a mistake. Seth didn't like sharing his wife with four children who weren't even his, and the feeling was mutual. He thought we were undisciplined little louts and we thought he was a complete bastard. We were probably both right," he admitted with bleak humor.

"We didn't make it easy for him, but his idea of discipline usually involved using his belt on one of us. I was thirteen and big for my age. He only tried to hit me once."

Nikki's heart ached for the boy he'd been. He might have been big for his age, but he'd still been a thirteen-year-old, still a child. It couldn't have been easy for him to stand up to a grown man.

"I warned him about hitting any of the others and I thought he'd listened. I told him I'd kill him if he hurt my brothers.'' There was something in his voice that told Nikki it hadn't been an idle threat. ''I thought things were settling down, but Mom came home one day and caught him beating the hell out of Cole for some minor infraction of one of Seth's rules. I think she already knew the marriage had been a mistake, but that was the push she needed to end things. She divorced him, but she was already pregnant with Shannon.''

He stared up at the darkened ceiling, remembering. Nikki was quiet, waiting for him to finish the story.

''I think we were all a little shell-shocked by then. First Dad dying, then Seth, then the divorce. Shannon was the first good thing that had happened to the family in a long time. We were all old enough that there was no question of resenting her, and we spoiled her rotten. It's a wonder she didn't become an obnoxious little brat. But she was a great little kid. As soon as she could walk, she'd follow one or the other of us around. We all adored her.''

He fell silent, as if lost in memories. Nikki wasn't sure she wanted to know what had happened anymore. Some memories were better left undisturbed. But now that he'd started, it seemed Sam intended to finish the story.

''Seth had visitation rights, of course. Not that he bothered to take advantage of them very often. But he popped in and out of Shannon's life, seeing her once or twice a year, just enough so that we couldn't forget him, which was probably why he did it.

''Shannon was about four when he tried to convince Mom to give the marriage another try. She wanted no part of him and told him so. He seemed to take it fairly well, but it must have rankled with him. A couple of weeks later, he came to pick Shannon up to spend the weekend with him. He never brought her back.''

He said it so simply that it took several seconds for his meaning to sink in.

"You mean he just disappeared with her?"

"Into thin air."

"And you haven't seen her since?"

"No."

"But that was years ago."

"Nineteen." The way he said it told her that the wound was far from healed.

"Didn't he call? Let you know that she was all right? Give some explanation?"

"No."

"Did you try to find her?"

"Sure. But thousands of children disappear every year and are never seen again. Shannon was one of them."

Nikki knew that tragedies like the one he'd just described were more common than anyone wanted to believe. But it was one thing to know it on an impersonal level, something else to hear about it happening to someone she knew. She thought of the family portrayed in the photograph, of the smiling faces. And then she thought of the pain in Rachel's face, in Sam's voice. Nineteen years later, the hurt was still close to the surface. There wasn't enough time in the world to get over something like that.

"I'm sorry." The words seemed hopelessly inadequate, but there was nothing else she could offer.

"Yeah. Me too," Sam said softly.

They didn't speak again. Nikki lay awake for a long time, staring into the darkness. She was sorry she'd asked about the child in the picture, sorry she'd brought up something so painful to him. It would be a long time before she forgot the pain that had roughened his voice.

When she'd married Sam, she'd seen him as the means to an end. She hadn't given much thought to him as a person. But she was starting to realize that it wasn't possible to share a house and a marriage license with someone and avoid coming to know them as an individual.

She turned over and tucked the pillow under her cheek, frowning at the wall opposite the bed. She didn't want to know him as a person. It made things more complicated. Meeting his family complicated things. And the fact that she liked them only made it worse. It had been simpler when she'd disliked him, when he'd been nothing more than an annoying necessity in her life.

Nikki closed her eyes determinedly. Tomorrow they'd be back in L.A. and things could get back to normal. She and Sam would go back to being nodding acquaintances. She preferred it when there was plenty of distance between them.

The sound of someone knocking on the door woke Sam out of a light sleep. He was momentarily disoriented when he opened his eyes and found himself staring at the carpet inches from his nose. But the fogginess lasted only a moment, and it hit him that, whoever was outside the door, he didn't want them to see him sleeping on the floor while his wife of barely a month had the bed all to herself.

He lunged to his feet, bringing his pillow and blanket with him. He threw them at the bed and bent to snatch up the bedspread that had served as a mattress. It hit the foot of the bed in a jumbled heap and slid off onto the floor.

Nikki had been more deeply asleep when the knock came, and she was just turning over and opening her eyes when she felt a solid weight hit the bed. Her eyes flew open and she found herself nose to nipple with a man's naked chest. She opened her mouth, but the startled shriek emerged as a muffled squeak as Sam's hand closed over her lower face.

"It's me," he hissed in her ear. With his free hand, he was shoving the pillow he'd used back against the headboard and trying to pull the covers into place. The knock came again, louder this time. He saw understanding in Nikki's eyes and moved his hand.

"There's someone at the door," she whispered.

"No kidding." Sam jerked the blanket into position. "Come in," he called. As the doorknob turned, he slid his arm under Nikki and pulled her solidly against his side. She immediately stiffened and tried to pull back.

"We're newlyweds, remember?"

"We're not *that* newlywed," she muttered between her teeth just as the door opened.

Keefe stood in the doorway. His dark eyes skimmed over the tangled covers and the couple nestled cozily in their midst. He arched one brow in silent commentary. Nikki blushed, looking more angry than embarrassed.

Sam scowled at the amusement in his brother's eyes. "What do you want?"

The amusement deepened. Keefe propped one shoulder against the doorjamb, looking as if he planned on staying awhile. "I can see being married hasn't made you a morning person. You're going to have to work on that, Nikki. See if you can convince him that life begins before noon."

"Actually, I'm not overly fond of mornings myself," Nikki said. Shifting subtly, she tried to wedge a little space between herself and Sam, but he kept her firmly clamped against his side.

"Obviously the two of you are well suited." Keefe blandly ignored Sam's furious look and slouched a little more comfortably.

"I'm glad you approve," Sam said through gritted teeth. He'd had precious little sleep the night before and was not really in the mood for the game his brother was playing. Talking about Shannon had brought up a lot of old memories and it hadn't been easy to shake them. And he'd spent more time than he cared to admit thinking about the woman sleeping just a few feet away.

Now he was actually in that bed with her. And she was pressed against him with very little between them. The cotton nightgown, for all its modesty, was not a very effective barrier. He could feel every inch of her along his side, the softness of her breast pressed against him, the smooth curve of her waist under his hand. Sam shifted uncomfortably and felt the silky length of her bare leg against his where the nightgown had twisted up.

"Was there something you wanted?" Sam asked, not troubling to hide his annoyance. Damn it all, Keefe knew, better than anyone, what the true situation was.

"Actually, I—"

"Good morning." Gage looked over Keefe's shoulder and grinned at the couple in the bed. "You two look cozy."

"Thanks," Sam muttered. Nikki shifted, seeking some distance between them. The softness of the mattress defeated her, and she succeeded only in rubbing her leg against his. Sam swallowed the urge to groan.

"If you guys don't mind—"

"Uncle Sam!" Mary darted between Gage and Keefe and ran over to the bed. "You're awake."

"Yeah." Sam conjured a smile for his small niece. "Good morning, rug rat."

"I'm not a rug rat," she told him firmly. "Babies are rug rats. I'm not a baby." She perched on the foot of the bed and studied Sam and Nikki with the open curiosity of the very young. "You're in the same bed."

The simple observation turned Nikki's face pink and brought a snort of laughter from the two men in the doorway.

"Yes, we are," Sam said, shooting a killing look at his brothers.

"Is that 'cause you're married?"

"Yes." Maybe this was a sort of cosmic punishment for the deception they were practicing. "We'd really like to—"

"I told you not to wake them, Mary." Cole's tall figure filled in what little space was left in the doorway. "Morning, you two."

"What is this?" Sam snarled. "Is someone selling tickets?"

"What kind of tickets, Uncle Sam?"

"I think he means that the room is getting a little crowded," Cole suggested. He grinned at his oldest brother. "Nikki might as well find out now what kind of a family she's married into."

"A bunch of voyeurs," Sam muttered in disgust.

"What's a voyer?"

"Never mind, urchin." Cole came into the room and lifted his daughter from the bed. "I think your aunt and uncle would like to be alone."

"So they can kiss?" she asked. "My friend Bambi

says her big sister just got married and all they do is kiss and kiss and kiss. Do you kiss Aunt Nikki a lot?'' Perched on her father's hip, she looked at them with bright-eyed curiosity.

''All the time,'' Sam managed in a strangled voice, torn between frustration and laughter.

''Can I watch?''

Gage and Keefe laughed out loud. Cole grinned. ''Kissing isn't a spectator sport,'' he told his daughter. ''That means it isn't for people to watch.''

''How come? People kiss on TV.''

''This isn't television,'' Sam told her. He didn't dare look at Nikki. From the rigidity of her body, he suspected she might be on the verge of bolting for safety.

''Don't you want to kiss Aunt Nikki?'' Once she'd gotten an idea in her head, Mary wasn't inclined to let go of it.

''Yeah, Sam. Don't you want to kiss Aunt Nikki?'' Keefe asked, his eyes gleaming with a wicked amusement.

Gage didn't know the truth about his brother's marriage, but he did recognize an opportunity for harassment. ''I'd certainly want to kiss Aunt Nikki if I were married to her.''

''What I want is to be an only child,'' Sam said, his glare encompassing all three of his brothers.

''But don't you *want* to kiss her?'' Mary asked, showing a tenacity at odds with her delicate appearance.

Sam stared at her helplessly. There was more truth in his answer than he would have liked. ''Of course I want to kiss her.''

He sucked in a sharp breath as Nikki's fingers found the skin over his ribs and pinched viciously. The message was unmistakable and enough to make him give up the half-formed thought of using his niece's innocent curiosity to satisfy his own not-so-innocent urges.

"But I don't want to kiss her with everyone staring at us."

"We'd close our eyes," Gage offered helpfully.

"I wouldn't," Keefe said, grinning at his older brother.

It was just as well that Rachel entered the picture just then, because Sam's response would probably not have been fit for Mary's young ears.

"What have you got going—a convention?" she asked, poking her head in the door. Her gaze went from Nikki's flushed face to the temper simmering in Sam's eyes to the pure mischief in her other sons' expressions. "Out," she ordered briskly. "Stop harassing Sam and Nikki. Keefe, did you tell them breakfast would be ready soon?"

"Gage showed up before I got a chance to," he said.

"I don't remember putting my hand over your mouth to keep you from talking," Gage protested.

"Don't start squabbling," Rachel told them.

"He started it," Gage said, doing a creditable twelve-year-old whine.

Despite the situation, Nikki found herself laughing. The sight of Gage, at six foot two and looking like a Greek god, whining like a preadolescent brat was too ridiculous. He grinned at her, blatantly pleased with himself.

"Don't encourage him," Sam muttered, less in the mood to be amused by any of his siblings.

"Out," Rachel said again, making shooing motions. "Keefe, there's bacon on the stove. See that it doesn't burn. Gage, you can scramble the eggs."

"He always overcooks them," Cole complained.

"Then you can cook the eggs," she said promptly. "And your brother can take care of the pancakes. Mary, you make sure your father and your uncles do as they're told."

"I've always envied only children," Sam grumbled as the room emptied.

"Can't say I blame you," Rachel said, with an exasperated look at her departing offspring. "I asked Keefe to wake you, but I didn't expect it to turn into a convention. I hope they didn't embarrass you too much, Nikki."

"Not at all," Nikki lied.

Now that they were gone, she was less concerned with Sam's brother's teasing than she was with the fact that she was still plastered to Sam's body. A very warm, muscular, male body, one that set off tremors she had no business feeling.

"Why was Keefe supposed to wake us?" Sam asked. He rubbed one hand over his face to conceal a yawn.

"Because I knew you wanted to get started early."

"We did?"

"Nikki needs to get back to L.A., remember?"

"She does?" He gave his mother a blank look that sharpened quickly when Nikki's fingers found the tender skin over his ribs again. "Oh yeah. I forgot."

Rachel gave him a questioning look, but all she said was, "Breakfast will be on the table in twenty minutes, if your brothers don't start a food fight."

The door had barely shut behind her when Nikki wrenched herself loose from Sam's hold. He watched with unabashed interest as she scrambled off the bed. He caught only a glimpse of long legs before she jerked the nightgown down and into place.

"If you ever manhandle me like that again, I'm going

to call the police,'' she snapped, shoving her hair back from her face.

"I am the police. Besides, I'm the one with bruises.'' Sam rubbed his side for emphasis. ''You've got finger-nails like a damned velociraptor.''

"You're just lucky I couldn't get to your throat. You didn't have to hold me so tight.''

"We're supposed to be newlyweds,'' he reminded her. He folded his hands under his head and watched as she stalked across the room to where her clothing lay in a neat pile.

"You had me squashed so close, we looked more like Siamese twins than newlyweds.'' But he noticed the heat had gone out of her voice.

"I wasn't the one who made up some story about having to leave early, which led to Keefe coming in to wake us.''

"I thought we'd want an excuse to get out of here this morning. I don't think we should push our luck with this whole charade we're playing.''

"Not a bad idea,'' he admitted. ''But if you'd let me know, I could have made it a point to be up and about before anyone was likely to come knocking on the door.''

Nikki turned to look at him, her fine brows drawn in a frown. Wearing the modest cotton gown, with her hair falling in tousled waves and not a scrap of makeup on her face, she didn't exactly look like a centerfold, but Sam had never seen a stapled-in-the-middle model who sent such a sharp stab of awareness through him. A quick surge of hunger made him want to pull her onto the bed again and not let her up until the sun went back down. Didn't he want to kiss her, Mary had asked. The problem was he wanted to kiss her too damned much.

"I think Keefe suspects something." Nikki's worried comment distracted Sam from his lustful—and completely inappropriate—thoughts.

"Keefe?" He stalled for time.

"There's something about the way he looks at us, as if he suspects something." Her teeth tugged at her lower lip. "Do you think he's guessed that we're not really married?"

"Guessed?" Sam hesitated, reluctant to tell her that Keefe hadn't had to guess. But she looked so worried and he was surprised to discover that he didn't like seeing her look that way. "Keefe doesn't suspect anything."

"How can you be so sure? The way he looks at us—"

"He knows the truth. I told him a couple of weeks ago."

"You *told* him? I thought we agreed that no one was going to know the truth about us."

"I suppose you didn't tell your friend Liz?" He arched one brow in question.

"I told Liz," she admitted.

"I told Keefe. We're even." He shrugged.

Nikki tried not to notice the way the movement drew attention to the furry width of his chest. For some reason, it was difficult to notice anything else. It wasn't as if she hadn't seen his chest before, she thought, exasperated by her wandering attention. It was an unfortunate reminder, bringing back memories of the day she'd walked into his room. She'd seen a great deal more than his chest that day.

She looked away, trying to marshal her scattered thoughts and drag them back to the conversation at hand. It probably didn't matter that Keefe knew the truth. And she could hardly blame Sam for telling his brother, when she'd told her best friend. Her eyes widened suddenly. "Keefe knows?"

"I thought we'd already established that." Sam stifled another yawn.

"Last night, when you dragged me onto your lap, you knew I was worried that he might suspect something, that that was why I sat down on the arm of your chair."

"I couldn't resist," he admitted without the least sign of repentence. "You were doing such a good job of playing the doting bride."

"You took advantage of me."

"You got your revenge," he reminded her. "You drove your elbow halfway to my spine, and I'm probably permanently crippled from the damage you did when you stepped on my foot."

"Good." She nodded in satisfaction. "Maybe that will teach you not to treat this situation like it's some kind of game."

She turned and stalked into the bathroom without giving Sam a chance to respond. He stayed where he was, his eyes on the closed door. The bed beside him was still warm and a trace of soft, floral scent clung to the sheets.

It occurred to him, not for the first time, that this marriage-of-convenience business wasn't nearly as simple as it had seemed at first.

# Chapter 10

The rain of the day before had given way to deep blue skies and warm sunshine. Breakfast was a noisy affair, involving a great many good-natured insults tossed back and forth about who'd burned the bacon and who'd undercooked the pancakes, both of which were perfect as far as Nikki could tell.

After the meal, Nikki helped to clear the table. She and Rachel talked easily as they worked, and any silences were filled in by Mary, who seemed to never run out of questions about anything and everything.

"You're very good with her," Rachel commented, after Nikki had fielded a particularly convoluted inquiry.

"I like children," Nikki said, her face soft with affection as she watched the little girl carefully carry a plate from the table to the counter.

"Mary could use some cousins. Not that I'm hinting or anything," Rachel added, smiling.

"I... We haven't really discussed that." Nikki was pleased by the steadiness of her voice.

"Well, there's plenty of time," Rachel said comfortably.

Nikki murmured an agreement and made her escape as quickly as possible, retreating into the living room, which was momentarily empty. She couldn't take much more. Her conscience was already screaming bloody murder. How could she have been so incredibly blind? To think that this marriage wouldn't affect anyone but her and Sam.

She wandered around the room, touching a knick-knack here and there but not really seeing anything. They'd be leaving here soon and she might never come back. It wouldn't be all that hard to avoid visiting Sam's family for the next eleven months. After all, she didn't care what they thought of her. Did she? She shied away from the answer to that question.

Finding herself next to the piano with its row of photographs, it occurred to her that there was probably a picture of Sam's wife. Seized by a sudden curiosity, she bent to look at them.

There it was. Picking it up, she carried it over to the window, where the light was better.

It was an informal shot, obviously taken at their wedding. Nikki guessed that Sam had been in his mid-twenties and the woman at his side looked a little younger. They were smiling at the camera, but there was something about them that suggested they were aware only of each other. They looked young and very much in love.

Her eyes skimmed over the quietly pretty brunette and focused on Sam's face. This was a different man than the one she'd married—younger, with fewer shadows in his eyes.

Nikki was so absorbed in the photograph that she didn't hear Sam's voice until he was right outside the living room. She couldn't be caught standing here with his wife's picture in her hand. In a panicked flurry, she stepped behind the open drapes. She regretted the move immediately. She was going to look like a complete fool if anyone caught her lurking behind the drapes like a second-rate burglar. But it was too late to change her mind.

"I don't want to argue with you about this. Just take the check," Sam was saying.

"I don't want it." It was Cole's voice, and he didn't sound happy. "I can come up with the money on my own."

"How? By selling your plane? Then how are you going to earn a living?"

"I'll manage," Cole said tightly.

"You don't have to manage. I've got the money. When the time is right for Mary's surgery, it will be paid for."

*Mary's surgery? What kind of surgery?* Nikki's heart clenched at the thought of something being wrong with the beautiful, dark-eyed little girl.

"Where did you suddenly come up with this kind of money?" Cole asked. "Unless they've started paying cops a helluva lot more than they used to, you don't have this kind of bucks."

"Nikki's rolling in the stuff. When I told her about Mary's surgery, she wanted to help." Nikki wondered if she was the only one who heard the strain in Sam's voice.

"No." Cole sounded adamant, and she heard him

move abruptly away and then back again, as if he couldn't stay in one place. "It would be bad enough if it were your money, but I'm sure as hell not going to sponge off your wife. I'll pay for it myself," he insisted stubbornly.

"Don't be an ass." Sam didn't trouble to soften the sharpness in his voice. "Nikki is family now. She wants to do this."

*Which was true, even if Sam didn't realize it.*

"No." Nikki didn't need to be able to see him to know that Cole was shaking his head. "Absolutely not."

"Swallow your damned pride and think of what's best for your daughter."

"What's best for her is to have a father who doesn't take charity," Cole said sharply.

"This isn't charity, dammit! I'm family. And don't tell me you wouldn't do the same damned thing if the situation were reversed."

"It isn't reversed and I don't want your wife's money. I'll do it on my own."

"So your pride is more important than Mary's health?" Sam snapped furiously.

There was a brief silence, and Nikki half expected to hear it end with the sound of Cole's fist connecting with Sam's jaw. But the next sound wasn't that of a fist against flesh. Cole sighed, a quick, harsh sound that held both anger and resignation.

"I hate it when you're right. No, my pride isn't more important than Mary's health. I'll take the money." The words sounded as if they'd been pulled from him.

There was a pause, and Nikki imagined Sam handing him the check.

"This...means a lot to me, Sam, to both of us. Thank you."

"You'd do the same for me."

"Yeah, but I wouldn't be so obnoxious about it." Nikki was relieved to hear a trace of humor in Cole's voice.

"I'm oldest. I get to be most obnoxious."

"You're very good at it."

"Thanks."

"I'll catch Nikki before you guys leave and thank her," Cole said.

"No!" Sam must have realized that his response was too sharp, because he softened it immediately. "She'd be embarrassed. I'll pass on your thanks."

"I'd really like to say something to her myself. This means a lot to Mary and me. I'd like to thank her."

"No, really. She's...very self-conscious about having money and...I know it would just make her uncomfortable."

Nikki bit her lip to hold back a chuckle at the blatant discomfort in Sam's voice. Obviously, she wasn't the only one finding herself floundering under the false pretenses they'd created.

"If you're sure." Cole sounded doubtful.

"I'm sure. I'll tell her how much you appreciate it."

There was another silence, and Nikki mentally urged them to leave. Her nose was starting to itch and she wasn't sure how much longer she could resist the urge to scratch it.

"I've got to ask you something, Sam." Cole sounded uneasy. "You didn't marry Nikki to get the money for Mary's surgery, did you?"

Her itchy nose was immediately forgotten. Nikki held

her breath, waiting for Sam's response. Would he tell Cole the truth?

"Have you looked at Nikki?" Sam's tone was rich with amusement. "Can you imagine anyone marrying her for her money?"

Cole's tone didn't lighten to match his brother's. "I can imagine you doing it if you thought it would help one of us," he said slowly. "You've been trying to protect us ever since we were kids."

"I was the eldest. There wasn't anyone else."

"Yeah, but we're not kids anymore. If you married Nikki so you could give me this money, I don't want any part of it. I can still figure out a way to pay for the surgery."

"I think you've seen too many movies." Nikki wondered that Cole didn't hear the false note in Sam's light tone. "I married Nikki because I wanted to. She's beautiful, she's intelligent, and the fact that she happens to be rich just worked out well for you and Mary."

"You're sure?" Nikki could imagine the searching look Cole gave his older brother.

"I'm sure. Now, will you put the damned check in your pocket? I don't think I've ever seen anyone so reluctant to take money. God help Ed McMahon if he ever tries to give you any."

Cole laughed reluctantly. "Maybe you should call and warn him."

"Maybe I should. I've got to find Nikki. We have to hit the road pretty soon."

Nikki waited until she was sure they were gone before leaving her hiding place. Thank heavens neither of them had seen her. It would have been a little difficult to explain why she was hiding behind the curtains with a picture of Sam and his first wife clutched in her hands.

She carried the photo back over to the piano, but before setting it down, she stared at it for a few more minutes, her thoughts spinning with all she'd learned. In the past couple of days, she'd seen the man she'd married in a whole new light. He'd been married and, from the way Rachel spoke, he'd loved his wife.

He was devoted to his family, enough so that he'd married a woman he didn't know to get the money for his niece's surgery. Why hadn't he told her that was what it was for? She'd assumed he was driven by greed, while holding her own motives up as pure and noble. The memory of her smug condemnation of Sam as a fortune hunter made her squirm inside.

"Sam's looking for you." Rachel's voice came from directly behind her. Nikki started and spun around, guiltily aware of the photo she held.

"I was just…looking at some of the pictures," she blurted out.

Rachel's dark brows rose in surprise. "You're family, Nikki. You're welcome to look at them all you like."

Aware that she'd reacted oddly, Nikki forced a smile. "Lena used to always accuse me of getting into things I shouldn't. I guess I still half expect her to catch me with my fingers where they don't belong."

Rachel smiled. "I haven't slapped anyone's fingers in a very long time."

"Oh, she never slapped my fingers. She just gave me this long-suffering look and then took me out to the kitchen and put me to work helping with dinner." Nikki's face softened with affection. "She spoiled me rotten, actually."

"Is Lena your mother?"

"Oh no. Lena is our housekeeper, only she's always

been more like a mother to me. Marilee is my mother, and I doubt if she'd notice if I had my hand in a tank of piranhas.'' There was amusement rather than condemnation in her tone. ''Not that she doesn't love me,'' she added, with more duty than conviction. ''But Marilee lives in her own little world and she doesn't pay much attention to anything outside it.''

If Rachel thought there was anything strange about the fact that Marilee's child apparently hadn't been a part of that world, she didn't comment. She held out her hand for the photo. ''Which one were you looking at?''

Nikki reluctantly handed it over, wishing she hadn't given in to the moment's curiosity about Sam's wife. ''I just wondered what she looked like. Sam…hasn't said much about her.''

Which wasn't a lie. Sam hadn't said *anything* about her.

Rachel studied the photograph for a few seconds before lifting her gaze to Nikki's face, her eyes shrewd. ''Did Sam mention Sara at all?''

Nikki opened her mouth to say that, of course, Sam had told her that he'd been married before. But she couldn't get the lie out. She shook her head.

''We…haven't really known each other all that long,'' she said quickly, trying to forestall the questions she saw in Rachel's eyes.

''Sam told me it was a whirlwind courtship,'' she murmured.

''I suppose it seems foolish to you—us marrying so quickly, I mean.''

''I'd known Sam's father less than a month when we got married and we were very happy. Sometimes you just know something is right,'' Rachel said slowly.

"Yes."

*And sometimes you know it's wrong and do it, anyway.*

Rachel hesitated a moment longer, her eyes searching. Nikki felt as if she had the word *phony* emblazoned across her forehead in flashing neon lights. But she obviously didn't look as guilty as she felt.

"I think Sam's about ready to leave." Rachel reached past Nikki to set the photograph on the piano.

"I'll go find him." She was vividly aware of Rachel's eyes following her as she left the room.

"I think Jason finds your mother attractive," Nikki said, glancing at Sam as the truck pulled away from his mother's house.

"I figured that when he decided to stay in Los Olivos over the weekend. Should I be asking to see his credentials?" He took his eyes off the road long enough to glance at her with a quick smile.

"They're impeccable. Besides, I don't think they're heading for Vegas quite yet."

"I don't know. Mom was blushing like a girl."

Nikki had noticed the same thing, along with the fact that Jason had seemed younger than he had in years.

"Would you mind if they fell in love?"

"Why should I?" Sam gave her a surprised look. "Jason seems like a nice guy and Mom could certainly use some happiness in her life."

"But what about when we get a divorce? If they get together, won't that be awkward?"

"Let's worry about that when the time comes," Sam suggested. "They aren't married yet."

"True." Nikki stared down at her wedding ring, twisting her hand back and forth to watch the way the light changed on the gold band. She hadn't planned on saying anything, but the words were suddenly there. "I heard you talking to Cole this morning."

Sam stiffened, and she felt the look he shot in her direction. "Talking about what?"

"About the money. About Mary's surgery. What's wrong with her? Why does she need surgery?"

He took his time answering. This wasn't a topic he'd ever expected to discuss with Nikki. But she knew enough now that there was no reason not to tell her the rest of it.

"There's a hole in her heart."

"Will she be all right?" There was real concern in her voice, in her face.

"The prognosis is very good. They'll do the surgery sometime in the next couple of years probably. I don't know what all goes into deciding when to do it. But they generally wait until a child is a little older. It doesn't cause her too many problems. And once the repair is made, she should be fine."

"And that's what you wanted the money for? That's why you married me?"

"Yeah. Max knew about the situation with Mary, and he thought it would be a good solution." He flicked on his turn signal. Nikki waited until he'd made the turn before speaking again.

"What about insurance? Wouldn't that pay for the surgery?"

"Cole runs a delivery service. A one-man, one-plane operation, and he's still paying off the plane. No insurance, not a lot of ready cash. We'd have come up with the money eventually. Gage is the only one of us with any money in the bank, but it wasn't enough. Keefe was trying to sell his ranch. Our marriage made things a lot simpler.''

''And you don't mind making that kind of sacrifice for your brother?''

''He'd do the same for me. We're family.'' The simple statement summed everything up for him. ''Besides, it's a pretty decent salary for a year's work, not to mention it's only a part-time job. And the living conditions aren't bad.''

He shot her a quick grin which she didn't see. She was staring out the windshield with an expression he couldn't read.

''Your family seems very close,'' she commented.

There was a wistful note in the comment that made Sam remember her surprise when he'd asked if her family would be getting together for the holidays. He hadn't given much thought to it at the time. He'd just been relieved that there was no conflict with spending Thanksgiving with his family. She'd commented that her family was not close. Apparently, she'd meant it. Which reminded him of something else.

''Did you mean what you said to Molly—about changing your name to Walker? I assumed you'd want to keep your own name.''

''I don't know. It might be nice to have a name that I didn't have to spell every time I make a reservation or order something over the phone, even if it is only for the next year. If you'd rather I didn't…'' She let the words trail off in question.

''I don't mind.'' In fact, he was finding that he minded less and less about this marriage. When it had begun, it had seemed like a year doing hard time. Once they'd called a truce, he'd begun to think of it as more of a minimum security sentence. But after the last couple of days, the prison analogy didn't seem apt anymore.

When he'd married her, he'd seen Nikki as a means to an end. But the longer he knew her, the more he saw her as a person, one he was coming to like.

He frowned at the highway in front of the truck. It was one thing to like her, but he didn't want to find her attractive. Unfortunately, he didn't seem to have much choice about it.

# Chapter 11

Sam picked up the phone, tucking it between his chin and his shoulder so that his hands were free to keep shuffling through the papers on his desk. Where the hell had he put that report? "Walker."

"Sam?" The woman's voice was vaguely familiar.

"Speaking."

"This is Liz Davis, Nikki's friend."

"I remember." The redhead with the cute kid and the suspicious husband. He moved another stack of papers in search of the elusive report. "What can I do for you, Liz?"

"I'm sorry to bother you at work, but it's about Nikki, actually."

"Is something wrong?" The report was forgotten as his attention focused sharply on the conversation. "Is Nikki all right?"

"She's fine," Liz said hastily. "She's just stranded. Her car won't start."

"It's a wonder that thing ever starts." Sam relaxed back in his chair. He tuned out the bustle around him with practiced ease. Nearly fifteen years on the job had given him the ability to concentrate on the matter at hand, regardless of what was going on around him.

"That's what Bill says. But Barney is more reliable than he looks."

"Barney?" Sam's eyebrows rose. *Barney who?*

"Nikki's car. Michael named him."

"The car has a name?" *That rolling junk pile is named Barney?* "Isn't there a puppet or something named Barney?"

"A dinosaur. The most irritatingly happy creature you've ever seen. He's purple. Nikki's car is purple."

"So your son named the car Barney," Sam finished for her.

"Children aren't always as imaginative as they're cracked up to be," Liz said dryly. "Anyway, Barney has the croup, and Nikki's stuck for a ride. She called me and I told her Bill would pick her up, but it turns out Bill's working late tonight, and I really don't want her there after dark."

"Want her where?" It seemed as if he'd spent most of the conversation asking questions.

"At Rainbow Place," Liz said, sounding surprised that he had to ask.

"Of course." What the hell was Rainbow Place? A shopping mall? A restaurant? And why would Liz assume that he'd know what it was?

"I was hoping you might be able to pick her up. If you can't, I'm sure she can get a cab."

Sam glanced at his watch. He'd put in a good ten hours and there was nothing urgent pending—at least, no more than there usually was.

"I'll pick her up. Can you give me the address? I don't have it handy." Which was true enough, since he didn't have it at all.

"I have it right here."

Sam's brows shot up at the address she was giving him. He suddenly understood Liz's concern about Nikki being there after dark. He wasn't sure *he* wanted to be there after dark. So what was Nicole Beauvisage Walker, pampered rich girl, doing in a neighborhood like that?

"I know Nikki will appreciate this, Sam," Liz said, obviously relieved to have the problem solved.

"No problem."

He hung up the phone and stared at the address scribbled on the outside of a fast-food bag that had been lying on his desk. What was Rainbow Place? And what was his wife doing there? There was one way to find out. He got up and reached for the coat draped over the back of his chair.

Half an hour later, he pulled the Bronco up to the curb in front of the address Liz had given him. There had to be a mistake. *This* couldn't be the right address. But painted across the front of the building, in bright, crayon colors were the words *Rainbow Place,* complete with rainbow arcing across the wall.

Sam shut off the engine and got out, careful to lock the truck. The neighborhood wasn't as bad as he'd expected it to be, a small pocket of tattered respectability in the midst of urban blight. The houses nearby were shabby but neat—it was obvious that the occupants might not have much money, but they hadn't stopped caring about their homes.

He stopped in front of the tall chain-link fence that surrounded Rainbow Place and studied the assortment of playground equipment that filled the small yard. The fence itself had been painted in a variety of bright colors, which made it look a little less starkly functional. The scene was bright and welcoming. And completely bewildering.

A nursery school? What was Nikki doing at a nursery school?

The gate was locked, but there was a bell with a hand-lettered sign that read Ring Me. Sam took the suggestion and pressed his finger on the bell. A moment later, the door of the house opened and a slender young African-American woman came out. She stopped on the other side of the fence and eyed him suspiciously. Seeing her up close, Sam realized she was younger than he'd thought—probably not more than seventeen or eighteen.

"We don't allow solicitors," she told him firmly.

"I'm not a solicitor. I'm here to pick up Nikki. I'm her husband." It struck him that the words came more easily than he might have expected. More than he'd have liked?

"Nikki doesn't have a husband," the girl said flatly.

Obviously Nikki hadn't felt it necessary to tell everyone in her life about her marriage. Sam was surprised by the sharp little pinch of annoyance he felt.

"Yes she does, and I'm it." He tried a smile and got nothing but a cool look in response. "How about if you tell her I'm here and we'll see if she admits to knowing me?"

"What name shall I give her?"

He thought of pointing out that it was unlikely Nikki had more than one husband, but remembered that even that was under dispute. "Sam Walker."

"Wait here."

"I'm not planning on scaling the fence," he muttered as she turned and walked back up the path.

He shoved his hands into the pockets of his denim jacket and hunched his shoulders a little against the chill in the air. Thick gray clouds hovered overhead, blocking the late afternoon sun. Rain was predicted sometime before midnight.

But Sam wasn't concerned with the weather, present or future. He kept looking at the cheerful playground and the brightly painted stucco building. Just where did Nikki fit into this picture?

A few minutes later, the teenager returned. "Nikki says you can come in," she told him. Her expression was slightly more welcoming than it had been before his identity had been confirmed. "I'm Jade Freeman. I'm sorry about making you wait, but Nikki hadn't told us about getting married."

"We've only been married a little while." Sam stepped through the gate, waiting while she relocked it.

"Still seems odd she didn't say anything."

It seemed odd to him, too, but he couldn't say as much. He smiled and tried to look unconcerned. The look Jade gave him suggested she was wondering if Nikki had had a reason for concealing his existence. Under other circumstances, Sam might have been tempted to drag his knuckles on the ground and maybe drool a little to confirm her obvious suspicions, but at the moment he was more interested in finding out what Nikki was up to.

Jade pushed open the front door, which was painted an eye-searing shade of pink, and led him into a narrow front hall. The walls were a soft white, the better to show off the rows of crayon drawings and finger-painted masterpieces that covered them like one-of-a-kind wallpaper.

"Nikki said you could wait in the office," Jade told him.

Sam glanced through the door at the tiny room, which was nearly filled by a battered wooden desk. A personal computer and stacks of paper concealed its surface. There were more examples of children's artwork tacked to the walls and several boxes of disposable diapers stacked in one corner.

"Where's Nikki?" he asked.

Jade had already started to walk away, but she turned back at his question. "She's with the children, but she said you should wait here."

"I'd like to see her, please." Seeing the refusal in her expression, Sam tried a coaxing smile. "I gave up devouring small children years ago."

There was a flicker of humor in her dark eyes. "Found a new hobby, did you?"

"Hanging by my heels from rafters."

A smile tugged at the corner of her mouth. "We don't have any rafters handy."

"Then you don't have anything to worry about."

She studied him a moment longer, and then, with a half shrug, turned away. It wasn't exactly the warmest invitation Sam had ever had, but he wasn't complaining. He heard Nikki's voice even before Jade stopped in the doorway of another room. She looked over her shoulder and put her finger to her lips.

The warning was unnecessary. Sam didn't think he could have found his voice if his life depended on it. There were a dozen children in the room, ranging in age from toddlers to perhaps five-year-olds. They were sprawled on the floor or seated in child-size chairs, their attention firmly directed toward the woman sitting cross-legged on the floor at the front of the room.

Sam found his own attention similarly riveted. This was a Nikki he'd never seen, never even imagined. She was wearing a pair of faded jeans and a jade green cotton shirt, both decorated with assorted smears, courtesy of overexuberant young artists. Her hair was pulled back in a simple ponytail, but a few pale gold tendrils had escaped confinement and lay against her forehead and neck.

This was not the woman he'd married. *That* woman wore silk suits, tailored trousers and impeccable makeup. She didn't wear jeans and sneakers and have a smear of red paint along her jawline. And she didn't sit on floors, reading to a group of fascinated children.

While Sam was staring at her, the story came to an end. Immediately, young voices were raised in a babble of comment and demands for her to read another story. She answered questions, told them that two stories were more than enough and fished a tissue from her pocket to wipe a runny nose, all the while looking cool and unflustered, as if she did this every day. Which, for all he knew, she did.

It occurred to him that maybe he didn't know as much about the woman he'd married as he thought he did.

"I had a hard time convincing your watchdog to let me in the gate," Sam said.

"Jade is very protective of the children." Nikki moved a stack of papers from one corner of the desk to the other. Her office was far from spacious at the best of times, but with Sam in it, the room suddenly seemed claustrophobically small. In fact, from the moment she'd looked up and seen him standing in the doorway, she'd felt as if there wasn't quite enough air in the building.

"She seemed surprised when I told her we were married."

His tone was neutral, but Nikki felt a surge of guilt. It was completely irrational. She didn't owe him any explanations, but she heard herself giving one, anyway. "I thought it would be easier if I didn't mention it. It might confuse the children when we...when the year is up, I mean."

It sounded weak even to her own ears. Her marriage and divorce would be nothing more than an abstract idea to a four-year-old, causing not even a blip in their lives. But she didn't feel comfortable telling him the truth, which was that she'd wanted—needed—this one place to remain un-touched by the charade her life had become. Ironic, really, since the charade had begun *because* of this place.

But Sam nodded as if it wasn't a completely ridiculous excuse. "Makes sense," he said. "If I'd known, I could have said I was your uncle from Australia or something."

"It's all right. It was a silly idea, anyway." She picked up the same stack of papers and straightened them by tapping them against the desk, concentrating on the task as if her life depended on having the edges perfectly aligned.

"You volunteer here?" Sam asked, probing carefully.

Nikki considered saying yes and leaving it at that. It was the truth—she *did* volunteer here. But she didn't want any more lies, even those of omission. Lately, it seemed as if her entire life was a tissue of lies.

"Actually, Rainbow Place is mine. Jade's mother manages the place, but I work here three or four days a week."

She wasn't sure whether or not to be insulted by the surprise in Sam's expression. Obviously, it had never occurred to him that she might do something useful.

"It looks like a great place," he said slowly, still trying to get his mind around the idea of her as a businesswoman.

"The kids like it." She set the slightly mauled stack of papers down. "I'm ready to go."

"It's not the greatest neighborhood," Sam commented as they walked to the gate. "Couldn't you have found a better location?"

"This is where there's need," she said simply. "Most of the children come from single-parent homes. Having a safe place to leave them makes it possible for their parents to work and stay out of the welfare trap. Some of our mothers are going to school full-time, getting a better education so they'll qualify for better jobs."

"Is this why you wanted the money your grandfather left you?" Sam asked slowly. That was a question that had lingered in the back of his mind—why Nikki would want the money so much that she was willing to marry him to get it.

She hesitated a moment and then nodded. "Yes. Inheriting that money means I don't have to spend my time fund-raising to keep Rainbow Place open. I may even be able to open a second day-care center somewhere else."

Sam considered what she'd told him while she unlocked the gate, relocking it after they'd stepped through. It was a new facet to the woman he'd married, one he'd never expected.

"It's a lot of work," he commented, trying to shift his thinking to encompass Nikki as a philanthropist.

"It needs to be done. Do you know how hard it is to raise a child alone? If you don't have family or friends who can help, you're virtually forced onto the welfare rolls, and once you're there, it's almost impossible to get back on your feet again."

She stopped abruptly, aware that she'd been all but lecturing him. "Sorry. I didn't mean to sound off like that. It's just so frustrating to me when I think of all the people who fall through the cracks in the system."

"I don't mind. Most cops have more than a few complaints about the system."

"I suppose you do. But at least you know you're doing something to help."

"Are we?" Sam's mouth twisted in a mournful half smile. "Sometimes I'm not so sure. What's wrong with your car?" he asked, abruptly changing the subject before she could comment.

"It won't start."

"Now, that's a good, detailed description." His grin took any criticism from the words. "Give me the keys and I'll see if I can come up with a more specific diagnosis."

Nikki handed him the keys, then stood on the sidewalk while he slid onto the front seat and tried to start the car. The engine turned over, almost caught, sputtered and coughed, but refused to start.

"I think it might be the fuel pump," he said as he got out and shut the door.

"Can it be fixed?"

"Sure." He stared down at the battered purple vehicle. "It might be kinder to shoot it and put it out of its misery, though."

"Absolutely not," she said indignantly. "Barney is perfectly dependable most of the time."

"Except when it doesn't start," he pointed out dryly. He lifted his head and glanced around the neighborhood. "Of course, no self-respecting car thief would be caught dead trying to steal something this old. In that respect, it may be the smartest thing you could drive."

"That had occurred to me. I know I can park Barney just about anywhere and find him still there when I come out."

"It would be safer still if you didn't come here at all," he said as he handed her back the keys.

"It's not as bad as it looks."

As if on cue, a car full of tough-looking youths drove by, radio blasting out a drumbeat so loud the ground seemed to shake under Nikki's feet. As they passed, a beer can sailed out the window, bounced off Barney's hood and landed on the grass between Sam and Nikki. He waited until the car had disappeared down the street before giving Nikki a dry look.

"An example of some fine, upstanding citizens, I presume."

"There are a few troublemakers," she admitted. "But most of the people around here *are* fine, upstanding citizens."

He glanced at the tidy houses across the street. "That doesn't make it any safer for you to be here. I don't like the idea of you coming down here alone."

Nikki started to tell him that it was none of his business, when an extraordinary thought occurred to her. *He's worried about me.* She tried to remember the last time someone had been protective of her, but nothing came to mind. Lena, certainly, when she was a child. But no one since then. The realization softened her response.

"I've been doing it for three years and nothing has happened to me."

"It only takes once."

"Do they teach you that positive attitude at the academy?"

"Yeah. Reality 101. Come on. Let's go home. We can call your friend Bill and arrange for him to pick up this junk heap and tow it to a shop. If you need a ride tomorrow, I'll bring you."

"Thanks, but I wasn't planning on coming here tomorrow. I just had some shopping to do, and that can wait."

She climbed into the Bronco, aware of a warm feeling in her chest and the vague thought that if she'd *had* to get married, she could have done worse in choosing a husband.

Sam woke suddenly, hearing the sound of a crash echoing in his head, like something half-remembered from a dream. Only the sound hadn't been part of a dream. He stood, grabbing a pair of jeans from the foot of the bed and dragging them over his legs. He had no particular desire to deal with a burglar in the nude. Lifting his gun from the night table, he pulled it from the holster on the way to the door.

The house had a good security system—not the most sophisticated, but more than enough to encourage the average burglar to seek out an easier target. Since he hadn't heard the alarm, if there was someone in the house, they were professional enough to have bypassed it. It couldn't be Nikki—she'd gone to bed hours ago.

Sam headed for the stairs with long, silent strides. He held the .45 beside his head, pointed at the ceiling, where he could bring it into action quickly if necessary.

A quick scan of the darkened living room revealed everything apparently in order. He stepped into the foyer and immediately heard a sound from the direction of the kitchen. A few seconds later, he'd found the intruder, as well as the cause of the noise that had awakened him.

Nikki stood in the middle of the kitchen. The tile floor in front of her was covered with a pool of sugar and a powdery brown substance he couldn't immediately place. In one hand she held a stainless-steel canister, slightly dented. In the other she held a dark brown box which, after a moment, he identified as having once held cocoa—until very recently, judging by the mess at her feet.

He lowered the gun to his side. Apparently, he wasn't going to need it. "If you're planning on stealing that canister, I should warn you that I'm a police officer."

At the sound of Sam's voice, Nikki jumped and jerked her head toward him. Great. Just what she needed. Not only had she made a world-class mess but now there was someone to witness it. And not just someone, but Sam Walker—the man who was and wasn't her husband, the cause of the sleeplessness that had brought her down to the kitchen in the middle of the night.

"Go ahead and shoot," she told him glumly. "It can't make any more of a mess than I've already done."

Sam grinned and came farther into the room. "I don't think it's worthy of capital punishment." He set the gun on the counter and studied the mess at her feet.

He hooked his thumbs in the belt loops of his jeans,

and Nikki tried very hard not to notice when the denim slid dangerously low on his hips. The only light was the small one over the stove, but it was more than enough to show every inch of his bare chest. It was a dream about that chest—not to mention everything that went with it—that had caused her to flee her bedroom in the middle of the night in hopes that a cup of cocoa would bring less disturbing dreams.

"How about half an hour hard labor with a broom?" Sam said.

With an effort, Nikki forced her attention back to the disaster at her feet. "Half an hour?" She raised her brows. "Do you know how far five pounds of sugar scatters when dropped?"

"Well, I didn't see any in the dining room, so I think it's safe to assume that the spill is at least partially contained."

"That's a relief. I can quit worrying about filing an environmental impact report."

"That's a safe bet. Do you mind my asking what happened?"

"Should I demand to have my attorney present?" Nikki set the canister and the nearly empty box of cocoa on the counter.

Sam grinned again, and she felt her pulse take a jump. "I'm asking as an interested bystander, not as an officer of the law," he assured her solemnly.

"In that case, I'll admit that I'm occasionally overcome by an uncontrollable urge to come down to the kitchen in the middle of the night and drop canisters on the floor."

"Ah, a canister dropper." The laughter in his eyes belied the serious set of his mouth. "We studied them at the academy, but I've never had to deal with one before.''

"Did your instructors offer any suggestions?"

Nikki couldn't remember having ever had such an utterly ridiculous conversation with anyone. If someone had told her that she'd be standing in a small sea of sugar, in the middle of the night, having such a conversation with the man she'd married, she'd have thought they were crazy.

"They advised us to use extreme caution," Sam said. He shook his head, looking worried. "Canister droppers are known to be unpredictable. You never know what they might do next."

"I don't suppose they said anything about helping them clean up the mess," she suggested hopefully.

"*That's* the worst possible approach. Sometimes they turn violent."

"But I'm unarmed," she protested, spreading her hands to emphasize her harmlessness.

Unfortunately, as far as Sam was concerned, Nikki didn't need a weapon to be dangerous. Someday, he'd figure out how it was that she managed to look so desirable wearing clothes that couldn't, even by the wildest interpretation of the word, be called *sexy*. The voluminous nightgown she'd worn Thanksgiving night certainly hadn't been designed with enticement in mind but he'd been enticed. Tonight she was wearing a pair of pink-and-white striped cotton pajamas that had an almost childlike sweetness about them. But there was nothing childlike about the body inside them. *That* was all woman.

And the response she inspired in him was all man.

Nikki saw Sam's eyes go over her in a slow, sweeping glance that started with her tousled hair and ended with her sugar-dusted, slippered feet. He took his time, letting his gaze linger on the way.

The look had the impact of a physical touch. When his look skimmed her breasts, it was as if he'd put his hands on her. She felt her breasts swell, her nipples hardening into tight peaks that pressed against the fabric of her pajama top, visible evidence of the effect he was having on her.

His gaze moved on slowly, tracing the curving indentation of her waist before sliding slowly across her hips and down the length of her legs. As if he hadn't already wreaked enough havoc with her breathing, he then proceeded to retrace his path.

By the time his eyes collided with hers, Nikki's knees were trembling so badly that she was in danger of sinking to the floor, sugar and all. The blatant male hunger in his look sent a wave of heat through her like nothing she'd ever felt before.

''I—I should get a broom.'' She spoke more out of a need to break the tense silence than out of housewifely concern for the mess at her feet.

''If you walk through the sugar, you're going to track it even farther.'' Sam's words were reasonable, but his tone and the look in his eyes suggested that tidiness was not the main thing on his mind.

Without giving her a chance to respond, he stepped closer, his bare feet crunching on the edge of the spill. Leaning forward, he closed his hands around her waist. Nikki gasped as he lifted her as easily as if she'd weighed nothing at all. To steady herself, she put her hands on his arms, feeling the corded strength of his muscles as he stepped back from the grainy brown-and-white pool on the floor.

Nikki's breath caught when he drew her close before

lowering her, so that her body brushed against his every inch of the way. Her eyes remained locked with his, mesmerized by the searing blue flame of his gaze. She felt that warmth as if it were a touch, spreading heat through her body, warming her in ways she'd never felt before, never imagined.

He was going to kiss her. She knew it as surely as if he'd stated the intention out loud. The thought sent a shiver of anticipation, mixed with something very close to fear, rushing down her spine. She couldn't analyze the fear—it wasn't physical. She knew, with every fiber of her being, that Sam would never hurt her. But there was a deep, emotional trepidation, a feeling that his kiss would change her life in ways she wasn't sure she was ready for.

"I don't think—"

"Don't think," he ordered, his voice a soft rasp. His hands, still at her waist, slid around her back, one pressing against her spine, the other sliding upward to tangle in the thick, pale gold of her hair. He tilted her head back. "Don't think at all."

The last word was a breath against her mouth. It was an unnecessary order. Every semblance of rational thought fled the moment his lips touched hers.

She'd been expecting him to take possession of her mouth, as much triumphant conqueror as lover. Instead, his lips were gentle, asking rather than demanding, coaxing her to let go of her uncertainties, to give him the response he wanted, to give herself to him in a way she'd never allowed herself to do.

Nikki was aware of a feeling oddly akin to despair. This was what she'd been afraid of—that once the door was opened, it might be impossible to close it again, to keep a safe distance. She felt as if carefully built walls were crumbling to dust. But it was impossible to resist. If she were honest with herself, she didn't *want* to resist. She wanted this, had wanted it from the first moment they'd met.

With a breath that was nearly a sob, she opened her mouth to him. Sam accepted her invitation immediately. His tongue tasted the fullness of her lower lip, brushed across the smooth surface of her teeth and found the honeyed sweetness of her mouth, taking possession.

Nikki's fingers dug into the heavy muscles of his upper arms, clinging to him as the world tilted and spun around them. It was everything she'd known it would be. It was the fulfillment of every guilty fantasy she'd had over the past few weeks. This was the dream that had driven her from her bed, that had sent her downstairs. She'd been seeking the gentle comfort of warm cocoa and found instead the hot passion of Sam's kiss.

She was everything he'd imagined she'd be, warm and soft, fitting in his arms as perfectly as if made to be there. Sam deepened the kiss, drawing Nikki closer until not even a shadow could have slipped between them. He could feel the fullness of her breasts crushed against his chest, the cotton of her pajama top proving a thin barrier at best.

He'd been waiting forever for this, waiting to taste her, to feel her against him. She'd created a hunger in him like nothing he'd ever known. One taste and he was rock hard and aching.

He slid his hand under the hem of her pajama top, flattening against the satiny skin of her back. Her skin warmed beneath his touch. His mouth slid restlessly from hers. Nikki gasped when his teeth closed on her earlobe. His tongue tasted the taut arch of her throat, settling on the pulse that beat raggedly at its base. He felt an echo of that pulse in his own heartbeat. God, he wanted her.

He wanted her here and now. He didn't care if she was sprawled beneath him on the table or sitting on the counter. Hell, he'd have her on the floor in the midst of the damned sugar, for that matter. As long as he could bury the aching heat of his arousal in the tender warmth of her. The thought of it made him shudder with need.

Nikki felt as if she'd been snatched up in a whirlwind. She could feel the hunger in him, feel herself being pulled into it, overwhelmed by it. Her skin felt sizzling hot beneath his hand. That heat radiated outward until her entire body was flushed with it. Her fingers curled into the thick dark blond hair at the base of his skull as her tongue came up to curl around his, teasing and tantalizing, fanning the heat higher still.

Sam shuddered against her. His hands shifted abruptly, and Nikki gasped in shock as she felt them slide beneath the fabric of her pajamas and flatten against her bottom. She started to protest, but all that came out was a soft moan against Sam's mouth as he lifted her half off her feet, pressing her lower body against his, letting her feel the swollen length of his arousal.

Nikki's bones seemed to melt. There was a throbbing pressure in the pit of her stomach, an aching emptiness that only he could fill.

"I want you." The words were a low growl against her throat, as much felt as heard.

"Yes." Nikki arched her head back, trusting Sam to keep them both upright. His tongue swirled across the pulse that beat wildly at the base of her throat.

"Come upstairs with me."

Yes. It was the natural conclusion to what they'd begun, and she wanted it as much as he did. She wanted
to lie in his bed, to feel him over her, within her. There
was nothing to stop them, no reason to hesitate. They
were married and, in a few short minutes, they would
be husband and wife in fact as well as name.

The thought penetrated Nikki's fevered absorption in
the taste and feel of the man holding her.

*Husband and wife? Married? For real?* That wasn't
the way it was supposed to work. This was a marriage
of convenience, not passion. If they made love, all the
rules would change. She'd be Sam's wife in every sense
of the word. There'd be no more pretending that they
were strangers linked by nothing more than their names
on a marriage license. No more pretending that, at the
end of the year, she was going to walk away untouched
by regret. No more pretending that she wasn't falling in
love with the man she'd married to get her inheritance.
The thought was terrifying.

"No." The word was barely audible, and she had to
repeat it, as much for herself as for Sam. "No."

"No?" He echoed the word against her mouth, and
Nikki was helpless to prevent a response. "No?" He
rocked his hips gently against hers, sending a shiver of
need racing down her spine. "No?"

It took every ounce of willpower she possessed to
turn her head away. Her hands slid from his hair to his
shoulders, pressing against him. "No."

Sam held her a moment longer. She wanted him. He
could feel it in her, in the way she trembled in his arms,
in the ragged edge to her breathing. He could change
her mind. It wouldn't take much to have her begging
for him there and then, to hell with going upstairs.

He shuddered as he eased his hands away from her,

steadying her until her feet were solidly on the ground. He drew an unsteady breath and stepped back. She was still too close for his peace of mind, but at least he didn't inhale the scent of her with every breath he drew.

They stared at each other across the rubble of their tidy marriage of convenience.

"It's going to happen," Sam said quietly. "Not tonight. Not until you're ready. But it is going to happen."

Nikki opened her mouth to deny what he was saying and then closed it without speaking. She knew he was right. She couldn't pretend otherwise. Now that the hunger, the need, was out in the open, it was inevitable that they'd come together.

She looked away from him, staring down at the fine white grains of sugar and the powdery brown cocoa that dusted the dark tile floor.

"I should get this cleaned up," she said. It seemed like the accident had happened a thousand years ago.

"Why don't you leave it till morning?"

"Lena will have a fit if she walks in on this in the morning. Besides, I'm...not really sleepy."

Sleep was the last thing on Sam's mind, but he wasn't such a glutton for punishment that he was going to offer to stay and help her. His self-control was stretched to the limit. As it was, it was going to take an hour or two in a cold shower before he'd cooled down enough to think about going back to bed.

"I'll leave you to it, then," he said.

Nikki nodded without looking up. Sam hesitated a moment longer before turning away. He picked up his gun on the way out of the kitchen. All in all, he might have been better off finding the burglar he'd been expecting. It certainly would have done less damage to his peace of mind.

# Chapter 12

"So, are you two sleeping together yet?" Liz asked, eyeing Nikki with cheerful curiosity.

Nikki choked on a mouthful of ice tea. When she managed to regain her breath, she glared at her friend out of red-rimmed eyes. "*What* did you say?"

"You heard me." Liz twisted her fork in the fettuccine Alfredo on her plate, looking as if she didn't know she'd just asked an utterly outrageous question.

"I heard you, but I thought I must be hallucinating."

"No, you didn't. We've been friends too long for me to surprise you." Liz popped the fork in her mouth.

"That's what I thought. But I can't believe you just asked me if...what you just asked me." Nikki couldn't bring herself to repeat the question. The images it brought to mind were simply too powerful. "You know this isn't a real marriage."

"I know he's a man and you're a woman."

"You sound like a bad pop song," Nikki muttered.

"And I know chemistry when I see it," Liz finished, ignoring the interruption. "There was definitely chemistry between the two of you at the wedding."

"All bad," Nikki snapped. "I despised Sam then."

"Aha!" Liz pounced on the weak point. "*Despised*. Past tense. Obviously, your feelings have changed."

"For heaven's sake, Liz, you've got to get out more. You're starting to sound like a talk-show hostess." Nikki dropped her voice in imitation of a television announcer. "'Today our show is about women who marry men they dislike in order to get inheritances that should have been theirs in the first place.' And I always thought they made all that stuff up."

"Truth is stranger than fiction," Liz said imperturbably.

"*You're* stranger than fiction." Nikki jabbed her fork into a broccoli floret.

She'd thought about canceling her monthly lunch with Liz but had decided she was better off occupying her time with something more productive than thinking about Sam. Now she wished she'd listened to her instincts. This conversation wasn't doing anything to help put him out of her mind.

It had been three days since The Kiss. Nikki had counted herself fortunate that her path and Sam's had crossed only briefly in that time. Sam was apparently putting in long hours at work, because he didn't seem to be home much. Either that or he was no more anxious to see her than she was to see him.

She had mixed feelings about that thought. He was the one who'd said that they were going to end up sleeping together, and she hadn't been able to deny it. Shouldn't he be putting some effort into convincing her? Not that she *wanted* him to convince her. At least, she didn't think she did.

And it really didn't matter, anyway, because she was very busy with the day-care center. With Christmas just around the corner, many of the parents were working extra hours, which meant Rainbow Place stayed open later, which meant everyone was putting in more time.

It was an unfortunate fact that, despite the additional work, it seemed there was still plenty of time to brood about Sam. And now, when she thought she'd be able to escape her own thoughts for a little while, her best friend was dragging him into the conversation.

"You can insult me all you like," Liz said calmly. "But I know you well enough to know when you're hiding something from me. You can tell me it's none of my business—"

"It's none of your business."

"But something's bothering you, and I think it's Sam. I thought it might be that the two of you were starting to get involved."

"We're married. I think that's plenty involved."

"You know what I mean."

Nikki knew exactly what she meant. She'd had a graphic demonstration a few days ago of what Liz meant.

"I don't want to get any more involved with Sam than I already am," she told Liz firmly. But even as she said it, she knew it wasn't entirely true. Her head didn't want to get involved with him, but the rest of her didn't seem to feel the same.

"What you want and what you get aren't always the same thing." Liz waved a forkful of fettuccine for emphasis. "Look at *me*."

"What about you? You wanted to marry a nice guy

and have one or two kids and a home of your own, and that's exactly what you got.''

There was a brief silence.

"Okay, so that wasn't a good example," Liz admitted. "But that doesn't change the essential truth of what I said. Life doesn't always go the way you plan."

"Tell me about it." Nikki looked down at the gold band on her finger. At the moment, almost nothing in her life was going as planned. Liz must have read something of that in her expression, because she dropped the faintly teasing tone she'd been using.

"Look, Nikki, all kidding aside, I worry about you."

"Why?" Nikki gave her a surprised look.

"You're so directed, so focused on what you want and how to get it. You always have been."

Nikki raised her eyebrows. "This is bad?"

"No, it's good," Liz said quickly. "You know how much I admire the work you do with Rainbow Place. I didn't even argue when you told me you were going to marry some guy you'd just met to get your inheritance so you'd have the money to expand the program."

"Maybe you should have argued," Nikki said. At least then she wouldn't have to worry about the possibility of falling in love with a man who'd only married her for her money. No matter how noble his intentions for that money, it still wasn't a comfortable feeling. Even now, he hadn't so much as hinted that he loved her, just that he wanted her.

"Maybe I should have," Liz agreed. "But I knew how much getting this money meant to you. And then I met Sam and I thought there might be other benefits besides just getting the money."

"You figured that because he was good-looking, we were going to fall in love and live happily ever after?"

"I figured that the two of you struck too many sparks off each other for this to remain a cold business deal. I was really hoping it might lead to something, if you'd let yourself be distracted."

*Distracted? That doesn't even begin to describe the effect Sam has had.* "The only thing I want it to lead to is me getting my inheritance a year from now," Nikki said firmly.

"What about Sam?"

"What about him?" Nikki toyed nervously with her silverware.

"Is he just going to walk out of your life? Disappear forever?"

The question caused a sharp pain in Nikki's chest. She swallowed hard. "That was the plan."

"But plans can change. That's what I mean by you being so focused. Sometimes I think maybe you don't look at the possibilities." Liz leaned forward, her hazel eyes intent. "Wouldn't it be wonderful if Sam turned out to be the love of your life?"

"I've only known him six weeks." Nikki's protest sounded weak, even to her own ears.

"I knew a week after we met that Bill was the only one for me."

"Not everyone has your ability to make snap judgments."

"You don't have to make a snap judgment. You've got a whole year to make up your mind." Liz poked her fork in a slivered carrot and then waved it at Nikki. "Think of how much time you could save if you and Sam stayed together. You wouldn't have to spend time dating another guy or planning another wedding."

"So you think I should try to fall in love with Sam

because it's efficient?'' Nikki's mouth twitched at the corners.

''It's as good a reason as any. Besides, you'll either fall in love with him or you won't. You won't have to *try* to do it.''

*That's just what I'm afraid of,* Nikki thought. She ran her thumb over her wedding band. She was very much afraid that she wouldn't have to try to fall in love with Sam at all.

It just might be happening already.

With an effort, she looked away from the ring and fixed Liz with a look that held both determination and warning. ''Enough about me. Tell me what my wonderful godson has been up to lately.''

To Nikki's relief, after only a momentary hesitation, Liz followed her lead and the topic of her marriage was dropped. But Liz's comments stayed with her.

She was still thinking about them a couple of hours later when she turned into the driveway and saw Sam's truck sitting in front of the house. She shut off the engine on the rental car—Barney was at Bill's garage awaiting a new fuel pump—but didn't immediately get out.

So Sam was home. She hadn't seen him since yesterday morning when they'd bumped into each other in the entryway, both on their way to work. They'd exchanged polite greetings, but she'd been vividly aware of the way his eyes had lingered on her lips, making her mouth feel as flushed and swollen as if she'd just been thoroughly kissed.

Of course, maybe she'd imagined the look. Maybe he didn't even remember the kiss and his promise that they were only postponing the inevitable. Or had it been a threat?

Muttering under her breath, Nikki pushed open the car door and got out. Accustomed to Barney's quirks, which included cranky latches, she slammed the door too hard and the little rental car shuddered under the impact.

"Wimp." She scowled at the car. It might have air-conditioning and a heater, but it was boring. But she knew it wasn't the rental car's lack of personality that was bothering her.

With a sigh, she walked up to the house. Maybe she'd be lucky and she wouldn't even see Sam. The door had barely shut behind her when she heard him call her name.

"Nikki? Is that you?"

She briefly considered the possibility of not answering. She wasn't ready to see him. Not when her head was full of Liz's comments about letting herself fall in love with him.

"It's me," she said.

"Could you come here a minute? We're in the living room."

*We? Who's we?* Her curiosity stirred. Nikki shrugged out of her coat, hanging it over the newel post on her way into the living room.

Sam was standing by the fireplace, and Nikki felt her breath catch a little when she saw him. He was wearing a pair of dark blue running shorts that came perilously close to qualifying for indecent exposure. He also wore a tank top that left his arms and a good portion of his chest bare. He looked like a poster boy for the benefits of working out.

Distracted by the flagrant display of muscle, she needed a moment to get her mind on what he was saying.

"This guy broke into the house and I caught him trying to get out with that vase." He nodded to a Sevres vase that usually sat on a side table. It was now lying on its side on the sofa. "I'd have hauled him off before now, but he claims he's your brother."

"My brother?"

A slightly stout young man of medium height rose from the wing chair where he'd been sitting and turned to face her. "Nikki, would you tell this ape who I am?" he demanded petulantly.

"Alan?" She stared at him in disbelief. She hadn't seen him since her grandfather's funeral. He'd put on at least forty pounds. Despite the extra weight, he looked smaller than she remembered. Or maybe it was just the fact that Sam loomed over him that made him look small. "I thought you were in Monte Carlo or Rio or some such place."

"So he was telling the truth?" Sam didn't trouble to conceal his disappointment.

"Of course I was telling the truth." Alan adjusted the lapels of his pale gray suit and drew his shoulders back, his soft mouth settling into a self-important little sneer. "Now you'll know what it means when I tell you that you're fired."

"It means the same thing it meant a few minutes ago when you threatened to fire me," Sam said, looking more amused than angry. "Nothing."

"You obnoxious, overbearing, overgrown—"

"Sam is my husband, Alan," Nikki said quickly. She came forward to stand next to Sam. "We were married six weeks ago."

The announcement cut through his tirade like a hot knife going through butter. "You're married?" His voice came out on a wheeze.

"We're married," she confirmed.

"I don't believe you." His eyes narrowed, and he shot an accusing look from her to Sam and back again. "You did this just to get around Grandfather's will. Just so you could keep your hands on my money."

"Your money?" Nikki felt a shaft of anger go through her, stiffening her spine. "*Your* money? Grandfather left you half of his estate, which you received on his death. The money I inherit when I marry is *my* money."

"That's a matter of opinion," he sneered. "But it really doesn't matter one way or another, because Grandfather's will specifically stated that it had to be a genuine marriage, not some stranger you picked up off the street and paid to marry you."

Nikki hoped he'd take her guilty flush as a sign of anger. He'd come uncomfortably close to the truth.

"Not that it's any of your business, but our marriage *is* genuine." Sam put his arm around Nikki and drew her against his side. The look he gave her held such blatant hunger that Nikki felt herself flushing again, but for a different reason. "*Very* genuine."

"I don't believe it." But Alan's protest was weak.

Just like the man, Sam thought, surveying him with unconcealed contempt. It was hard to believe that this whiny little specimen was Nikki's brother.

There was, he supposed, a certain physical resemblance. Both were fair, and Alan's eyes were a slightly paler shade of green than his sister's. But the resemblance ended there. It didn't look as if Alan had any of his sister's strength and determination.

"Maybe you'd like to tell us why you broke into our home and tried to steal that vase," Sam said to his brother-in-law.

"I don't have to tell you anything," Alan snapped.

"Okay." Sam dropped his arm from Nikki's waist and took a step forward. He pretended not to notice when Alan flinched away from him. "Keep an eye on him, honey, while I call 911."

"You wouldn't," Alan said. He took one look at Sam's expression and all the bluster drained out of him.

"I needed some money," he muttered. "I was going to sell the vase."

"You were going to sell Grandfather's favorite vase?"

"He's not around to care anymore," Alan said. "I didn't know you'd cooked up this marriage thing, and I figured it was going to be mine in a few months, anyway."

Sam considered arguing with his choice of phrasing, but he didn't think Nikki had any desire to drag out this scene.

"Well, now you know it isn't going to be yours, so unless Nikki wants you to hang around to reminisce about old times, why don't you leave?"

"I can't."

"Why not? You know your way to the door, don't you? Or do you normally enter houses through the window?"

Alan shot Sam a resentful look. "I came by cab," he said sullenly.

Sam's brows rose. "You had a cab bring you here to commit burglary? That's one I haven't heard before."

"Burglary!" Alan looked alarmed. "What are you talking about?"

"When someone jimmies a latch, climbs in a window and tries to make off with valuable items, that's what it's usually called."

"I had to come in the window because I lost my key," Alan told him furiously. "But this is my home and I have a right to take anything I want. This should all be mine, anyway. If she hadn't married you, it *would* be mine." The look he shot Nikki was venomous. "She owes me."

It took Sam a moment to control his temper. With every fiber of his being, he wanted to plant his fist in Alan's face. He might even be doing the jerk a favor. A broken nose might add some character to Alan's pretty-boy looks. On the other hand, Alan obviously had no character, so it would be false advertising, and from the sick look in Nikki's eyes, he suspected that the best thing he could do for her was to end this scene as quickly as possible.

"Nikki doesn't owe you a damn thing," he said, keeping his tone level with an effort. "I want you out of here and I don't ever want to see your pasty, overfed face in this house again."

"You can't throw me out. I have just as much right to be here as she does." Alan jerked his head in Nikki's direction.

"Does he have any legal rights to the house?" Sam asked, without taking his eyes from Alan's.

There was a moment's pause, and then, out of the corner of his eye, he saw Nikki shake her head slowly. "Grandfather left the house to me. Alan has no legal claim on it."

"Then that makes this a definite case of breaking and entering." Sam's smile held all the friendliness of a wolf contemplating a particularly juicy rabbit. "Isn't it handy that I'm a cop."

"You're a cop?" Alan paled to the color of skim milk. He glared at Nikki. "You married a cop?" He made it sound as if she'd committed a heinous social solecism.

"It happens in the best of families," Sam said cheerfully.

"How could you marry a cop?" Alan seemed to be taking it as a personal affront.

"I wouldn't worry too much. I don't expect we'll be seeing much of each other." Sam dropped the good-humored facade. "Out. And don't come back."

"Are you going to let him do this, Nikki?" Alan turned an appealing look in his sister's direction. "We're family. Are you going to let this gorilla you married force me out of your life?"

Nikki looked at her older brother and felt nothing but a cold emptiness inside. They'd never been close, but she'd always felt a certain tie to him. It was obvious that she was the only one who'd felt that bond. Alan's sole concern was for himself, just as it always had been and just as it always would be. "Goodbye, Alan."

Shock flashed across his face. "You're choosing him over your own family?"

"We've never been a family," Nikki told him. She thought of the Walkers, of how close they were, of how they'd opened their arms to her. She'd never known what a family was until she became part of theirs.

He must have seen the finality in her eyes because he didn't attempt to argue any further.

"Can I at least have the vase?"

"I don't believe you!" Sam's hand closed over the smaller man's shoulder, and from Alan's sudden pallor, Nikki assumed his grip was no gentler than it looked. She considered—briefly—protesting on Alan's behalf.

"Out!" Sam ensured Alan's obedience by marching him from the room. A moment later, Nikki heard the door slam shut, cutting off Alan's protest that he needed to call a cab.

"We could have let him call a cab," she said as Sam reentered the room.

"The walk will do him good," Sam said without the least sign of remorse. "Are you okay?"

"If you mean, am I devastated by the loss of my only brother's warm affection, no. I told you before that we weren't really close."

"I guess that's an understatement."

"I suppose it is." It was only recently that she'd realized just how much of an understatement it was. "I hope he wasn't too obnoxious before I got here."

"He wasn't exactly charming, but I doubt I'd have won any awards in that respect myself." Sam shrugged. "When I caught him trying to make off with the vase, I guess I wasn't as civil as I might have been."

Despite the nasty scene just past, Nikki found a smile tugging at her mouth. She walked over to the sofa and picked up the vase to return it to its place. "Don't they teach you to be civil to burglars at the academy?"

"I think I was sick that day."

Sam watched her walk around the room, straightening things that didn't need straightening. Whether she wanted to admit it or not, the scene with her brother had obviously upset her. He wished he knew what to say to make her feel better, but he couldn't think of anything.

She finally turned to look at him. "I think I'm going to go for a run. I need to blow the cobwebs out of my brain."

"It's almost dark."

Nikki followed his glance out the window and hesitated, but she was desperate to get out and feel the fresh air in her face.

"It'll be okay. This is a pretty safe area."

"No area is safe, especially not for a woman alone. I'll go with you."

"No, really, Sam. I'll be all right." Since he was part of what she was running from, it wouldn't do much good to have him with her. But she couldn't tell him that, so she sought another excuse. "I've been running for almost five years and I set a brisk pace."

She realized her mistake immediately, but it was too late. There was a slight but visible stiffening of Sam's spine. Male pride radiated from every inch of him.

"Do you think I couldn't keep up with you?"

"Do you run?"

"I've done my share," he hedged, not wanting to admit that it had been almost ten years since he'd run on a regular basis. "Besides, I'm in damn good condition. I bench-press two-twenty before breakfast. In fact, Alan's arrival interrupted my workout, so a run sounds like a good idea."

Nikki hesitated a moment and then nodded. "Let me get changed."

Sam watched her climb the stairs, hoping he hadn't just bitten off more than he could chew.

# Chapter 13

"I feel much better," Nikki said brightly. "A good run always clears my mind and leaves me with so much energy. Isn't this great?"

Sam glared at her. He didn't have the breath to spare to answer her and, even if he had, his mother had taught him not to use those kinds of words in front of women. He was about to die right here on the street, and she was still bounding along like a damned gazelle.

He'd never been so grateful to see anything in his life as he was to see the familiar driveway up ahead. He knew he just might make it that far without humiliating himself by collapsing in a heap.

"I feel good enough to make another round," Nikki chirped.

Sam's heart dropped. His knees threatened to follow suit. He'd never make it. One more hill—up or down—and he was going to die. There was no question in his mind.

"I guess it's a little late for that, isn't it?" she asked.

"Yes." He put as much force behind the word as possible with his lungs on fire. When had he gotten so out of shape? Or was this a symptom of encroaching age?

To his enormous relief, Nikki turned in the driveway. The thought of reaching the end of this torture renewed Sam's energy to the point where he was able to keep from staggering his way up the drive.

"I always do a little bit of cool-down out by the pool," Nikki said, bounding past the house.

Sam gave the front door a longing look, thinking of the hot showers, cold beers and soft beds that lay beyond it, but he forced himself to follow Nikki.

"You look a little tired," she said as she began a series of stretches that made him ache just to look at.

"It's...the damned...hills," Sam got out between gasps for air. He braced his hands on his knees, his back rising and falling in a rapid rhythm as he struggled to catch his breath.

"Am I hearing correctly?" Nikki asked incredulously. "Is the iron man saying that a little run was more than he could handle?"

"That wasn't a 'little run.' We must have covered at least six miles."

"Three and a half," she corrected. She jogged in place a little. "I've measured it."

The look Sam shot her suggested that he didn't appreciate her precision. "And it wasn't more than I could handle. I'm just a little winded, that's all. Would you stop bouncing up and down!"

With a barely concealed grin, Nikki stopped. She stretched out one leg and leaned her weight toward it, stretching the muscles. There was a brief silence filled only by the sound of Sam's ragged breathing.

"Shall I get you an oxygen mask?" she asked politely.

For a moment, Sam remained in the same position. Nikki waited, her teeth tugging at her lower lip as she fought the urge to grin like a clown. After his comments about what great condition he was in, she couldn't help but enjoy the picture he made.

"You have just made the mistake of your life," Sam said as he straightened. The look he gave her held the promise of retribution.

"Now, Sam, there's no reason to get hostile." She took a cautious step backward.

"No reason? You just tried to kill me by running me up and down every hill in Los Angeles and now you're making fun of me?"

"I ran up and down those hills, too," she protested.

"Yeah, but don't think I haven't figured out your secret." He moved toward her. Nikki backed away.

"Secret?"

"You're wearing rocket-powered running shoes."

"Rocket-powered shoes?" She bit her lip to hold back a giggle.

"That's the only possible explanation. And after taking unfair advantage of me, you had the nerve to laugh."

"But, Sam, I wasn't laughing *at* you. I was laughing *with* you."

"Do you see me laughing?" he demanded sternly.

"If you hadn't made such a point of what great shape you were in and how you could bench mark a thousand pounds, I wouldn't have cracked so much as a smile."

"That's bench-*press* two-twenty," he corrected her.

She thought she saw a smile tug at his mouth, but he suppressed it.

"Can't we talk about this?" She held out one hand in a pleading gesture.

Sam seemed to hesitate, as if considering the possibility.

"No, we can't." He moved with a speed that left Nikki blinking, his hand closing over hers and dragging her forward. She squeaked in surprise as she felt her feet leave the ground and she found herself cradled against his chest, his blue eyes only inches away.

"I know a really quick way to cool down," he said, smiling wickedly. Nikki glanced over her shoulder and saw where he was heading. The tiled pool was only a few feet away.

"Don't you dare!" She threw her arms around his neck, determined to take him with her. It was a wasted effort.

Instead of dropping her in the pool, Sam simply stepped off the edge and into the water. Nikki held her breath as the water closed over her head. Sam released her when they hit the water and Nikki surfaced first, drawing in a deep breath. She jerked her head to the side to flip the hair out of her eyes and saw Sam surface next to her. Acting on pure instinct, she put her hand on top of his head and promptly dunked him.

She brought her legs together in a scissor kick, heading for the side of the pool, but her fingertips had barely brushed the tiled edge when she felt his hand close over her ankle. Her shriek was abruptly silenced when he dragged her under.

For the next few minutes, they played like a pair of children, chasing each other through the water, laughing and shouting. They called an unofficial truce just long enough to toe off their running shoes, letting them sink to the bottom of the pool for later retrieval. And then the game was on again. Sam's greater strength and longer reach were balanced out by the fact that Nikki was a better swimmer. Her speed and agility made the contest more even than it would have been on land.

"You'll never catch me, copper," she cried defiantly as she swept her hand across the water, sending a miniature tidal wave in Sam's direction.

When he ducked underwater to avoid it, she took the opportunity to make a wild escape dash toward the shallow end. Her feet had just touched bottom when a long arm caught her around the waist, jerking her backward against a hard, male body.

"You'll never take me alive!"

She struggled to escape, but Sam used his superior height to unfair advantage. With his feet planted solidly on the bottom, he controlled her effortlessly. He turned her to face him and wrapped his arms around her, stilling her wild struggles.

"You're cheating," she protested breathlessly. She thrust out her lower lip and glared up at him. "The water's too deep."

"Funny, it seems about right to me." He grinned down at her, his teeth gleaming in the shadowy illumination of the pool lights. "I should have warned you that I always get my man."

Nikki shoved experimentally against his chest. It was like pushing a solidly built wall. Next, she tried to touch the bottom of the pool. With her foot pointed, her toes just brushed the tile, which wasn't nearly enough to give her the leverage she needed.

Her movements, small as they were, were enough to make Sam aware of the soft curves he was holding. His hold shifted, gentling subtly. One hand flattened against the small of her back as he widened his stance. The pressure of the water brought Nikki's hips against his.

Her head came up, her wide green eyes meeting his blue eyes. In the space between one heartbeat and the next, the playful mood was gone. In its place was a sharp awareness, a vivid realization of how close they were, of how fragile a barrier their clothing was.

And hunger—hard and powerful and overwhelming.

"I don't want to play any more games," Sam said huskily.

Nikki knew he wasn't talking about their childish romp in the pool. She swallowed hard, trying to gather her thoughts together. Hadn't she spent the past few days considering just this possibility? She should have had a response ready, known just what she wanted to say.

But the choice wasn't one she could make based on careful thought. It was made for her by the aching need deep inside her, by the desire to feel his touch again, to finally assuage the hunger that had haunted her for so long. She was tired of playing games, too. She wanted him, had wanted him from the very beginning. There was no more lying to herself, no more lying to him.

She didn't need to say anything. Sam saw the answer in her eyes, felt it in the way her body softened and molded itself to his. With a muffled groan, his mouth covered hers.

There was a rapacious hunger in the kiss. They couldn't get enough of each other. The need they'd been denying, once acknowledged, exploded into a white heat at the first touch.

Nikki didn't realize Sam had moved them into shallower water until she felt the bottom of the pool come up under her feet. His hands were impatient with her clothing, stripping her T-shirt and bra over her head, without bothering to unhook the latter.

Nikki whimpered with pleasure when his hands closed over her bare breasts, his thumbs flicking across nipples already puckered by the coolness of the water. A moment later, her shorts and panties floated languidly toward the deep end.

"Aren't you overdressed?" she whispered.

He was most definitely overdressed, Sam thought, staring at her naked body beneath the water. He could strip off his shorts and take her right here and now. He'd never made love in a pool before, but he was sure he could handle the logistics.

On the other hand, he'd spent the past few days fantasizing about having her in his bed and he wasn't quite ready to give up that fantasy. Besides, the pool might be heated, but it wasn't exactly balmy.

"Not like this," he groaned.

"I don't mind." Nikki reached for the waistband on his running shorts. She was impatient with the last barrier between them, impatient to feel him against her.

"I mind." Sam's hand closed over her fingers, stilling them. He waited until her eyes lifted to his face. "I want our first time together to be in a bed, where I can hold you and touch you and not have to worry about one of us drowning. I want to make love to you all night without risking hypothermia."

"I don't think you can get hypothermia in a heated pool," she whispered, dazed by the intensity of his look.

"You can if all your body heat is being used elsewhere." He scooped her up against his chest and started up the steps. "And for what I have in mind, we're both going to need plenty of body heat."

The darkly sensual promise in his voice warmed Nikki so that she hardly noticed the chill of the night air against her bare, wet body. She planted nibbling little kisses along the line of his shoulder. His skin was cool and damp beneath her mouth. She licked the droplets of water from his collarbone, smiling with satisfaction when she felt him shudder.

Later, Sam wondered how he'd made it as far as his room. The feel of her, wet and naked and trembling in his arms, made it difficult to remember basic skills like putting one foot in front of the other. It seemed like forever before he pushed open the door of his room and carried her inside.

"Hurry," she whispered.

Sam didn't need her urging. He was nearly shaking with the need to be inside her. He couldn't remember ever wanting a woman this much, so that it was a gnawing hunger, an all-consuming need that drove out all rational thought.

He had to have her.

Now.

He tumbled Nikki onto the bed. Hot as the flame burned, he didn't immediately move to join her, but stood over the bed, looking down at her, savoring the knowledge that she was there, that she was about to be his in the most elemental way possible.

Nikki flushed beneath the heat in Sam's eyes. Feeling suddenly shy, she reached out to turn off the light. He stopped her with a word.

"Don't."

She hesitated, flicking him an uncertain look.

"I want to look at you," he said. "I want to see your

breasts swell under my mouth and the way your skin flushes when I touch you. I want to watch your face when you take me inside your body.''

Nikki's hand dropped to the bed, all the strength gone from her fingers. The erotic images he'd painted in her mind were as powerful as a touch. Her skin felt hot and sensitive and a throbbing ache settled deep in the most feminine heart of her.

''Aren't you overdressed?'' she whispered again, her voice trembling.

He hooked his thumbs in the waistband of his shorts and slid them down over his hips. His erection sprang free of confinement, thick and hard, visible proof, if she'd needed it, of just how much he wanted her.

''Oh my,'' Nikki breathed, feeling the words catch in her throat.

''I'll assume that's not a complaint,'' Sam said, with a grin that suggested he already knew the answer. Nikki couldn't imagine he'd ever had any complaints. There was pure male arrogance in his smile, in the way he stood there, hands on his hips, without a stitch of clothing—or modesty.

At another time, Nikki might have felt compelled to take a jab at that arrogance, to deflate it just a little. But at the moment, she had much more important things on her mind.

''Now,'' she said fiercely, opening her arms and legs to him.

Sam groaned. ''Give me a second.''

Nikki waited with barely controlled impatience while he opened the nightstand drawer and took out a condom. Later, she'd appreciate his responsible behavior. At the moment, the small delay seemed almost unbearable. But it was only a matter of moments before he came to her.

There was no need for further foreplay. It was as if all the weeks since their marriage had been a kind of extended foreplay, leaving them both aching and ready now that the moment was finally here.

Sam tested himself against her. Nikki groaned and arched her hips in a wordless demand. A demand he answered immediately, sheathing himself in the moist heat of her body with one thrust. He shuddered with pleasure as he felt her close around him.

Nikki felt herself filled, completed in a way she'd never known, never imagined possible. The pleasure was more than physical. It was as if a piece of her soul had been missing and was now found. Her fingers clung to Sam's back as he began to move over her and the world rocked around her.

The fire was too hot to burn long. They strained together in a headlong rush toward fulfillment. And when they found it, it was shattering in its power, tossing them both toward the stars, leaving them breathless, able only to cling to each other in the aftermath.

This was what he'd ached to know; this was what he'd had to have. She was made for him and him alone.

This was what she'd ached to know, had to have. He was hers and hers alone.

# Chapter 14

"I've got a great idea. Let's spend the rest of the day in bed," Sam suggested.

The morning sunlight filtered through the curtains, creating intriguing patterns of shadow and light across Nikki's bare body. With his fingertip, Sam traced an imaginary line from Nikki's belly button up between her breasts to the hollow at the base of her throat. He let his finger rest there, feeling the delicate flutter of her pulse.

"Sounds great, but I can't," she said on a sigh.

"Why not? It's Saturday. They can do without you at the day-care center. I have the day off, and unless the criminal element rises en masse and lays siege to city hall, I don't have to think about work. Play hooky. I'll make it worth your while."

He provided a vivid demonstration of just how worth her while it might be by leaning over to replace his finger with his mouth. He retraced the path he'd blazed moments before, with a few side trips along the way. Nikki shivered as he swirled his tongue over the side of her breast, teasing but not quite touching its peak.

"You're…very persuasive." For some reason, it was suddenly difficult to form a coherent sentence.

"I took a course in negotiation at the academy." The tip of his tongue teased her nipple.

"You're…you're very good at it." She arched her back in a silent plea.

"Not everyone has the necessary skills." His breath brushed across her damp nipple, like a feather going over her skin. "You have to know when to be gentle." He stroked the taut bud with the tip of his tongue. "And when to be more firm."

Nikki moaned as his mouth opened over her breast, drawing the nipple inside and suckling strongly. Her fingers slid into the dark gold thickness of his hair, pressing him closer.

Sam's original intention had been more teasing than passionate. After all, they'd made love not more than an hour ago. And last night—

Just thinking about last night made his head spin. They'd slept in each other's arms, woke to make love again and slept again, only to wake in the dark hours after midnight, ravenously hungry. They'd raided the refrigerator, feasting on cold chicken, marinated artichoke hearts and a package of Twinkies Nikki found in the pantry.

Watching her lick traces of sticky filling from her fingers, Sam had felt desire rise as fast and hard as if it had been months rather than hours since he'd touched her. She'd seen the look in his eyes, and her own had grown heavy and slumberous, her mouth parting a little as if she were having trouble breathing.

Nikki hadn't offered any objection to the hardness of the table against her back.

They'd staggered upstairs, giggling like a pair of guilty children, and fallen into bed and gone instantly to sleep, wrapped in each other's arms. When they'd awakened less than an hour ago, they'd made love again.

Yet he had only to touch her, to feel her arch beneath him, feel her skin heat beneath his fingers, and he wanted her again. It was as if he could never get enough of her, as if he were trying to slake a lifetime of hunger. With a groan, he dragged his mouth from her breast.

"Do you give in or am I going to have to get tough?" he asked unsteadily.

"I think you're going to have to get tough." She tugged his face up to hers.

A considerable time later, Sam collapsed on the bed next to Nikki. A fine sheen of sweat coated both their bodies. Sam slid his arm under her and pulled her close so that her head was cradled on his shoulder.

"Maybe next time you won't force me to take such drastic measures."

"I think I may be one of those habitual criminals," she confessed. "The kind that can't be rehabilitated."

Sam groaned. "I can see this is going to be a tough assignment."

"I'm counting on you not to give up." Nikki threaded her fingers through the crisp hair on his chest.

"I'd better start taking more vitamins," he muttered. "Extrastrength."

They fell into a comfortable silence. Sam eased his fingers through the tangled gold of Nikki's hair. He tried to remember when he'd last felt so utterly content. It had been years. Since before Sara died.

The thought of his first wife brought a sharp pinch of guilt. Not at the idea of betraying Sara. She'd neither expected nor wanted him to spend his life tied to her memory. No, the guilt wasn't for Sara, it was for Nikki, who didn't even know that he'd been married before.

His previous marriage had held no relevance when they'd made their original deal. Now everything was changed, but that change had come about so quickly there hadn't been a moment when it seemed appropriate to bring up the fact that he'd been married before.

This certainly wasn't the time or the place. But soon. Very soon. He didn't know where the two of them were headed, but he didn't want any big surprises coming out at an inopportune moment.

Nikki shifted slightly, settling into a more comfortable position against Sam's large body. She'd gone to sleep wrapped in his arms and awakened the same way. But it seemed the more he held her, the more she wanted him to hold her. It was as if she'd been starved for this, for having his arms around her, his body pressed against hers.

She slid her fingers through the hair on his chest, watching the lazy movement through drowsy eyes. Her body was satiated, replete with satisfaction. There was a pleasantly tender ache that spoke of thorough loving and a certain awareness just beneath her skin. She felt exhausted, fulfilled, full of energy and thoroughly indolent, all at once.

Underlying it all was a stunned awareness of the drastic change that had just taken place in her life. She hadn't just gained a lover. She'd gained a husband in fact as well as in name. In one night, all her plans for a marriage of convenience and a tidy divorce had crumbled to dust.

Wherever they went from here, they couldn't go back to the way they'd been. There'd be no returning to separate bedrooms and polite nods as they passed in the hallway. Last night had changed everything, and only time would reveal all the ramifications of that change.

Nikki searched her mind for some sense of regret and found none. Other than the fact that Lena was going to be unbearably smug when she found out how well her matchmaking had turned out, there was nothing to regret. How could she possibly regret something that had felt so right? She felt an uneasy twinge. There was more to that feeling of rightness than the purely physical satisfaction she'd experienced. She felt a sense of completion that went much deeper than that. Half-afraid of what she might find, she decided not to examine her feelings too closely. At least, not right now.

"So it's settled," Sam said, interrupting her thoughts. "We're spending the rest of the day right here, pursuing your rehabilitation."

"I really can't." Nikki sighed with regret and rolled away from him to sit up on the edge of the bed. She glanced back over her shoulder. "I promised Liz I'd take Michael for the day to give her and Bill a little time alone. I'm taking him to the zoo."

Sam thought briefly. "It's not exactly what I had in mind, but I haven't been to the zoo in a while."

"You'd go with us?" Nikki hadn't even considered the possibility that he might want to join them.

"If you have no objections."

"*I* don't have any objections, but I don't know how you'll feel after a day with Michael. Kids his age aren't exactly restful."

"I like kids," Sam said easily. "Mary tells me I'm her very favoritest uncle." He frowned slightly. "Of course, I've heard her tell Gage and Keefe the same thing, but I know she means it when she's talking to me.''

Nikki grinned. ''I'm sure she does. If you're sure you want to come with us, you're welcome.''

Actually, it might be interesting to see him with Michael. Her godson had seemed to take to Sam at the wedding and Sam had been good with him, but it would be interesting to see how Sam's patience lasted over the course of an entire day. In the back of her mind, unacknowledged, was a deep curiosity to see what kind of a father Sam might make.

If it was possible to judge by a day at the zoo, Sam would make a wonderful father. His patience with Michael seemed endless. He answered questions, wiped sticky hands and laughed at terrible, five-year-old jokes. But he also didn't hesitate to pull Michael up short if he threatened to get too wild. Michael might not know Sam very well but he knew the voice of authority when he heard it, and Nikki was disgusted to find him much more inclined to listen to Sam than he was to her.

''It's a manly thing,'' Sam told her with a grin. ''You wouldn't understand.''

Nikki shook her head. ''I think it's just that you're bigger than I am. He probably thinks you'll squash him like a bug if he doesn't obey. You've terrorized him.''

Since Michael was currently perched on Sam's shoulders, his small fingers firmly entwined in his mount's hair, the terror theory seemed a little shaky, but Nikki stuck with it, finding it more palatable than some secret man-to-man understanding.

When they reached the tiger enclosure, Michael demanded to be set down.

"I wanna see 'em up close."

Sam obediently deposited him on the ground but kept a close eye on him, suspecting that the boy's idea of "up close" might not stop at the railing. He was aware of a feeling of quiet contentment.

He'd been disappointed when Nikki had told him that she already had plans that precluded spending the day in bed. But he had to admit that he was enjoying himself. Michael was a handful, but he was a great little kid.

"You meant it when you said you liked kids, didn't you?" Nikki asked suddenly.

"What's not to like?" He reached out and caught Michael by the back of the collar before the boy could attempt to work his way through the barrier surrounding the tiger enclosure.

"How about the endless stream of questions, the demands to possess every item they see, the fact that they never stop talking?" Nikki reeled off promptly.

Sam chuckled. "I didn't say they were perfect. But I kind of like their questions. It makes you look at things in a different way. Who else but a kid would ask why polar bears have fur instead of feathers?"

Nikki laughed. "True. But you've got to admit that children aren't exactly restful creatures."

Sam kept his hand firmly on Michael's collar, but took his eyes off the boy long enough to shoot Nikki a curious look. She seemed awfully interested in his opinion of children. Was she pondering his suitability as father material? The thought was intriguing. What would it be like to have a child with Nikki?

He had a sudden image of her, her stomach rounded with his child, and felt a wave of hunger so powerful that it nearly staggered him. Good God, when had he started to think of Nikki in those terms? A few weeks ago, he would have said he didn't even like her. Now he was picturing her as the mother of his child and finding the picture startlingly right.

"I always planned on having a couple of kids," he said slowly. He glanced to make sure Michael was still fully occupied with watching the big cats. He returned his attention to Nikki. "I never told you that I was married before."

The zoo wasn't exactly the setting he'd envisioned for telling Nikki about Sara, but maybe handling it casually was better than anything he could have contrived.

She looked surprised but not particularly shocked. "I know. Your mom mentioned it. She was surprised that I didn't already know."

Sam winced. "That must have been awkward. If it had occurred to me that Mom might mention it, I would have told you myself."

Nikki shrugged. "I don't think she suspected anything out of the ordinary, if that's what you're thinking."

"It isn't. I was just thinking that it was a hell of a position to put you in—we're supposed to be madly in love and you didn't even know about Sara. What did she say?"

"Not much. Only that your wife—that Sara—died." Nikki was pleased by the even tone of her voice. They might have been discussing the weather. Certainly, no one would have guessed that there was a knot the size of a small car in her stomach.

"She had cancer," Sam said, speaking almost as if to himself. "By the time we knew she was sick, it was too late to stop it."

"I'm sorry," Nikki said sincerely. "That must have been terrible."

"I've had better years." He was looking at Michael but Nikki had the feeling he was seeing something—or someone—else.

"You must have loved her very much." As soon as the words were out, Nikki wished she could call them back. She wasn't sure she wanted to hear what he might say in response.

He took his time about answering, and shook himself free of memories. When he looked at her, his eyes seemed clear of shadows.

"I loved her deeply," he said simply. "When she died, I couldn't imagine ever loving anyone that much again. I figured it was a once-in-a-lifetime kind of thing."

Nikki struggled to conceal the effect his words had on her. Better to know now, she told herself. Better to know before she let her heart get any more involved than it already was. But Sam wasn't done speaking.

"I'm not so sure anymore," he said slowly, his eyes searching her face. "I wonder if it can happen twice, after all."

Nikki's heart stumbled, her breath catching in her throat. Was he saying what she thought he was? That *she* was the reason he was changing his mind? That he might be falling in love with her? The possibility was enough to make her feel light-headed.

She didn't know whether to be relieved or sorry when Michael interrupted.

"I want to see the elephant," he announced, having seen his fill of the tigers. "Can I ride, Uncle Sam?"

Sam's eyes held Nikki's a moment longer and then he dragged his gaze to Michael's pleading face. "What do you think I am—a horse?'' he complained as he swung the child up, settling him easily on his shoulders. Michael giggled happily.

''Giddyap,'' he cried, apparently taking to the idea of Sam as a two-legged horse.

''I had to mention it,'' Sam said, throwing Nikki a rueful look.

She smiled, but it didn't reach her eyes. Walking beside Sam and Michael, she listened with half an ear to Michael's endless stream of commentary and questions and Sam's patient answers.

Nikki tried to sort out what had just happened. Had Sam implied that he was falling in love with her or was that wishful thinking? And how could it be wishful thinking when she didn't even know if she *wanted* him to be in love with her?

If she hadn't been in the middle of a busy walkway, Nikki might have been tempted to tear her hair in frustration. This wasn't the way it was supposed to work. She'd had everything planned out, and falling in love with Sam—and she wasn't saying she had—wasn't part of that plan.

Perhaps Sam sensed something of what she was feeling. He stopped in the middle of the crowded pathway, oblivious to the eddy they created. He reached out to catch her hand in his, and Nikki had no choice but to stop also.

''We're causing a traffic jam.''

''Los Angelenos are used to traffic jams. Makes them feel at home.''

''I'm not so sure,'' Nikki commented, catching the exasperated look thrown them by a mother who had to push a stroller around them. ''Is there a reason we're halting traffic?''

"Yes. A very important reason."

Nikki waited and, when he didn't continue, she looked at him, raising her brows in question. She caught just a glimpse of his smile, and then his lips covered hers in a kiss that made only marginal concessions to the fact that they were standing on a public pathway in broad daylight. When he finally lifted his head, Nikki had to set her hand against his chest for balance.

"What was that for?" she asked, blinking up at him.

"Just a little something to tide us both over until tonight."

If he'd been looking for a way to distract her, he'd certainly done a good job, she thought dazedly. The distant future didn't seem nearly so worthy of concern when the near future held so much interest.

"Are you guys gonna do mushy stuff? Can't ya wait till after I see the elephants?" Michael asked in a tone of such disgust that both his companions burst out laughing.

"We'll try to hold off until after the elephants," Sam promised, but there was another, sensual promise in his eyes for Nikki.

Maybe Liz was right, she thought as they continued to walk. Maybe she did spend too much time planning her life. It seemed that there were some definite advantages to allowing the unexpected to happen. Perhaps it was time to try living life one day at a time and see what happened.

Though there was no discussion, it seemed as if both Sam and Nikki had the same idea. Over the next couple of weeks, there was no discussion of the future, no questioning what might lie ahead, no speculation about where the sudden change in their relationship might be going, if anywhere. Like lovers on a desert island, with no expectation of rescue, they lived life wholly in the present.

They made love. They talked about everything, from politics to movies, sometimes agreeing, sometimes agreeing to disagree. They made love. They swam in the pool. They made love.

Sam talked Nikki into trying her hand at weight lifting. Her brother, Alan, had bought the gym equipment when he was in high school, installing it in an unused bedroom on the ground floor. Probably the only useful thing he'd ever done, in Sam's opinion.

Nikki was a little uncertain about picking metal bars up only to set them down again, but Sam was persuasive, promising that she'd love it once she got the hang of it. He'd guide her every step of the way. He was true to his word, giving her an extremely hands-on demonstration of technique, which resulted in the discovery that an exercise mat was soft enough to make possible aerobic activities beyond the ones for which it had been intended.

Nikki sprawled across Sam's chest, listening to the rapid rhythm of his heartbeat beneath her ear. Her body tingled with the aftershocks of their lovemaking. They were still joined together, and she liked the feel of him inside her.

She'd never in her life felt so utterly replete as she had in the days since she and Sam had become lovers. He'd shown her a side of herself that she'd never known existed, a deeply sensual side that she found just a little shocking.

"I never realized that lifting weights was so much fun." The words came out just a little breathless.

"Building strong muscles is an important part of a

solid program of health improvement,'' Sam said in a pedantic tone that made her giggle.

She suddenly laughed harder. "I just thought of something."

"What?" Sam smoothed his hand down her back, less interested in what she'd thought of than in the interesting vibrations caused by her laughter.

Nikki lifted her head and looked down at him, her green eyes bright with laughter. "I finally understand the meaning of the term *pumping iron*."

Sam stared at her for a moment before her meaning sank in, and then he started to laugh.

Having someone to laugh with was one of the things he'd missed most after Sara died, Sam thought hours later. And it was one of the best aspects of his relationship with Nikki—a relationship that had yet to be defined. Nikki was sprawled on her stomach beside him, taking up a ridiculous amount of room for a woman her size.

They'd eaten dinner together, then watched an old movie on TV, arguing all the while about who the killer would turn out to be. When the ending had proven him right, he hadn't been able to resist the urge to point out his superior powers of deduction. Nikki had proven herself a poor loser by hitting him with a pillow. The ensuing battle had ended with him carrying her upstairs draped over his shoulder, issuing threats in between giggles and demands to be put down.

The sex was certainly spectacular, he thought. And he'd be a liar if he said it didn't add a considerable amount to his current contentment, but he'd lived without sex before and could do so again, if necessary. But he really needed someone to laugh with, someone to talk to.... He hadn't realized how lonely he'd been until now.

But that was all in the past. At least, he thought it was in the past. Sam frowned at the darkened ceiling, considering the unsettled state of his marriage. A marriage in the legal sense of the word, but not yet one in the less easily defined terms of commitment.

He eased onto his side and looked at Nikki. Her face was turned toward him, and he let his eyes trace the smooth lines of her profile. She really was a beautiful woman, but it wasn't her beauty that he'd fallen in love with. And he was through pretending to himself that he didn't love her.

He loved her. He wasn't sure just when it had happened—maybe even that first time he'd met her in Max's office. Maybe that was why he'd disliked her— because he'd looked at her and seen his own personal Waterloo.

Now that he'd admitted to himself how he felt, he wondered how *she* felt. Sam frowned and reached out to brush a lock of hair back from Nikki's cheek. It curled around his finger like a pale silk ribbon, like the most delicate of chains.

Chains of a sort were part of marriage, bonds that tied two people together, creating a whole that was stronger than its separate parts. They'd started out this marriage with the intention of avoiding all but the most superficial of those ties. But everything had changed.

At least, it had for him. He knew what he wanted. He wanted Nikki as his wife. For now. For always.

The question was: Did she feel the same?

With Christmas almost upon them, it was easy for Sam and Nikki to postpone any discussion of their future together, a discussion they both knew was inevitable. But neither wanted to disturb the idyll they'd been granted. And the upcoming holidays gave them as good an excuse as any to avoid rocking their personal boat.

Christmas with the Walkers was like no Christmas Nikki had ever known. Feeling as if she wanted to return the hospitality she'd received at Thanksgiving, Nikki had invited the family to Pasadena for the holiday, broaching the subject very hesitantly over the phone with Rachel, afraid the other woman might think she was intruding. But Rachel had cheerfully consented to the change of venue, as long as Nikki allowed her to help with the food.

Since Lena was to spend the holidays with her son's family in Detroit, Nikki was more than happy to have the assistance. Though she was a better than average cook, thanks to Lena's tutelage, she'd never cooked a meal for so many people before.

Her own family's holiday celebrations had been modest. Her grandfather had not been fond of lavish celebrations of any sort. Nikki had sensed that even the tree seemed a bit much to him. A pleasant meal, a restrained exchange of gifts, a glass of fine sherry, and he'd considered the holiday sufficiently celebrated.

There was nothing restrained about the Walkers' Christmas celebration, however. They arrived together the afternoon of Christmas Eve and immediately seemed to fill the big house. There were hordes of presents, most of them haphazardly wrapped.

The tree had been put in its stand but had yet to be decorated, a lack that was soon remedied. Lena had been the one to decorate the tree, which was invariably small and sat neatly in a corner of the entryway. Lena decorated a tree the way she did everything else—with care. One strand of tinsel at a time, carefully chosen ornaments and the lights arranged just so.

This year, Sam had chosen the tree, a huge affair that swallowed half the living room. And it didn't seem to occur to anyone in the Walker family that tinsel had been designed for any purpose other than *hurling* at the tree, where it settled in drifts and occasional clumps that no one seemed to mind. Bulbs were hung with a similar abandon, and no one seemed to care if three red lights happened to wind up in close proximity to one another.

When it was finished, Nikki thought it was the most beautiful Christmas tree she'd ever seen.

Lying in bed that night, cuddled against Sam's side, she realized she couldn't remember a time when she'd been happier than she was right at this very minute. She couldn't imagine ever wanting anything more than what she had right here and now.

Nikki felt a twinge of worry at that thought, but she was already half-asleep, cradled close in Sam's arms.

Christmas morning began early. Mary saw to that. She woke her father at six o'clock. Cole made sure everyone else got up.

"I'm not suffering alone," he announced firmly.

There was some obligatory grumbling, but no one wanted to be anywhere other than where they were, which was emptying stockings and opening presents. The mound of presents turned out to contain everything from hand-knitted sweaters to a rather greasy drill that Cole had borrowed from Sam and decided to return as a Christmas gift.

Jason Drummond arrived in time for Christmas dinner, and Nikki was amused to see the usually unflappable Rachel flush like a schoolgirl when she heard his voice in the hall.

Dinner was reminiscent of Thanksgiving—everyone seemed to talk at once and yet no one seemed to lose the thread of the conversation. The food was wonderful, and Nikki flushed with pleasure at the compliments she received.

After the meal, there was a general slowdown. Cole tried to coax Mary into lying down for a nap. She consented only after everyone obediently promised not to do anything fun while she was gone. She was so obviously humoring her father that it was all Nikki could do to keep from laughing out loud.

But she felt a lump in her throat as she watched Cole carry the little girl upstairs. It just didn't seem possible that there could be anything wrong with Mary. She was suddenly quite fiercely proud that Sam had cared deeply enough about his niece that he'd been willing to make a marriage of convenience to ensure that Mary got the help she needed.

Even if it did leave Nikki with a niggling sense of uncertainty about the future of a marriage that had begun on such a basis.

By the time Mary got up from her nap and demanded to go in the pool, her uncles had recovered enough from their overindulgences at the table to accommodate her. With the temperature in the mid-seventies and not a cloud in sight, it seemed the perfect way to celebrate the holiday in true Southern California style.

Nikki, Rachel and Jason chose to remain on dry land, but they did move outside to the comfort of heavily padded redwood loungers, choosing a vantage point where they could watch the antics in the pool without running the risk of being splashed.

"I want to thank you."

Nikki took her eyes off the group in the pool and

looked at her mother-in-law. Jason had gone into the house, and she and Rachel were more or less alone.

"Thank me?" Nikki asked. "For what?"

"For making my son smile again." Rachel's eyes were on the pool, where her sons and granddaughter were all happily attempting to drown each other. "It's been a long time since I've seen Sam so happy."

"I can't take any credit for that." Nikki shifted uncomfortably on the lounger, her contented mood shaken. She didn't want Rachel thanking her, not when her very presence in the woman's life was based on a lie.

"I think you can." Rachel's dark eyes settled on Nikki. "I was worried when Sam told me he was getting married so quickly and that he hadn't known you very long," she admitted quietly. "Sam's never been the impulsive type. I think it comes of him feeling that he had to try and take his father's place."

Rachel smiled a little, remembering. "He grew up so early. I worried about it, but I'll admit there were times when I leaned on him a bit, too. All my boys are strong, but Sam was the eldest and I depended on him, maybe more than I should have."

"I'm sure he didn't mind." Nikki reached out to touch the older woman's hand, which was restlessly smoothing the cover of the lounge pad. "I think Sam was very lucky to grow up in a family like yours. I think anybody would be," she added a bit wistfully.

"I think so, too," Rachel admitted. "It's not that I think Sam's life was blighted, but I do think he learned to control any impulsiveness in his nature at a young age. When he married you, it was so unlike him that it worried me."

If only Rachel knew that she'd had every reason to

be worried, Nikki thought. And she still did. "It was rather sudden," she said simply.

"But obviously, it wasn't *too* sudden. It's been years since I've seen Sam laugh the way he has this weekend. Not since..."

"Not since Sara?" Nikki finished the sentence for her.

"Not since Sara," Rachel confirmed quietly. Her dark eyes were searching. "I thought he might have made a mistake, but you've helped him find the joy in life again and I thank you for that."

"What are you two looking so serious about?" Jason's voice preceded him as he walked toward them from the direction of the house. He was carrying a tray that held a pitcher of ice tea and a stack of colorful plastic glasses. "You're both much too lovely to be frowning," he chided as he set the tray down.

Gracious of him to include them both, Nikki thought, especially when he couldn't take his eyes off Rachel. From the delicate flush that rose in the woman's cheeks, Nikki assumed that Rachel had noted—and was not averse to—Jason's distinct partiality.

As far as Nikki was concerned, the interruption couldn't have been more timely. A few more minutes and she'd probably have been on her knees confessing the truth to Rachel.

She stared at the pool, picking Sam out easily, feeling something twist inside her when she heard his shout of laughter. For the past couple of weeks, she'd been pretending that everything was as it should be, that her marriage was just like anyone else's. It had taken Rachel's words to remind her of how false that was.

The dreams she was building were like houses built in an earthquake zone. And she just might find those dreams crashing around her ears.

## Chapter 15

Sam felt the mattress shift and opened his eyes a crack, watching as Nikki got out of bed. A week ago, he might have grabbed her around the waist and dragged her back into it. But a week ago, he'd have known exactly how she'd react. There'd be a brief, laughing struggle, and it would be at least a half an hour before either of them made it out of bed.

But this morning he watched her tug on a soft cotton robe and tiptoe from the room without even letting her know he was awake. The soft snick of the door closing behind her sounded almost painfully loud. Sam opened his eyes and stared at the ceiling

Something had changed. He didn't know what it was, but he could almost see the walls she was building between them. Whatever it was seemed to have begun at Christmas, but, no matter how he racked his brain, he couldn't come up with a reason for it. Nikki had appeared to be enjoying herself. His family liked her. She liked them. As far as he could tell, it had been a terrific holiday.

But something had obviously happened, because in the week since then, he'd felt Nikki starting to slip away from him. It was a subtle change. She was still sharing his bed, still responsive to his touch, but there was a new element in their lovemaking. He couldn't put his finger on exactly what was different, but he knew it was there. She was holding herself back from him, keeping a little distance.

Sam swung his legs off the bed and stood. He'd spent too many hours lying awake the night before, trying to figure out what was wrong, and his eyes were gritty from lack of sleep. Naked, he crossed the bedroom and pushed open the bathroom door. He braced his hands on the counter and stared at his reflection, grimly satisfied to see that he looked just like he felt—tired and rumpled.

He suddenly thought of a conversation he'd had with Keefe late Christmas day.

"Looks like your marriage of convenience has turned out to be a lot more convenient than you'd expected," Keefe had said, nodding to where Nikki sat cross-legged on the floor, intent on the Lego tower she and Mary were building.

Gage was offering suggestions on the tower's construction. Normally he charged for this kind of consultation, he'd pointed out. Cole was sprawled in an easy chair, unabashedly asleep. Rachel and Jason were playing a game of gin rummy, and, from the barely audible complaint, she seemed to be beating him quite soundly.

Sam had directed his look to where Nikki and Mary sat, and his face creased in a smile that said more than words possibly could have. "She likes kids. Did I tell you she runs a day-care center?"

"Twice." Keefe's tone had been dry, but there was a smile in his eyes.

"It's worth repeating," Sam had said unrepentantly. He returned his attention to the bottle of wine he was opening, twisting the corkscrew into place.

"You're in love with her." The words were more comment than question, but Sam answered him, anyway.

"Very much." Applying steady pressure, he eased the cork from the bottle with a muffled pop. He set the bottle aside to allow the wine to breathe before looking at Keefe. "I wish I could say I was clever as hell and planned it this way."

"I haven't noticed that planning does much good when it comes to love," Keefe said. From the shadows in his eyes, Sam knew he was thinking of his own marriage and subsequent divorce.

"I thought you and Dana were going to make it," Sam said quietly.

"Yeah. So did I." Keefe's smile held a bitter edge. He reached for his cigarettes, remembered where he was and let the pack drop back into his pocket. "Lousy habit," he muttered. "One of these days I'm going to have to quit again. Tell her you love her," he said abruptly. He gave Sam an intense look. "Don't wait."

Sam had muttered something about it being too soon, but Keefe had simply repeated his advice. Maybe Keefe had been right, Sam thought now. Maybe he should tell Nikki how he felt. He'd planned to wait. Married or not, they hadn't known each other very long. It wasn't that he doubted his own feelings, but he didn't want to rush Nikki.

"Face it, Walker," he said to his reflection. "You're scared to death she doesn't love you. *That's* the real reason you don't want to tell her how you feel."

The man in the mirror offered scant reassurance. After a moment, Sam turned away, no closer to an answer than he had been. He pushed open the shower door and turned the water on full blast. His jaw was set as he stepped under the hot spray.

The only thing he was sure of was that he wasn't going to let Nikki slip away. He didn't know what had caused the change in her. Hell, maybe there *was* no change. Maybe it was all in his head. But he wasn't going to lose her, not without a fight. He hadn't been able to fight Sara's illness. He'd had to stand by and watch her slip away from him. But that was different. Nikki wasn't dying of cancer. And whatever the problem was, they could solve it.

Unless he was the only one who wanted it solved.

Everything had just happened too quickly, Nikki thought as she dressed. They'd gone from cordial foes to tentative friends to lovers in a few short weeks. It was too much, too soon. She wasn't ready for this.

She tugged a soft gold cashmere sweater over her head, tucking it into the waist of a pair of slim black trousers. This wasn't supposed to have happened. It hadn't been part of the plan.

Nikki stopped, a hairbrush suspended over her head, hearing an echo of Liz's comments about her being too wedded to her plans, about missing out on something wonderful because it wasn't part of her plan. But that wasn't what she was doing.

Was it?

She scowled at her reflection and yanked the brush

through her hair in a quick, jerky stroke that pulled at her scalp. There was nothing wrong with having plans, nothing wrong with trying to direct your life. People who didn't have plans generally ended up going in circles.

Look at her mother. Marilee wouldn't know a plan if it slapped her in the face, and she'd spent her entire life drifting from one marriage to another, looking for something she probably wouldn't recognize even if she found it.

And Alan. Another perfect example of someone who just let life happen to him. He certainly hadn't planned to run through his inheritance the way he had. But because he hadn't planned on doing anything else, that's what had happened. Now he was reduced to trying to steal vases from his own sister. And if he'd done a little planning before attempting to rob her, he might have gotten away with it. But he'd just stumbled into burglary the way he stumbled into everything else in his life, and the result was he'd ended up with nothing. Even committing a decent crime required a plan.

Nikki brushed her hair back from her face and secured it at the base of her neck with a soft black ribbon. There was nothing wrong with having a plan and nothing wrong with trying to stick to that plan. It wasn't that she was going to walk away entirely from whatever it was she and Sam had together—she just wanted to step back a little. She didn't want to rush into anything.

She'd planned to get married, not to fall in love. Contrary to what Liz thought, it wasn't that she was so focused on her goal that she couldn't let anything intrude on her plans.

"I just want to be sure that what I think is happening is really happening and not just some flash-in-the-pan attraction,'' Nikki told her reflection. "After all, how do I know I'm *really* in love with Sam? It could be propinquity or animal magnetism or...or practically anything.''

The woman in the mirror looked doubtful. Something in her eyes suggested that she thought Nikki was hiding her head like a scared rabbit, making excuses for her own cowardice.

"What do *you* know?'' Nikki snapped. "It's my life and I know exactly what I'm doing.'' She turned away from the mirror, not wanting to see the doubts in her reflection's eyes.

She picked up her watch and slipped it on. She needed to talk to Sam, needed to try and explain how she felt, how she wanted just a little distance. Though how they were going to manage that when the terms of the will said they had to live in the same house, she didn't know.

Pushing her feet into a pair of black loafers, she remembered that it was New Year's Eve and Sam had to work. Which meant she could put off talking to him for a little while longer. He'd understand. She knew he would. If he loved her—which he hadn't said he did—he'd understand.

Nikki left her room and went downstairs. She'd planned to spend the day at the day-care center. If she was lucky, maybe she could grab a quick breakfast and be out of the house before Sam came down.

The phone rang just as she reached the bottom of the stairs, and she detoured into the living room to answer it.

"Nikki? It's Alan.''

Nikki's brows rose. After the way Sam had nearly

thrown him bodily out of the house, she hadn't expected to hear from her brother this soon, if ever.

"This is a surprise."

"I know. I...ah...wanted to see how you were."

Nikki's brows rose. "You called to ask how I am?"

"Don't sound so surprised. I *am* your brother."

"I am surprised, Alan. After grandfather's funeral, it was a couple of years before I heard from you, and then it was only because Sam caught you stealing from me. This sudden concern for me is a bit unexpected."

"I *wasn't* stealing it," he snapped. "And that gorilla you married had no business treating me the way he did. He's lucky I didn't press charges."

"Seems to me your case would have been a little thin." Nikki didn't trouble to hide the amusement in her voice. "He did catch you breaking into the house. What would you have charged him with?"

"I don't know. Police brutality, maybe." Alan's tone was sullen, and Nikki could envision the pouty, dissatisfied expression on his face. "I'm sure a good lawyer could have come up with something, but I didn't want to cause any trouble for you."

"Gee, thanks," she said dryly. "I appreciate the brotherly concern."

"Well, I am your brother." Her sarcasm seemed to have gone right over his head. "I know we haven't always been close—"

"Try *never*."

"—but that doesn't mean I don't care about you," he persevered, ignoring her interruption. "With Grandfather gone, I am the man of the family—"

"God help us."

"—and it's my duty to look after—"

"Cut to the chase, Alan," Nikki interrupted ruthlessly. "What do you want?"

There was a short silence on the other end of the line, and she knew that Alan was running through his options, debating whether to stick with the concerned-brother act or to try a new tack.

"I need money," he muttered sullenly, apparently deciding that honesty was the best policy.

"You expect me to give you money?" Even knowing him as well as she did, Nikki found it hard to believe his gall. "After you tried to steal from me, you turn around and hit me up for a loan?"

"The money would have been mine if you hadn't gotten married." He made it sound as if she'd committed a crime.

"But I *did* get married, and that makes it *my* money."

"I was counting on that money."

"Didn't you ever hear the phrase 'don't count your chickens before they're hatched'? What did you do? Spend money you didn't have?"

If he thought she was stupid enough to give him money, he had another think coming. Undoubtedly, he was going to try and bully her into giving him what he wanted, the way he'd bullied her when they were children, the way he'd bullied his way through life. But she wasn't a child and she wasn't afraid of him anymore. She waited, her jaw tight and angry.

"I'm in trouble, Nikki." There was no bravado in Alan's voice, no bluster. Just fear, real and startling.

"What kind of trouble?" Nikki felt her stomach clench.

"I owe money to some people. I told them I was going to inherit a bunch of money next year, and they were willing to wait. But now that you're married, they know that's not going to happen and they don't want to wait anymore.''

"Gambling?'' she asked, her voice softening despite herself.

"Yeah. I know it was stupid, but I can't go back and change anything now. I know we haven't been close—''

Nikki's snort of laughter cut him off. *Close?* They'd barely been civil.

"How much?''

He named a figure and she winced.

"Must have been a hell of a poker game.''

"Roulette,'' he muttered. "I lost most of it playing roulette.''

"Oh, well, that's different, then. Roulette is much more respectable than poker.''

Alan didn't respond, and she stared blindly out the window, her fingers knotted around the receiver. She couldn't shake the suspicion that he was suckering her, that this sincere act was just that—an act he could put on or take off at will. Maybe he didn't owe any money; maybe he just wanted more money to gamble with.

But what if he was telling the truth? What if he really did owe a lot of money to people who didn't like to wait. She didn't like him, but she didn't want him to end up at the bottom of a river wearing cement shoes, either.

"Give me one good reason why I should give you that kind of money.''

"I'm your brother. We're family.''

Nikki closed her eyes. She heard an echo of Sam saying much the same thing about his willingness to do whatever it took to get the money for his niece's surgery. *We're family,* he'd said, as if that answered all questions. And maybe it did.

"Okay," she said wearily. "I'll give you the money, Alan. Give me an address and I'll see that you get it in the next few days. But this is the only time," she added, ignoring his whoop of pleasure. "Don't come to me again. I'm not going to spend the rest of my life financing your gambling habit."

He ignored that comment and gave her the address. "I need it right away," he said, and she was almost amused to hear the old arrogance back in his voice. He hung up the phone without saying goodbye.

Nikki set the receiver slowly back in place, wondering if she'd just saved her brother's life or been played for a fool. It was something of a moot point, since she'd agreed to give him the money, but it would be nice to know, one way or another.

She turned away from the phone and found herself looking straight into Sam's eyes.

"Did I just hear what I think I heard? Was that your brother? And you just agreed to give him money?" He sounded both disbelieving and angry.

Nikki immediately felt like a child caught with her hand in a cookie jar and was just as immediately furious with herself for feeling that way. She didn't have to ask Sam's permission to give Alan money. She didn't have to ask anyone's permission to do anything. "That's exactly what you heard."

At another time, Sam might have heard the cool tone of her voice and taken heed, recognizing that this was not the time to pursue the subject. But he'd spent the past week feeling as if she were slipping away from him, and his sense of judgment was not what it might have been. "I can't believe you're actually going to give money to that jerk." Sam paced away from Nikki and then spun on his heel to look at her as if not sure who he was talking to.

"He's in trouble." It sounded weak. Worse, it sounded as if she were making an excuse. Nikki felt a quick flare of anger. It was her money and she could do anything she wanted with it.

"Guys like him are always in trouble," Sam snapped impatiently. "It's like pouring water into a bottomless pit. You give him money now and he'll just come back for more. If not next week, then next month or three months from now or six months from now. Are you going to give him more money every time?"

"Maybe." It wasn't the strong, mature response she would have liked. It was more the response of a sullen three-year-old.

He was right, of course. Alan wasn't going to suddenly become a model of fiscal responsibility. He was, always had been and always would be the kind of person who avoided responsibility of any kind as if it might be injurious to his health.

"Maybe?" Sam repeated. "So you're thinking of supporting him for the rest of his life?"

"I don't know. I haven't thought that far ahead."

"Well, you should. Because after setting a precedent like this, you're going to have him banging on your door every time he runs out of pocket change."

"I'll deal with that when the time comes."

"Why deal with it at all? Why not just nip it in the bud now?"

"I've already told him I'd give him the money." And even if she regretted it—and she certainly wasn't saying she did—she wasn't going to go back on her word, especially not with Sam insisting that she do just that.

"Call him back and tell him you've changed your

mind.'' He knew immediately that he'd made a mistake. The words had come out like an order, and he saw Nikki's spine stiffen in response.

''I'm not doing anything that you wouldn't do,'' she said in a painfully controlled tone. ''You'd do the same for any one of your brothers.''

''None of my brothers would break into my house and try to steal from me,'' Sam snapped. ''He's using you, Nikki. He doesn't give a damn that you're related—all he cares about is that you're loaded.''

Though it was nothing that she hadn't thought herself, hearing Sam sum up her relationship with Alan so bluntly stung. She struck back. ''I seem to bring out that tendency in people,'' she said softly. ''You can't exactly throw stones at my brother. At least Alan doesn't have to marry me to get money from me. And at least he's not pretending to feel something he doesn't, just to stay close to my checking account.''

The minute the words were out, she'd have given anything to call them back. Sam's face whitened, his eyes a stark blue against the sudden pallor. His jaw tightened until it looked as if it had been carved from solid granite.

''I apologize,'' he said levelly. ''It's none of my business whether or not you give your brother money.''

Nikki stared at him, trying desperately to come up with the words to say she was sorry, that she hadn't meant anything she'd said.

Sam glanced at his watch. ''I've got to get going.''

''Sam, I—''

He looked at her, looked through her, and Nikki found the words drying up in her throat. He nodded as if she were a casual acquaintance. A moment later, she heard the door close quietly behind him.

What had she done?

Feeling as if she were running in quicksand, Nikki ran to the door, dragging it open just as she heard the truck's engine roar to life.

"Sam. Wait!"

Either he didn't hear her or he chose to ignore her. She didn't know which it was, but the truck pulled away even as she stepped out onto the porch. She stood there, watching it disappear down the driveway and turn out into the street. After a moment, she turned back into the house, shutting the door behind her and leaning against it.

How could she have accused Sam of pretending to care for her just for her money? She'd had her doubts about the speed with which things were moving between them, but she'd never thought he was a fortune hunter—not since she'd found out about Mary's illness, anyway.

How could she have hurt him like that?

Ten hours later, Nikki was still asking herself the same question. She'd finally decided that it had been less Sam's autocratic tone that had triggered her response than all the fears and uncertainties that had been plaguing her recently. She'd resented him telling her what to do, but that had been simply the spark that lit the fuse. She'd lashed out at Sam because she was afraid. She'd felt her life slipping out of her control and she'd responded like a frightened child.

She owed him an apology. She just hoped he'd be willing to listen to it.

Lena was still on vacation, so Nikki spent the afternoon and evening setting the table and cooking a special meal. The way to a man's heart was supposed to be through his stomach. She didn't think it was that simple, but perhaps a little candlelight and wine would help make her apology more vivid.

Once the meal was in progress, she went upstairs and changed into a little black dress—a very little black dress. She wasn't above using a touch of seduction if it would help soften Sam's mood. She didn't know what she'd do if he refused to accept her apology.

Nikki dabbed a touch of perfume behind her ears, carefully avoiding her reflection in the mirror. She was afraid of what she might see in her own eyes, afraid she might see something that would make it impossible to pretend there was any doubt about her feelings for the man she'd married.

She glanced at her watch as she left her room. If Sam had mentioned what time he expected to be home, she didn't remember. Since it was New Year's Eve, she assumed he'd be working late. But she'd wait up. The New Year didn't really start until after bedtime, and she wasn't going to bed until she'd talked to Sam. She didn't want to start the New Year off with those hurtful words between them.

She'd just reached the bottom of the stairs when someone rang the doorbell. Sam. She felt her heart slam against her breastbone as she hurried across the foyer. Maybe he'd forgotten his key. Or maybe, after the fight they'd had, he'd hesitated to use it.

Nikki wrenched open the door, ready to throw herself into his arms, all her plans forgotten for once.

But it wasn't Sam standing on the porch, though it *was* a police officer. Two of them, in fact. She stared at them blankly for a moment, trying to shift her thinking to encompass the fact that they weren't Sam.

"Mrs. Walker?"

"Yes." Their solemn expressions set off warning bells. Her fingers tightened around the edge of the door, and she had to fight the urge to slam it in their faces. She didn't want to hear what they had to say.

"I'm afraid we have some bad news."

# Chapter 16

It was the waiting that was the worst, Nikki thought. It gave her too much time to think, too much time to wonder what was happening. Sam was somewhere beyond one of those doors, and it was all she could do to keep from jumping up and running down the hall, pushing open doors until she found him.

He was in surgery, the nurse had said. No, she didn't know the extent of his injuries. Officer Walker had been shot in the chest, but no one could tell Nikki anything beyond that. She huddled deeper into the plastic chair, only vaguely aware of the two police officers who shared her vigil. They'd introduced themselves, but she couldn't remember their names. Friends of Sam's, fellow officers. They didn't talk much to each other and they didn't seem to expect her to talk, which was just as well. Polite conversation was beyond her right now.

She'd lost track of how many hours she'd been sitting there, waiting, praying, when the door opened. Nikki jerked upright in her chair, hoping desperately to see the doctor and just as desperately frightened of what she might see in his face. But it wasn't the doctor. It was Rachel.

Nikki was out of her chair and in the other woman's arms in a heartbeat. They clung to each other for a long moment, not crying but drawing strength from the contact.

"Keefe and I asked at the desk, and they said he's still in surgery," Rachel said as she drew back.

"Keefe. I didn't see you." Nikki held out her hand but found herself drawn into his arms. He gave her a solid hug before setting her away.

"Sam's going to pull through," he told her firmly.

"Of course he is," Rachel added, her voice sounding a little shaky around the edges.

Nikki nodded, hoping her fear didn't show. "I know."

"Cole is in Oregon and Gage is somewhere in Africa," Rachel said. "I spoke to Cole and he's on his way home, but I didn't want to worry Gage. He's so far away. By the time he got my message, I'm sure Sam will be back on his feet."

When Rachel said it, Nikki could almost believe it. Rachel looked past her and saw the two officers. "You must be friends of Sam's," she said, moving toward them. "I'm Rachel Walker."

Nikki envied her her ability to keep up a facade of normalcy, to hide the fear she must be feeling.

"Don't look so scared," Keefe said quietly. "Sam's too mean to die."

"He's been in surgery for hours," she whispered, her eyes haunted. "And we quarreled right before he left. I had dinner planned and I was going to apologize."

"Must have been some apology," Keefe said, eyeing her dress. "Sam will definitely appreciate it. I'd try a different pair of shoes, though."

"What?" She looked at him blankly and then followed his glance to her feet. With the skimpy little black dress and cobweb-fine black hose, she wore a pair of battered brown loafers.

"They really spoil the look," Keefe said solemnly.

Despite herself, Nikki gave a snort of laughter. "Maybe I'll start a new fashion trend."

"I wouldn't count on it." He put his arm around her shoulder and hugged her again. "I should warn you that Sam's really obnoxious when it comes to accepting apologies. He can never resist the urge to rub it in that he was right and you were wrong."

"He can rub it in all he wants, as long as he comes through this." Nikki glanced to where Rachel was talking with the two officers. She looked up at Keefe, her eyes haunted. "I...I accused him of pretending to care about me because of my money."

Keefe winced. "You don't pull any punches, do you?"

"I was upset. Nothing's gone the way I planned it," she wailed in a whisper. "This was supposed to be a business arrangement. I didn't plan on falling in love with him."

Keefe's mouth twisted in a sympathetic smile. He brushed a lock of hair back from her face with gentle fingers. "Sam said just about the same thing to me at Christmas."

"He did?" Nikki's eyes widened with a mixture of fear and hope.

"I'll tell you the same thing I told *him*, which is that

I don't think planning does much good when it comes to loving someone. I don't think you can schedule it.''

"I just didn't think it would happen like this. I wasn't ready.''

"Who is?''

Before Nikki could respond to that, the door opened again. This time it was the doctor, a tall, thin man, who looked much too young to have Sam's life in his hands. Nikki felt Keefe stiffen and knew that, for all his positive words, he was just as worried as she was.

"Mrs. Walker?''

Nikki took a half step forward, feeling as if her knees were going to collapse at any moment. "How...how is he?''

"He's going to be fine," he told her immediately. "It took us a while to get the bullet out and repair the damage, but the prognosis is excellent.''

"Thank God.'' Nikki felt light-headed with relief. She barely heard the others' exclamations. All she could think of was that Sam was going to be all right.

"When can I see him?''

"It's going to be a few hours before he regains consciousness," the doctor said. "I'd suggest that you all go home and get some rest.'' He read the immediate refusal in her expression and held up his hand. "I'd suggest it, but I know it wouldn't do any good. You're welcome to wait here. Someone will let you know as soon as you can see him.''

It seemed like days, rather than hours, before a nurse finally came to say that Sam could have a visitor. But just one, and only for a short while, she added hastily when Keefe and Rachel and Nikki all stood. After a moment's hesitation, Rachel sat back down.

"Give him our love," she told her daughter-in-law, forcing a smile.

"I will." Nikki gave her and Keefe both a grateful look and followed the nurse from the room.

Maybe she wasn't being fair. Maybe she shouldn't be the one to see Sam. After all, Rachel and Keefe were his family. She was the woman with whom he'd made a marriage of convenience. But it was so much more than that now. She loved him now. And Keefe had said that Sam loved her. She clung to that thought as the nurse pushed open the door to Sam's room and waved her inside.

"You can only stay for a few minutes," she said before she stepped back into the hallway.

Nikki barely heard the warning. All her attention was focused on the man lying in the bed across the room. As she walked toward him, she had to keep reminding herself that the doctor had said he was going to be fine. Connected to an assortment of tubes and equipment, he looked anything but fine.

She stopped next to the bed and looked down at him. His eyes were closed, and for a moment she thought he might be asleep. Needing reassurance, she put her fingertips against his arm, which lay on top of the sheets. Immediately his eyes flicked open.

"Sam? It's me. Nikki."

"Nikki."

She'd spent so many hours thinking she'd never hear him say her name again that she felt tears flood her eyes. She hadn't planned on saying anything; she'd just wanted to reassure herself that he was really all right. They could wait until later to straighten everything out. But the words came tumbling out. "Oh Sam, I'm so sorry. I didn't mean it. I know you wouldn't pretend you cared for me because of the money."

He blinked, trying to clear the lingering drugged haze from his brain. It took him a moment to remember the quarrel they'd had. It seemed a thousand years ago.

"What day is it?"

"What?" Nikki stared at him as if he'd lost his mind.

"What day is it?" he repeated, more clearly.

"January first. Why?"

"You don't expect me to remember something that happened last year, do you?"

"Last year? But it was just yesterday."

"Last year," he repeated firmly.

His chest felt as if an elephant were sitting on it and his entire body ached. He knew he'd been shot and he supposed he should be demanding to know what happened. But at the moment, that didn't seem as important as the fact that Nikki was standing next to his bed, looking rumpled and beautiful and—surely it wasn't the drugs that made him see love in her eyes.

"It's a new year. Let's start over again. Hi. My name is Sam Walker."

Nikki stared at him for a long moment. He saw her throat work as she swallowed, saw a flush come up in her pale cheeks and saw uncertainty in her eyes.

"I don't want to start over," she said. "I liked where we were, before we quarreled."

"It's not a bad place to start," Sam agreed. "But it could use some fine-tuning."

He wanted to pull her into his arms, but was limited by the assortment of tubes that tied him to the bed. He turned his hand up and waited until she threaded her fingers through his.

"What kind of fine-tuning?" she asked quietly.

"The kind that starts with me telling you that I love you." Maybe it was the drugs, but it suddenly seemed incredibly easy to say. He decided to say it again. "I love you, Nikki."

She was silent so long that he began to think he'd misread her, that it hadn't been love in her eyes. The sudden pain in his chest had nothing to do with the bullet he'd taken and everything to do with his heart cracking.

"This wasn't the way I had it planned," Nikki said slowly. "But I guess maybe it's time to change my plans a little." She lifted her eyes to his face, and Sam was dazzled by the love he saw there. "I love you, too."

She squeezed his hand, her heart swelling with love.

She'd never dreamed that her marriage of convenience would turn out to be so perfect.

# *Epilogue*

If anyone had told Sam that something good could come out of taking a .38 slug in the chest, he would have thought they were crazy. But if he hadn't been shot, God knew how long it might have taken he and Nikki to admit their feelings for one another. He wasn't exactly *glad* he'd been shot, he thought a week later, but he couldn't say he was entirely sorry either. Getting shot seemed a relatively small price to pay to find out that Nikki loved him.

As if thinking about her had conjured her up, the door to his hospital room opened and she came in. Looking at her, Sam wondered how it was possible that he'd gotten so lucky. He married for mercenary reasons and ended up with something money could never buy.

"How are you feeling?" Nikki asked as she approached the bed.

"Like a rat in a trap." He caught her hand in his and tugged her down for a kiss. "If they don't let me out of here this afternoon, I'm going to make a break for it."

"If the doctor thinks you should stay another day…"

"I'm still coming home," Sam interrupted. "I can't take another day in this place. Every time I turn around, someone's coming at me with a needle or a thermometer. It's a wonder I have any blood left, considering the amount they've drawn off."

"Poor baby." Nikki gave into the urge to brush his hair back from his face, loving the feel of it beneath her fingers. She'd come too close to losing him to take even the simplest of contacts for granted. "I'm sure they're taking good care of you."

"And I'm sure the nurses are some kind of coven of vampires," Sam muttered.

"I don't think vampires come in covens."

"They do at this hospital. They've obviously got some kind of competition going to see who can draw the most blood out of me—the night shift or the day shift.

When Nikki laughed, he gave her an indignant look. "Go ahead and laugh but, I tell you, one more night in this place and I'm not going to have enough blood left to shake a stick at."

"What are you complaining about now?" Rachel Walker asked as she entered the room.

Nikki turned to smile at her mother-in-law. "He thinks the nurses are bloodsucking vampires."

"They probably are," Jason Drummond said as he followed Rachel into the room. "The one time I was in the hospital, they seemed to have a sadistic fascination with my veins. I was lucky to escape with my life."

"And you thought I was imagining it," Sam said.

The triumph in his voice was at odds with the laughter in his eyes.

"Don't encourage him, Jason," Rachel said as she bent to kiss her son's forehead. "I suspect he's making the nurses' lives hell. He always was a terrible patient."

"Thanks for the sympathy, Mom," Sam said with heavy sarcasm.

"You're welcome, dear," she said serenely. She moved to the foot of the bed to stand next to Jason. "Nikki, you have my sympathy when it comes to seeing that he obeys doctor's orders when he gets home. I suggest you buy a whip and a chair if you expect to keep him in bed for more than a few minutes."

"I bought some good strong rope," Nikki said. "If he gets out of hand, I'll just tie him to the bed."

"Now that's the first interesting suggestion I've heard in days," Sam said, giving her an exaggerated leer.

"Behave yourself," Nikki told him, flushing a little. "If I tie you to the bed, it will be for strictly medicinal purposes."

"That's what they all say." Sam's grin was wicked.

"I still think the whip and the chair are your best bet," Rachel commented, watching the byplay between her son and daughter-in-law. "You're going to have your hands full with him."

"I don't mind." Nikki brushed her fingers against Sam's cheek and he caught her hand in his, bringing it to his mouth and pressing a soft kiss into the palm. The look they exchanged was so full of love that it seemed almost an intrusion for anyone else to witness it.

There was a moment's silence and then Jason cleared his throat. "Seems like the two of you made a better bargain than you expected."

"Bargain?" Nikki looked at him curiously.

"When you decided to get married. Your marriage of convenience," he clarified when they continued to look at him blankly.

"You know?" Nikki asked incredulously.

"I know. We both do," Jason added, glancing at Rachel.

"When did you figure it out?" Sam asked.

"I suspected before I met you," Jason told him. "When Nicole called to tell me she was getting married, I did some checking and couldn't find any connection between the two of you. It was pretty well confirmed for me when I saw the two of you together. Next time you're pretending to be madly in love with someone, Nicole, you'd do well to avoid grinding your heel into his foot," he suggested kindly.

She was too shocked to appreciate the humor. "But…if you knew… You gave us your blessing."

"You mean I knew you weren't fulfilling the terms of your grandfather's will? I suppose that's true, in the strictest of legal terms. When Lyman told me he wanted that provision in the will, I told him I'd have nothing to do with it. I told him he was going to force you to make a marriage of convenience, that you were too stubborn to let him beat you out of your inheritance. He said it was strictly up to me to decide whether or not you were making a mistake."

"And after I stepped on Sam's foot, you thought I *wasn't* making a mistake?" she questioned, bewildered.

"That wasn't exactly the moment when I made my decision," he admitted. "But there was something between the two of you that made me think you might have a chance. I'd never seen you so interested in a man, Nicole."

"Interested? I detested Sam then!"

"It was more reaction than you'd ever shown before. I'd learned enough about Sam to know you'd be safe with him, even if the two of you continued to detest each other. I decided to take a chance. And I was right," he added, nodding to their linked hands.

There was a silence while Sam and Nikki adjusted to the idea that their secret hadn't been a secret at all.

"Mom?" Sam didn't have to complete the question.

"Oh, I figured it out pretty early on. The way you got married without so much as introducing Nikki to the family. And the fact that you hadn't told her anything about the family, not even that you'd been married before. And of course, when Cole told me you'd given him the money for Mary's surgery, that cinched it. You've always had such a strong sense of responsibility toward the family, Sam. I guess I wasn't really surprised that you'd take such a drastic step."

"Why didn't you say anything?"

"Well, it was really none of my business. Besides, I liked Nikki and I hadn't seen you look so alive since before Sara died. I thought there was a pretty good chance that you'd find out that you'd made a better deal than you knew."

Sam looked up at Nikki, seeing his own shock reflected in her eyes. "So much for our acting abilities," he muttered.

"I guess we aren't going to have to prepare that Oscar speech after all. We thought we were fooling everyone." She giggled. "And they knew all along."

Sam grinned, looking from his wife to the older couple at the foot of the bed. "I suppose the two of you feel very smug, figuring out that we were meant for each other before we knew it ourselves."

"Actually, I did comment to your mother that you seemed a bit slow-witted," Jason admitted with a smile.

"I told him you'd come to your senses eventually," Rachel assured them.

"Gee, thanks." Sam's hand tightened over Nikki's.

He thought of his mother's comment that he'd made a better bargain than he knew. Looking up at his wife, he knew that he'd never heard truer words. He'd made the best bargain of his life.

\* \* \* \* \* \*

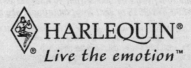

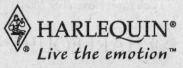

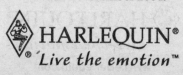